Martyrs of Science

Martyrs of Science
and Other Victims of
Devilry and Destiny

by
S. Henry Berthoud

translated, annotated and introduced by
Brian Stableford

A Black Coat Press Book

Visit our website at www.blackcoatpress.com

ISBN 978-1-61227-229-0. First Printing. November 2013. Published by Black Coat Press, an imprint of Hollywood Comics.com, LLC, P.O. Box 17270, Encino, CA 91416. All rights reserved.

TABLE OF CONTENTS

Introduction

Samuel-Henri Berthoud, who anglicized the spelling of his familiar name as an affectation when he elected to sign his literary works "S. Henry Berthoud," was born on 19 January 1804 in Cambrai, in Flanders in north-western France. He was the son of a printer and bookseller who also had the first name of Samuel, that being traditional in the family. Samuel-Henri was educated at Douai, as the beneficiary of a bursary. It is unclear how far that education extended, but there is no evidence that he ever obtained any advanced qualifications. Although he later adopted the representation "Dr. Sam" in some of the fiction he wrote specifically for children, that too was an affectation; he probably had no right to any such title.

It is, alas, necessary to use the word "probably" a lot in the course of any attempt to reconstruct the story of Berthoud's life and career, which was scantily documented while he was alive, and almost completely ignored thereafter. Very few studies of the French Romantic Movement mention his contribution to it, or even his presence within it, and he would probably have gone entirely unmentioned in that context had it not been known that he was an early acquaintance of Honoré de Balzac and that he is mentioned in passing in a story by Théophile Gautier. He is described as a popularizer of science in an entry devoted to him in Pierre Versins' *Encyclopédie de l'utopie, des voyages extraordinaires et de la science-fiction* (1972), where a complimentary description is offered of two of the stories in his children's book *L'Homme depuis cinq mille ans* [Humankind over Five Thousand Years] (1865), and mention is also made of an earlier story, "Voyage au ciel" (1841; tr. herein as "A Heavenward Voyage").

Versins' hint was presumably responsible for Francis Valery taking advantage of the Bibliothèque Nationale's website *gallica* to locate "Voyage au ciel." Valery's expertise and judgment immediately allowed him to recognize the significance of the story as an item of "proto-science fiction," and he subsequently reprinted and publicized it, but he does not seem to have been moved to make further investigation of the four-volume set of *Fantasies scientifiques de Sam* [Sam's Scientific Fantasies] (1861-62), in which "Voyage au ciel" is reprinted, although he might have concluded, if he did take a brief look, that they were not very interesting, as very few of the other inclusions contain any speculative content.

Without the indexing facility provided by *gallica* and the similar facility offered by Google Books, it would be impossible to research Berthoud in any methodical fashion, and that would have been the situation for more than a century after his death, when it would have been nearly impossible to gather any information about him or assemble even a partial collection of his works. The record remains extremely patchy even today, but the combination of those two sources does allow ready consultation of a small fraction of his output in volume form and the location of a few fugitive secondary references. It also permits access to a tiny fraction of his unreprinted contributions to periodicals, although the vast majority of the publications to which he contributed remain unavailable as yet. In consequence, attempting to piece together a general overview of the author's career and productions is am matter of trying to deduce the general appearance of a picture from a handful of jigsaw pieces. Even so, the narrative that can be pieced together from the fragments in question is an interesting one, in spite of its uncertainties.

Berthoud obtained his first publication in 1822, when his father published his *Premiers essais poétiques* for him, and his talent was independently endorsed in 1823, when he won a competition organized by the Societé d'Émulation de Cambrai, the literary society of his home town, with a poem entitled "Le Fugitif" [The Fugitive]. His father printed a pamphlet version of that for him too. He published at least one other item in the Societé d'Émulation's annual bulletin: a story entitled "Le Fou" [The Madman] (1829), a fanciful historical romance in which Michel de Montaigne and Peter Paul Rubens lend a helping hand to Torquato Tasso after discovering him in dire straits. Many years later, he wrote another story with the same title—the latter is the one translated herein a "The Madman"—which has a very different cast and is set in a different era, but which shares something of the same method, building a fanciful and fervent romance around a small nucleus of historical fact.

By 1929, Berthoud was the permanent secretary of the Societé d'Émulation de Cambrai, and he was also editing a periodical founded the previous year by his father, the *Gazette de Cambrai*, where more of his early publications probably appeared. He had probably been working for his father since leaving school, in the family business. Whenever his formal education had been suspended, however, it certainly did not prevent him from thinking of himself as a scholar. His first passion was natural history, but he was also interested in literature, music, history and local folklore. In literary terms he was undoubtedly an adherent of the Romantic Movement from the very beginning, taking in German and English influences as well as French ones. Ernst Hoffmann is featured as a character in some of his historical romances and he was undoubtedly an admirer of Lord Byron, probably to the extent of adopting some affectations of dandyism—but not the "satanism" that made such a deep impression on many French Romantics, as Berthoud never compromised the devout Catholicism that had doubtless made a deep imprint on him while he was at Douai.

Berthoud moved to Paris in 1830, in which year "Prestige" was published in the *Revue des Deux Mondes*. He appears to have met Balzac in that year, and undoubtedly became part of the curious community of would-be writers so graphically described by the latter writer in *Illusions perdues* (1837-43; tr. as *Lost Illusions*). Exactly where Berthoud fitted into the spectrum of types identified by Balzac's novel is unclear, except for the fact that he was one of those who "sold out" by falling prey to the temptations of journalism, perhaps

9

compromising his original ideals and ambitions in the process. Before then, however, he must have written the bulk of the items in his first collection, *Contes misanthropiques* [Misanthropic Tales] (1831), whose contents leave no doubt about the fact that, whatever illusions he might have bought to Paris regarding literary life and the prospects of finding success therein, he had none at all about life in general and the roles played therein by love, marriage, fickleness and recklessness.

It is difficult to determine exactly when Berthoud first met other leading members of the Parisian Romantic Movement; although he was certainly acquainted with Jules Janin and Petrus Borel by 1833, he might not have known them in 1831, but whether there was any communication between the three or not, Berthoud's *Contes Misanthropiques* have very strong thematic, methodical and philosophical links with the many short stories that Janin began collecting in 1832 and those that Borel collected in *Champavert: contes immoraux* (1833; tr. as *Champavert: Immoral Tales*) and. Although Berthoud's work lacks the fire and ferocity of Borel's and the slick dexterity of Janin's best work, there is no doubt that it is Berthoud who was the true originator of the rich tradition of what eventually came to be known as *contes cruels*. Indeed, the brevity and relative laconism of Berthoud's work in that vein makes his stories even more closely analogous to the works produced in the heyday of the tradition by such writers as Octave Mirbeau, Léon Bloy, Jean Richepin, Guy de Maupassant and Edmond Haraucourt than the more high-profile foundation-stones provides by Janin, Borel and the writer who gave the genre its most popular label, Villiers de l'Isle-Adam.

Had it not been virtually impossible to find for such a long time (and it is still unavailable on *gallica* as I write, although Google Books offers a full view), *Contes misanthropiques* would surely have been recognized as a crucial contribution to the *conte cruel* tradition. Its fall into oblivion was doubtless aided by the fact that Berthoud never produced another volume like it, although the present sampler will hopefully make it very obvious that he never fully overcame the extreme and studied disillusionment that fueled those early stories, and that it continued to influence all of his works—even the children's stories in which he evidently made great efforts to conceal it. In particular, it colors his scientific journalism and his "scientific fantasies" in a distinctive fashion, which distances his work in that vein considerably from that of such fellow pioneers of the popularization of science as Camille Flammarion and Henri de Parville.

That element of disillusionment gave almost all of Berthoud's work a downbeat inclination that cannot have helped his popularity, and probably contributed to his eventual oblivion. There is no way of knowing how much it affected his personality in social intercourse, but the fact that he was so rarely mentioned in memoirs by all the people who undoubtedly knew him at least slightly might be revealing. He apparently intended to call his first novel *Bah!* but was overruled by the publisher, who imposed the title *La Soeur de lait du vicaire* [The Curate's Foster-Sister] (1832). The title of *Le Régent de rhétorique, moeurs flamandes* [The Regent of Rhetoric; Flemish Mores] (1833) restored an element of sarcasm, and *Le Cheveu du diable* [The Devil's Hair] (1833) and *Mater dolorosa* [Mother of Tears] (1834) also offered a clear implication of their downbeat inclinations.

Le Cheveu du diable has no fantastic content, although it does include mention of the folktale reference from which the title is borrowed in an introduction. *Mater dolorosa*, which describes the trials and tribulations of a writer and artist who leaves Cambrai to settle in Paris, also includes a mock folktale supposedly written by its hero, as well as a historical romance starring Ernst Hoffman and Carl-Maria Weber, but it is impossible to assess the extent to which the frame narrative mirrors Berthoud's own tribulations. All four of those early novels attempt naturalistic representations of provincial life, seen from a quasi-sociological viewpoint, and have strong affinities with Balzac's work in a similar vein.

11

By the time *Mater dolorosa* appeared, Berthoud had completed publication of the work that won him his first real success, the three volumes of *Chroniques et traditions surnaturelles de la Flandre* [Chronicles and Supernatural Traditions of Flanders] (1831-34). The collection does include some genuine items of folklore, only slightly modified in giving them literary form, but it also contains a considerable number of works that do not even bother to mimic the form of folktales, simply being items of modern supernatural fiction based on the kinds of materials found in folktales, and at least some of those that do mimic folktales are original compositions—"fakelore" rather than "folklore."

Such mixtures are not unusual in collections of that sort, but Berthoud is further removed from being an authentic folklorist than the most prominent Romantic contributors to the field, including the brothers Grimm in Germany, Robert Hunt in England and Anatole Le Braz in France; the French successor with whom he had most in common was probably Julie Lavergne. In a single-volume reprint of the collection published as *Légendes et traditions surnaturelles de Flandres* (1862), Berthoud added the novella *Asrael et Neptha*, originally published separately in 1832, to the series—a move serving to re-emphasize the fact that its contents are far more readily considered as literary works that draw some inspiration from Flanders folklore than attempts to record the folklore in question in anything resembling its "original" anecdotal form.

As with the *Contes misanthropiques*, Berthoud never made any concerted attempt to write more supernatural fiction in the same vein as the *Chroniques et traditions surnaturelles de la Flandre*, but as with the former volume, its legacy left an indelible legacy on his future work, where folklore and fakelore continued to occupy a situation "in the wings," always available for recruitment, at least for the purposes of comparison and subsidiary reference. Just as the present sampler illustrates the lingering effects of the author's deep disillusionment, so it represents his continual tendency to cite the

Devil's dealings with humble folk for other literary purposes than straightforward recycling and orthodox transfiguration.

Berthoud's literary production slowed markedly after 1834, at least so far as the production of books was concerned, but that was largely because he found employment as an editor, probably aided by his experience on the *Gazette de Cambrai*, under the auspices of Émile de Girardin. Girardin, a writer who eventually carved out a more significant career as a politician, founded several important periodicals, with a particular emphasis on popular education. His first periodical, *La Mode*, was supposedly a women's magazine with an emphasis on fashion, although Berthoud's contributions to it included "La Bague antique" (1831), the item of mock-folklore here translated as "The Antique Ring." More typical of Girardin's projects were the enormously successful *Journal des connaissances utiles* (founded 1831), published under the banner of La Societé nationale pour l'émancipation intellectuelle, of which he was the secretary, and the *Almanach de France* (founded 1834), and he made a highly significant contribution to the popular daily press with *La Presse* (founded 1836), which helped to found the tradition of popular feuilleton fiction that brought about a revolution in French popular fiction in the 1840s.

Berthoud probably contributed to all these projects, although exact data is scarce, and was probably a member of the Societé nationale pour l'émancipation intellectuelle; his commitment to the cause of mass education played a major role in shaping the remainder of his literary and journalistic output. The only one of Girardin's periodicals of which a significant number of issues is currently reproduced on *gallica* is, however, the illustrated *Musée des Familles*, founded in 1833, of which Berthoud was hired as its first editor; it was a pioneering "family magazine" on which Jules Hetzel was later to model his endeavors in the same line, which made a highly significant contribution to the founding and shaping of the tradition of French children's literature—many of whose early classics were produced on request by key members of the Romantic Movement.

In 1833 as "children's literature," in the sense of books and magazines designed for children to read by themselves, hardly existed; it was still assumed that children would provide an audience for adults readers, and even the *Journal des Enfants* founded in that year with Jules Janin as editor, was aimed at parents rather than the supposed "end consumers." The *Musée de Familles* was by no means designed with child listeners exclusively, or even primarily, in mind, but the whole point of it was to construct an all-inclusive audience, addressing content to children, women and poor people as well as to the adult males who had previously constituted the core of the audience for periodicals, thus adding significant impetus to the crusade for universal literacy—which was proceeding more rapidly in France in the 1830s than any other nation. Berthoud did, however, produce a three-volume series of studies of *La France historique, industrielle et pittoresque* [Historic France, Industrial and Picturesque] (1835-37) aimed more specifically, if indirectly, at children, and he went on to contribute several volumes to a more general collection of didactic works entitled *Petits livres de M. le curé* [The Parish Priest's Little Books] in the late 1840s.

It was in connection with the crusade for universal literacy, and in trying to cater to it with his editorial policy, that Berthoud apparently first became intensely interested in the popularization of science, as something that would probably interest children and would be good for them to know. It was in the *Musée des Familles* that his career found the fundamental orientation that it would maintain for the rest of his life. Berthoud also edited the *Musée*'s short-lived companion, the *Mercure de France*—one of several periodicals to bear that name—in 1835-36.

As an editor, Berthoud, like Janin in the *Journal des Enfants*, actively helped to further the careers of several members of the Romantic Movement; he published work by Balzac, Charles Nodier and Alexandre Dumas, and although they were not in need of his assistance, he also published Théophile Gautier and George Sand, who must have been grateful for it at the time. Although very little information is presently recoverable about Berthoud's social life, he probably became a regular at the famous salon hosted by another of his leading contributors, Émile de Girardin's wife Delphine, a notable writer in her own right and the daughter of Sophie Gay, a significant precursor of French Romanticism and important commentator on the growth of the movement.

Berthoud's most successful book after the *Chroniques et traditions surnaturelles de la Flandre* was probably his account of the life of *Pierre-Paul Rubens* (1840), initially published as a supplement to the *Musée des Familles*, but he followed it up with a long series of novels, most of which were "domestic melodramas" slanted at the same audience as the *Musée des Familles*, beginning with *La Bague antique* (1842), a title confusingly attached to two two-volume novels (neither of which has any connection with the similarly-titled short story translated herein) and continuing with *Berthe Frémicourt* (1843), *L'Enfant sans mère* [The Motherless Child] and *Le Fils du rabbin* [The Rabbi's Son] (1844), *Daniel* (1845) and *Mémoires de ma cuisinière* [My Cook's Memoirs] (1846). He did other work alongside the series that reflected his wider interests, including *La Palette d'or* [The Golden Palette] (1845). The series of his publications might well have continued unabated had it not been brought to an abrupt halt by the revolution of 1848, when—as Berthoud points out in one of the mock-autobiographical stories included herein—men of letters suddenly found themselves with a lot of leisure time because the entire economy had ground to a halt.

Berthoud undoubtedly kept up his journalistic work throughout the decade prior to the 1848 Revolution, and was active as a *feuilletonist* too, although the evidence of that activity thus far reproduced on *gallica* is patchy. Several of his works were, however, reprinted in the annual omnibuses *Echo des Feuilletons* and the *Revue des Feuilletons*, some volumes of which are available on *gallica*. The samples include "Voyage au ciel," originally published in Girardin's *La Presse* in 1841; how extensive his contributions were to that paper it is presently impossible to tell. One publication that is partially reproduced on *gallica* to which Berthoud made numerous contributions, however, is the devoutly Romantic *Revue Pittoresque*; among the three stories he published there in 1844 were "Le Maître du temps," here translated as "The Master of the Weather," and "Le Fou," here translated as "The Madman," both of which have evident thematic links with "Voyage au ciel."

All three stories are accounts of scientific obsession, but they are distanced somewhat from precious tales of "mad scientists" by virtue of their treatment of the theme. All three stories feature scientists who are, to begin with, not merely sane but exceptionally so—more so, in fact, than the uncomprehending neighbors whose incomprehension and diffidence routinely play a part, sometimes crucially, in driving them mad. Their eventual and seemingly inevitable annihilation by overwhelming compulsive obsession is presented as stark tragedy, akin in a more than merely metaphorical sense, to martyrdom.

There might have been other stories in that group published in other periodicals; *Fantaises scientifiques de Sam*, which reprinted "Voyage au ciel" and "Le Fou"—the latter in a section revealingly headed "Martyrs"—contains another possible candidate that has close thematic links with them, "Le Second soleil," here translated as "The Second Sun," which slots in between "Voyage au Ciel" and "Le Fou" in developmental terms; it is possible, however, that that appearance is deceptive, and that it was a later addition to the group.

The longer of the two stories that Berthoud contributed to the *Revue Pittoresque* in 1845 also belongs to the set, and adds further layers of complication to the basic pattern, thus becoming a very peculiar story indeed. Although it is impossible to tell, at present, whether Berthoud added any further stories to the sequence thereafter, there certainly seems to be an element of conclusion about the story in question, "Le

Chaudron de Bicêtre" (1845), here translated as "The Cauldron of Bicêtre," which not only complicates and confuses the thread running through the series but almost seems to break it off deliberately and throw it away.

"Le Chaudron de Bicêtre" can easily be imagined as a pivotal work in Berthoud's career; it is a kind of summation of his more exotic endeavors so far, being an extended *conte cruel* in a form that as later to become one of the standard templates of that genre, and a tale of diabolism, the force of which is only slightly diminished a frame narrative placing it in the mouth of an inmate of the lunatic asylum at Bicêtre. It is also, however, an account of fatal compulsive obsession and frustrated scientific discovery, in exactly the same fashion as its three (or perhaps four) recent predecessors.

"Voyage au ciel" and "Le Maître du temps" both feature fictitious scientists—as does "Le Second soleil"—but "Le Fou" broke that pattern by using an actual scientist as its protagonist, after the fashion of so many of Berthoud's historical romances, although the story constructed around his name and career is a drastic distortion of the history of the real individual. "Le Chaudron de Bicêtre" continues that pattern, again featuring an actual historical individual as its doomed inventor, but again playing fast and loose with actual history in a fashion that would seem extraordinarily reckless even without the supernatural element. It might conceivably have been complaints about such cavalier distortions of fact that persuaded Berthoud to take things a little easier in future; while few of his other stories featuring real individuals can be commended for their accuracy and authenticity, most are far more conscientious in treating their heroes than "Le Chaudron de Bicêtre."

In order to avoid spoilers I shall say no more about "Le Fou" and "Le Chaudron de Bicêtre" here, but I shall add afterwords to both stories to explain the actual histories of their central characters, neither of whom would have been a household name in Paris in 1844-45 and who will almost certainly be unfamiliar to modern readers. It is, however, worth making in advance the general observation that what seems to have struck Berthoud most forcibly when he began to investigate the history of science in the 1830s and 1840s was the extreme disillusionment suffered by some scientists as a result of society's misunderstanding of their endeavors and indifference to their achievements. That, at least, seems to have the chief aspect of scientific endeavor with which he identified himself imaginatively.

The five stories that I have gathered into the "Martyrs" section of the present sampler are certainly Berthoud's most interesting attempts to invent a form of "scientific fiction," and are all the more interesting because they remain so distinctive—indeed, effectively unique; there is nothing else in the historical record of precursors of modern science fiction quite like them. They are interesting both because of the detail in the accounts they offer of the allegedly-typical psychology of scientists, in terms of their obsessiveness and social awkwardness—"Voyage au ciel," in particular, contains what would now be recognized as a textbook description of Asperger's syndrome—and because of their insistence on the hostile manner in which the scientists' fellow men react to their eccentricities. As to why Berthoud found that kind of plight ripe for passionate identification, we can only speculate, although the attitude and depth of feeling of the *Contes misanthropiques* and such cynical items of fakelore as "Saint-Mathias l'ermite" (here translated as "Saint Mathias the Hermit") probably offer a clue.

Because all his accounts of hypothetical scientific discoveries are set in the past, Berthoud had to find narrative means of obliterating them all from the historical record: a strategy that prevented him from extrapolating their possible social and intellectual consequences, and thus prevented him from inventing a kind of fiction more akin to modern science fiction. What it did enable him to do, however, by way of partial compensation, was to construct a striking account of the frustrations of genius occasioned by ambient incomprehension, and to give that account a particular dimension of tragedy. That achievement is certainly not without interest, and it is worthy of praise as well as attention.

Berthoud's popularity and perceived importance in this phase of his career is reflected in the fact that he was appointed a *chevalier de la Légion d'honneur* in 1844, but it is likely that his endeavors on behalf of the education of the masses had more responsibility for that award than his reputation among his literary peers; at the very best, he would have been ranked alongside some of the other "foot-soldiers" of Romanticism who contributed extensively to the *Revue pittoresque*, such as Joseph Méry, Jules Janin and Léon Gozlan, and he might well have been ranked some way beneath them because of the increasing banality of his didactic novels. In that context, the short stories he did for the *Revue Pittoresque* can probably be considered his most ambitious work, and might also be considered as a peak of aspiration that he did not attempt to scale again.

It is profoundly unclear, from the record provided in *gallica*, exactly what Berthoud was doing throughout the 1850s, although he certainly resumed regular publication once the most difficult months of the Second Republic were over. He published the Algeria-set *The Zéphir d'El Arouch* [The Soldier of El Arouch] (1850)—one of two books he published about that country, which he might well have visited in the mid-1840s—and *La Vierge de Tasse* [Tasso's Virgin] (1851) in spite of the continued economic difficulties, and had a number of plays produced during the Second Republic, including *L'Anneau de Salomon, légende hollandaise* (1850 at the Théâtre des Variétés). It appears that he became a regular contributor to the newspaper *Le Pays* in 1849, although he subsequently transferred his primary allegiance to *La Patrie*, where the bulk of the non-fictional materials reprinted in the *Fantaisies scientifiques* probably made their original appearance.

It seems to have been in the 1850s that Berthoud settled down to work primarily as a popularizer of science and commentator on scientific progress, but he did other work as well, including a good deal of fiction for children, and might well have been active as an editor in that field, although the evidence for that is indirect. By that time, the Romantic Movement as such was a thing of the past and all of its leading contributors had moved on, although those who became and remained famous all maintained its ideals in one form or another.

Many of the leading members of the Movement had a hard time after 1951, especially those who had accepted positions in the government of the Second Republic, including Victor Hugo, Edgar Quinet, Alphonse de Lamartine (its first, provisional, President), Jules Hetzel and Eugène Sue. Many were formally exiled following Louis-Napoléon's *coup d'état*, and not all of them consented to return when offered amnesty a few years later. Where Berthoud stood is not entirely clear—his works exhibit an almost total disregard for contemporary politics—but his long-time employer, Émile de Girardin, started out as one of Louis-Napoléon's most enthusiastic supporters when he was a candidate for the presidency of the Republic, and then became one of his diehard opponents when he proclaimed himself emperor. Berthoud's association with him must have been potentially problematic, and it might have been the case that Berthoud found it politic to distance himself from Girardin; at any rate, his eventual association with the conservative and imperialist *La Patrie* suggested that he accommodated himself comfortably within that camp. If so, that might help to explain why Jules Hetzel, when he accepted amnesty and returned from exile, does not seem to have had any dealings with Berthoud, who would otherwise have seemed an ideal contributor to, if not a collaborator with, the "family magazines" that Hetzel founded and promoted so enthusiastically in the late 1850s and 1860s.

When there was a new boom in periodical production, book production and the popularization of science in the early 1860s, however, Berthoud was more than ready to capitalize on it on his own account, and his publications in volume form became prolific again throughout the decade. With specific regard to the popularization of science, he became the editor of and leading contributor to the annual *Petites chroniques de la science* (1861-72) and in addition to the four volumes of *Fantaisies scientifiques* he published several other volumes of popularizing fiction, most notably *Contes du Dr. Sam* [Tales of Dr. Sam] (1862), *L'Homme depuis cinq mille ans, Les Féeries de la science* [The Enchantments of Science] (1866) and *Les Soirées du Dr. Sam* [Dr. Sam's Evening Entertainments] (1871), all of them slanted toward juvenile readers. *Les Cassette des sept amis* (The Seven Friends' Casket] (1869) is similar in structure, although its inclusions are mostly unconcerned with scientific themes. He also published a series of orthodox non-fictional popularizations, including *Causeries sur les insectes* [Conversations about Insects] (1862), *Le Monde des insectes* [The World of Insects] (1864), *L'Esprit des oiseaux* [The Intelligence of Birds] (1867) and *Les Os d'un géant, histoire familière du globe terrestre avant les hommes* [A Giant's Bones: An Informal History of the Terrestrial Globe Before Humankind] (1868).

These works were, however, part of a veritable deluge. Having published no volumes at all in the later 1850s, and only one in 1860, he published no less than thirteen in 1861, and half a dozen more in 1862, many of which must have been written during the 1850s; which of them had appeared in periodicals and merely awaited reprinting and which had simply been stockpiled, it is difficult to tell. Few of them are readily available for consultation, but the titles suggest that most of them were children's stories—at least ten appeared in a series of publications for children—and that others continued the series of sentimental melodramas developed in the 1840s. Those that appear to be novels include *La Belle limonadière du Palais-Royal* [The Beautiful Lemonade-Seller of the Palais-Royal] (1861), *Étienne le Manchot* [One-Armed Étienne] (1861), *Histoire d'un meunier et ses enfants* [The Story of a Miler and his Children] (1861), *La Petite Columbelle ou Aventures d'un tisserand* [Little Columbelle;

or, The Adventures of a Weaver] (1861). *Le phénomène vivant: histoire de la Saint-Barthélemy* [The Living Phenomenon: The Story of Saint Bartholomew] (1861), *Quinze ans de la vie d'une femme* [Fifteen Years in a Woman's Life] (1861), *L'Enfant du mystère, un tyran en jupon* [The Mystery Child: A Petticoat Tyrant] (1862) and *Les Femmes vengées* [The Avenged Women] (1863), while volumes of shorter works include *Les Aventures d'un bossu, suivies de l'histoire du lion Daniel* [The Adventures of a Hunchback and The Story of the Lion Daniel] (1861), *La Fidèle servante, suivi des Aventures de Burgett* [The Faithful Maidservant, and The Adventures of Burgett] (1861), *Lectures des soirées d'hiver* [Readings for Winter Evenings] (1862), *Contes à Dodo et à Dedele* [Tales for Dodo and Dedele] (1863) and *Histoires pour les petits et pour les grands enfants* [Stories for Little and Big Children] (1863).

In addition to these works of fiction, Berthoud also published several non-fiction works unrelated to his studies of natural history, including three works on what might loosely be termed "marriage guidance," which suggest that he must have contributed to the specialist women's magazines of the 1850s. "Le Château de Heidenloch," translated herein as "Heindenloch Castle" was published in the June 1962 issue of the *Journal des Demoiselles*—a long-running magazine aimed primarily at teenage girls—without a by-line before being reprinted in *Contes du Dr. Sam*, and it is impossible to guess how many other unsigned contributions he might have made to that and other publications of a similar sort. Other works that were probably based on articles in women's magazines include *La Nouvelle et veritable Morale en action* [The New and True Morality in Action] (1861), *Le Nouveau jardin d'amour, précédé du Conseiller conjugal* [The New Garden of Love, preceded by the Marriage Guidance Counselor] (1861) and *Le Veritable tableau de l'amour conjugal d'après les écrivains le plus célèbres de l'antiquité et des temps modernes* [The True Depiction of Conjugal Love, According to the Most Famous Writers of Antiquity and Modern Times] (1863).

Other areas represented in his non-fiction publications of the 1860s include an interest in the occult fringe of the history of science, represented in *Le Grand Albert et ses secrets magiques et merveilleux* [Albertus Magnus and His Magical and Marvelous Secrets] (1861) and further illustrated by *Le Dragon rouge ou l'Art de commander au démon et aux esprits infernaux* [The Red Dragon; or, The Art of Commanding Demons and Infernal Spirits] (1865), which is presumably either a reprint of or a commentary on the eponymous grimoire, from which Berthoud had quoted in some of his fakeloristic tales, including "Saint-Mathias l'ermite." *Le Baiser du diable* [The Devil's Kiss] (1861) might conceivably belong to this group, although it might as easily be a novel whose title is purely metaphorical.

This glut of book publication obtained Berthoud a second round of popularity and celebrity, and a promotion to the rank of *officier* in the Légion d'honneur in 1867. The brief description of his lifestyle contained in "L'An deux mille huit cent soixante-cinq" (1865; herein translated as "The Year 2865") is confirmed by one of the few journalistic sketches available, contained in Jules Brisson and Félix Ribeyre's *Les Grands Journaux de France* (1862); he really did live in a house cluttered with books and his various collections of specimens, in company with a dog named Master Flock and a pet lemur he called Mademoiselle Mine.

As in the 1840s, however, history interrupted his career yet again, and the Franco-Prussian War of 1870 brought further economic and political upheavals. Once again he continued his career as best he could, but he was now getting old, and he slowed down drastically; apart from reprints of earlier works, he only published a handful of books during the Third Republic, of which the most significant are *La Botanique au village* [Village Botany] (1874) and *Histoires et romans des végétaux* [Histories and Romances of Vegetable Life] (1882). By the time he died, on 26 March 1891, he was virtually forgotten, and remained so throughout the 20th century.

It is arguable that everything Berthoud did in the course of his checkered career was done better by other people—that he was, in effect, a second-rate writer of limited interest. That certainly seems to have been the prevailing view within his lifetime as well as thereafter. Even if that were true, however, it would not detract from the fact that he was a genuine pioneer, and that he did at least do several significant things before the people who then went on to improve on his efforts. In fact, though, he was a writer of considerable ability, who might have spent a great deal of his time "free-wheeling" in the comfortable production of routinized work, but whose best efforts are certainly meritorious. His *Contes misanthropiques* are occasionally awkward in construction, but they do have a genuine bite as well as an experimental verve. The same is true of the best of his supernatural stories, which are not necessarily shown off to their best advantage by being buried in a supposed collection of antiquarian folklore.

The most remarkable of Berthoud's works, however, are undoubtedly his historical romances, especially those featuring real or imaginary scientists. Those that pretend to be based on fact—"drama-documentaries" in modern parlance—are more extensively fantasized that most of the similar items nowadays produced for the television medium, but it is arguable that that makes them all the more interesting, and certainly makes them more extensively "personalized." Looking back from the viewpoint of a literary archaeologist interested in precursors of modern speculative fiction, Berthoud might seem to be a deeply frustrating case-study, as a writer who came close to inventing "science fiction" in the 1840s but failed to do so, ultimately producing only one futuristic story in the 1860s, conscientiously offered as a Mercieresque dream, more in a spirit of parodic frivolity than serious anticipation. It is, however, rather unfair to assess him in terms of what he did not do rather than what he actually did.

The items he collected in *Fantaisies scientifiques de Sam* now seem extremely eccentric to modern eyes educated by a very different notion of what "scientific fantasies" might be.

Many are items of offbeat journalism, only lightly fictional-
ized, and many of those that are more solidly cast in a fictional
mold are brief historical romances devoid of any scientific
content, or primitive exercises in what would now be called
"animal fantasy." Those that do deal with contemporary scientific research and discovery, however, often do so from an odd
and perhaps seemingly-perverse perspective. I have only reproduced a handful of them in this sampler, attempting to give
a hint as to their range, but the group is hopefully varied
enough to illustrate their eccentricity as well as their scope.

The collections of children's stories Berthoud assembled
after the *Fantaisies scientifiques* frequently recycle stories
therefrom—especially the longer stories that probably predate
the articles reprinted from *La Patrie*—but usually add new
items intended to round out their themes. The latter are usually
presented in a supposedly child-friendly manner, but that does
not always serve of conceal the author's cynicism, and certainly does not suppress the pioneering surges of his imagination.

In those more extravagant endeavors, Berthoud was inevitably working under the handicap of the imperfect
knowledge of his era and the limitations of his own particular
idols of thought. He was by no means the only writer to become interested in contemporary paleontological discoveries
in the 1860s, or to attempt to find ways of dramatizing those
discoveries in fictional form, but the limitations of the fossil
record as a basis for fictional reconstruction are painfully obvious to the modern eye in "Le Château de Heidenloch" and
we now know that Berthoud was on the losing side of the ar-
gument in sticking to Georges Cuvier's insistence on main-
taining belief in the special creation of humankind in accordance with Biblical chronology in spite of the overwhelming
evidence of the Earth's antiquity and the mounting evidence
that humankind's Stone Age must date back much further than
Biblical chronology allowed. It is, however, worth remembering that modern readers only have access to the second, revised edition of Jules Verne's *Voyage au centre de la Terre*,
written in 1867 in order to take aboard the conversion of Louis

Figuier, its principal source, to the latter viewpoint, and that the first version of the novel, published in 1864, had accepted the creationist account to which Berthoud adhered.

All the English versions produced as *Journey to the Centre of the Earth* reproduce the revised edition. It is true that the depictions of the plesiosaur and the ichthyosaur contained in Verne's novels are far more accurate that the earlier descriptions contained in Verne's novelette, but Verne's description of a prehistoric human, presented (as a vision) in the second version is as wide of the mark as anything in Berthoud's work, and Berthoud's pioneering account of Stone Age humankind, "Les Premiers habitants de Paris" (1865; translated herein as "The First Inhabitants of Paris"), although inevitably primitive by comparison with the prehistoric fantasies produced in the 1890s by J. H. Rosny and others, nevertheless remains something of a *tour de force* for its time, having been produced a full decade ahead of the next significant attempt to do something similar—which was almost certainly inspired by Berthoud—in *Le Monde inconnu* [The Unknown World] (1876, tr. in 1879 as *The Pre-Historic World*) by his fellow veteran *feuilletonist* Élie Berthet, which was subsequently revised in 1885 as *Paris avant l'histoire*.

Jules Verne was a considerably better writer than Berthoud, and seems much more important to historians of science fiction because he did write a handful of genuine items of speculative fiction that extrapolate the possibilities of scientific progress far more robustly than anything Berthoud did, but it is worth remembering that Jules Hetzel did his level best to restrain, if not actually to suppress, that aspect of his star writer's work, and that Berthoud, mostly working for editors far more conservative than Hetzel, was certainly not operating in an environment hospitable to that kind of endeavor.

It is still impossible to judge the full extent of Berthoud's endeavors in pioneering his own varieties of "scientific fiction," because many of the periodicals for which he worked have vanished from human ken, and it is highly unlikely that *gallica* will ever be able to reproduce even scattered samples of them, but the few samples that have been revived by that means indicate that he really was an interesting and accomplished writer in that context. The work in question would have been as difficult for contemporary readers to assess properly as for modern ones but their esotericism should not be allowed to detract from its achievement, which is as remarkable for its fervor as for its uniqueness.

The translations from *Contes misanthropiques* included in the present collection's section of Misanthropic Tales were made from the Google Books version. Most of the translations of items from the *Chroniques et traditions surnaturelles de Flandre* in the Folklore and Fakelore section were made from the versions reproduced on the Biblisem website at biblisem.net, because they are easier to read than the originals contained on *gallica*, but the items not available on Biblisem were taken directly from the *gallica* version of the first edition. The translation of the three stories in the Martyrs of Science section reprinted in *Fantaisies scientifiques de Sam* and all the stories in the Scientific Fantasies section were made from the *gallica* versions of that four-volume set. The translations of "Le Maître du Temps" and "Le Chaudron de Bicêtre" were made from the *gallica* copies of the *Revue Pittoresque*. The translation of "Le Château de Heidenloch" in the Stories for Children section was made from the *gallica* version of *Contes du Dr. Sam*; the translations of the other two stories in that section were made from a copy of an undated Garnier edition of *L'Homme depuis cinq mille ans*.

Brian Stableford

MISANTHROPIC TALES

PRESTIGE

> May Our Lady aid me, good sire! A tattered
> rag instead of an entire mantle of new fabric!
> Père Mathias, *La Querelle des Chevaliers.*[1]

> My daughter is young, she is pretty;
> And her mother has trained her
> In economy since childhood.
> I'm rich, it's true, but I have many children;
> It's time I married her off.
> S. Henry Berthoud. *Le Projet de mariage.*

It was four o'clock; the sea, leaving the shore dry, was only audible as a dull murmur, and only a few waves were perceptible, still swaying on the edge of the horizon.

The greatest activity reigned in the port of Dunkerque; troops of fishermen, their baskets on their back and their nets in hand, wearing their skirts of thick red cloth rolled up to their knees, were advancing barefoot in the midst of the hardened sand that the ebb-tide had uncovered; their confused and singular cries mingled with the racket of carts, the oaths of mariners in their various languages, the plaintive and rhythmic songs of sailors unloading ships, and other confused noises. Cabin-boys in tarred hats, tradesmen, foreigners, women

---

[1] Like many of the citations with which Berthoud liked to preface his stories, this one is invented; it probably relates to the imaginary Père Mathias featured in "Saint Mathias the Hermit."

wrapped in the grey or black mantillas known locally as "capes," and others elegantly dressed in fashionable costumes, were moving around the harbor, crossing paths, forming groups, moving apart, advancing on to the jetty; and the rays of the setting sun displayed their ruddy light through the furled sails, rigging, flags and masts that rose up in all directions.

Picturesque as the spectacle was, it did not attract the slightest attention from a young man who was making his way along the harbor precipitately.

I should think so! All his sensations were absorbed by one of those ardent and unrestricted joys that arrive so rarely in life to dilate the breast of a young man, although it suffices, in order for it to happen, that he is young and in love.

Far from noticing the effects of the light, Paul, for that was his name, did not even think about looking where he was going. That would have been a good idea, however, for on two occasions he attracted energetic protests, and he finally found himself in the arms of someone who demanded in a phlegmatic tone, with an unequivocal English accent: "Paul, have you done mad?"

"Sydney, my friend, you, here? I thought you were in London. It's my good angel who's sent you! Oh, I'm the happiest of men!"

After that beginning, which a professor of rhetoric would have called an exordium *ex abrupto*, Paul linked arms with the friend that he had encountered in such an opportune fashion, and set about telling him the cause of his joy. Nothing befits and animated conversation like a precipitate pace, and Paul dragged his listener along so rapidly that the latter exclaimed: "God damn it! Don't you know that I've got a bullet lodged in my leg?"

That interjection slowed Paul's march for a few seconds; even so, he gradually resumed his hasty pace, and when they both arrived at the hotel where Sydney was staying, the islander's face was covered with sweat.

"My friend," he said, stopping with an entirely British gravity, "I see that felicity is at least as loquacious as misfortune. You've asked for Mademoiselle Tréa's hand in marriage; her father, Monsieur Vandermoudt, has promised it to you. Thank God: there, in one sentence, are your confidences of five quarters of an hour.

"Personally, I left London the day before yesterday and Calais this morning. My business affairs will keep me here for two weeks. I'm going to have dinner; will you join me?"

Paul accepted, laughing, talked about nothing all through dinner but Tréa, the charming Tréa, and would not give Sydney a rest until he had consented to be introduced to Monsieur Vandermoudt. Sir Edward Sydney finally gave in, and after having retired to a room whose door he took extreme care to close, he emerged again dressed with an elegance and taste that the most committed dandy would not have disavowed.

Sir Edward might have been forty years old. At first sight, his distinguished bearing, teeth of admirable whiteness and regularity, beautiful blond hair and graceful manner produced the favorable impression that disposes people to great benevolence. It was only after a more attentive examination that one discovered a discordance in his gaze and bizarre effects that lingered.

Furthermore, he expressed himself in French with great facility, albeit with a certain hoarseness and awkwardness in his pronunciation. The limp occasioned by the wound in his leg was hardly noticeable, perhaps not even lacking in a certain grace, and, far from harming him, reflected upon him the interest that a soldier's wound almost invariable produces. Let us add, too, that the wound in question was not his only one, for he experienced some difficulty in making use of his right arm, the hand of which remained constantly covered by a glove.

The portrait of Mademoiselle Tréa will not be as long: an only daughter, a spoiled child, delightful caprices, and a whimsicality that might drive a husband to despair or render him the happiest of men; nourished on novels like all the young women of the province, and in consequence, excitable; incorrect in judgment and imagining the ideal type of happi-

31

ness in the features of a cavalry officer with an epaulette and medal, whom every sentry salutes.

At any rate, she was allowing herself to be married to Paul without regret, but without joy, saying to herself: *He's a nice fellow who loves me as much as he's capable of loving— which is to say, very gently—and with whom I'll find a negative kind of happiness.*

The rank that gave Tréa's father his consideration and his fortune were only secondary; according to the conventional expression, it placed him among the well-to-do bourgeoisie and nothing more; the young woman's vanity felt flattered when Paul, with a solemnity unaccustomed for him, introduced, first to Monsieur Vandermoudt and then to Mademoiselle Tréa Vandermoudt, "Colonel Sir Edward Sydney of Sydney Hall."

Sir Edward's distinguished manners, which made a contrast with Paul's blunt and bourgeois manners, initially inspired in Tréa a kind of suspicion of herself and respect for Sir Edward; she did not indulge that evening in her customary chatter, a delightful profligacy overflowing with mischief and candor; she maintained a certain reserve, and replied timidly.

It was a major occasion for her, when Sir Edward arrived the following day on his own. Paul had left that morning on important business, which would keep him absent for at least a month.

On the one hand, she did not want to appear silly, and on the other, she could not overcome the impression of superiority that Sir Edward made on her; she was flattered to be associating with a man of his rank and merit, and yet the man in question imposed himself upon her in the most cruel fashion.

There was in Sir Edward's character that exaltation that, far from being incompatible with experience and disenchantment, is rather the companion of then, if not the consequence.

Utterly smitten with the Tréa's grace and naivety, he had promised himself the previous day that the charming creature would not be Paul's. Rich, powerful and accustomed to satisfying his slightest whim, Paul's departure served his purpose marvelously; it was up to him to do the rest. He set to work with the confidence of a man whose experience and intelligence guaranteed success, and the wariness of a lover who is very much in love and who is staking too much on success not to be afraid of failure.

The colonel had observed, without seeking to destroy, the impression of superiority that he had made on Tréa; far from being unfavorable to his plans, it was to serve them. He showed himself to be so witty and so amiable that Tréa felt attracted to him by a gentle charm that would temper, but without diminishing, the sentiment she experienced of the colonel's merit.

The next day and on the days after that, Sir Edward continued to surround Tréa with the most assiduous attentions. However, he never mentioned love; he did better than that: he let her see that he loved her.

It was necessary to lead Paul's fiancée insensibly to renounce the man to whom she and her father had granted the right to her. That was a treason that would go against and revolt the young enthusiast's romantic ideas, and such a rupture would be bound to cause a scandal. All the small town gossip! To have fingers pointed at one, to be subjected to sarcasms and mealy-mouthed atrocities!

The colonel read Tréa's mind. He therefore continued his skillful seduction, always putting himself, by indirect means, in parallel with Paul; that was to establish his value and to denigrate, perhaps doom, the man who, although younger, admittedly, did not possess any of Sir Edward's brilliant qualities.

Even so, he would never have triumphed if he had not dissipated the ideas of treason to which Tréa's romantic character was opposed, making them disappear beneath generous sentiments.

Naturally melancholy in his character, he took advantage of that disposition. He allowed it to be glimpsed that a profound chagrin was consuming him. That somber despair, about which he never uttered any complaint, inspired that tender interest in the young woman which, quite different from pity, only differs from love by an imperceptible nuance, and whose effect is all the more sure because one is less wary of it, and the mystery in which its attraction is clad.

The progress of that sentiment was rapid in Tréa, but it was necessary to hasten it further, because Paul was going to return, along with the forgotten scruples and the shame of saying to his face: "I love someone other than you, whose wife I have promised to be."

The opportunity for a decisive struggle presented itself the next day. The colonel was alone with Tréa. Tréa yielded with charm to one of those conversations which relaxation, confidence and a tenderness as-yet-unadmitted or concealed render so delicious.

The subject turned to happiness; she cited someone as an example of a happy man.

"Happy!" he said.

"Yes…there are many who are said to be happy."

"And yet, if one knew that they were suffering, perhaps one wouldn't want to change places with them, at the price of the softness of luxury, the glamour of rank and the glory of renown. Perhaps one wouldn't want to, if one had to sleep on straw and eat black bread.

"I knew a man whose lot everyone envied; amiable, it was said, learned, a great name, and rich enough to satisfy the vastest desires. He was, however, very unhappy. There was no ostentation or exaggeration in his dolor; he allowed himself to drift in the midst of life's pleasures, insouciantly, without receiving any beneficent impressions therefrom.

"An atrocious and prolonged dolor numbed his moral faculties, as it can dull the physical faculties, except that the latter are sometimes cured, the former never can be. He loved, he was beloved; a woman had sacrificed everything for him: happiness, the past, the future, conscience! He was worthy of such sacrifices. He was worthy, because he did not regard love as a frivolous struggle of pleasure and vanity a duel in which one deploys cunning, which one refines with skill, and after which one departs cold and indifferent.

"To love, to unite oneself with another for life, in spite of misfortune and despair, he for her and she for him: that was what he understood by love; that was what she understood by love. Poor fools!

"She belonged to another, and he knew of their love, and cruelly avenged himself for his misunderstood rights. She had only given her friend a tenderness that he alone could understand, that he alone could inspire; it did not matter; she belonged to another, body and soul; her thoughts, imagination, desires and dreams all belonged to another. That other claimed them. He claimed them by virtue of the pact she had signed, as a poor girl devoid of experience whose parents had guided her hand.

"He proposed to the unfortunate—the man whose story I'm telling—either exile for him or opprobrium for her. Opprobrium for her! The world would have laughed at that fall as at the fall of an angel.

"He exiled himself.

"For five years, only two people in the world knew where he had taken refuge: a sure friend and her.

"Finally, she became free again; the pact that bound her to another was broken, for death alone can break such a pact. And he received a letter that said: *Come back; I can be yours*.

"Yours! What, together! Always together! No longer to be apart, no longer to await as a boon letters sent at long, uncertain intervals—letters, not from her but from another, saying: *I've seen her; she loves you and is weeping...*

"Yours!

"Together now, together forever, arms entwined, lips seeking one another out!

"To admit his love to the entire universe; to say: *I surround you, I protect you with my tenderness!* She is mine! I am hers. She is my wife. She will be the mother of my children. Oh, what delight, children! To see them born, to be gripped by new bonds. Children who will love me as much as she loves me, whom I will love as much as I love her.

"Come on, come on, faster! Here's gold, press your horses, hurry up!

"No distance was ever crossed with as much urgency as the two hundred leagues that separated him from her.

"He arrives, he runs. 'Where is she?' He's stopped; people try to speak to him. 'Let me go! Let me go! Her! I want no one but her!' He shoves them all away, moves them aside; he succeeds in reaching her. There she is!

"She's asleep. Next to her is the crucifix before which, yesterday, she prayed for him, for now she can pray for him; her love is chaste and virtuous.

"He dare not wake her; her sleep is so pure, her beautiful face is relaxed with so much grace.

"How pale she is! There are the traces of what she has suffered for him—for she has suffered a great deal, suffered as much as a woman can suffer; despair, anguish, opprobrium...and all that for love of him!

"In his arms! In his arms! It's necessary that he press her in his arms!

"Her cool lips...her closed eyes..."

"Dead!"

"The unfortunate man!" cried Tréa, violently moved by the story.

"Oh yes, very unfortunate," said Sydney. "very unfortunate...for, after ten years of despair, after having thought his heart broken forever and incapable of love, the unfortunate fell in love again...with an angel like her. But that one, who could have made him forget all his sufferings, that one, who could have made a heart withered by despair palpitate with joy again...

"Tréa, she loves another! Another will possess her!"

With both hands, he covered his eyes.

The young woman allowed her head to fall upon Sydney's breast, and hid her face therein. And he gently picked up a hand that she abandoned to him, and covered it with kisses and tears.

A few moments went by.

"Tréa," he murmured, then, emotionally. "Tréa, my Tréa…"

Trembling, joyful, troubled, she raised her eyes tenderly toward him…

An exclamation expired on her lips; her cheeks paled and tightened.

Sydney's mouth was wide open, open as no human mouth ever opens; convulsive efforts were reddening his face, his expression was strange and staring. He looked like a vampire ready to feed…

Sydney ejected the young woman from his arms, and ran out.

He came back almost immediately, a smile on his lips. Joy, he claimed, had caused him to experience a violent convulsion, but the fresh air had sufficed to cure it.

Soon, and gradually, his grace and amiability dissipated the terrible impression that the bizarre incident had produced; he ended up causing it to be forgotten by means of gentle pleasantries, which he gradually transformed into tender words and passionate protestations.

The following day, at dawn, Sydney went to Paul's house as the latter was getting down from a carriage, had a long conversation with him, left him, and went to meet him again an hour later outside the town, armed with pistols and accompanied by two witnesses and two domestics.

At the first shot, Sir Edward fell; a bullet had broken his left leg, the leg that was already wounded. He was seen to crumple at knee height, the heel forward.

Paul fled, and the witnesses hastened around the colonel, but he wrapped himself up in his cloak, obstinately refused their help, and had himself taken away by his domestics in a carriage that was waiting a short distance away.

A courier was sent to London during the night by the colonel, and as soon as he returned, the servants marveled to see their master quit his bed and go to see Tréa's father, without limping any more than he had limped before the duel.

A fortnight later, the marriage took place of Sir Edward Sydney, colonel and baronet, and Mademoiselle Tréa Vandermoudt.

The newlyweds left immediately for London, to the great regret of the idlers and scandalmongers of Dunkerque, the sort of people who thrive in little towns and for whom gossip is the greatest joy—except, of course, for the pleasure of spreading a slander.

For a year, Tréa has been Sir Edward's wife.

To bear his name, to be his, she has sacrificed everything, including her own conscience and the pledge made to another, and left everything, including her father and the beautiful land of France.

She is unhappy! In buying that name at such a price, she believed that she was buying happiness; alas, she has only bought two things to which she had never given any thought: rank and fortune.

Tender and sweet caresses, words of love murmured and repeated by lips so close to one another that they quiver with the warm vapor of their confused breath...never to be apart...two in one...that, oh, that was the happiness of which she had dreamed with him!

Instead of that, a mysterious and inexplicable constraint! One would think that he is afraid of being broken by her hugs, devoured by her kisses!

Spending nights alone, far from her, in an apartment that no one but he enters, had ever entered! Never, for him, a spouse who sleeps peacefully in his arms, murmuring words of love; never, for him, the awakening of a spouse whose dreams and sensuality have left her white shoulders bare and her breast palpitating!

Always a desperate reserve, always stripping love of its sweetest prestige, its most intoxicating charms, repressing voluptuousness to the point of outrage!

He has just left her; he has just retired to that apartment whose mysteries he alone knows, that apartment that Tréa cannot open either with supplications or tears.

What are the mysteries that unfold there?

Already too much that is strange and menacing surrounds her: that fixed and satanic gaze…that horrible convulsion, that gaping vampiric mouth, which she saw one evening…that mortal wound miraculously cured…

Why that hidden life? Without being superstitious, Tréa cannot help believing that there is something supernatural about it.

But let what comes of it come! There is too much despair, too much doubt, too much anguish. She is his wife; she has the right to penetrate where the sacred title that she holds on the part of Heaven and the law is perhaps being outraged…

She gets up, she takes a step…and then, frightened of what she wants to do, she stops…

At length, she arms herself with all the resolution of which she is capable, and marches with slow and unsteady steps to the door of the mysterious apartment.

There, she hesitates again.

She leans over, she listens: not a word, not a movement, not a sound!

She is about to draw away when the moon, suddenly emerging from behind a cloud, causes a key to gleam. A key! He has forgotten to take it out.

She can go in.

Hesitation and anguished twitches take possession of her again.

Finally, she turns the key; she pushes the door slowly; she goes in.

A profound darkness…no other sound than the breath of her mouth, and the palpitations of her heart.

If she dared to lift the thick curtain over the window! She reaches out her hand; the fabric yields, falls, and the moonlight inundates the fantastic apartment.

Then a slobbering voice threatens; then a bald and naked head looms up, a bald head, one of whose eyes is nothing but an empty hole; a bald head, whose flaccid cheeks dangle to either side of a jawless mouth; a bald head, the rightful complement of a mutilated trunk to which only one arm and one leg remain...

Now, she is mad.

THE PAINTER GHIGI

> I have never understood very clearly,
> in a satisfactory fashion, how some
> people can cut a man's throat as if he
> were a pig, and pay no heed to their
> crime after committing it, while
> others suffer horrible remorse.
> I have referred in vain to differences
> in nervous organization, to differences
> in education; it has remained evident to
> me nevertheless that remorse, like disease,
> destroys some people while leaving others
> untouched.
> D.-M. Fabien, *De l'Organisation morale de l'Homme*,
> ch. VII.

Happy is he who feels no remorse! If he throws himself on his bed, he soon abandons himself to a refreshing and peaceful sleep; he does not pant in the grip of a nightmare; he does not wake up with a start; he does not dart wild glances in all directions.

He does not yearn for daybreak as a blessing; and during the day, he does not have one implacable idea, and one alone, a frightful phantom that attaches an insupportable gaze to him, which never lowers the accusing finger extended toward him.

He does not reply in a brusque tone to the loving words of his young wife; he does not push away his child, who comes to kiss him; he is not irritated by his noisy games.

He has no remorse!

People envy me my renown and my glory: it is a crown of red hot iron that burns my head, and which I cannot tear off.

People envy me my palazzo, my villa, my domains, my carriage, my horses: I would give them all, I would give everything, to whomever could take away my remorse.

But that is impossible, alas. No, that is quite impossible, for I have done everything to rid myself of my remorse.

I have never been able to do it!

I have knelt in a priest's confessional; I uttered such sobs there; I struck my breast there with such despair that the man of God said: "My son, there is no sin that cannot be redeemed by such great repentance."

I spoke; the priest fled.

After that, young artists sometimes demanded why I was pale, why my lips never wore a smile any longer. "Come with us; a secret pain is eating you away, but there is no pain that joyful orgies cannot cure; come to lewd songs repeated in chorus; come to wine that will intoxicate, to semi-naked women who will intoxicate even more; there—that is what you need!"

I followed them, and when their speech became noisier; when, tottering, they were rolling on the grass in the arms of their mistresses, I drank, I drank, and I drank more, for I said to myself: What joy! I shall be like them! I shall no longer have reason!

Alas, wine has no drunkenness for me.

Once, I saw a hermit who lived far away from men; he boasted to me of the calm he had found in his retreat, and I ran away into a desert.

I prayed, in vain; I imposed the greatest austerities upon myself, in vain; I tore myself with blows of the disciplinary lash, in vain: there, always there, my execrable idea!

I was told that women have marvelous secrets to render peace to those who have lost it; that no one in the world knows how they are able to put dolor and despair to sleep; I was told that, cradled in their arms, with one's head laid on their bosom, one becomes placid again, devoid of remorse; that they purify and enable forgetfulness.

I married Marianna, an angel of beauty, tenderness and love, the most celestial of creatures who ever murmured intoxicating words in a man's ear.

Her caresses make me feel sick; they are killing me; I have no response to make but gestures of refusal, indifferent, harsh words.

She calls me Ghigi.

Ghigi, Ghigi! Always and everywhere that execrable name!

Romans, foreigners, my wife, my son, always Ghigi, always Ghigi!

If they knew how much it hurts me, what dagger they're showing me, what muffled death-rattle they're causing me to hear!

For I'm not Ghigi. Antonio Ferragio is my name. Ghigi is a name I've stolen, a name in which there's ingratitude, treason, adultery, theft and murder!

Oh, if there were no Hell, if death were oblivion, how immediately I would die!

But a life without end, a life of eternal punishment, a life in which I always hear that name: Ghigi! Ghigi!

Never can my head, never can my soul conceive an idea with which that name is not alloyed; it has become inherent in my nature; it torments me; for me, it is a necessity. And now that I'm alone here again, alone in the midst of darkness and silence, tell me how it is that I find, in writing ideas that drive one to despair, a horrible pleasure, a torment that Hell does not have; tell me how an imperious force is attaching me to this table, is making this pen move.

Oh, may you never experience remorse!

There was once a time when I never experienced remorse myself. I was a young man then, with a slim figure and black curly hair, a young man who abandoned himself with delight to a precarious and nonchalant life. Pleasure was my great, my only affair: I enjoyed the present moment, and never had a care for the quarter-hour that would follow it, much less for the next day.

One night, one single night, arrived, however, to change my destiny, and make me the most rascally and miserable of men.

I had spent a part of that fatal night in debauchery; my head heated by wine, I was wandering aimlessly in the ruins of Palermo with a friend when we encountered a senora escorted by two cavaliers. "I'll wager," I cried, that I can lift the veil of that unknown beauty!"

"I'll help you," replied the madman who was accompanying me.

That cost the lives of two men—one of the cavaliers and my friend were killed.

In the meantime, I lifted the senora's veil; it was the governor's mother.

"Antonio Ferragio," she said to me, your head will expiate my brother's death."

Where could I find refuge? Already, sbirri were running in response to the senora's screams, those implacable screams that never ceased naming Antonio Ferragio.

I fled aimlessly, and when day broke, I was alone a few leagues from Palermo, on the shore of the sea.

I let myself fall on to the sand, in a stupid torpor produced by fatigue and despair. I resolved to wait there for the fate that I could not escape. For I could not deny my murder; one of the victims had recognized me. I could not leave the country; I did not have a sequin. I could not find a refuge; anyone who had given me shelter would have perished with me.

A man, still young, passed by on horseback. Seeing me pale and unmoving, he thought that I had been robbed and stabbed by thieves, and came to help me. His questions and his pity wearied me. "Leave me alone," I said. "I've murdered the governor's uncle."

"Climb up on the rump of the horse with me," He said. "I'll give you a safe hiding-place where I defy the governor to find you."

My death was inevitable, death on the scaffold! Imagine what I experienced in hearing those words, which gave me hope! I leapt on to the horse, and after riding for three hours, we arrived at a villa of meager appearance.

The interior of the villa matched its exterior: poor walls with no wallpaper—but they were partly covered by paintings worthy of a celebrated master.

Then the stranger said to me: I have your secret, and to reassure you as to my fidelity, I'll give you mine. You've heard mention of the Neapolitan painter Ghigi, whom some say has been dead or ten years and others say has gone to Mexico. I'm Ghigi.

"After having studied my art for a long time in foreign lands, I returned to Naples, where no one recognized me, for I was an orphan, and fifteen years of absence and traveling have changed me considerably. I was nevertheless about to take up residence in Naples and devote myself to works of art, when I saw the young daughter of Count Rienzi, when I succeeded in becoming Paola's lover.

"Then all my plans changed; I liquidated my fortune, abducted Paola and, fleeing the vengeance of a noble family, we came to seek refuge in Palermo under assumed names. I bought this villa, where I live a happier existence with Paola than I can say.

"Yes, the mystery that surrounds us, never being apart from one another, living only for one another, cultivating the art that I adore—unknown, it's true, but also without being harassed by envy—all extends over our existence a peaceful, inexpressible charm. I've exchanged glory for happiness, and the deceptive amity of men for Paola's love; not a day goes by when I do not bless Heaven!

"I've revealed to you what no one in the world knows, other than myself and Paola; you can see now that your refuge is safe."

Wretch! I destroyed that happiness, destroyed it irredeemably! Oh, Ghigi, how have I repaid you for your kindness!

My idleness and my solitude in that retreat, set my Sicilian blood on fire. One day, beside myself, I took the sleeping Paola in my arms. She was mine.

Attracted by the poor woman's screams, Ghigi came running to take revenge. A dagger-thrust laid him at my feet.

Then I thought I heard infernal laughter; I thought I heard a voice whispering in my ear: "Leave for Rome with Ghigi's gold; take his paintings. Say: 'I'm the painter Ghigi; I've come back from Mexico.'"

Yes, it was the Demon that gave me that advice, for what man could conceive such a sin? Yes, it was the Demon; I felt his burning breath exhaling into my ear!

But that woman! Ghigi's body...he might yet revive; his tongue might speak; his hand might write...

A delirious rage, a fiery vertigo took possession of me...and when I recovered my reason, I was aboard a ship whose cannon was saluting the port of Nettuno, and I was sitting on a crate that contained all of Ghigi's paintings.

Arrived in Rome, I exhibited a few of the paintings; I said that I had painted them. Soon, the name of Ghigi was being repeated enthusiastically; his paintings were snatched up. I had glory; I became rich, and the intoxication of glory and fortune stunned the memory of my crime; it sometimes came back, at long intervals, to persecute me, but the whirlwind of pleasure and prestige stifled it.

I thus had, for nearly ten years, a kind of happiness.

I had sold all my paintings except for one, representing a Madonna nursing her son; Prince Borgia saw it, gave me a considerable sum for it, and immediately had it transported to his gallery. The painting was not covered by any veil during the journey, and, gripped by admiration, a crowd soon assembled around the masterpiece and started following it to the prince's gallery, saluting wildly the name of Ghigi. The excitement went so far as to require me to participate in that improvised triumph and follow the painting in the prince's uncovered carriage, in the midst of enthusiastic shouts.

There were so many people that a cart carrying a victim to execution could not get past; it was a mute beggar who, driven by need, had stolen a loaf of bread. At the sight of me, and hearing the name of Ghigi, he stood up, extended two mutilated hands toward me, tried to say a few words with his severed tongue…and fell back in despair.

It was Ghigi.

Oh, may you never feel remorse!

THE DAY AFTER THE WEDDING

> There are good marriages;
> there are no delightful ones.
> La Rochefoucauld, *Maximes.*[2]

> Alas, neither reason, nor imagination,
> Nor intelligence, nor the heart
> can render happiness; I understand that now.
> *Lettres d'amour.*

Cologne, 25 September 1820.

So, my dear Frederick, you are abandoning me at the moment when, according to your advice, I have to sacrificed my most cherished errors to reason!

You're leaving for Mexico!

If, at least, your letters had been able, once a week, to continue to encourage me, to persuade me, to make me persevere…but alas, they'll only reach me henceforth at long intervals! No more fixed day to receive them, no more desirous waiting for the post! Immense seas will separate us; you'll be living in another world!

It's no longer letters that I'll be writing to you; it's a journal that you'll receive, God knows when…perhaps never…

If you knew the courage it required for me to break the links that bound me to Madame Narscheid! Poor Louise, who sacrificed to my love her future hopes, her conscience, her domestic joy, and her reputation!

I admit it: twenty times, during that last meeting, I felt close to renouncing my marriage to Fraulein von Reistadst.

---

[2] The Duc de Rochefoucauld's *Maximes* were first published in 1665, although more were added in later editions.

Yes, Frederick, I would have done it; but, after fits of the most frightful despair, Louise suddenly armed herself with a resignation that I no longer had. "I love you more than my happiness," she said. "Be happy, Eduard, since you can be, with someone else."

Then, after that, without saying another word, she went to collect everything that had come to her from me, and threw it all into the fire.

Frederick, I bought very dear, that evening, the happiness that you promised me in a marriage of convenience! What interior peace, what wellbeing of fortune, can be worth the love that I'm losing, Louise's love? It was surrounded by perils, by despair, I know, but it was burning, devoted, sublime.

Poor fool that I am! Look, there's my imagination running away with me again!

I shall not see Louise gain; her husband arrives this evening, and, as you know, my mere presence in Cologne can move him to the most frightful fits of jealousy; since the discovery of one of my letters to Louise, four years ago, he's capable of anything.

I'll leave at daybreak for Aix-la-Chapelle, and I shall finally see my wife.

Aix-la-Chapelle, 26 September, 3 p.m.

I've just seen her; she's a pale and rosy-cheeked young woman; a great freshness, beautiful blonde hair, an ingenuous smile. Her name is Fanny.

Her parents made a big occasion out of our meeting; they introduced me to my fiancée with solemn ostentation.

It's a singular thing to find oneself among so many unknown people, that I'll be calling brother, sister, father, mother and wife tomorrow!

My wife! A lover who will lavish the mot tender caresses; the only one it will be permissible to love henceforth; a faithful friend in happiness as in adversity; a companion from

49

who death alone can separate me! And I've never seen her before today! And it's tomorrow that she'll become my wife!

You're wiser than I am; I recognize the superiority of your reason over mine; you judge things with a much greater justice than I can contrive; you love me as much as one can love a friend, and it's you who have proposed to me, have advised me, who have made this marriage,

Frederick, I need to remind myself of all that; I need that, for otherwise it won't be tomorrow that she'll become my wife.

The same day, 6 p.m.

I've just had a long conversation with her, after supper. Her ideas seem to me to be more solid than extensive; her imagination is as pure as a virgin's, her soul as affectionate as that of a young woman who has never been parted from a good and wise mother. She has had a prudent education, and has been brought up in great principles of economy.

The conversation has done me good; yes, my friend, I'm beginning to understand that you were right: a calm, placid, uniform happiness without the slightest shock; peace, repose, a good wife who surrounds you with kindness and tender attention; a fresh and naïve smile always ready to form at your first words; a delicate hand that prepares and presents the beverage when fever burns you and your breast is oppressed... It's not Louise; it's not the ideal, impossible happiness of which I once dreamed; but it's real happiness.

Yes, the conversation with Fanny has done me good; yes, her smile has calmed my unbearable agitation.

Frederick, were you telling the truth?

27 September, 4 a.m.

I've slept, Frederick, slept peacefully until now; yes, I'm going to be happy.

Yes: until now, I had not sought happiness where one might find it, and, blasphemer that I was, I said: "There is no happiness."

A young woman as beautiful and pure as the angels; her innocent caresses, her ineffable tenderness; and then, soon, children who will tighten the solemn bonds more narrowly; children who, with their dear little voices, will cause the delightful name "Father" to resound in my ear, in my intoxicated soul.

28 September, 6 a.m.

The virgins of Heaven do not have her purity; the fiery cherubim do not have her tenderness! Oh, Frederick, Frederick, I'm happy, happy forever, and I owe that happiness to you.

She's getting dressed at present, and then we're going to take a long walk in the countryside that surrounds us. Frederick, Frederick, we'll be alone, alone with nature and its sublime beauties; we'll exchange sensations in a glance, a smile, the pressure of a hand. Frederick, my friend, do you comprehend fully the happiness that I possess? Tell me, do you comprehend?

15 October, same year.

I'm alone in my room, lying down. Is it a dream I've had—a horrible dream? Oh, if it were only a dream!

Madman that I am, it can't be otherwise; such misfortune isn't possible; no, no!

Can you imagine that I dreamed going for a walk with my young wife, with Fanny; I'd never seen a more beautiful sunrise. That's because I'd never seen the sun rise while my Fanny was giving me her arm.

We were on the bank of a river. Suddenly, I saw something floating in the water, something indistinct...it came closer...a woman's corpse...Louise!

Oh, what a dream! What a frightful dream!

I don't know what I experienced at that moment: a convulsive rage set all my limbs ablaze and trembling; my eyes could no longer see; my ears were deafened by an execrable ringing...

I seized, I clutched tightly, obstinately, something warm and delicate; then I felt a flaccid weight fall upon my breast and slide to my feet with a dull sound.

Then people surrounded me; they were uttering cries of horror; I struggled against those numerous man; they tied me up and took me away, through an immense crowd.

And I saw two female corpses on a stretcher that was being carried in front of me: Louise and Fanny.

Oh, what a dream! What a frightful dream!

My God, what an impression it has made on me! I've just looked in the mirror; I saw myself livid, emaciated.

But everything around me is in chaos, broken, strewn with debris...

My clothes! They're no more than tatters!

Iron bars on my windows! Enormous bars at the door!

Ah...it wasn't a dream! It isn't a dream...

THERIAKI[3]

Better one grain of opium than twelve gourds full of rice.
(Oriental proverb.)

Happiness? It's drunkenness that takes away reason.
(Anonymous.)

"Alas, my feeble and convulsive hands can scarcely raise this cup to my lips; the shaking is making its contents spill. Oh, I would bless the angel of death if he would extend his redoubtable blade over my mouth! Life weighs upon me so heavily! There is no true believer more miserable than me; my contracted muscles are inclining my heavy head toward me left shoulder; a cup seems a burden in my trembling hands; my stiff legs are buckling beneath my paltry body and the slightest light closes my eyes, too weak to support it.

"I would like to be in a shroud on which the pious hands of a dervish has inscribed verses from the Koran; I would like the servants of Mohammed to prostrate themselves on seeing my abode illuminated by funeral lamps; yes, I would like them to repeat, while striking their breasts: 'The Aga Massoud is no more! There is no God but God and Mohammed is his prophet.'

"What is there left for me to do on the earth?

"In vain the most delicious dishes are set forth before me; they only excite my disgust.

"What use is it to me to have slaves in my seraglio from Georgia with white shoulders, Kaffirs with passionate move-

---

[3] This term, referring to opium, was exceedingly esoteric in 1831 and has fallen into disuse since, but Honoré de Balzac was fond of it and used it in several stories, including one reference to a cadaverous face with "a theriaki smile."

ments and coppery complexions, Africans with large eyes and black breasts? Their smiles leave me cold; their voluptuous dances weary me; it is necessary for me to lower the triple bans of my turban over my ears when they marry their voices and play the lute or the Persian flute; the softest sounds shake my debilitate brain and are too noisy for it.

"Yes I would like to be in a shroud on which the pious hands of a dervish has inscribed verses from the Koran; I would like the servants of Mohammed to prostrate themselves on seeing my abode illuminated by funeral lamps!"

Such were the thoughts of the Aga Massoud.

Lying sadly on a vast sofa, pale and motionless, his eyes half-closed, one might have mistaken him for a corpse if one had not heard the rattle of his slow respiration.

Soon, the effects of the opium that he had drunk began to manifest themselves: a more rapid breath elevated his bosom; all his limbs quivered with a convulsive frisson; his swollen face became red; a wild expression caused his eyes, previously dull and bleak, to scintillate.

At the same time, a coolness, an indescribable wellbeing circulated in his veins and rendered an artificial existence to that demi-cadaver; a magical influence caused reflections of dazzling light to gleam in his eyes from all the surrounding objects.

Suave visions rose up, passing back and forth, rotating before his charmed gaze; there was the vertigo if an intoxication, not like that produced by the fermented beverages of Europe, but a divine intoxication, an inexpressible, sublime ecstasy.

"Oh," he murmured, in a halting voice, "Oh, what sensations of happiness are inundating all my senses! They are too delightful for the strength of a mortal: it's necessary that I succumb to them!

"A soft languor is half-closing my eyes; my warm and supple limbs allow themselves to relax into the sweetest abandonment. Make the celestial melody sounding around me stop…take away those houris who are fluttering and smiling at me and lifting up garlands of flowers entwined around their semi-naked breasts…leave me alone, beautiful phantoms, oh, leave me alone! Do you want to make me die of voluptuousness?

"I need to get rid of these fantastic images…it's necessary to flee…

"A magic power is dragging me away and making me glide lightly over meadows enameled with flowers, shores sparkling with light, without me having the fatigue of having to lift my feet, without my will directing my body: a delightful sensation in which the inertia of repose is mingled with the wellbeing of movement…

"I'm no longer gliding now; a vague and languorous swaying is cradling me voluptuously, and mysterious beings are lifting me slowly into the clouds.

"They're angels who are supporting me in their interlaced arms, they're the angels of the divine Allah! I can glimpse their smiling heads over my shoulder; their warm breath exhales over my forehead, and the blond curls of their beautiful hair gently brushes my lips.

"Will I never be able to stop, being borne away forever and ever by the unknown impulsion that it drawing me? No, divine messengers of the prophet, not even to visit those innumerable palaces sparkling with emeralds and carbuncles, which flee before my gaze, not even for those houris whose modulated voices are calling to me!

"No, no, don't stop! One is rocked so softly in your arms, one palpitates with such sweet ecstasy, on breathing the air with which this region is embalmed. The air of mortals makes me die. Keep flying! Let's fly without stopping, like the rapid arrow of the angel of wrath! Let's fly and fly, further…let the celestial wind that is blowing over my face never cease to blow…"

And Massoud's voice, fading away and becoming inarticulate, no longer murmured any but rare and inconsequential words; and his eyes closed; and he went to sleep: a profound sleep excited by fantastic and voluptuous dreams.

The next day, when he woke up, Massoud was pale and suffering; his extenuated voice could hardly make itself heard by his slaves. He summoned them so that they could give him another dose of opium.

NOCTURNAL TERROR

I am one of those who are most sensible of the power
of the imagination: everyone is jostled by it,
but some are overthrown by it.
(Montaigne, ch. 11.)[4]

"Ha ha! You make me laugh uproariously!
Boasting about your reason and your courage!
It only requires the most ridiculous accident to
put the latter in default and ruin the former forever."
(Anonymous.)

Oh, what a delightful day Lord Edgard was about to
spend! To depart at daybreak for the ruins of the priory of
Saint Ruth, to depart with the naïve Miss Arabella, and the
witty and piquant Duchess MacMoran! And to have the mild
and indulgent Milady Tornson's carriage for a conveyance,
and for a guide the jovial and knowledgeable Dr. Raleigh!

Let's go then! Forward ho! Farewell to old Edinburgh!
There isn't a cloud in the sky; the refreshing wind is making
the foliage of the oaks tremble gently. Let's go! Onwards,
onwards!

And there was, to begin with, a merry mélange of frivolous remarks, tender words, ingenious pleasantries; I would
have defied the most careworn brow not to have cleared; I
would have defied the most phlegmatic of men not to have felt
the electric gaiety that sprang forth from every direction in
sparks.

But a cloud has formed at the extremity of the horizon; it
is extending like a lugubrious veil; instead of the light of a

---

[4] In fact, these are the opening words of chapter 20 of volume I of
Michael de Montaigne's *Essais*.

little while ago, of the radiant day that ornamented nature with a soft and living glare, everything becomes dull and inanimate; one can no longer breathe freely, one no longer experiences an indescribable wellbeing; and I don't know what sadness comes to squeeze the heart and freeze the imagination. Still, if one were to shiver at the sudden glare of lightning, which flashes, dies and is reborn, with the majestic din of thunder...

But no; it's a slow, gray, monotonous rain that clutches the limbs with an icy inconvenience.

They do not have their picnic on the grass; the semi-ruined arcades of the monastery do not resound to their joyful bursts of laughter; shut up in a poor cottage where an old woman is dying hoarsely on a wretched bed, they spend two long hours of rain, disappointment and sadness, without saying a word.

Finally, the horses are rested; they can leave, and quit that black dwelling where the fetid air makes it so difficult to breathe, where they have been embarrassed and inhibited beside the bed of a dying woman. A few gifts are left to a tall, pale and thin young woman, the only creature weeping by the invalid's beside. She murmurs, by way of thanks: "This will serve, my ladies, to bury my mother."

To complete the misfortune, the roads have become bad; the horses' feet slip, the wheels sink into profound ruts. Night will have fallen by the time the berline reaches Edinburgh.

Night? No, it will be tomorrow, for now it's the axle that has broken; the carriage is lying on its side in a ditch...

Thank God no one is injured! A great fright for the ladies; for everyone, a rainy night spent under the stars: those are the only inconveniences of the accident that has just occurred. It's necessary, however to seek shelter. In which direction? They are five miles from any habitation, and how are they to reach one, with frail footwear, along muddy roads, in rain like this?

Luckily, a short distance away, there is an old ruined manor house, whose owners, if there are any, have not been in residence there in living memory; today, the only living beings to be found there are an old Scots woman and her daughter; they have come to set up home in the ruins, rather like swallows taking possession of the corner of a window to build their nests.

After holding a discussion, they decided unanimously to go seek a refuge in the old manor while one of the domestics would keep watch on the carriage and the other would go on horseback in search of laborers.

The hospitality was not as poor as might have been feared; the good woman in the manor received the strangers as best she could; dealing, as she could easily see, with people of high status, who would reward her zeal generously, she displayed the utmost reverence, and put her abode and the manor at the disposal of her guests.

To begin with, the ladies exchanged their sodden clothes for the Sunday garments of the old woman's daughter, Betty. The travelers' cheerfulness was briefly reanimated: that was when they saw the two young ladies dressed in scarlet skirts, whose Scottish cut allowed the sight of their legs clad in blue stockings and shoes with big buckles; for headgear they had muslin bonnets, which fell over their shoulders and were certainly not unfavorable to their charming features.

The entire evening was spent around a large fireplace where a peat fire was burning. Insensibly, the conversation became sad and lugubrious, and they began to tell terrifying ghost stories.

It was the old doctor who, seeing his audience marvelously disposed to feel the somber impressions of that kind of story, amused himself greatly in following the progress of the vague and insurmountable terror that gradually took possession of the ladies during the narrations, and even attained the gentleman, Edgard.

It must be said that the irritations of the journey, the memories of the cottage and Saint Ruth, the howling wind, the deceptive light of the fire and the walls charged with Gothic sculptures could not have seconded the doctor any better; never had he had such a satisfactory audience.

The hoarseness of his voice, and Lady Tornson eyes, which were beginning to close, indicated that if he wanted to keep such a great success intact, it was time to bring it to an end, so, taking out his watch, he announced that midnight had chimed some time ago.

The ladies then took possession of the only lamp that their hostess had in the house, and the doctor and Sir Edgard went their separate ways to lie down on pallets of straw set down in the only two rooms in the manor into which the rain did not penetrate through the dilapidated roof.

Hazard had placed Edgard in the remotest part of the building; his tender imagination, inclined to excitement, had experienced the effect of the doctor's tales keenly. Then again, after having groped his way through a long, narrow corridor, he was alone, far away from everyone else, in the large deserted hall of a ruined building; he could not, therefore, prevent himself feeling a kind of mysterious dread.

While recognizing the absurdity of such a sensation, he was nonetheless subject to its effects; wrapped up in is cloak and lying in a corner, in the midst of a profound obscurity, he felt his heart beating forcefully. The only glimmer of light he perceived was that which the moon sometimes projected through the large clouds, which the wind as driving rapidly; the only noises that reached his ears were the hooting of an owl and the roaring of the wind.

He was nevertheless dozing off when the badly-closed door flew open with a bang. He woke up with a start: the moon half-lit the place where he was...

Great God! A white phantom was standing over him!

He tried to cry out, but his voice failed; he tried to fell, but a powerful, inexorable hand held on to his garments...

He fell unconscious.

The next morning, at daybreak, the domestics brought the berline to the old manor house, restored as best they could to a condition in which it could reach Edinburgh. At that good news, everyone assembled—but Edgard was missing.

"He's asleep, the idler. Come on, we need to go and wake him up."

They found him pale and motionless, with the pocket of his jacket caught on the foot of an old stone statue. His hair had turned white.

They had a great deal of difficulty bringing him round. As for his reason, he was never able to recover it.

ALICE

And the evils that endure, and the evils one suspects,
And those that I have sung, will not prevent anyone
From loving as they loved before.
(Émile Deschamps, "Conclusion")[5]

Alice was the daughter of a poor country minister. She was eight years old when her mother died; at twelve she was an orphan.

The only relative that remained to her in the world, Miss Abigail Lawton, a retired seamstress in the city, took Alice into her home, making a great issue of the extreme charity she was displaying in not putting her brother's only child in the orphanage.

No benefit was ever more dearly bought, for little Alice had to satisfy the demands of a shrewish, eccentric, exacting old woman, and the angelic resignation, loving character, gentility and precocious intelligence of the poor girl could not find any mercy from Miss Abigail.

Alice worked from dawn to dusk, and if, stealing a few moments' relief, she took refuge in her little room to read a page or two of an old edition of *Pamela*,[6] the sole legacy that she had inherited from her father, Miss Abigail immediately

---

[5] Émile de Saint-Armand Deschamps (1791-1871) was one of the early leaders of the French Romantic Movement; with Victor Hugo he founded the periodical La Muse Française. "Conclusion" was included in his collection *Études française et étrangères* (1828).

[6] Samuel Richardson's work was very popular in French translation, especially *Pamela; or, Virtune Rewarded* (1740), which provided a key model of the kind of "moral fiction" to which the cynicism of Berthoud, Janin and Petrus Borel—not to mention the Marquis de Sade—provided conscientious opposition.

came to throw her out again, protesting against the "lady-like airs" that her niece was putting on.

"Isn't this," she said, in the harshest voice that had ever been heard to screech in the city, "a fine occupation for a girl who doesn't have a farthing? Learn to earn your daily bread with your arms, for I won't live forever, and when I'm gone you'll soon have dissipated the savings that I've had so much trouble amassing. Who'll feed you then?"

At these unjust reproaches and gross outrages, Alice shed many bitter tears, which it as necessary for her to strive to conceal, for they would have occasioned a further diatribe. Without saying a word, she went back to work.

Constrained to the most servile tasks, to the most repulsive work, Alice never let slip a murmur, but not because Miss Abigail's persecutions had produced in her the kind of indifference that might have rendered such an existence tolerable; the extreme pallor of her physiognomy and her habitual sadness revealed how profoundly she felt the misfortune of her situation.

Two years had gone by when an old naval officer came to lodge in Miss Abigail's house. Touched by Alice's sad situation, the old man became her friend, and thanks to the protection of Sir John Clapperstuck, the orphan's fate became a little more tolerable.

The former long-haul captain was a learned man; he took great pleasure in cultivating Alice's fortunate dispositions; his pupil's rapid progress filled him with joy. Miss Abigail often shook her head, murmuring, on seeing her niece wasting her time, as she put it, with the old mariner, but she dared not complain too loudly, because the captain had sworn that, if his pretty protégée were harassed, he would immediately leave Miss Abigail's house and take lodgings at the other end of the street with Miss Southey.

Now, Miss Southey was the owner of a well-stocked lingerie shop, and had established a redoubtable competition with Miss Abigail. There was no sacrifice that the latter would not have made rather than lose a guest like the captain—a guest who was sometimes visited by lords. If she had ever seen their carriages stopping outside Miss Southey's boutique, she would have fallen ill with chagrin. Alice, therefore, spent all her recreational time with Sir John.

Glad to receive testimony of affection that reminded her of the days when she had had a father, Alice loved the old man with all the abandon of her age, and surrounded him with the most tender cares and most delicate kindness. The captain often said, with tears in his eyes, that the child would fill his final years with happiness.

Alice was eighteen when the venerable old man yielded his last sigh peacefully, in her arms.

For her, everything then became sad, bitter and empty again. Miss Abigail had counted on the old man making her his heir, but he did not bequeath anything to her or to Alice but trivia of little value. That disappointment returned all its original bitterness to the old woman's character—a bitterness further augmented by the chagrin of seeing the captain's room remain unoccupied for a long time.

Finally, a young man from Exeter presented himself as a tenant for the late Sir John's apartment. Teddy Wolsey did not take long to get into his landlady's good graces; he was a young medical student, jovial, tidy and studious, and extremely polite to Miss Abigail. He soon acquired a considerable intimacy within the household; nothing was done without asking his advice, and if the old woman had a fit of ill-temper, Teddy's cheerful remarks were able to dissipate it and restore calm and gaiety.

Gradually, a pleasant intimacy was established between Alice and Teddy; the young woman yielded to the vague and indecisive sentiment that she was beginning to feel, without seeking to examine it closely. She knew that the affection she had for Teddy was not the same as that the captain had once inspired in her, but because the mixture of sweet languor and melancholy pleasure gradually took possession of hr entire being did not give rise to any alarm, she was already in love with the young man before she had given any thought to explaining the nature of her new sensations.

Imagine her terror when, one evening, she saw Teddy come home covered in blood, with a wound on his head! Oh, what a horrible despair clutched her heart when the doctor who was summoned examined the wound for a long time, silently, and sadly shaking his head. Imagine her anxiety when, that night, sitting up with the invalid on her own, she interrogated the feeble palpitations of his heart, dreading that she might feel it stop!

For eight days and nights they trembled for the life of the injured man, and for eight days and nights Alice kept vigil by his bedside; she scarcely closed her eyes for a few minutes from time to time in order to sleep, and her slumber was so light that, at the slightest moan, she would be standing over the invalid, offering refreshing beverages to his burning lips.

Finally, they ceased to fear for his life, but it was necessary to surround him with long, attentive, persevering care. When the doctor announced that, Alice was distressed to earn that Teddy had a long time still to suffer, but was gladdened by the thought that she would be close to him for a long time yet.

With what a mixture of modesty and tenderness she rendered him the kind and gentle cares that only women are able to offer so affectionately! He never had time to formulate a desire; she was already offering whatever he was about to request; she interpreted his vaguest gaze reliably.

One evening, she had helped him to sit in an armchair, and, as her hand placed the pillow that was to sustain the convalescent's head, Teddy took that hand in his stiff fingers and raised it to his lips. A fiery redness, and then a sudden pallor, covered the poor young woman's cheeks in turn, and she had to lean on the back of the chair, having become unsteady on her feet.

Teddy put his arm around Alice's elegant waist; he tried to speak, but, too emotional, could scarcely proffer an exclamation. They both kept a long silence, and that silence was delicious, for Alice's pretty head rested on Teddy's shoulder; their hands were entwined, and the young woman's tears fell one by one on to the convalescent's knees.

Then their lips met, and they swore to love one another forever.

Afterwards, they set about making long and pleasant plans for the future, and confiding to one another the most secret thoughts of their souls. Alice told Teddy about the chagrins she had suffered since her mother's death; then, her eyes bathed in tears, with a celestial smile, she said: "I shall be very happy now."

He drew her gently to his bosom. "My Alice! My Alice! We shall soon belong to one another. When my mother knows that she owes her only son's existence to the tender care of my Alice, she'll leave Devonshire and come to call you her daughter."

The three months of the convalescence went by so quickly for the two lovers that they were struck motionless by surprises when the doctor said to Teddy: "Nothing more is needed now to render the cure perfect than to go and breathe the air of your natal county. You can support the fatigue of the journey; I've written to tell your mother the good news, and this is her response—she wants you to leave the day after tomorrow."

He left.

Unfortunate children! Large tears formed in their eyes, and they threw themselves into one another's arms, sobbing. "Oh no!" Teddy exclaimed. "I don't want to leave you!"

"What about your mother?" poor Alice murmured, affecting a firmness that was far from real. "How disappointed she would be."

He left, and only four days had gone by when a letter from Teddy arrived to console Alice and render the isolation in which her friend's departure had left her less frightful.

Tomorrow, he wrote, he was going to confide his love and the promise he had made to marry Alice to his mother.

Two days later, another letter arrived, and Alice opened it with a hand agitated by hope and anxiety. Misfortune! Teddy's mother had forbidden him even to think about a marriage so disproportionate. "But," he said, "I'll keep my promise. I'm going to leave for London in secret; we'll go to Gretna Green, and a marriage will be made there by the Scottish blacksmith, without which I'd have nothing else to do but die."

On reading that letter, Alice shed bitter tears, but she did not hesitate for an instant.

"My Teddy, I have only you in the entire world to love poor Alice, and Heaven is my witness as to how dear you are to me, but I would rather lose your tenderness than buy the name of your spouse at the price of the remorse that such a disobedience would cost you. Let us defer, my Teddy, a marriage that could not be happy, since it would be a bad deed; and let us hope for the future."

Such was Alice's reply.

And she was well-rewarded for so great a sacrifice, for every week she received letters from Teddy expressing the greatest tenderness; as she read them she thanked heaven for having blessed her because she had listened to the voice of duty.

Alas, Teddy's letters soon became less frequent and less tender. Then they stopped altogether.

Six months went by.

It was evening. Sitting in his study, beside a large fire, Teddy was formulating dreams of marriage and happiness; but the image of Alice was not, alas, associated with those future projects. A young miss with blue eyes, a dowry of a thousand pounds sterling and, perhaps even more than that, the numerous and lucrative clientele of his fiancée's father, the celebrated surgeon Olbarn—such were the ideas caressing Teddy's imagination. In becoming Miss Olbarn's husband, he would clear at a single stride all the discouraging hindrances that a young debutant in the healing art must overcome; protected by his father-in-law's name, associated with his work, he would effortlessly acquire a reputation and the abundant advantages that would flow from the acquaintances that he would make in London.

A sudden groan made him tremble; he raised his head. A woman, Alice, was standing before him, pale and hardly able to stand.

At the sight of the unfortunate woman, alas, one sole dread agitated the ingrate Teddy's heart: the dread that Alice's unexpected arrival in Exeter might trouble his marriage to Miss Olbarn.

And when, making an effort, she advanced toward him, and her lips, contracted by a convulsive movement, tried to pronounce a few words, he said to her, harshly: "What are you doing here?"

A cold sweat was streaming over the unfortunate woman's brow. She uttered an inarticulate groan. Despair had annihilated all the faculties of her being.

Teddy went outside, precipitately, for a few moments. The night was dark and the street was deserted. He went back in, took Alice by the hand, and led her away silently. She did not offer any resistance, but numbly allowed him to take her wherever he wished. They walked for a long time, and when they had arrived at the road that led to London he put a purse full of money in Alice's hand and abruptly fled.

There's an inn a short distance away, he said to himself. *She can spend the night there, and go back to London tomorrow. It's a violent remedy, but what else can I do, in the circumstances?*

Soon, the agitation caused to Teddy by Alice's unexpected arrival gave way to a profound depression, the common result of an extreme determination. Alice's presence, the cruel manner in which he had treated the unfortunate woman, now appeared to him as a bizarre and deceptive dream; he would not have believed it, if the remorse of his sin had not weighed heavily upon his heart.

He made the greatest efforts, in vain, to snatch himself away from the ideas that were stabbing him; he gathered all the faculties of his soul, in vain, to concentrate, as before, on his dreams of ambition. Alice alone, always Alice, remained in the forefront of his thoughts. A burning fever circulated in Teddy's veins; a circle of fire gripped his head...

He got up, and repose became an intolerable fatigue to him; he walked, and his limbs, worn out by an unaccountable lassitude, obliged him to fall back into the armchair that he had just quit. He tried to read, and forced his eyes to scan the pages, but it was without the characters translating themselves in his imagination; and his hands turned the pages mechanically, without any other idea replacing the one that was obsessing him: Alice, Alice.

No sleepless night had ever been longer or more dolorous.

At about two o'clock in the morning someone hammered on the door. He pricked up his ears. Could that be Alice— Alice returning? Oh, this time, he would listen to her pitiful cries; this time...

The knocker rapped again; a hoarse voice made itself heard. It wasn't her. No, he knew who it was.

He opened the door, and let in two men of sinister physiognomy; their ferocious smiles were a horrible parody of the satisfaction of a merchant seeking to talk up the merchandise he is offering.

"Oh, for this one you'll have to pay no less than fifteen guineas—we've paid more than two thirds of that."

"Yes," his companion added. "It cost us dear."

Teddy paid the two men the money they were demanding; then they deposited, on a long table, a burden whose form it was difficult to discern, because it was wrapped in a vast sheet, and the only lamp that was lit in the apartment was giving out very little light.

When the two men had gone and he had closed the door on them, Teddy unwound the cloth; it enveloped a corpse, the black and disfigured features of which were half-covered by a mask of pitch.

"They've murdered her!" cried the young man, shivering with horror and indignation. "Oh, those villainous

69

resurrectionists! I'm going to denounce their crime and demand vengeance for it!"

He brought the lamp closer in order to try to identify the
victim.

It was Alice.

FOLKLORE AND FAKELORE

Introduction
(From an appendix to "The Barn at Montcouvez")

[These] are legends of French Flanders, a land so fecund in memories, so rich in traditions. Visit any one of its villages, any one of its hamlets, and people there will tell you these stories; there, among bizarre events, an energetic, somber and wild imagination sparkles, in which the influence of our foggy atmosphere, our cold and rigorous landscapes and our superstitious customs is recognizable.

In the warm climate of Spain, the peasants sing joyful *seguidillas*, an expression of the voluptuous indolence that gentle and fecund sun engenders; in Italy, an azure sky and a bewitching nature inspire amorous and tender *canzonetti*; but in Flanders, everything that surrounds us is grave, monotonous and austere in appearance; the eye sees nothing in the countryside but marshes, valleys and fields rich in agriculture but not very picturesque. The earth there only yields its fruits to persistent labor.

To make an impression on organs hardened by fatigue, and to interest people used to seeing nothing but severe scenery, it requires stories of sinister marvels, which acquire a kind of plausible in being attached to familiar objects and places. It requires stories in which terror is taken to an extreme, and which leave a profound impression in the memory. They are retold in the long winter evenings. At the moment when interest reaches its peak, the spinning-wheels stop; the silent circle draws tighter; nothing can any longer be heard but the deep, hoarse voice of the story-teller, while the gazes of those surrounding the speaker glance behind fearfully, as if the evil spirits of which mention has been made, evoked by the nocturnal tales, were standing there, terrible pitchforks in hand.

THE DEVIL'S CHESS GAME

> Seigneurs and ladies who have heard good stories told,
> if it pleases you to listen and remember, I have a good
> one to tell. So, please pick up this little book, correcting
> its faults if you find any, which is newly translated from
> old rhymes and prose.
> Prologue to *Histoire de Richard-Sans-Peur*[7]

The Sire de Clairmarais had been out hunting since the early hours. His wife, the chatelaine, was occupying the leisure of a long autumn evening in her oratory, embroidering a veil of precious golden cloth destined to ornament the miraculous reliquary of the blessed Saint Bertin.[8] Her ladies in waiting were working around her in silence, for their mistress was too haughty to chat with vassals, and even to permit them to raise their voices in her presence except in response to her request.

An hour after the wind had ceased to bring the last chimes of the curfew rung at the belfry of Saint-Omer, a village about half a league away, to the château, the blast of a horn was suddenly heard at the manor's postern. There was

---

[7] *Histoire de Richard sans Peur, duc de Normandie, fils de Robert le Diable* was a chapbook originally published by Garnier in 1736, popularizing a sequel to the popular legend of *Robert le Diable*, which became the basis of a famous opera by Giacomo Meyerbeer, premièred in Paris in 1831. Berthoud appended versions of both legends to his collection of *Chroniques et traditions surnaturelles de la Flandre.*
[8] The ruined Benedictine abbey founded in the seventh century and dedicated to its second abbot, St. Bertin, in Saint-Omer, was one of the most famous monuments in the region that Berthoud calls Flanders. In the period when Berthoud wrote the story its stone was being plundered in order to built Saint-Omer's Hôtel-de-Ville, completed in 1834.

something strange and wild about the fanfare that made the chatelaine and her ladies tremble. A page went to enquire as to who it was, and came back to inform his mistress that a knight of noble appearance, who called himself Sire Brudemer, was requesting hospitality.

If some poor laborer in mortal danger had been lamenting on the far side of the moat, the chatelaine would not have had the drawbridge lowered to give him shelter in the manor, but a noble lord was another matter entirely. She gave the order that he should be admitted to the château and introduced to her presence.

Then, in accordance with custom, she set about preparing with her own hands the hypocras that one had to offer guests as a gesture of welcome. She had just finished pouring the beverage into a silver cup when Sire Brudemer was brought in by the page.

He advanced toward the chatelaine with the charming and noble courtesy typical of a high-born knight, and began by thanking the lady politely for the hospitality that she had granted him.

"I have lost my way in the domain," he said. "A little while ago I was cursing the impetuosity of my horse, which, separating my from my huntsmen, drew me into marshes and ravines and the deepest thickets; but since I have been fortunate enough to be admitted to the presence of such a marvelously beautiful lady, I no longer take any account of fatigues, danger or anxieties."

At first, the stranger's voice had something bitter and coarse about it, but that was soon forgotten thanks to the honeyed grace of his words.

The ladies in waiting, who, in accordance with custom, had retired to the far side of the room, in such a way that they could see what was happening without being able to hear anything that was said, exchanged remarks in low voices regarding the richness of Brudemer's vestments, the elegance of his bearing, the symmetry of his features and the grim expression in his fiery eyes. Thus, it was not surprising that the chatelaine found an inexpressible charm in the society of her guest. She had had no other companions than vassals since birth, and her conversations had been limited to long accounts of her aged husband's battles and tournaments, he being a better wielder of the lance than an amiable gallant.

Profiting skillfully from his advantages, Brudemer did not take long to mingle with his discourse something more flattering and more affectionate than the chivalric mores of the era permitted. The chatelaine, ordinarily so proud and disdainful, subjugated by an unknown power, listened to him without anger, and then with ever-increasing emotion.

Then, placing himself unceremoniously in such a way as to hide the Dame de Clairmarais from her ladies in waiting, he took possession of a hand that she did not think of withdrawing, and raised it tenderly to his lips; then, his knee pressed gently upon a knee that was trembling.

It would be difficult to describe the chatelaine's sensations: a harsh, infernal fire was circulating dolorously in her veins; it gripped her forehead and caused her bosom to heave. She did not experience any of the sweet languor and the ineffable intoxication that are the gentle and cruel symptoms of love-sickness; there was, instead, anguish, a cold sweat and the frissons of a sinner at fault; there was, instead, the horrible stupefaction of a pilgrim whose sees the mortal gaze of a basilisk fixed upon him.

In her disturbance, the Dame de Clairmarais dropped the veil that she was embroidering. "Oh, if I were granted the gift of such a scarf, said Brudemer, "if the lady whose beautiful hands have fashioned it took me for her knight, how many lances I would break in her honor on the tourney-field and in battle!"

She picked it up with a convulsive movement and said to him: "Here it is!"

Brudemer raised the scarf to his lips, in order to hide a horrible smile that he could not repress—but he suddenly threw it away with a frisson of terror, as if it were made of fire. The chaplain had examined it the previous evening, after vespers, with his hands still moist with holy water.

Immediately recovering from his emotion, however, he drew nearer to the chatelaine and lowered his voice to say: "I was guided to your chattel by an old man in great haste to see the Sire de Clairmarais. He's waiting at the postern to tell him an important secret, which concerns you."

The chatelaine went pale at those words.

"I asked," Brudemer continued, "about the motives that caused him to seek out your husband in such a hurry. His purpose, he told me, is to reveal a mystery to him—a mystery that might well lead to changes in the manor of Clairmarais. 'The chatelaine,' he said, 'has expelled me ignominiously from the château; she has threatened to have me thrown in the moat if I return. The ingrate! I'll deprive her of her titles and her wealth, of which she is so proud.'

"As I did not want to add faith to these threats, he told me that his wife had been the nurse of the daughter of the Comte d'Érin; that the nursling had died without anyone in the world knowing it except him; that he had put you, his own daughter, in the dead young comtesse's crib, and that you had been brought up and married as the child of the Seigneur d'Érin. He furnished me with numerous and irrefutable proofs of his fraud.

"One this mystery is known, the Sire de Clairmarais will not take long to repudiate a vassal, the daughter of an ignoble serf by whom he had been duped."

The chatelaine wrung her hands in despair .

"Listen," Brudemer continued, lowering his voice even further, but in such a manner that the Dame de Clairmarais would not miss a single word. "The old man, wrapped in his cloak, is asleep outside the postern: take this dagger…come…"

"My father!"

"No, you're right," Brudemer replied, with an ironic coldness. "Who knows? Perhaps, out of pity, you'll be admitted among the ladies in waiting of the Sire de Clairmarais' new wife. At the worst, you'll only be shaved and locked up in a convent..."

The chatelaine rose to her feet swiftly, made a gesture to her women forbidding them to follow her, and gave her hand to Brudemer. They both went down to the postern.

After having hunted all day, the Sire de Clairmarais came back, where he expected to find himself before long before a roaring fire, beside his wife, the beautiful chatelaine.

He was in such haste to arrive that he was preceding his huntsmen by a short distance when his horse suddenly refused to advance any further, rearing up and giving sins of great fear. The old seigneur was forced to dismount. Oh, how surprised and chagrined he was to see his wife's foster-father lying there, unmoving, with a deep wound in his breast.

People hastened around the old man, and the care that they lavished upon him had not been in vain. He opened his eyes, raised himself up effortfully, and, leaning close to the ear of the Sire de Clairmarais, murmured a few words that had made the castellan shudder with horror; then he fell back and died.

Without proffering a single word, the old seigneur marched straight to the oratory, where he found his wife. Her forehead coved by a mortal pallor, she was sitting in front of a narrow table, and, in order to conceal her trouble, was pretending to play chess with Brudemer.

The latter, at the sight of the Sire de Clairmarais, emitted a horrible burst of laughter. The chatelaine shared that execrable hilarity, and must have been suffering a great deal to laugh like that.

Then the Sire de Clairmarais had no further doubt as to his misfortune—for until that moment, he had been unable to believe in the crimes of which the dying man had accused the chatelaine. "Satan!" he cried, at the peak of indignation and despair. "Satan! I abandon the parricide, the adulterous spouse and the château she has soiled with her presence to you."

"I accept," said Brudemer. At the same time, a crown of flames sprang forth around his head, and he reached out for the chatelaine's white shoulders with two terrible hands that were suddenly armed with infernal claws.

It was more than two hundred years after the Sire de Clairmarais had died in an odor of sanctity in the abbey of Saint Bertin when, one evening, a monk of the order of Saint Benedict asked an inhabitant of Saint-Omer what the manor was whose towers could be seen in the middle of a wood surrounded by immense marshes.

"May Our Lady and the saints protect you!" the townsman replied. "That's the Château de Clairmarais, an accursed place haunted by the Demon. Every night, it lights up with a sudden glow; every night, the Devil and I don't know how many revenants arrive there in their chariots of fire."

"If the old people of the region can be believed, the demon that inhabits the château is named Brudemer, and forces the insensate individuals who penetrate his abode to play chess for their souls, in exchange for the property of the domain and all the treasures it contains. As you can imagine, no one, as yet, has been able to beat the devil, and, in consequence, no one has come back from Clairmarais.

The monk listened to the townsman in silence, and then, after having reflected briefly, he marched at a firm step toward the diabolical manor.

He got in without meeting any obstacle, and went to sit down in a richly-furnished oratory, in the middle of which there was a narrow table on which a chessboard was set and all the pieces for a game.

While the monk was examining these objects, which nightfall was beginning to render indistinct, a bright light suddenly flooded the oratory and the monk was surrounded by a crowd of varlets, pages and ladies-in-waiting dressed in an antique style. Al of them carried out their duties in silence, without their footsteps being audible, and, marvelously, without their bodies producing a shadow when they passed in front of the light.

Shortly afterwards, a richly-dressed seigneur advanced, who wore on his blazoned doublet, by way of an armory, a divided shield forked with sable, with the device: *Brudemer*. On his arm there was a woman, still young, whose beautiful features were covered with a cadaverous pallor; then came eight pages, bowed down beneath the weight of four heavy coffers filed with gold.

Brudemer sat down at the chessboard and made sign to the monk inviting him to sit opposite. The monk obeyed, and they commenced playing without either of them saying a single word.

By means of clever strategy the monk believed that he had checkmated his adversary when the pale lady, who had remained standing behind Brudemer and leaning on the back of his large armchair leaned over and pointed at a pawn. Then the game changed its aspect, and it as the monk who found himself in danger of being checkmated.

Having brought off that coup, Brudemer and the lady burst out laughing, and all the people in the oratory gathered around the players, taking part in that frightful fit of gaiety, which no human words can describe.

The monk began to regret his temerity. Cold sweat formed on his brow, and he would have given anything in the world to find himself back in his convent at that moment. Nevertheless, he did not despair of divine bounty, and he appealed mentally to his blessed patron Saint Benedict, for only a miracle could get him out of the dangerous pass. Suddenly, thanks to a celestial inspiration, he perceived that a new stratagem might yet enable him to win the game, and he was about to advance the pawn that would ensure him of it when the bursts of laughter that were resounding around him changed into frightful howls. Then he heard and saw no more.

The monk, after having spent all night in prayer, finally saw dawn break with a joy that is easily imaginable. He found, in the place occupied by the pale lady, a skeleton covered in ragged shreds of rich women's clothing.

Left the owner of the château and the wealth it contained, the monk made the accursed place into a monastery, of which he was appointed the superior. No more of it remains today that meager vestiges of the cloister, destroyed in the epoch of the revolution.

How I regret not having been able to recount the story in the native dialect and with the expression of credulity of the old woman who told it to me, in a poor cottage lit be a single lamp and the red glow of the hearth, while the rain fell in torrents and the roaring wind plunged into the immense wood of Clairmarais.[9]

---

[9] In fact, the village of Clairmarais, near Saint-Omer, owes its name not to some Feudal overlord of that name but to a Latin improvisation by Saint Bernard the founder of the Cistercian abbey that was established in the marsh in 1140. The last vestiges of the abbey are still visible, but it was destroyed during the Revolution, in 1790, when Clairmarais became a commune.

THE MOUTH OF HELL

> My good seigneur, have compassion on the
> piteous people shivering at the door of your
> dwelling, in the cold and swirling wind, and
> torrents of rain that lash their faces.
> "When one enters here; one does not leave again."
> Père Mathurin. *L'Oeuvre de miséricorde.*

At present, the Trou-d'Enfer is a hideous quarter of Cambrai: tortuous streets, paltry house, a stinking atmosphere, a filthy and narrow arm of the Escaut.[10]

It has never enjoyed a heyday, and when she has to traverse that reprobate quarter, an honest woman hastens her steps, not raising her eyes, and only breathes easily when it is safely behind her.

I can well believe it! One sees no one at the doors of black hovels but infamous prostitutes crouched on the step; one meets no one there but old women torn from the decrepitude of prostitution, who engage drunken soldiers and men in rags in execrable battles of words.

On certain days of the week a meager and badly-tuned orchestra strikes up in the Trou-d'Enfer; that adds a further sinister note to the unwelcoming place. If you feel brave, go into the open sewer where the fiddlers are playing, and upon my soul, you'll see a strange spectacle. You'll see a cabaret of evil appearance. I've seen it myself, and shivered in disgust and horror.

---

[10] When Berthoud lived there, there was an area popularly known by this name in Cambrai, whose appellation caused some discussion among antiquarians, recorded in the publications of the Societé d'Émulation de Cambrai. Its main thoroughfare had already been officially renamed the Rue Sainte-Barbe.

One can only breathe an air laden with tobacco-smoke there, darkening by coal ash and the reddish dust that is produced and kicked up everywhere by the friction hundreds of pairs of shoes on the bricks with which the main room is paved. Add to that the nauseating odor of beer, the voices that mutter and yap, the screech of violins and the nasal cries of the clarinet. Imagine yourself, then, in the yellow light of sparse Argand lamps, a confused movement of men, women and soldiers, coming, going, mingling, circulating, forming groups, dispersing, long tables garnished with drinkers, the rattle of pewter tankards and the clink of glasses, and you'll have an almost precise idea if the appearance of a cabaret: an appearance that dazzles and strikes the indecisive sight of the spectator with a sort of vertigo.

The Trou-d'Enfer is not a better place to be during the night, Most of the time, plaintive cries, the sounds of stunning blows and raucous voices proffering oaths rise up relentlessly. Then, when a patrol appears, attracted by the tumult, everything disappears; the door slam shut; there is now only one single noise amid that great deceptive calm: the slow and measured tread of the guardsmen. Scarcely have those footsteps faded into the distance like an indistinct murmur, however, than confusion and disorders spring forth noisily from all directions, and insomnia begins again for peaceful folk, if there are any in such a place.

Isn't it the truth? The Trou-d'Enfer, as I have depicted it, is a hideous quarter.

Well, seven hundred years ago, it was even worse.

There were no streets to be seen there, no houses at all. It was a vast marsh of evil renown, in the middle of which were vast ruins. No Christian ever dared set foot there, because, as its name clearly indicates, the Trou-d'Enfer was haunted by the Evil Spirit, and frightful marvels were recounted in that regard, which probably did not measure up to the verity. Lend me your ears, pay attention, and judge whether I'm telling the truth.

The ruins that lay in the heart of the Trou-d'Enfer were those of a fortified château, inhabited a long time ago by a Seigneur named Truandre, whose mother had sold him in his cradle to the Demon and his power.

The chronicler relates that the miscreant in question worshiped the Father of Evil, and committed a thousand lubricious and impious horrors to please his god. Young women of good lineage were abducted from their families and kept captive in horrible warrens; the throats of infants were cut in order to prepare diabolical unguents from their body-fat, and pilgrims who had the misfortune to ask for shelter at the château found themselves forced to deny the holy name of God or die of starvation in dungeons more frightful than one can describe.

But it was priests in particular, and the bishop most of all, that Truandre hated. He had all the servants of God who were not extremely careful apprehended, and when they refused to tell him where he treasures of the church were hidden and did not want to surrender the rents of their abbeys to him, he whipped them, personally, until they fell dead beneath his blows, or laid them out on hot coals and burned them slowly thereupon.

Heaven finally took pity on the misfortunes of Le Cambrésis,[11] and during a violent storm, Truandre was struck by lightning, along with the accomplices of his crimes and all his men-at-arms. Only a few servants were spared.

Those servants went to find the bishop, and offered him large sums of money to bury their dead lord, as befitted a nobleman of high lineage, in holy ground—but the bishop did not even want to listen to them, and ordered that the corpse should be thrown into the moat of Truandre's château, next to an enormous gibbet. In addition, he declared excommunicate and expelled from the holy church anyone who touched the body other than to spit in its face and damage it.

---

[11] Le Cambrésis was one of the ancient provinces of France, of which Cambrai was the capital.

There was no need for that excommunication, for the body had no sooner been thrown where the bishop had ordered than the earth all around began to catch fire and to emit continuous jets of flame; and, horrible as the rains were that fell during the next four years, they were incapable of extinguishing them. A thousand petty demons were working incessantly, throwing oil and pitch to aliment the fire of that inferno, the approach to which was guarded by a huge dragon.

The clamors of Truandre and the laments of his servants were heard night and day; their souls were seen, trying to flee, and demons armed with pitchforks pitilessly hurling them back into the midst of the flames. Songs such as human mouths could never have produced, such as the human mind could not conceive, and bursts of laughter suggestive of the ripping of thunder mingled with the cries of the damned; often, too, the demons seized them with their burning hands and forced them to join in with their dances and whirl with them in mid-air, from which they suddenly dropped them to the ground.

The worthy bishop, touched with compassion by the sufferings of Truandre's soul, persuaded a vassal of the dead man to do penitence for him, by relieving the necessities of the poor and giving all the wealth that he had inherited from his master to the church. That pious vassal had no sooner accomplished the bishop's good advice than the marsh, which had vomited fire for four years and caused to appear everything that Hell, demons and reproofs had of the most hideous, resumed its somber verdure and its still, stagnant waters.

No one, however, had the courage to go and live in a château in which the angels of darkness had held their sabbats, and it remained deserted for a long time.

Nevertheless, little by little, poor people who had no hearth or home became bold enough to take a few stones from the manor house to build houses, and, as no harm came to them, others did more, and built their houses near to the châtel, even in the midst of the ruins, although there was always a kind of reprobation attached to the place.

Such is the origin of the quarter known nowadays as the Trou-d'Enfer, which continues to justify its name by its sinister aspect.

THE DEVIL'S SONATA

There was once a musician in Augsbourg named Niéser, who was equally skilled at making instruments, composing tunes and playing them; his reputation still extends throughout the region of Swabia. It is true that he was immensely rich, and that does no harm to artistes, even the most skillful ones. His less fortunate colleagues sometimes said that his opulence had been achieved by less than honorable means, but he had friends who were able to rely that those were nothing but the words of the envious.

Niéser's only heir was a daughter whose innocence and beauty would have appeared to be a sufficient dowry, even without the attractive prospect of her father's possessions. Esther was no less celebrated for the softness of her blue eyes, the grace of her smile and a thousand amiable qualities than old Niéser was for his riches, the perfection of his instruments and his prodigious talent.

Now, in spite of old Niéser's fortune and the consideration that he drew from it, and in spite of his musical celebrity, he was tormented by a great chagrin. Esther, his only child, the sole representative of a musical family extending over generations, could scarcely distinguish one note from another, and it was a source of painful reflection to Niéser not to be able to leave an inheritor of his talents, which he held in equal esteem to his wealth. As Esther grew up, however, he consoled himself with the idea that, if he could not be the father of a family of musicians, he might at least be the grandfather of one.

In fact, as soon as his daughter was old enough to marry, he made the singular resolution to give her, with a dowry of two hundred thousand florins, to the man who composed the best sonata and was best able to play it. His determination as immediately published throughout the town and the day fixed

86

for the competition. It was even said that Niéser had affirmed on oath that he would keep his promise, even if the sonata were composed and played by the Devil himself. Perhaps it was only a joke, but it would have been better for old Niéser never to have said those words. It was obvious, some said, that he was a wicked man, with no respect for religion.

As soon as the musician's resolution was known in Augsbourg, the entire town was in a stir. Several people who had never before dared to raise such high ambitions presented themselves without hesitation as competitors for Esther's hand; for, independently of her charms and Niéser's florins, their reputation as artistes was at stake, and where there was a lack of talent, vanity stood in for it.

In brief, there was not a musician in Augsbourg who did not hasten, for one reason or another, to enter the lists of which beauty was the prize. Morning, noon and night the streets of Augsburg resounded with melodious chords. At every window the sounds of a sonata in progress could be heard; there was no longer any topic of conversation in the town than the imminent competition and its probable result. A musical fever reigned over all social classes; favorite tunes were repeated by instruments or voices in every house in Augsbourg; sentinels hummed sonatas at their posts; shopkeepers beat time on their counters with their yardsticks and their customers, when they came in, forgot what they had come to buy in order to join in. It was even said that the priests were murmuring allegros as they emerged from the confessional, and that a few bars of a rather lively movement had been found sketched on the reverse of the bishop's homily.

In the midst of all that agitation, however, one single man remained unafflicted the general epidemic. That was Franz Gortlingen. With as little disposition for music as Esther, he had the most noble character and was reputed to be one of the best-dressed cavaliers in Swabia. Franz loved the musician's daughter, and the latter, for her part, would have preferred hearing her name pronounced by Franz, with a few amiable compliments, to the most beautiful sonatas ever composed between the Rhine and the Oder.

On the eve of the great musical competition, Franz had not yet attempted anything for the accomplishment of his desires. How could he have done so? He had never composed a note of music in his life. To sing a simple tune to the accompaniment of a harpsichord was the *nec plus ultra* of his science.

That evening, Franz came out of his apartment and went down to the street. The shops were closed and the town entirely deserted. A few lights were still burning in windows, however, and the sound of instruments being prepared for the struggle that might deprive Franz of Esther struck his ears sadly. Sometimes he stopped to listen, and was even able to distinguish, through the panes, the faces of musicians satisfied with the success of their efforts and animated by the hope of triumph.

Gortlingen wandered at random, so that he eventually found himself in a part of the town that seemed entirely unfamiliar to him, although he had spent his entire life in Augsbourg. He could no longer hear anything but the roar of the river. Then, suddenly, the distant chords of a supernatural harmony reminded him once again of all his anxieties. A light coming from an isolated house proved that the reign of sleep as not yet general. Gortlingen assumed, judging by the direction of the sound, that some musician was still preparing for the next day's ordeal.

Gortlingen went on, and as he came closer to the light, such brilliant bursts of harmony were launched into the air that, ignorant as he was of music, the chords exercised a charm upon him that increasingly aroused his curiosity. He moved forward rapidly, without making any noise, all the way to the window. It was open, and inside, an old man was sitting at a harpsichord with a manuscript in front of him. His back was to the window, but an antique mirror allowed Gortlingen to see the musician's face and movements.

He had an expression of infinite gentleness and benevolence: a physiognomy of which Gortlingen could not remember ever having seen the like, but which one could have desired to see often. The old man was playing with marvelous expression; he stopped from time to time in order to make a few changes to his manuscript, and when he had appreciated their effect, he testified his joy in words that were incomprehensible, and resembled gestures of thanks, but in an unknown language.

To begin with, Gortlingen could hardly contain his indignation at the thought that that little old man might dare to present himself as one of Esther's suitors, but as he watched him and listened to him he sensed himself becoming reconciled to him by virtue of his singularly gentle physiognomy, and also by the beauty and particular character of his music.

Finally, at the conclusion of a brilliant passage, the artiste perceived that he was not alone, for Gortlingen, no longer able to restrain his admiration, had stifled the moderate exclamations of the old man with his applause. Immediately, the old man got up and opened the door.

"Good evening, Herr Franz," he said. "Sit down and tell me how you like my sonata, and whether you think it can win the prize."

There was something benevolent in the old man's face, and something soft in his voice. Gortlingen felt all jealousy disappear, and he listened.

"Does my sonata please you?" said the old man, as he finished.

"Alas!" replied Gortlingen. "If I were only capable of doing as much!"

"Listen to me," said the old man. "Niéser has made a criminal oath in swearing that he would give his daughter to whoever composes the best sonata, even if it were the Devil himself, and played by his hand. Those words been heard, and repeated by the echo of the forests, have been carried on the wings of the wind and night all the way to the ears of the one who dwells in the valley of darkness; the Demon's cries of joy burst forth. But the genius of good was alert; so, without taking pity on Niéser, the fate of Esther and Gortlingen has touched him. Take this score; go into Niéser's drawing-room; a stranger will present himself to dispute the prize; two others will seem to be accompanying him: the sonata I have given you is the same one that they will play, but mine has a particular virtue: watch for an opportunity, and substitute this one for his."

After this extraordinary speech, the old man took Gortlingen by the hand; he led him through unfamiliar streets to one of the gates of the city, and left him.

As he returned home with his scroll of paper, Gortlingen lost himself in his reflections regarding that bizarre adventure and conjectures relating to the next day's event. There had been something in the old man's physiognomy that he could not mistrust, and yet it was impossible for him to comprehend how he could obtain any advantage from the substitution of one sonata for another, since he was not one of the suitors for Esther's hand.

He went up to his room and went to bed. While he was asleep, Esther's image danced before his eyes, and the old man's sonata resonated in the air.

The next day, at sunset, the Niéser house was opened to the competitors. All the musicians of Augsbourg were then seen, hurrying along with scrolls of paper in hand, while a crowd gathered at Niéser's gate to watch them pass by.

When the time had come, Gortlingen, taking his score, also went to Niéser's door. All those who knew him felt sorry for him, because of his love for the musician's daughter; they said to one another: "What's Franz doing with that piece of paper in his hand? Surely he isn't thinking of entering the lists? Poor fellow!"

When he entered the room, Gortlingen found it full of suitors and the music-lovers of Augsbourg, who had been invited to the session. When Gortlingen crossed the room with his musical score, smiles appeared on the faces of the musicians, who all knew one another, and also knew that he could hardly play a march, much less a sonata, even if he were able to compose one. On seeing him, Niéser smiled too, but when Esther's eyes met his, she was seen to wipe away a tear.

It was announced that the rivals could come forward to inscribe their names, and that the order of play would be decided by lot. The last to present himself was a stranger, for whom everyone made way as if by instinct. No one had seen him before and no one knew where he had come from. His physiognomy as so repulsive and there was something so extraordinary about his gaze that even Niéser could not help whispering to his daughter that he hoped that the man's sonata would not be the best.

"Let's begin the trial," said Niéser. "I swear to give my daughter, whom you can see sitting beside me, with a dowry of two hundred thousand florins, to the man who composes the best sonata and can play it most perfectly."

"And you'll keep your word!" said he stranger, advancing to face Niéser.

"I'll keep my word," said the musician of Augsbourg, "even if the sonata is composed by the Devil in person and played by him."

Everyone fell silent and shivered; only the stranger smiled.

The first name presented by the ballot was that of the stranger, who immediately took his place and unrolled his score. Two men whom no one had noticed previously placed themselves by his sides with their instruments, awaiting the signal to begin. All eyes were upon them. The signal was given, and when the three musicians raised their heads to follow the music, everyone perceived, with horror, that their faces were similar.

A frisson ran through the audience. No one dared speak to his neighbor, but people began to draw their cloaks more tightly about them and slip silently away. Soon, the entire audience had disappeared, with the exception of the three who were continuing to play the sonata and Gortlingen, who had not forgotten the old man's advice. Old Niéser was still in his seat, but he was trembling at the memory of his fatal oath.

Gortlingen was standing close to the musicians; as they approached the finale, he boldly substituted his paper for theirs. An infernal grimace contracted the faces of the three artistes, and a distant groan resounded like an echo.

A few hours after midnight, the old man was seen leading Esther and Gortlingen out of the room, but the sonata was still continuing.

The years went by. Esther and Gortlingen were married, and reaching the end of their lives; the strange musicians, however, were still pursuing their task, and old Niéser, it is said, was still sitting in his seat, beating time.

THE SABBAT BOW

Mathias Wilmart was the best fiddler in the town of Hesdin. In no village for ten leagues around would people have danced with such a good heart if anyone other than Mathias Wilmart were playing the bass violin. Thus, he was an individual of no small importance; he sat down at the relatives' table at weddings; the bride—who, following local custom, served the guests during the meal—never failed to give him the choice morsel. Furthermore, when he began to speak, everyone lent him their eras, for no one knew better than he did how to tell a story, sing a song or make a witty remark.

One winter evening, there was a wedding in Auffin. The dancing went on very late, and night had fallen long ago when Mathias, loading his bass violin, which he had played with so much talent, on to his back, announced that he was going to go. All imaginable efforts were made to dissuade him from that resolution.

"Stay with us, Père Mathias," everyone said, "the wind's blowing cold; there's a frost fit to crack stones; the forest of Hesdin, which you have to pass through, doesn't enjoy a good reputation; it's a haunt of wolves and highwaymen, who are no less dangerous, not to mention witches, who come to hold their Sabbats there."

"I have a goblet of excellent wine in my belly," the stubborn old man replied, "a god fur cloak covers my shoulders, and here's a stout iron-tipped staff in my hand. With that I can defy the cold, the wolves and the thieves. As for witches and devils, if I meet any, I'll make them dance to the music of my bass violin. Why, they can tell me whether the fiddlers in Hell can ply the bow as well as Mathias Wilmart of Hesdin!"

He had scarcely been on the road for a quarter of an hour when the sky, starry until then, was suddenly covered by immense clouds. The darkness became terrifying. Then the fiddler surprised himself by regretting the good bed that he had been offered in Auffin—but it was too late to retrace his steps. Besides which, after the boasts he had made, they would be bound to mock him, saying that fear had brought him back. So he continued walking. To cap his chagrin, it did not take him long to notice that he had gone astray.

What should he do? To keep going might only be to go further astray. To wrap himself up in his cloak and lie down at the foot of a tree did not appear to be a safe things to do; the wolves would undoubtedly come to rip out his throat; besides which, if he escaped the carnivorous beasts, he would surely perish of the cold. Meanwhile, with both hands gripping his staff, he remained in a state painful anxiety; then a light suddenly appeared in the distance.

It's shining in some woodcutter's hut, he said to himself. *Thank God!*

He tried to head in the direction in which the light was shining, but it had disappeared. He struck the ground with his iron-tipped staff and uttered a horrible blasphemy. The guilty words were scarcely out of his mouth when the light reappeared.

It was not without much difficulty and after a long and perilous journey that Mathias reached the place from which the light toward which he had been marching for so long was coming. His surprise became extreme when he arrived, for he found himself outside a château of magnificent appearance, of which he had never heard mention. Lively music was resounding there in all its parts, and the dancers who were continually passing in front of the windows cast their swift black shadows on the curtains, which were rendered translucent by a red glare.

He circled around the immense building several times, but in vain, searching for the entrance door. He was despairing of finding it when an old man suddenly appeared and started blowing a horn. A drawbridge, which Mathias had not seen until then, was abruptly lowered, and the fiddler, following the old man, went into the manor.

He was utterly astonished to find it filled with an inconceivable multitude of people. Some were taking part in a splendid feast, others were playing games of chance, but the largest number were dancing and uttering deafening cries.

Mathias marched boldly toward a tall man whom he recognized as the master of the abode by the manner in which he was giving orders and the respect with which he was treated.

"Lord Castellan," she said, "I'm a poor fiddler lost in the woods; deign to permit me to spend the night in a corner of your manor; I'll leave tomorrow at daybreak."

The individual to whom Mathias was speaking only replied with a benevolent gesture of assent. On his order, a page took the fiddler's bass violin and hung it on one of the golden nails shining in the rich wall-hanging of the room. While he attended to this task the page smiled in a strange manner, and the place where his hand touched the instrument immediately blackened, as if the hand were made of fire.

Mathias began parading his gaze around and examining the place in which he found himself, but he sought in vain to recognize any of the people surrounding him; every time he fixed his eyes on the face of one of them, a kind of light mist veiled the face in question and deceived the old man's curiosity. While he was trying to fathom this prodigy, he perceived a bass violin, and the instrument seemed to him to be so beautiful that the desire gripped him to make use of it and go to play with the other fiddlers, to whom he would not be sorry to demonstrate his skill. As he raised his eyes to look for the staircase that would take him up to their gallery, however, he was astounded to recognize among them Barnabé Malassart, who had died thirty years before, and who had given him his first lessons on the bass violin,

"Blessed Virgin, have pity on me!" he exclaimed.

At the same instant, everything—the musicians, the dancers and the château—vanished before his eyes.

The next day, the people of Auffin who, more prudent than the fiddler, had deferred the day of their departure for the town, found the poor man lying unconscious at the foot of the gibbet, with a white bow in his hand.

"Père Mathias," one of them said, has chosen to sleep in a rather unattractive location.

"And an even less attractive nail on which to hang his bass violin," another replied. "Look—the bass violin and the bow are attached to the big toe of the foot of a hanged man."

"Was he afraid that the cadaver might be cold?" asked a third. "He's covered its desiccated shoulders with his cloak."

"He's a careful man, Père Mathias," added a fourth, who was attempting to revive the old musician. "He'd brought two bows, in order not to be left short if one of them happened to break."

Having come round, thanks to the care lavished on him, Mathias put the blame for his accident on the cold, and was careful not to say a word about the infernal visions that he had experienced during the night.

When he got home, however, he carefully examined the bow of which he had become the possessor in such a strange manner. A frisson of terror followed that examination. The bow was nothing less than the bone of a dead man, carved with extreme care; one could also read in its rich silver ornamentation the name of a resident of Hesdin who was reputed in the town, with good reason, to be a spell-caster and sorcerer.

Mathias waited for nightfall and then went to the house of the man of ill-repute.

"Neighbor," he said, bowing deeply, "This is a bow that belongs to you, I think. I found it by chance and I'm returning it to you."

The neighbor went pale at these words, and stood there momentarily without saying a word, so great was his emotion.

"Uh oh, Mathias!" he finally murmured. "You've discovered that singular things happen by night, and a word from you could do me harm."

"May God please that I don't speak it, Neighbor!"

"You're a worthy man, Mathias, but you'd do well to keep silent. If I'm burned alive—which they would surely do if they knew that you'd seen me you-know-where—something bad might happen to you."

Mathias got up to go, but the owner of the bow made him sit down again, and moved nearer in order to whisper in his ear in a very low voice: "Neighbor, tell me who your enemies are; I'll cast a spell on their livestock tonight, or I'll give them some wasting disease that will rid you of them."

"I have no enemies, Neighbor, and may God please that I wish no evil on my peers!"

"In what way can I be useful to you, then?"

"In none, Neighbor," the fiddler replied, already wishing that he was outside. "None at all. I'm just glad to have been able to return such a beautiful bow to you."

"A very precious bow, to be sure—but it's necessary that I make you a gift, Père Mathias."

"Give him this purse—no matter how hard he tries to empty it, it will always contain six Parisian francs in solid money."

These words had been pronounced by a man with a sinister face, who had certainly not been in the sorcerer's study when Mathias arrived there. How had he got in? That was incomprehensible, for the doors had been carefully closed by the master of the house, in order that his conversation with Mathias could not be overheard.

"This is some work of the evil spirit," exclaimed the fiddler, "and I won't risk my salvation by accepting it!"

"It's a talisman," replied the unknown individual. "A talisman of which a Christian can make use without fear." As he pronounced the word "Christian" a frisson ran through all his limbs. He added, laughing bitterly: "If this purse is the Devil's work, then I'm damned!"

Half-reassured, Mathias succumbed to the temptation of becoming the possessor of such a treasure.

He emptied the marvelous purse so often that he soon acquired a nice house, and started to live as the richest townsfolk of Hesdin were able to do. Every day there were parties and feasts that never ended. He continued to play for the dancers at weddings, but he now had a good mule to take him to the homes of the newlyweds, which walked at a brisk place, and a servant to carry his bass violin.

The fiddler's new lifestyle excited considerable comment in the town of Hesdin. The most general rumor alleged that Mathias had found an immense treasure, which he kept hidden in some secret place in his house.

Now, Mathias had four nephews, bad lots of whose conduct no good had ever come. One day, they said to one another: "Uncle Mathias has become rich; there's no one but us to inherit his great wealth..."

Apparently, one word suffices for scoundrels to understand one another, for they each went home to fetch an arbalest, and came back to hide at a crossroads in the woods through which Mathias was due to pass that evening.

The fiddler was unable to avoid his destiny; four arbalest darts struck him dead; his servant, who was luckier, ran away.

Without giving any thought to the witness to their crime, the four brothers ran to the cadaver to rob it, expecting to share the inheritance. A tall man with a sinister face stopped them, leapt upon the corpse, took a small purse from the dead man's wallet and disappeared, shouting: "That's how people profit from my gifts!"

Execrable laughter followed those words.

While the murderers stood there, motionless and bewildered, the provost of law and his archers suddenly surrounded them. Mathias' servant had met them in the woods as he fled and had come back to deliver his master's murderers to them.

Given the evidence of the crime, justice was not slow in being rendered to them. The provost had the rascals hanged from the trees behind which they had hidden, arbalests in hand—for which reason the place in question is known today as the Crossroads of the Four Brothers.

THE ANTIQUE RING

> Oh, tell me that it's a dream.
> Isn't it true that all of this
> is a dream?
> *Owen*

> Poor human reason,
> which cannot distinguish dream
> from wakefulness, or illusion from reality.
> *Alfred Mercier*[12]

My dear Édouard, or fifteen years the most devoted amity has linked us to one another.

Which is to say that, for fifteen years, you have sustained me and consoled me; which is to say that, for fifteen years, you, so grave, so positive, so superior to the impetuous distractions of our age, have listened patiently and consoled with perseverance the chagrins of an unhappy young man whom a disorderly imagination has dragged incessantly far from the real and the reasonable, whom an irresistible, deadly, extraordinary force never wearies of delivering to the consequences of a Romantic sensibility full of exasperation.

Édouard, Édouard, now more than ever I have need of that amity.

Listen, for I shall write to you; I dare not go to find you to tell you in person, so ashamed am I. I shall write you a story in which you will not be able to believe. It gives birth to laughter and scorn on the visage of anyone who hears it; they treat me as a madman. But you, my friend, you won't laugh, will you? You won't tell me that I'm a madman, a maniac, a

---

[12] Both of these quotations appear to be invented, as well as their supposed authors.

dreamer; that would hurt me a great deal, and you're so afraid of hurting me.

Then again, it doesn't matter that they call me by all those insulting names, which drive me to me despair, which make me clench my firsts in rage and stamp my foot on the ground; it doesn't matter that they slander my belief; I still experienced what I experienced, and I still saw what I saw. Oh, if it were permissible, for me, to call it into doubt...but the memory of that execrable scene pursues me so relentlessly...

I can't get away from it...it's impossible. It's there, always there!

You know, Édouard, when one is suffering as I am suffering, one has every right to lament that no one can believe in his suffering! Yes, yes, one has every right to complain!

My friend, you don't know everything about my difficulties. You know about the obstacles that were opposed to my marriage to Laura, and how they became more numerous and more insurmountable every day, but what you don't know is that the young woman was frightened by seeing love accompanied by so many torments. She raised her eyes with terror toward the future, and then she looked behind her with regret. I read it in her heart; she preferred a negative but peaceful happiness to the bitter intoxication of a sublime and ardent tenderness full of trouble and agitation.

In consequence, I took the decision to suffer alone, and not to associate that frail creature with the bleak destiny that weighs upon me. I wrote to tell her that I was renouncing her, since my love was causing her so much anguish. She replied in a letter moist with tears, in which she accepted my sacrifice.

Oh, I offered it to her in all sincerity—Heaven is my witness! And yet, Édouard, my dear Édouard, I cannot tell you how much harm she did me by accepting that sacrifice!

You have often told me that a good deed, a great act of courage, sustains the soul and renders the sacrifices imposed by duty less harsh. I confess, my friend, that that has not been my experience. But at least I have recognized the justice of another of your observations: that study is the only charm that soothes mental troubles. When one identifies with imaginary individuals, when one appropriates their chagrins, when one makes them weep over their misfortunes, when one softens sensations and torments that have become communal to them and us, it seems that one is not alone in suffering, that one is pouring out one's suffering into the bosom of a friend and that a secret voice is sympathizing, encouraging and consoling.

Two months ago I was spending the night writing beside a blazing fire. My ideas were flowing rapidly; pages covered in my large untidy scrawl had piled up on my desk. They were full of lugubrious thoughts, bizarre events and inconsequential, conflicting sentences of no interest to anyone but me, or you—you, Édouard, to whom a unique friendship has rendered my extravagant ideas, the impetuosity of my imagination and my fits of despair familiar.

When morning came, my blood was not refreshed and my head had not become any less heavy, but I had escaped from myself for a whole night, and that was a good deal. The day before, I had ordered that a bath should be prepared for me, Dr. Fernand having recommended me more than ever to make frequent use of it. I only just had time to go into the bathroom because my lamp, for lack of oil, was about to go out, and I was scarcely in the water before it threw off one last gleam and left me in complete darkness.

Here, my dear Édouard, I renew the plea I made just now: don't laugh at me, don't call what you're about to read into question, for you'd be doing me an injury!

I didn't take long to relax into the comfort of the bath. A soft warmth refreshed my limbs, tensed by long sleeplessness, by relaxing them. My forehead, burning with chagrin, was enveloped by a benevolent moisture. My ideas were suspended, without ceasing entirely, and my eyes closed under a gradual drowsiness.

I had been in a delightful situation for a few moments, when I thought I could hear a vague murmur somewhere in the vicinity. It even seemed that some unknown light was visible through my eyelids, although I felt so content that I didn't have the strength to open my eyes, to move or to stammer a single word; however astonishing the commotion might be that was happening close by, I could not pluck up the resolution to discover the reason for it.

A shock burst forth like a thunderbolt, but sharper and more harrowing.

I woke up with a start; in front of me stood a mocking and intimidating individual. He was looking at me as no human eye has ever gazed.

The sight of him suffocated me; it made me suffer indescribably.

He advanced his left hand and showed me the antique ring that, as you know, I bought from a Jew.

Then the specter passed the ring before my eyes, as if to prove to me that it really was mine; he gave me time to consider the fluting of the large ring and the two animal figures engraved on the black stone.

After that he raised his right hand; he showed me three fingers; he pronounced the word "Three," struck me hard on the head and disappeared.

When I recovered consciousness I was in bed, surrounded by people who were caring for me. Attracted by a piercing scream, they had come running; I had been found in the bath, half-drowned; a few seconds later, and it would have been all over. Why, alas, did they bring me back to life?

My first words were to ask my manservant for the casket in which my jewelry, including the fatal ring, was kept. On receiving that order, he went pale and trembled in every limb. A bitter laugh contracted his features.

"May Satan strike me dead!" he stammered. "You know everything!"

I thought that the wretch was referring to the dream I had had shortly before, because I still thought that it was a dream.

Then, suddenly, another idea—an absurd idea—passed like a flash of lightning through my imagination. I clung to it urgently. The apparition of a little while ago was a joke, played by one of my friends; they must have involved Antoine.

"Yes, I know everything!" I exclaimed. "You shall be punished as you deserve."

Antoine went out, in despair. Five minutes later I heard an explosion. I ran to my servant's room. He had blown his brains out.

He had left a note for me: *Monsieur, I'm a wretch. I've stolen your jewels. I'm dishonored; I shall die.*

On reading that, I was overtaken by an unbearable distress, and a fever. I had to take to my bed, in a pitiful state.

Édouard, as truly as I believe in God, the figure that I had seen the night before leapt to my gaze all night long—except that he only showed me two fingers, and his vibrant voice pronounced the word "Two."

Now, his mysterious speech and gestures were only too clear to me. The fatal ring was to cost the lives of three people. One of them had already met his fate.

During my convalescence, I was told that a young woman, poorly dressed and carrying a small child in her arms had come several times to ask for me. She had begged insistently that she be allowed to speak to me. I ordered that she should be brought to me if she came back again.

An hour later, she was shown into my room.

Casting my eyes over that unfortunate woman, pale, save for her eyes reddened with tears, hardly able to stand up, I understood that she had suffered a great deal, even more from moral troubles than physical ones.

"Antoine loved me," she said—and her knees buckled underneath her. If an armchair had not happened to be there, she would have fallen on the floor. "It was for me that he stole. It's because of me that he's dead. I'm…this is his son…"

The poor young woman's sobs broke my heart.

"Here, Monsieur, take this ring back. It's the only gift of his that I have left. I hadn't yet sold it in order to live. Take it back, Monsieur, but don't denounce me to the law. What would become of my child, the only thing that remains to me?

What would become of Antoine's son, if they threw me in prison?

She handed the ring to me, and I, overwhelmed by the memory of my vision, despairing in the realization that she had told the truth, chilled by fear at the thought of the misfortunes that she was still anticipating, remained motionless, absorbed by my lugubrious thoughts.

Poor creature! She thought that I was rejecting her supplications; she threw herself at my feet, seized my hand and bathed it with tears.

The unfortunate woman's agony brought me out of my reverie. "That ring must be destroyed," I exclaimed, "in order that it should not be deadly to anyone else. Hurry up, give it to me!"

The child had taken it from his mother's hand, in order to play with it; she had surrendered it listlessly. He had raised it to his lips.

Suddenly, he uttered a groan, stiffened convulsively and fell back. His mother was no longer holding anything but a cadaver.

The ring enclosed a mortal poison in its gem.

And the horrible figure that was pursuing me appeared above the despairing mother. This time, he did not speak, but his long finger held up a single digit.

Who will the third victim be?

Édouard, this is an idea that has lit up within me for the first time: an idea inspired in me by Heaven, I'm sure of it.

What if I were to put an end to the misfortunes caused by that infernal ring? I've lost everything that attached me to the earth. Existence weighs upon me; it has burdened me. What if I were to deflect the fatality that threatens someone else and draw it down voluntarily upon my own head?

The phantom has predicted it, and I am only too forcefully compelled to believe its predictions. It still needs another victim—only one! Will Providence punish me for sacrificing myself in this situation?

Already, for a long time, I've wanted to free myself from life. The fear of celestial wrath held me back. Now, God will bless me for dying.

Look! Here's the phantom coming back; he's giving me a sign that I can die.

Adieu!

THE LADY OF THE COLD KISSES

In the year 1187, Godescalque, Abbbé de Vaucelles,
weary of his burden and wanting to plunge more
deeply into the contemplation of Heaven, resigned it
to Jean, who was obliged to return it to him two years
later, because he did not feel strong enough or rigorous
enough to remedy the deplorable debauchery,
mutiny and confusion of its monks.
Le Carpentier, *Histoire de Cambrai*, vol. I,
Abbaye de Vaucelles.[13]

To my transports she yielded about to die,
And her happiness was but one long sigh.
F. Délacroix, "The Rape."[14]

The valley of the Escaut is one of the most picturesque
locations in Flanders. There is no traveler who does not marvel at it and ask: "What is that vast building whose three
wings, iridescent with windows, stands amid the ponds, meadows and woods?"

At present, it is a factory; once, it was the Abbaye de
Vaucelles.[15]

---

[13] *Histoire Genealogique des Pais-Bas, ou Histoire de Cambray, et
du Cambresis* (1664) by Jean Le Carpentier.

[14] This citation is probably invented; Berthoud could not have known
in 1831 that the Romantic painter Eugène Délacroix would produce a
famous painting of "Le Rapt de Rebekka" in 1858. Delacroix father,
a statesman, was named François, but he was not a poet.

[15] The Cistercian Abbaye de Vaucelles, some 13 kilometers from
Cambrai, was founded in 1131 by Saint Bernard. Destoyed in the
Revoluton, it was partly restored in the 20th century.

Once, the woods that crown the immense valley extended much further than they do today. Then, numerous pathways, contrived with extreme artistry, did not allow the monks to lose a single one of the amazing views that extended in every direction.

Flocks, the property of the abbey, covered those green meadows, through which the Escaut runs; its source is not far from Vaucelles. The virgin waters of the river, still a stream, alimented the ponds that you can see. At all times their tranquil surface cradled gondolas surmounted by awnings, on the cushions of which the monks, sprawling limply, enjoyed the pleasures of fishing and the delights of fresh air.

The Abbaye de Vaucelles offered the reality of the retreats of which the Epicurean imagination dreams, retreats that one would love to possess in order to live there, far from the anxieties and fatigues of the world, a life without cares, a life of idleness and wellbeing.

The monks' habits were made of fine white silky cloth; their hair, lightly fastened behind the head, was exquisitely neat, falling over a black scapular; and the elegance of their ingenious footwear had become proverbial.

Under the episcopate of Maximilien de Berghes in the year 1569, a man carefully hidden in the folds of a voluminous cloak was wandering by night around the Abbaye de Vaucelles, advancing with precaution, moving along the wall in order not to be seen. He circled the building in that fashion and, having reached the dormitory, coughed lightly. Suddenly, a ladder fell from a window, to which it remained attached at one end. The unknown man climbed up slowly and was received by two half-naked monks. The young man, whose garments included a mixture of religious and secular costume, set about recounting some adventure or other to them in a low voice, in which the name of a woman continually cropped up. Afterwards, they separated, and each one went away to go to bed in his own cell.

The young monk, for he was a member of the Vaucelles community, returned like the others and threw himself down breathlessly on his bed. Agitated by memories that he could not chase away, however, he unsuccessfully tried to go to sleep. In vain, he got up to bathe his forehead in cold water; in vain, he opened the window of his cell to let in cooler air; nothing could reconcile him with sleep.

Then, lighting a small lamp that he brought to his bed-side, he took up a thick manuscript whose parchment pages were overloaded with gilt ornaments and the most vivid colors. He read at random, at the place where the book had fallen open, and happened upon these pages, which recounted the foundation of Vaucelles:

Christian readers, it is necessary for you to read attentively and meditate upon this true story, if you want to know when and how Monseigneur Hugues d'Oisy, Seigneur de Crèvecoeur and Vicomte de Cambrai, after having contested with his bishop as his ancestors had done, after having had none but his own interest in recommendation, after having measured the just and the unjust for their utility, and concluded that a good consciences was importunate to his designs, was suddenly moved to compunction and horror of his crimes. You shall see after that in what fashion he caused the glory and advancement of the House of God to march at the head of all his actions, and took such tender care of all the churches and hospitals of Cambrésis and its surroundings regions that he is revered there everywhere as a benefactor and a founder.

But it is necessary for you to know that Monseigneur Hugues d'Oisy possessed, in the location where the Abbaye de Vaucelles now stands, a fortified château with four crenellated towers, guarded by men-at-arms as miscreant and harsh as their seigneur was at that time.

The most evil of them all was, without a doubt, an old squire whom no one could look at without fear. There was a wicked and lubricious expression in his little shining eyes, and to see the burned color of his skin one might have thought him a demon escaped from the fires of Hell or a sorcerer that the executioner had allowed to flee the pyre. That villainous man claimed to have fought in the Holy Land and attributed his suntanned complexion to the burning sky where Our Lord Jesus Christ did for the salvation of men.

But if his body had borne arms for a holy cause, it had not worked to the profit of his soul, for old Pecquigny—such as his name—addressed ugly blasphemies and insults to all the saints in paradise without even excepting (may Our Lord pardon me for relating such things!) the Blessed Virgin Mary herself, the mother of the savior and the pure and immaculate source of all merits and blessings.

In spite of having so many bad habits—among which we have omitted drinking to the point of drunkenness, unrestrained thievery, wrath and rebukes—Pecquigny had been able to find means to be in great favor with his young master, Hugues d'Oisy. It is true that he employed the experience of his old age and the cunning of his inventive mind to serve the impetuous passions of the young lord; then again, he excelled at taming horses, it being sufficient for him to murmur a few words, or merely to dart a glance, to render the most intractable horse as docile as a timid lamb.

Now, Monseigneur Hugues d'Oisy reckoned nothing superior to the pleasure of riding a fine palfrey or embracing a pretty girl, and with Pecquigny and his shrewd and deceitful advice, Hugues found as many restive fillies as chargers.

It happened one day that Sire Hugues met a young woman who had come from the estates of Espienne to accomplish in a convent in Cambrai the pious desire that Heaven had given her to enter a cloister and spend her life in perpetual prayer on the road to salvation. Fortified by her blessed resolution, she was walking alone, rosary in hand, having taken the veil in advance and put on a wimple.

Monseigneur Hugues d'Oisy doffed his hat, more out of habit than in a spirit of devotion, when he encountered the blissful young woman. Seeing that, Pecquigny burst out laughing, so loudly that he nearly fell off his horse. "By the Devil in Hell!" he exclaimed, "by his fork and his tail, it's my opinion, my young master, that you'll soon be dressing in a cowl and hood, and instead of feeling the edge of a blade against your thigh you'll be whipping your bare shoulders with the cords of a disciplinary lash. Far be it from me to let the girl pass with my hat lowered as if she reeked of holy incense—I'd pay her a different compliment, myself."

And, setting off after the young woman, he brought her back to his master.

She told him, naively, for what reason she was going to the town of Cambrai, and Monseigneur Hugues d'Oisy felt ill at ease on hearing that voice, so soft, pronounce simple words, and seeing large dark eyes full of sensuality and languor.

He sighed, and, fearful of evil thoughts, told the young woman to go on her way.

She was already obeying when she heard Pecquigny call out to her. "Hey!" he shouted. "Don't venture any further at thus hour. The road is dangerous, and thieves and lechers might do you harm. As you can see, we're pious folk, who doff our hats before a blessed veil." He cast a mocking glance at Hugues. "Come to the manor close by; you can spend the night comfortably there with no mishaps, and tomorrow, if it suits you, you can continue on your way."

The young woman followed this bad advice.

Merciful God, Blessed Virgin, model of purity, what happened at the manor during the night? Female laments, moans and cries for help were heard at about midnight, and the following day, a coffin was buried, without the priest naming, after the oblation—as is usual—the deceased for whom it was necessary to say prayers.

A year after that sad adventure, Monseigneur Hugues d'Oisy espoused in legitimate marriage Heldiarde de Beaudour. The wedding-party was held at the Châtel de Vaucelles, and the moment when the spouses were left alone, after the blessing of the nuptial bed, finally arrived—too slowly in Hugues d'Oisy's opinion.

Left with his spouse, he advanced in all haste toward the bed in which the beautiful Heldiarde lay, but he had scarcely arrived there than icy arms embraced him, an icy breast made contact with his and frozen lips kissed his lips.

Then the apartment was lit by a faint gleam, and he saw the pale cadaver of a woman lavishing caresses upon him, shoving aside Heldiarde—who was dying of fright—with one hand and only interrupting her caresses to say: "Hugues, it's me that you have married. I lost my chastity for you; I lost my divine spouse Jesus Christ for you; I lost the salvation of my soul for you; you belong to me; I am your wife."

The funereal bride did not disappear until daybreak.

She came back the following night, and the one after, and she came back every night, with her cold caresses, her stiff embraces and her horrible words of love.

It was in vain that Hugues left with Heldiarde for his Château de Crèvecoeur; the lady of the cold kisses followed him everywhere, and every time he looked at his wife, every time he extended his hand to her, the specter loomed up between them, and repeated: "It's me, and me alone that Hugues has espoused."

Hugues and Heldiarde would both have died, if the blessed Abbé de Clairvaux, Saint Bernard, had not come to Cambrésis. He heard mention of the frightful marvel that has just been related and had no difficulty in recognizing that, for so great a punishment, there must have been a crime even greater.

Wanting to return peace to the Châtel de Vaucelles, and banish forever the demon that was desolating the place, Saint Bernard came to find Monseigneur Hugues d'Oisy, and found him in a state that would have moved the harshest man to pity.

"There is a means," said the man of God, "to make the persecutions of the evil spirit stop; devote yourself to a holy monastic life; trample the vanities of the world underfoot, put on the robe of a hermit. The cloister and its pious austerities cure the soul of its criminal habits, purify the conscience of its iniquities, raise a rampart between the faithful and the tempter, console the most profound troubles, and open the way to eternal life."

Redoubling his energy, he continued: "Imitate Jesus Christ, our savior. He spent forty years upon the earth in chastity and continence; his happiness was solitude, meditation and prayer. Embrace the life of the cloister, wretched sinner covered in iniquity, and bless the Almighty, who, in his mercy, permits weak and unworthy mortals to imitate a God, an immense, omnipotent God who died for your salvation.

"I tell you this, and I repeat: there is no paradise outside the cloister. Is it not written in the gospels that it is easier for a camel to pass through the eye of a needle than for a powerful man to enter the kingdom of Heaven? Embrace the life of the cloister, then; do penance, and the kingdom of Heaven will come to you, and Satan will fall, vanquished, and the head of the serpent will be crushed."

Heldiarde uttered a profound sigh, for she could not consent to renouncing Hugues' love. At that sigh, her spouse felt his heart break, and he remained motionless, making no reply.

The old squire Pecquigny, whose discourteous gaze had not turned aside before Saint Bernard, then took it upon himself to speak.

"By my old blind mule!" he said, his fists on his hips, sniggering, "what you say is enough to make me die laughing. Bounty of the Devil! To listen to you, he'd have to tie up and lock away his spurs, and become an impotent wretch, like those they make among the infidels that people go to fight in distant lands, and let himself perish alive—unless he engenders bastards, as many monks do who repent of the vow they've sworn. By my good sword, I too have read and commented on the scriptures you call holy, and written there in all clarity is: *Be fruitful and multiply*. What do you say to that, my bald-headed friend?"

A holy indignation turned the blessed cheeks red. "*Vade retro, satanas!*" he cried, in a tone of authority and wrath—for he suspected that the Devil alone, in person, could be pronouncing those impious words at such a point.

Pecquigny trembled, and lost his audacity.

"*Vade retro, in nomine patris et filii et spiritus sancti!*"

Saint Bernard had not yet pronounced the name of the savior when a harrowing noise, like thunder, suddenly burst forth, and nothing more remained in the place where the squire had stood than a heap of ashes exhaling an odor of sulfur sufficient to make one feel sick.

It was necessary for the Comte d'Oisy and his wife to yield to that final prodigy, and they obeyed Saint Bernard's orders in every detail.

The reader will see in the sequel to this edifying story how Monseigneur Hugues d'Oisy donated the Château de Vaucelles, in order that an Abbaye might be built there endowed with great wealth, and how Saint Bernard brought a dozen monks there to live a god life, who all died in an odor of sanctity. He will marvel at the account of miracles contrived by the blessed Abbé de Clairvaux; for instance, a spring that surged forth to slake the thirst of the workers, and a chariot of fire to transport the stones, trees and other objects without being drawn by horses or other visible beings. When the Abbaye was built, the chariot of fire returned to the woods, where, since that day, no one has ever seen it again, in spite of the most assiduous searches that were made.

The lady of the cold kisses disappeared on the day when Abbé Raoul, English by nationality, came to live in the convent with his monks.

Monseigneur Hugues d'Oisy and his wife, Madame Heldiarde, proposed to retire to a cloister, in obedience to Saint Bernard's admonitions, but the aforesaid saint saw Our Lord Jesus Chris in a dream, who ordered him not to separate the two spouses, and they lived together for a long time in the fear of God and the most edifying devotion.

Since that time, the lady of the cold kisses has reappeared again, and comes to embrace sinners, whom she fills with terror, in her icy arms. It is when the monks of the Abbaye de Vaucelles break the vows of chastity that they have sworn...

At that moment, the impact of an invisible being struck the young monk's lamp, inundating his face and breast with some kind of icy liquid, and left him in profound darkness. He thought that it was the lady of the cold kisses, and uttered screams of terror.

Monks came running, and found him pale and distraught, covered from head to toe in the oil from his lamp. Then a bat came to flutter around the candles they were holding.

The young monk smiled, asserting that he had had a bad dream, during which he had knocked over his lamp.

After that, he went to sleep, soundly.

THE BARN IN MONTECOUVEZ

It happened, I am told, about four hundred and fifty years ago. The harvest had been bad and, to complete the despair of the unfortunate farmers, heavy rain began to fall in torrents in the month of September, gravely imperiling the hayricks that covered the fields; the trusses of wheat could not even be stored in the mill, as usual; the rain found means of getting in and rotting everything. There was a general desolation.

A young peasant, married a few months before, felt that calamity more than anyone else, for, confident of the fine days that normally arrive at reaping time, he had put off, for the time being, building a barn to shelter his harvest. The old men of the neighboring villages had even given him that advice. "Go into the fields," they had said, "and watch the harvesters; the master's eye makes the ricks grow, diminishes the share of the gleaners, and gives a third arm to the hirelings."

He listened meekly to these precepts of white-haired men whose hands had been put to the plough for sixty years. Misfortune arrived nevertheless, as I have said, but those who had spoken thus and caused the ruination of the poor young farmer, did not come to his aid in consequence, and left him to despair alone.

One evening, Pierre Margerin—that was his name—came back to his abode with death in his heart; he thought that his harvest would not bring in thirty écus; that it would be impossible for him to pay his rent; and that it would be necessary to hire himself out as a ploughman to some farmer in the neighborhood. Heaven was witness to the fact that it was not for himself that he felt the greatest affliction but for his wife and the child that she was due to ring into the world four months hence.

He found in such thoughts what is necessary to drive a man to an evil deed. He threw himself down at the foot of a

115

tree and, taking a large knife out of his pocket, he examined it in silence; then he put it to his breast.

At that moment, a stranger appeared, who asked Margerin which path let to the Château de Câtelet. He had to repeat his question, because the farmer was thinking so profoundly that he did not hear the dry and mordant voice interrogating him.

"I'll take you there," he said, the second time. "Come this way, Monseigneur." He gave him that title because the stranger, richly dressed, was wearing a sword, and his manners were indicative of a man of high status.

While Margerin was walking with him, the man he was guiding said: "You seem sad, my good man; has some misfortune struck you?"

"It has indeed! My crop is rotting there in the fields; it's rotting at its leisure, exposed to the rain, for I have no barn to shelter it. For a week now, workmen have been trying to build one, but they haven't made much progress, and when it's finished, what they've built will be no use to me, for I'll have nothing to put in it but compost. I'm ruined forever, unless God sends a miracle to save me."

The stranger went pale and shivered. Margerin thought he saw the sudden emotion in his eyes that is a sign of great compassion, and resumed telling him his troubles.

"You are indeed in a bad fix, and I can only see one way of getting you out of it."

"One means! What? Tell me what it is. If there is one, I'll accept it, whatever it might be, even if it costs me my life—just as long as my wife and child are saved from poverty."

"Well," the stranger went on, coolly, "I'll give you a hundred louis d'or, I'll have your barn built, and I'll fill it with dry wheat of good quality, worth seven écus a mencaud."

"May Heaven bless you, my generous Seigneur!" cried Margerin, passing from the most bitter despair to the heights of joy. My gratitude..."

He suddenly stopped, because a ray of moonlight slipping through a gap in the clouds at that moment lit up the stranger's pale face and gave his physiognomy a frightful expression. One might have thought that he was a cadaver of his dark eyes, small and sunken, had not been glittering with a supernatural gleam and an odious joy.

"I need guarantees, however; let's see, are you prepared to sign a contract with me? These are my conditions: before the first cockcrow, you shall have everything I've promised you, but you must consent to be my vassal and swear to come with me in a year's time to my own jurisdiction."

"Is your jurisdiction far away?"

"It only takes an hour to get there."

"It goes without saying that you'll give me lodgings there as good as my own, and that my wife and child will come with me?"

The stranger had difficult suppressing a burst of laughter. "Let's include your wife and child in the contract. I'll give you a hundred louis for the wife and fifty for the child."

"Done!" replied Margerin. "Let's go to the notary to sign the document."

"There's no need for a notary in this arrangement, and I carry parchment and a pen about my person. Besides which, I'm in a hurry to reach the château, and I can't waste any more time on such a minor transaction. Make a slight prick on your left hand, and we'll use blood instead of ink.

"As you wish."

When the contract had been drawn up and signed, and the gold counted and handed over, the stranger headed for the château and disappeared in the middle of the path, to Margerin's great surprise. The latter went home; on the way, he felt tormented by a secret anxiety with regard to the bargain he had just concluded.

Who was that nobleman, then? he wondered. *His jurisdiction is no more than a league away; apparently, he's the son of the Sire de Villers-Outréaux, Esnes or some other village in the neighborhood. My word! Two hundred and fifty louis and a barn full of good wheat is certainly worth the trouble of moving to another village.*

When he arrived at the farm, he found the unknown man's workmen already fulfilling the conditions of the contract. They were working with a marvelous promptitude; while some were setting up the beams and woodwork, others were laying the bricks, and they only had to set their hands on the mortar for it to dry and harden incontinently. A ruddy gleam illuminated the whole scene, although it was impossible to see any torch producing it.

What was even more incomprehensible, however, was the profound silence that reigned in the midst of such activity, involving a hundred and fifty masons, carpenters and others. There was not such a silence is an abandoned cemetery at midnight. The hammers struck without resonance, the saws scraped, causing clouds of oak sawdust to rise and fall, but the tearing of the wood and the respiration of the workman were equally inaudible.

Gripped by an expressible terror, he went into the house. He found his wife surprised and consternated; the domestic animals, agitated by a secret terror, were huddling together and trying to get into the main farmhouse, as if to escape some great danger. The dogs were howling lamentably, adding even further to the horror of what was happening.

There was a cockerel of rare beauty at the farm, of which the mistress of the house was particularly fond. The animal in question, which seemed even more alarmed than the others, suddenly flew into its mistress' lap.

Surprised by that abrupt and unexpected irruption, she screamed, made the sign of the cross and thrust the cockerel away, which began to crow.

Suddenly, there was a noise like a clap of thunder; the earth trembled and the workmen disappeared, leaving the barn unfinished.

The following day, the people of the village were amazed to see the barn, which had not only been built in one night but filled with corn-ricks, without any carts or laborers being employed to transport them. Margerin was careful not to say anything about it.

After having confessed to a holy priest and thanked Heaven for the peril from which God had saved him—for he knew now, belatedly, alas! that the stranger was none other than Satan in person—he set to work to finish a gable left incomplete. When he tried to place a brick there, however, he fell, suddenly knocked over by a supernatural force; he was never able to finish the gable, which remains to this day in the state in which the infernal workmen left it.

And since that time, too, a cockerel starts to crow at the farm in question long before daybreak, at the time when Satan's masons took flight.

Margerin did at a ripe old age, with sentiments of fervent piety.

THE WEDDING AT CAVRON-SAINT-MARTIN

If I live for another hundred years I shall still remember Jean Saveux's wedding as I remember it today.

I left my village early in the morning, because I had to go through the forest of Hesdin in order to pick up, in accordance with my uncle's request, our old friend Nicolas Meuron, the shepherd, who had been invited to the wedding.

He refused obstinately to accompany me, saying that he would not be seen at such an espousal even if he were paid a hundred ducats, but he did not want to tell me why.

I was already at least four *ave*s away from his house when he ran after me and called me back in order to hand me a little bottle which he asked me at least twenty times not to be separated from it for an instant throughout that time I was in Jean Saveux's house in Cavron-Saint-Martin. It would, he said, preserve me from the evil Spirit's ambushes, which would not fail to be laid.

Alas, the old shepherd's prediction was only too true, you shall see in due course.

I did not know my cousin Marguerite's future husband, and when I saw him on my arrival, I felt myself becoming quite sad that that he was marrying such a pretty girl. He was, I must admit, a handsome fellow, but there was something in his pale face and his eyes, sunken beneath bushy brows, the sight of which caused a sensation of unease. He was not much liked in the village because he was very careful with his money, never went to enjoy himself at the tavern and sometimes went an entire week without saying a single word to anyone. That became the cause of various speculations; some thought that he was under a spell; others, on the contrary, took him for a spell-caster. Thus, in spite of the goodly sum of money and the large farm with three barns that he brought as a marriage-portion, my cousin Marguerite was still criticized for making the marriage, and more than one person said: "Marguerite is marrying Jean Saveux; that will be quite some marriage."

The wedding-feast began, and everything went well until the time came for dancing. Now, it happened that the fiddler of Hesdin, the joyful Mathias Wilmart, had not been invited. Everyone was lamenting such the inconvenience when the groom was told that an unknown man was asking to speak to him.

Jean Saveux, who was chatting and joking with his wife, and who had never been seen, so far as anyone would remember, in such a good mood, got to his feet, cursing the importunate individual who was disturbing him thus. As the sight of the stranger, however—who, weary of waiting, had taken it upon himself to come in—he went as pale as a corpse and nearly fell over.

"I hope that I'm welcome?" said the unknown man, coldly, to the groom.

"You have the right to be here," Jean Saveux replied, but his pale face and the trembling of all his limbs gave the lie to the welcome that he forced himself to give to the newcomer.

The latter was not put off by it. He sat down cheerfully at the table, poured a full measure of beer into a tankard the size of a boot and drank it in a single draught—after which he served himself a ham, of which he left nothing but the bone, and then ate several enormous tarts, drinking in proportion. No one had ever seen a thirst so dry or an appetite so voracious.

In the meantime, there was a more profound silence among the guests than at a funeral dinner. The stranger was completely at his ease, however, and paid no heed to the concern that his arrival had caused; he crossed his legs with difficulty and, unbuttoning his waistcoat, which was hindering his digestion, turned his head and saw Jean Saveux, still standing there, paler than ever.

"Ha ha!" he said, in a familiar fashion. "You haven't introduced your wife to me yet, comrade. Damnation! I've been a reckless fellow in my time, like anyone else; I've drawn more than one pretty girl to sin—but other times, other tastes.

Now, as you know, Jean Saveux, it isn't young women I catch in my net, is it?"

Jean Saveux, albeit reluctantly, took Marguerite by the hand and led her to the strange man.

"She's a charming creature, Jean! You have good taste. My word, it's unfortunate that this evening...for it is this evening..." He added the last few words in a whisper, almost in Jean's ear. Jean shivered from head to toe.

"But what's the meaning of this?" the stranger went on, without paying any attention to the groom's distress. "This is a singular wedding; there isn't even a single violin."

Someone hazarded the remark that they had neglected to incite Mathias Wilmart, and that even if he had been invited, the rain that had been falling since midday would gave rendered the marl roads surrounding Cavron-Saint-Martin impracticable.

"Why, if that's all that's preventing you from dancing," said the stranger, "I have a violin, and without claiming to be an excellent musician, I hope that you won't regret the absence of this Mathias Wilmart, whom you're praising so loudly, too much.

He went out, and came back in with a violin. That surprised me somewhat, for I had chanced to see him, when he had knocked on the door on his arrival, and I would have sworn on my share of paradise that he did not have a violin in his hand or under his arm. Nor could the instrument have been in his traveling-bag, for he was not carrying one.

At any rate, the stranger put a chair in the middle of a table, climbed up to it, and started playing the violin as if he had never done anything else in his life. He could easily have been mistaken for a veritable fiddler, for he was a short fat man with a cheerful attitude and an exceedingly mocking manner; he tapped his foot, exclaimed, fidgeted and drank like Mathias Wishart.

Everyone took their places, except for the husband, who stood in a corner, taciturn and pensive, and tried to prevent his wife from dancing.

The violin-player perceived that. "What does this conduct signify, Jean Saveux?" he asked, sniggering. "Today is the most beautiful day in your life, and you're standing there like an owl! Come on! Cheer up, comrade, and take your place!"

This time, however, Jean Saveux refused to obey. With a single bound, the stranger leapt off the table and placed his hand on the recalcitrant's shoulder. Immediately, a frenetic gaiety took possession of Jean, previously so gloomy. He started to talk, to jump, and to laugh—but all of it in such a sinister manner that one would more ready have taken him for a man possessed that a man who was due, in half an hour, to find himself in private with a charming bride.

To tell the truth, the music that the unknown man was playing produced a sort of dolorous joy that I only ever experienced that once. During the dance, I sensed a thousand singular and guilty thoughts; it was as if I were drunk and having a bad dream. And yet, the air we were breathing in the room became heavy and hot, and a strong odor spread into every corner, acrid and suffocating, like that produced by a red-hot iron when one plunges it into water.

Midnight chimed; then, the unknown man put his violin under his arm, got down from his chair and approached Jean Saveux.

"Now" he said to him.

"One more night! Just one more night!" Jean pleaded, all of whose limbs were trembling in a frightful manner.

"No," the unknown man replied.

"At least grant me an hour, one more hour!"

"No," replied a dull and implacable voice.

"Give me a quarter of an hour!" said Jean, then, in a piteous manner.

"No," said the stranger. He added, after enjoying Jean Saveux's despair momentarily: "I'll take pity on you. If your wife signs it, I'll grant you another week."

Jean took the scroll of red parchment with golden letters that his guest handed to him—but he threw it back at him in horror.

"Then I'll bid the company farewell, and you can see me out."

The short man bowed to everyone, and, putting his arm around Jean Saveux's neck in an amicable fashion, he said to the bride: "Adieu. Don't hold it against me too much that I'm taking your lover away: you'll soon be seeing him again, my beauty."

It was, however, not until the next day that she saw him again, and he was no more than a cadaver struck by lightning. He was found like that, after a long search, lying at the foot of an oak-tree in Hesdin forest.

When he was taken to the church, the blessed candles all went out at the same time, and I'm told that the grave in which his coffin was deposited was found to be empty the following day.

THE SIRE WITH THE BROKEN ARMOR

At one time, the Château d'Esnes was the most beautiful in Cambrésis. Now, nothing remains of it but ruins, which are mingled with rustic and very modern constructions that give it an even sadder appearance.

Instead of broad crenellations, two paltry gabled roofs raise up their slate triangles on the towers flanking the draw-bridge. Windows have been hollowed out irregularly in the thickness of the ramparts, and a heavy layer of thatch makes them resemble a dilapidated farmhouse.

No more deep moats, no more angular fortifications; the plough has transformed he former into fields of wheat, which the wind agitates like waves; the others have collapsed, and there is not a single hovel in the village whose walls their rubble has not served to construct.

An immense dung-heap fills the court of honor; the ruins of the perron lead to a kitchen, and the vast ostentatious halls have been transformed into stables. Nothing is any longer heard but the clucking of the poultry-yard and the lowing of cattle in those places where the echoes once repeated so many times over the songs of the trumpet, the rattle of horses' hooves, the masculine cries of men-at-arms and the soft words of demoiselles.

To the right of the main gate, all that remains intact of the old manor house is a slender sandstone tower raising its bare gray head in the midst of the ruins. A Medieval sculptor has engraved on the summit, in 15th century characters, the twelve hours of the day: a clock, the marvel of the region, parades its thick gilded hand around the stone circle, indicating the duration of the day to the castellan and his vassals—for the artist, to achieve that double result, had placed the frame in such a manner as to be visible both from inside and outside the courtyard.

It was the year of our salvation 1440, at the feast of Pentecost, at the moment when the bell in that tower was sounded noon, that Messire Jean d'Esnes set forth in order to make a rather long sojourn on the estate of his old companion in arms, Messire Jacques de Crèvecoeur. Everyone was amazed to see the septuagenarian castellan undertaking such a perilous journey, because, for nine full years at least, he had only left the great reception-hall to go to the moustier,[16] and even for that he had to request the aid of two vigorous varlets, who carried him rather than led him to the velvet bench armoried with the silver shield and the sable border.

After seven days, Messire Jean returned to his estate. The first thing he asked was why his son, Messire Eustache, was not there to pay his respects and welcome him home, as was his duty.

The old chaplain, Master Claude Watremez, replied that the young sire had departed for the Château d'Élincourt a week ago, adding that he was sure to return after vespers, as he had send word to that effect the day before via his squire Simon Guyot.

Indeed, it happened as the worthy priest had said, for Messire Jean had not emptied his second goblet of hypocras when his son came into the hall, reverently, and knelt down to request a blessing from his father.

The old seigneur, however, neglectful for the first time in his life of the decorum of etiquette, kissed the young man tenderly on the cheeks without placing his hands on him and set about exclaiming rather than saying: "I've had a good journey, Eustache, a journey that will provide merriment and grandeur for the old and noble family of Esnes. God and the Blessed Virgin by praised! The Comte de Crèvecoeur has promised the

---

[16] The term *moustier*, resurrected by various members of the French Romantic Movement, including Edgar Quinet, was a Medieval synonym of monastery, surviving in numerous place-names, but Berthoud seems to be using it in a different sense, to refer to an oratory.

hand of his only daughter, Emme, for you, Eustache—for you, to the detriment of many a noble suitor."

Eustache's cheeks suddenly became pale; he wanted to speak but could not.

Then, without paying any heed to that great emotion, Messire Jean began relating how he had been able to make such an alliance, and counting on his fingers—of which he did not have sufficient—the rich lands that made up Emme de Crèvecoeur's marriage portion, not to mention that she would bring her spouse and suzerain the right to add to his coat of arms an emblem of gules with three gold chevrons and the motto *Tour Landry!* After which he sent his son away, smiling secretly at the trouble he foresaw.

At his age, he thought, *such news would have made me dance with jubilation, but he becomes pensive and confused. It's true to say that I was a different man, as alert as could be and known for ten leagues around for my jovial and facetious humor.*

Ruminating such thoughts of his youth, Messire Jean d'Esnes summoned his varlets by means of his silver whistle, who came running, had had himself put to bed immediately, where, he believed, fatigue and joy would have prepared him a sound sleep until sunrise.

But that was not the case.

In the middle of the night he woke up with a start. He had heard slow and solemn footsteps rustling the foliage with which, in accordance with custom, the parquet of the bedroom had been covered. To find out who it was, he lifted the curtain of his bed.

Jesus, savior of men! A knight of piteous appearance was standing before him, bare-headed, his face bruised, his armor broken, and his robe covered with mud and blood.

He fixed on Messire Jean d'Esnes a compassionate gaze, after which he knelt down, struck his breast despairingly, like a *mea culpa* for some great sin, and, turning toward the old sire he proffered these words in a deep and mournful voice: "Whoever does as I did is bound for Hell."

Then he disappeared.

Messire Jean then made such a noise with his silver whistle that his son, his varlets and even the old chaplain came running anxiously. Messire Jean told most of them to go away, only retaining with him the almoner Claude Watremez, begging the latter to recite prayers before anything else, and to sprinkle holy water liberally.

When the almoner had done that, Messire Jean told him every detail of the marvelous vision that he just come to him.

The chaplain listened gravely. When the monseigneur had finished, he said: "It's the sire with the broken armor who has appeared to you. There must be some projected marriage in your family that is against the wishes of the fiancés, for the terrible phantom only appears in such circumstances. You have just seen Ulric de Landast, sire of Sommaing and Esnes, one of your ancestors."

Monseigneur d'Esnes' physiognomy took on an unequivocal expression of ill-humor.

"By my patron Saint Jean! What crack-brained nonsense are you jabbering? I'm an old warrior, and you can be sure that the tales of a shaven-head won't make a fool of me."

The priest, who was accustomed to the castellan's rude manners, replied in the following terms:

"You were placed as a page at an early age with Monseigneur le Duc de Bourgogne, and for that reason, I see, you have not heard the legend of the sire with the broken arms in your childhood. I'll relate it to you as the good folk of the domain tell it on long winter evenings. May I be burned in the utmost depths of Hell if I change a single word of it.

"A long time ago—if my memory serves me right it was in the year 1153 of our Redemption, Monseigneur Liétard then being Bishop of Cambrai—Ulric de Landast, sire d'Esnes et de Sommaing, wanted to marry his son Alard to the Châtelaine de Walincourt, who had been left a widow by the death of her noble spouse. But Alard was in love with Gillette de Glimes, the orphan daughter of a poor knight of noble lineage, who had died without leaving his daughter any wealth but a stainless renown and the aid of a few rich burgers who had taken compassion on her distress. Now, the poor creature was carrying in her loins the fruit of the love that Alard had sworn on his share of paradise to sanctify by marriage.

"When he learned of this news, so destructive for the plans he had made, when Sire Alard had begged his father to unite him in legitimate marriage, not with the Dame de Walincourt but with his beloved Gillette, Messire Ulric swore an oath that, so long as he should live, nothing would come of it. Prayers and laments, far from soothing him, redoubled his fury; he banished his son from the manor and declared him cursed until he consented to marry the Dame de Walincourt

"Alard wandered in the country all night, and when daybreak came he left for the town in order to see Gillette one more time and then to die.

"As he approached the drawbridge of the Episcopal châtel he saw a large crowd gathered around the moat, and laments and maledictions were emerging from the assembly. He spurred his horse, for the presence of such great misfortune had stirred his already-broken heart, but the crowd surrounded him incontinently, throwing stones at him, and he fell, struck down by a stone, next to the corpse of Gillette, who had died the previous night after hurling herself into the moat.

"People were saying: 'He's broken!' 'He's down!' 'He's dead!' 'That's good!' 'It's quite enough to have caused Gillette's death—we couldn't let him come to laugh on seeing her pale face and rub his hands in glee as if to signify: I'm acquitted; God be praised!'

"It's necessary to say that the rumor had spread through the townspeople that Sire Alard had consented to marry Madame de Walincourt. Belief in such villainous bad faith had thus caused the death of the young man, who had arrived at a bad time, just as Gillette's body was being pulled out of the water, after she had drowned herself in despair at the false news of her lover's infidelity.

"Alard had scarcely rendered up his soul, however, when one of his men-at-arms, piercing the crowd, threw himself on the body, weeping, saying that his young seigneur had been wickedly slain, and recounting the manner in which he had preferred to suffer his father's curse rather than abandon Gillette.

"You can imagine how contrite the hotheads of Cambrai were when they heard that! The townspeople picked up the two lovers and bore them devotedly, bare-headed and bare-footed, into the church of Saint Jean and Saint Paul on the Mont des Boeufs, in order that prayers could be said and the *Requiem* sung for the repose of their souls.

"Meanwhile, Sire Ulric, having heard word that his son Alard had left for Cambrai in order to se Gillette again, summoned four men-at-arms and rode out with a slack bridle in order to prevent them from going away. As he came into the town, however, howls of rage even louder than the previous ones burst forth on every side.

"His men-at-arms were attacked, and they fell dead in less than no time. As for Sire Ulric, he was tipped from his horse, his hair and beard were torn out; even women were seen rushing upon him to pinch him and rake him with their fingernails. He was taken to the public square wearing nothing but a tattered chemise. Some pelted him with mortar and mud, others rained down blows with clubs on his head, others pricked him with awls and skewers. In brief, all the Cambrésians came to fall upon him and hung him up by his feet from the gibbet, where the coup-de-grâce was administered.

"Since that fatal day, whenever anyone in your noble family wants to make a marriage against the wishes of the fiancés, the sire with the broken arms appears in the Château d'Esnes until the death of the abetters of that marriage."

The chaplain had just finished that marvelous story when young Eustache came slowly into the Monseigneur's room and confessed to him the love that he had avowed to de Demoiselle d'Élincourt, saying that he would rather die than place the nuptial ring on the finger of another, even one a thousand times more noble and better endowed than the Demoiselle de Crèvecoeur herself.

He waited to see his father's wrath burst forth, but the Sire d'Esnes went back to bed, silent and pensive.

The next morning, when he got up, the old man was pale, trembling with an extreme emotion.

The sire with the broken armor had appeared to him again.

He sent the chaplain to the Château de Crèvecoeur, and as soon as Master Claude Watremez had returned, he made it known to his vassals that Eustache de Landast, Sire d'Esnes, was betrothed to Demoiselle Perrette d'Élincourt, and that henceforth, the shield with the sable border would be combined with a shield of gules on squares of ermine.

THE FARMER'S SUPPER

If your door suddenly opens, without anyone appearing to enter the house, be very wary of saying, either jokingly or otherwise: "Come in and make yourself at home."

Be wary, because what happened to the farmer Eustache Gosselin, of Élincourt, who had invited two friends to a lavish feast, might happen to you.

He had invited his guests to sit down at table before mid-day, and vespers had rung without either one of them having appeared.

He strode back and forth, looking out of the window, grumbling that no one was coming, then went to the window again and looked out again. In the end, he proffered an oath ill-befitting a Christian, and swore that he would offer a seat at the table to the first person who came along, even if it be the Devil himself.

Suddenly, the door of the dwelling opened wide, but there was no one there to come in.

Eustache Gosselin, without thinking that anything was wrong, having already forgotten the indecorous words he had spoken, and believing that it was one of his friends, shouted: "Come in and you'll be fed as appropriate, although, to tell the truth, you're later than it's permissible to be."

At these words, three unknown men, whose doublets, hose, boots and plumed hats were black, came through the doorway and bowed deeply, although they were having difficulty, in Eustache Gosselin's judgment, in stifling a strong desire to laugh.

The farmer had a strong desire to teach them not to make mock of him in his own house, but just as he was about to speak in an irritated fashion, he looked at the unknown men and, without knowing why, felt such a frisson of fear that he dared not say a word.

Then the guests, still in profound silence, surrounded the table, took their seats and helped themselves to the various dishes that were set out there.

No Christian had ever eaten as they ate.

Throughout the time that the meal lasted, Eustache Gosselin did not hear the slightest sound.

When they had finished, they looked at one another in a sinister fashion, and the farmer, still petrified by fear, dared not make a move or call for help.

From that day forward, no one ever went into farmer Gosselin's house, because, that night, a ruddy gleam appeared at all the windows in the house, and in the midst of that radiance, black shadows, which seemed to be holding plates laden with food in their clawed hands, passed back and forth rapidly with all the expedition of varlets serving at a feast. Bursts of laughter were heard and frightful words. An old shepherd, who, it is said, took the precaution of equipping himself with holy water and relics in order to approach the house, saw farmer Gosselin inside, sitting motionless and watching the demonic feast.

Many years passed, and Eustache Gosselin's house had fallen into ruins, without anyone ever wanting to go into it; they scarcely dared work the land around it, for it was isolated in the middle of a field.

Now, nothing remains of it, but at certain times, travelers who chance to pass that way by night still see the gleam of that infernal feast and hear the laughter of terrible guests.

So, therefore, as a true Christian, ever wary of the ambushes of demons, keep in mind this wise maxim. If your door opens suddenly without anyone appearing to come into the house, be very wary of saying, either jokingly or otherwise: "Come in and make yourself at home."

Be wary, because what happened to the farmer Eustache Gosselin of Élincourt, who had invited two friends to a lavish feast, might happen to you.

SAINT MATHIAS THE HERMIT

> One should not call any man holy and virtuous
> until he is dead.
>
> Sermon by Père Mathias.[17]

> To a great man, nothing is sufficient; because he can
> obtain anything, his desires increase with his fortune;
> everything that is more elevated than him makes him appear
> small in his own eyes; he is less pleased to leave so many men
> behind him than distressed to have less, as yet, than those who
> preceded him; he does not believe that he has anything until
> he has everything. His soul is always arid and thirsty.
>
> Massillon, *Petit Carême*.[18]

Monseigneur le Comte de Flandres, Robert—the third of
that name, named de Béthunes because before becoming a
Comte he had the title Seigneur de Béthunes,[19] had retired to
his town of Ypres, discontented with the king of France,

---

[17] This invented quotation is a variation of Herodotus' dictum: "Call
no man happy until he is dead."

[18] The sermons of the famous bishop of Clermon, Jean-Baptiste
Massillon (1663-1742) were collected after his death; Berthoud
would undoubtedly have made their acquaintance at Douai. "Petit
Carême" is one of those delivered during Lent.

[19] Robert III, Comte de Flandres, also known as Robert de Béthune
(1249-1322) had the title of Comte de Flandres passed on to him by
his father in 1299 but spent the next six years imprisoned by Philippe
IV, and was only able to assume the position in earnest in 1305. He
was not, in fact, involved in the battle of Coutrai or Courtray, otherwise known as the Battle of the Golden Spurs, in 1302, although
Berthoud was not the only writer to put him there; the Flemish writer
Hendrik Conscience did likewise in *Die Leeuw van Vlaanderen*
(1838; tr. as *The Lion of Flanders*), of which Robert is the hero.

Philippe le Bel. For, in spite of the fact that he had first been married to the late Catherine d'Anjou, the daughter of Charles, king of Sicily and brother of the king of France, Louis IX, and in spite of the fact that he had plied the lance valiantly with his father-in-law against the bastard Manfroi, whom he had slain with his own hand, Philippe le Bel had not taken care to reward such loyalty given to his relatives. On the contrary, taking issue with some light words of Monseigneur's Robert's, he had fought a great battle with him at Courtray—but he had received the punishment for such disloyalty in his army's bloody defeat.

Far from losing heart at such a rude blow, the king of France soon set about making clever use of cunning deceit; he beguiled Monseigneur Robert so well with fine words that the prince, more bold and valiant knight than crafty cleric, let himself be taken in by those fine semblances, and was deprived of his beautiful cities of Lille and Douai, which he handed back to the king of France.

The thing had scarcely been done, irredeemably, the Monseigneur Robert began stamping his feet and grumbling in a furious fashion; but it was already too late. A swarm of French men-at-arms, with redoubtable engines of war, were already guarding the two cities in question, well provisioned with food, capable of sustaining for year after year the harshest siege that it might please the largest possible army to lay.

Regretful of his simplicity, Monseigneur Robert retired to Ypres, where he was eaten away by worry and repentance. And, as there had been no issue of his marriage to the late Catherine d'Anjou but a single son whose health was precarious and who had undertaken a journey to Bourgogne for that reason, Monseigneur Robert heeded the advice of his noble vassals, who urged him to make certain of a sure lineage. He therefore sought the hand of Madame Iolente de Bourgogne, the only daughter of Monseigneur le Duc de Bourg, Odon, Comte de Nevers, who, still young and magnificently beautiful, was the widow of Jean de France, known as Tristan, the son of King Louis IX.[20]

The Duc de Bourg acquiesced willingly to Comte Robert's request, and Madame Iolente found herself incontinently betrothed, without being consulted and to her great regret. She dared not complain, however, for her father was stubbornly implacable, and never went back on a decision. In any case, if she had said that she was in love with young Charles de Flandres and had sword eternal fidelity to him, the old seigneur would simply have laughed, and hastened the marriage of Iolente to the father of her beloved.

Now, the marriage request had been made by Master Mathias, who had once been a poor hermit spending day and night in prayer in a cave near the gate of the town of Ypres. Everyone praised his devotion and everyone took him for a friendly arbiter in pleas and disputes; he always did so with wisdom and justice, such as is no longer seen nowadays.

One day, Mathias had been very surprised to see Comte Robert come to his pitiful lodging, who had, after conversing with him for some time, requested him to come and reside in his palace in order to render justice there and help him to govern his estates.

It was not easy for the holy man to resolve to do what was requested of him, for he rightly regarded as great wealth, worth more than palaces and power, sleeping peacefully on fresh straw, eating his fill of black bread, drinking fresh water, days without any cares and the ineffable joy of prayer. In the end, however, he gave in to the seigneur's persistence, and all the townsfolk of Ypres, on hearing the news, set forth to escort the new administrator of justice to the Comte's palace, shout-

---

[20] In fact, Robert had married Yolande, or Iolente, de Bourgogne in 1272 and she died—after giving birth to six children—in 1280, so the chronology of the story is inaccurate. Charles, the only son of Robert's first marriage, had died in infancy, but had he survived he would only have been six years old when Robert married Yolande, so that aspect of the story is entirely fanciful. The characters of Mathias and Bauderic are imaginary.

ing loudly: "God bless Monseigneur Robert and the holy man Mathias forever!"

The hermit performed the duties of his position as best he could, and by way of recompense, the Comte de Flandres gave him the mission mentioned above.

Madame Iolente de Bourgogne was brought to her fiancé, enclosed in a rich litter drawn by eight white hacks. A hundred men-at-arms marched in front and rear, to defend her against highwaymen and other vagabonds. The hermit Mathias followed, mounted on a benign horse, reciting paternosters and threading the beads of his rosary through his fingers one by one.

One evening, when Madame Iolente was lodging in the domain of a suzerain dependent on Monseigneur Robert, Père Mathias encountered one of the most renowned astrologers in the world, Master Bauderic de Nozenback, German by nationality, so old that it was said that he had predicted the future of King Philippe Auguste in the days when he was still a child.[21]

The astrologer was surrounded by people marveling at his science, so great that no one else knew as much as he did, and the suzerain himself, at supper, gave Bauderic the place of honor, much higher than that of Mathias the Hermit.

The hermit was secretly annoyed, for until that time, he had always seen everyone give preference to Madame Iolente herself, and had always heard his own virtues and sanctity praised at length. The next day, he was even sadder, because Madame Iolente invited Bauderic to accompany her to the town of Ypres, and instructed Mathias to make the savant astrologer welcome, professing in a loud voice that such great science was worth as much as sanctity. "If not considerably more," she added in a low voice to one of her ladies in waiting, who were ever ready to frolic at the expense of the hermit's critical expression and disapproving comments.

---

[21] Philippe II, known as Phiilipe Auguste, born in 1165, was king of France from 1180 to 1223.

On the other hand, the astrologer felt envious of the respect and renown that the hermit enjoyed. He therefore brought his horse into step with Père Mathias' hack, not with the intention of edifying himself with the latter's pious speech, but rather to find fault with him and try to bring about his fall.

"Thrice blessed are you, Father," he said, passing a withered and sinewy hand over his bald and wrinkled brow, "for you've never known any of the cares of study and the fatigues of science. Yes, by the seal of Solomon, I've wished many a time to be a placid and ignorant hermit—and yet I have the secrets of great works, demons obedient to my orders, and people would pay immense treasures for the least of my secrets.

"It's necessary to say, although it's prideful, that there's a great and beneficent joy is saying that one is superior to other men, and that one owes that superiority entirely to one's studies and the force of one's determination. One burning regret pursues me, however—which is that no one will inherit my science, and that my gravestone, which will not be long delayed in falling upon my body, for I'm older than any living mortal, will bury forever secrets that no one will ever rediscover."

At these words the hermit's heart beat rapidly. "A human life would not be sufficient," he said, "to learn those beautiful secrets."

The savant read the thought in the depths of the hermit's heart. "A week would be long enough," he said, "for all my science is enclosed in a parchment that I carry rolled up at my breast. But there are mysteries to accomplish—mysteries that would make the bravest of men tremble."

"A week would suffice?" asked the hermit.

"A week, and even less than a week—but then, it would be impossible to find a disciple capable of supporting the necessary ordeals, and paying for my science the price that I have paid, for I bought it from the Demon."

The hermit shuddered and crossed himself.

The astrologer smiled pityingly. Then he took out the parchment hidden in his bosom and began to read the secrets that it contained:

"The *sancturum regnum*, or the veritable manner of making pacts with the names, talents and power of superior spirits, and also the manner of making them appear by the force of the great appellation, which forces them to obey whatever operation one whishes them to carry out.

"Fortunate and unfortunate days.

"The composition of death, or the philosopher's stone.

"To charm weapons..."

"One week! One week!" the hermit repeated, anxiously,

Without paying any heed to the interruption, the astrologer continued:

"To speak to spirits on St. John the Baptist's Eve.

"To make oneself beloved by whatever maiden or woman one wishes.

"To render oneself invisible.

"To make seven-league boots."[22]

"And it's at the price of your soul, of eternal salvation, that you've bought this science!" murmured Père Mathias, after a profound reverie.

---

[22] Author's note: "This list and all the details of magic encountered in this legend are scrupulous in their exactitude and printed in various works of sorcery, in particular: *Le Dragon rouge, ou l'Art de commander aux esprits célestes; Questionum magicarum libri sex* by Père Delrio; J. B. *Neapolitani magiae naturalis libri vigenti: Un livre de l'imposture et tromperie des diables*, translated by Jean Vivier, by Jacques Grenin; *Commentarius de praecipius generibus divininationum*, by Gaspard Peucerus; *Malleus maleficarum*, by Jacobi Sprenger; *La Physique occult, ou Traité de a baguette divinatoire*, by de Vallemont; *Le comte de Gabalis, ou Entretien sur les Sciences secrètes*, etc., etc." The list mingles supposed grimoires and books penned by witch-hunters with one title (the Grenin volume) that appear to be invented. *Le Dragon rouge* was the best-known mock-Medieval book of spells; Berthoud later published a book with the same title, which is probably a new edition of it, but which is not available for consultation on *gallica* or Google Books.

"And who tells you, earthworm, that you have a soul?" replied the astrologer, ironically. "Before birth, what were you? After death, what will you be? Nothing. You were formed from atoms scattered in the air, combined with water, hidden in the earth; they will return after you to air, water and earth. The soul is the heat of the limbs; it is the principle that makes grass grow plants bud and animals live.

"Tell me, you who speak of the other world of the soul, have you not been engendered like all other beings? Have you not been carried like them in the loins of a female? Have you not remained, like them, feeble and imbecile until the atoms wandering in nature have nourished you, and you have grown and developed? Is your existence not like theirs? Is it not sustained as theirs is? Eating and rendering excrement, sleeping and reproducing: that is their life, and it is yours. Do they also have an immortal soul, then?"

A few hours earlier, this miscreant speech would have made the hermit cry anathema, but he heard them almost without horror, because he was going open-mouthed after the hook of pride and the knowledge of what the first man had lost in the terrestrial paradise.

"Why," he asked, although he as almost entirely convinced, "if that is the case, would the Demon wish to purchase our souls?"

"In the formula and prayer of invocation, the great Adonai means by the soul the sap of the body; it is also necessary to add that he is given the heart, the entrails, the hands, the feet and the sighs. It is a trivial homage, which he desires to be rendered to him by the vassal, who releases it to him in exchange for knowledge, magical power and the mysterious secrets of nature."

"And God? What about God? Jesus Christ?"

The astrologer shivered and paled at that thrice holy name.

"Error! Lies! Two spirits dispute the universe, Adonai and Jehovah; I serve Adonai, for Adonai has science and the spirits of the Inferno in his power."

"Would it please you, Master Bauderic, to receive me as a disciple?"

A joy that was harmful to behold shone in the astrologer's red eyes.

"Sign this pact with your blood, to be my faithful disciple, discreet to any proof, and before the dark of the moon you will be like me; I swear it by Adonai."

Père Mathias, in the greatest emotion, submissive to a strange power, as if he were having a bad dream, allowed himself to be pricked on the wrist by the point of a dagger and signed his name on the vellum inscribed with red letters.

"As soon as we reach Ypres," said the astrologer, "come to find me. It will be the first quarter of the moon, and you will not be long delayed in entering the way of life."

While everyone in Ypres was rejoicing at the arrival of the new Comtesse, and the betrothal was being celebrated with ostentation at countless feasts; the oaths of guilds were representing mysteries by the light of thousands of torches; and young women, nude in the fashion of sirens, were singing languorous motets and throwing flowers at noble husbands when they passed close by on returning from the moustier to their palaces, Père Mathias went in secret to meet Master Bauderic in a wood.

The astrologer was waiting, dressed in bizarre fashion. He was on a large stone sitting in the middle of a forest crossroads. After meditating for a long time he said the following words to Père Mathias:

"Gird yourself, my beloved disciple, with the courage of the lion and the prudence of the serpent, in order to be able to bring to a worthy and appropriate conclusion the great work on which I have spent sixty-seven years of my life, working night and day to arrive at the success of that admirable objective.

"Listen, then, and do as it will be said.

"You will spend an entire quarter of the moon without frequenting any woman or maiden.

"You will promise the great Adonai, the chief of all the spirits, only to take two meals a day, or every twenty-four hours, of the aforesaid quarter of the moon, which you will take at noon and midnight, while saying the prayer that I shall teach you."

And he recited a mysterious prayer replete with strange words that it was impossible to comprehend.

"Do not undress yourself and sleep as little as possible, thinking continually of the great work. Go my do, and do as it is said. Conserve with care this bloody stone called ematille,[23] and come to meet me here on the first night after the first quarter of the moon."

A fortnight having passed, the hermit came to meet the astrologer again at the same crossroads in the wood where he had met him the first time.

Bauderic was holding on a leash a goat-kid whose head was dressed with verbena, and had a red ribbon around its neck in the guise of a necklace. Without saying a word, he bared his right arm to the shoulder, brandished a blade of pure steel, and killed the kid with a single stroke, saying: "I make you this offering, O great Adonai, great Eloim, great Arcil, to the honor, glory and power of your being, superior to all spirits; may it please you to accept it!"

After which he skinned the kid, and put its flesh and bones on to a large fire. When everything was reduced to ashes, he brought them out and threw them in the direction in which the sun rises.

Then, with the dagger with which he had slain the kid, he cut a forked hazel branch, cut a circle from the skin of the victim, traced a triangle in the middle, and mysterious characters and signs, lit two candles, and poured a yellow-tinted liquid, incense and camphor into a bowl where willow wood was

---

[23] A term used in alchemical documents, which retains some fashionability today in occult circles, referring to heliotrope or "bloodstone."

burning. Finally, he threw a silver coin on the ground and murmured long invocations.

The hermit, pale, his hair bristling, stood in the circle, greatly excited and white with fear.

Suddenly, he felt the earth quake. A fiery figure sprang from the forest and cried: "Here I am! What do you want of me?"

"Science for this man, in exchange for his soul, his heart, his entrails, his dexter and his sinister, his feet, his sighs and his being."

The hermit felt a dolorous quiver in all his limbs; the voice roared: "I accept!" and darkness and solitude returned to the crossroads in the forest.

From that moment on, Mathias—for it is no longer appropriate to honor him with the holy name of Père—did not have a singly good thought in his soul. He sold justice, judged cases not on the weight of evidence but on the weight of gold, and paid no heed to the distress of orphans and the tears of widows.

The townsfolk of Ypres began to murmur, and even addressed remonstrations to the Comte, but the latter paid no heed to them, saying that they were troublemakers and only acting thus out of jealousy of the holy man.

In consequence, Mathias became more powerful than ever, and it did not take him long to display the science for which he had paid with the salvation of his soul. As he was careful not to say that it was the work of darkness, but claimed, on the contrary, that it came from the heavenly spirit, his renown increased in proportion, and, in spite of his prevarications, it was said throughout the region that he must be a very holy man, because the good God had suddenly granted him knowledge that many years would not have sufficed to amass.

The spirit of the Inferno rejoiced in seeing him yield to the impious joys of pride, and put into his heart a worse design than all those with which it was already filled. That was to make him feel the impure spur of the flesh for the young Comtesse Iolente, the wife of his suzerain and benefactor.

In order to succeed in his vile objective he employed every trick that a debauched hypocrite devoid of a soul can invent, but to no avail. He put diabolical invocations and exorcisms to work, but to no avail. And the fire in which he was burning roasted him more and more every day, driving him in his unhealthy desires.

In the meantime, Monseigneur Charles, Comte Robert's son, had returned to Ypres, and the first time he found himself in the presence of his stepmother, with whom he had been in love before Comte Robert had taken her in marriage, the poor young sire could not help weeping, and Madame Iolente did likewise.

Jealousy promptly divines secrets that wound it, and Mathias read in the aforesaid tears both love and regret.

She's mine! He thought, inwardly. And that night, putting her ladies in waiting, varlets and pages to sleep by means of his magic powers, he obtained entry to Madame Iolente's bedroom.

She was still weeping, and writing on a parchment, for she had learned that base and vassal science from an old cleric, even though her father had scolded her for it many a time.

Mathias, who had arrived stealthily, seized the vellum, where there were words of love addressed to Monseigneur Charles, and a plea that he should depart in exile.

He demanded that Madame Iolente grant him amorous mercy, or he would tell Comte Robert everything.

The lady bravely picked up a dagger with a golden hilt and tried to fight Mathias off. The latter was forced to retreat, because he was a coward and only had the heart for crimes devoid of danger. As he fled, he found a means to introduce a small packet into Madame Iolente's pouch, which she did not notice because of the emotion that was agitating hr.

After that, Mathias ran to Prince Charles' apartment, saying that he needed to speak to him as soon as possible. Admission was immediately granted to the sovereign Comte's favorite and dispenser of justice, and a page took him to the room where the young Sire Charles was asleep.

On seeing the prince, Mathias cried: "The revelation that I have just had in a dream is all too true! The young sire has been poisoned! Quickly, fetch water as fast as you can, milk if you can find it. It's a matter of life and death!"

And while the prince, pale and stupefied, remained motionless and everyone ran around, bewildered and not knowing what to do, Mathias presented a cup to Monseigneur Charles, into which he had secretly put poison.

The prince drank, in the belief that he was receiving relief for the malady that he did not yet feel but which Mathias had prognosticated. He drank, lay down, and died.

Feigning great despair, Mathias dropped the cup that he was holding, kicked it away and said: "Blessed Virgin! I've arrived too late!"

And, surrounded by the prince's servants, he went to find Comte Robert, whom he found preparing a chamfron with his own hands for his favorite horse. As he went in he crossed his arms over his breast, lowered his head and pronounced he name of Prince Charles.

Comte Robert understood that mute admonition. "Dead!" he cried. "He's dead!"

"May Jesus Christ and the Holy Virgin be your aid and consolation," the hermit said, "For he died a martyr rather than commit the deadly sin of incest."

As he pronounced these wicked words, he handed over the parchment he had snatched from the Comtesse's hands, in which, by means of his perfidious art, he had caused a few words to vanish and added several others, thus envenoming evidence that was weak but not criminal, and enabling the belief that she would have the love of the young Sire Charles or his life.

As the Comte's chaplain, more dead than alive, finished reading the fatal parchment, the Comtesse came in, crying for justice against the hermit, who had tried to rape her during the night.

Far from listening to her, however, Comte Robert, struck her a mighty blow on the head with the chamfron he was holding, and struck her again and again. She fell without uttering a moan, and rendered up her soul,

The hermit ran to the cadaver, opened her pouch and took out the poison, saying: "This is righteous justice!"

And everyone repeated: "That is righteous justice!"

The Comte's courtiers and the townspeople marveled at the admirable revelation that Our Lady had made to the saintly hermit regarding the fatal poisoning of Monseigneur Charles, and he was even more venerated than he had been before.

Four years later, he disappeared one evening in a whirlwind of flames, at the crossroads in the forest. No one had the slightest suspicion that it was the Devil who had taken one of his own to Hell; on the contrary, the general belief was that the angels had taken him to Heaven, like the prophets Elijah and Elisha, and ever since, the hermit Mathias has been invoked as a benevolent and powerful intercessor.

The cadaver of Comtesse Iolente was not buried in holy ground, but for pity's sake she was put in a corner of the garden of an abbey whose benefactress she was.

MARTYRS OF SCIENCE

A HEAVENWARD VOYAGE

In 1803, in the city of Altona, the capital of Holstein, there was a scientist named Ludwig Klopstock. When I say scientist, I am not expressing the general opinion of his fellow citizens in that regard, for they generally claimed that the poor fellow possessed no other merit and no other ability than bearing the great name of Klopstock. His sole entitlement to interest, according to them, consisted of being the nephew of the author of the *Messias*.[24]

In appearance, at least, Ludwig justified the low esteem in which he was held. Always distracted and dreamy, he sought out solitary places, spent hours with his eyes raised toward the heavens, had no fixed meal-times, and had no idea how to earn an écu by means of his labor. He lived as best he could on the modest returns of a farm that he owned in the village of Oltenzen, and an annual income of about eight hundred livres, produced by capital invested with a merchant in Pallmailstrasse. At any rate, neither his meditations in the open air nor his uninterrupted twelve-hour sessions in the study in which he locked himself away had ever produced the slightest known result. Whenever he was asked what he was doing among his scientific instruments, or what he saw

---

[24] The German poet Friedrich Gottlieb Klopstock (1724-1803), who considered that his vocation was to be "the Christian Homer," spent 25 years writing and publishing his epic *Messias* (1748-1773; tr. as *The Messiah*); he produced other Biblical epics thereafter, but they never attained a similar prestige.

through the large telescope installed on the roof of his house, he became disconcerted, blushing and stammering, and the questioner went away shrugging his shoulders, convinced that Ludwig was nothing but an imbecile.

This conviction became even more unanimous in Altona when it was learned that Ludwig Klopstock was going to marry. His marriage must, indeed, have seems very singular, for the young woman that the poor scientist was marrying was an orphan of sixteen; the death of her father had left her abandoned and destitute.

In spite of the mockery of all those who knew about his plan, Ludwig led his bride to the altar. Ebba took over the management of the scientist's household; order and propriety—which had been banished from the residence for some time, if they had ever entered it—flourished therein, and gave the desolate dwelling a cheerful and celebratory appearance.

Ludwig himself appeared in the city in clean linen, stocking without holes and garment that did not disappear in myriads of stains of all colors. His pallid complexion and livid thinness gradually gave way to a plumpness that gave his appearance a freshness and gaiety. He was still seen, every evening and well into the night, taking long walks in the country, but, instead of wandering at hazard, he was guided—or rather led—by Ebba. With her gaze directed at the ground, while her husband kept hers raised toward the heavens, she sustained him, after a fashion, like the angels of which the psalm speaks, in order that his feet should not be injured by the pebbles of the path.

Gradually, Ebba's figure rounded out, and one morning, Ludwig, sitting by his life's bed with his eyes full of tears, heard a little child utter that first cry, which causes so much emotion in a paternal heart. From then on, the scientist devoted himself less exclusively to science; he even forgot his telescope in order to dandle the new-born on his knees; he looked out with greater patience and greater happiness for the little creature's smile than he had ever done in discovering the mysterious conjunction of two stars.

The child grew; he was as beautiful as his mother, and his broad forehead indicated to Ludwig the promise of a powerful intelligence. Simply to say that concern was manifest around the crib in which the pale angel slept would be an understatement. Ebba gazed at him incessantly and Ludwig's calculations were confused by the slightest cry emitted by the infant's rosy little mouth. Alas, one night, the child's respiration became halting, his gaze lit up with a strange flame, and his cheeks became red. He had the croup! When day dawned, there was no longer anything but a cadaver on Ebba's bosom.

The poor mother thought of dying herself. It would surely have been better if God had reunited her body with that of her baby son in the same grave, as he had reunited their souls in Heaven. Ebba's soul never came back down to Earth. Her body acted at hazard; her voice no longer proffered any but inconsequential words. She was an idiot.

Ludwig's friends advised him to send his wife to a lunatic asylum, by which means, in consideration of a modest boarding-fee, he would be rid of the annoyance and the sad spectacle that the presence of a madwoman in his house occasioned. Ludwig became indignant at this suggestion, and persisted in caring for the insane woman with the tenderness and devotion that she had shown him when she had enjoyed her reason. There was no more studying for the scientist; he lavished his intelligence, his time, his days and nights, in humoring the bizarre caprices of the maniac. People ended up believing that he was going mad himself.

Nothing discouraged Ludwig for five years; nothing diminished his devotion to Ebba. At the end of that time, he fell victim to a further misfortune. The merchant in Pallmailstrasse, with whom he had invested the capital that yielded an income of eight hundred livres, went bankrupt and fled. That event left Klopstock with no other resource than the meager returns of his farm in Oltenzen. That would still have been sufficient for the scientist, who would not have minded being subject to privations, but the privations in question would affect poor Ebba. He decided to apply for a chair in astronomy that had just fallen vacant at the College of Altona.

Imagine what anguish, annoyance and distaste a poor timid man who never went out, and who only maintained rare and distant relationships with two or three friends, must have experienced when he had to solicit employment, explain his request to the burgomeister and submit to the disdain of the councilors. No one took his request seriously, and a professor was summoned from Drontheim. When Ludwig learned that, he sold his little house in Altona and set out for his farm in Oltenzen, taking nothing with him by his scientific instruments and his telescope. Ebba followed him mechanically, without knowing what she was doing. Her soul, as you know, was in Heaven, with her child.

Ludwig's farm was near Oltenzen church. From the window, he could see his uncle's tomb, shaded by a linden tree that the great poet had once planted. Ludwig sent his tenant farmer away and set about cultivating the land, with more intelligence, and even more strength, than anyone could have expected of him. The peasants began by laughing at his experiments and innovations, but they ended up copying him. The time that Klopstock did not spend harrowing and laboring, he devoted to study. The telescope took possession of the roof of Ludwig's farm; he hardly slept—for sleep is like friendship; it only lavishes its favors on the fortunate—and spent his nights studying the stars. During these vigils, consecrated to the admiration of celestial marvels, Ebba lay her head on the scientist's knees and descended into a dreamless torpor that resembled death.

One morning, on descending from his observatory, Ludwig, who was ordinarily sad and absent-minded, manifested an unusual and heedless joy. The scientist's manifestations of happiness could not have been more energetic if Ebba had recovered her reason. He spent six nights writing a long letter, with which he was never satisfied; he began it over, annotated it, consulted his telescope again...

Finally, the important work complete, he placed his memoir carefully in an envelope and posted it in Altona, after taking the precaution of franking it and obtaining a receipt from the Post Office. The package was addressed to the director of Hamburg Observatory, and contained the discovery of the axial rotation of Saturn in ten hours thirty-two minutes.

This is the reply he received:

If your letter is not a hoax, Monsieur, you are a little too late to claim a discovery made and published a fortnight ago by Frederick William Herschel.[25]

In response to this cruel disappointment, which stole all the glory of which he had dreamed for his name, Ludwig only manifested his chagrin by his habitual sad smile.

Let us admit, however, that in the meantime, that obscure and timid man had been devoured by a thirst for celebrity. He dreamed night and day of making a name for himself. He sensed a mysterious force within himself that elevated him above vulgarity and only required to manifest itself to be resplendent forever. Poverty and misfortune, however, rendered that manifestation impossible.

When, two years later, he announced that it was possible to solidify carbon dioxide, no one even wanted to read his memoir, nor examine the diagrams he had attached thereto for the construction of the machine necessary to carry out the experiment. The Hamburg Academy remembered the belated discovery of the rotation of Saturn, and treated as fantasy the great operation that was to be reinvented a few years later, by our illustrious scientist Monsieur Thilorier.[26]

---

[25] Frederick William Herschel (1738-1822) published his discovery of Saturn's period of rotation in 1790, which seems inconsistent with the date in the following note—and neither sits well with the date of 1803 given at the beginning of the story—so Berthoud is evidently employing a certain poetic license here.

[26] Adrien Thilorier (1790-1844) first produced "dry ice" (accidentally) in 1834. Berthoud knew Thilorier personally and wrote a eulogy after his death, categorizing him as a "martyr" because he was a casualty of one of his own experiments.

Several years went by without Ludwig leaving the village of Oltenzen or making any further attempts to publish the results of his studies.

One day, when the aeronaut Bitorff,[27] in the midst of an immense crowd of spectators, was getting ready to depart from Hamburg and make an aerial voyage, he saw a little man in a large threadbare black coat coming towards him. Without any preamble, the man proposed that he should accompany him on the excursion that he was about to make by balloon. At first, Bitorff thought that he was dealing with a madman, but as the unknown man insisted and even offered the aeronaut several handfuls of gold to obtain what he desired, he ended up giving his consent, all the more willingly because the strangeness of the proposition and the discussion keenly excited the general curiosity. Like a good speculator wanting a double return, however, he told Ludwig that his ascent would only take place two weeks hence, because the balloon—he alleged—was not yet powerful enough to carry two travelers. Ludwig consented to this delay, and calmly went back to Oltenzen, from which he returned on the appointed day.

During the two weeks, Ludwig Klopstock's project had been the only topic of conversation in Hamburg. The old story of the axial rotation of Saturn, discovered a month after Herschel's publication, was exhumed, and a thousand jokes were told. Bitorff had never attracted as many spectators as he did on the day when the ascension of his travelling companion was to take place. Ludwig, intimidated by the crowd, the eyes of which were fixed on him, approached the gondola awkwardly and almost tore the balloon by bumping into the scientific instruments with which it as laden, in order to carry out experiments during the voyage. To his great regret, the aeronaut obliged him to leave part of his luggage on the ground.

---

[27] The death of a German balloonist named Bitorff on 17 July 1812, recorded in German newspapers, was noted in the *Encyclopédie Catholique*, where Berthoud probably found the name.

They both took their places, the ropes were released and the balloon rose up rapidly like a bird.

Ludwig's first sensation, when he felt himself borne away by the frail machine, was terror. The immense abyss gaping beneath his feet furrowed the scientist's brow and surrounded him with swirling dizziness. Each commotion was succeeded by a sort of perfidious satisfaction. He leaned over the earth, attracted by a mysterious force, and was about to launch himself forth when his companion seized his arm and held him back. Once extracted from this peril, Ludwig recovered all his composure, armed himself with resolution and set about looking down with a freedom of spirit by which the aeronaut could only be astonished.

There is no way to describe the sensations that the scientist experienced. As they drew further away from the earth, one might have thought that his soul separated itself, disengaging itself from its original clay and freeing itself from the bonds of his body. An indescribable well-being penetrated every part of him; a gentle warmth enlivened him; his mind worked powerfully; he forgot all his misery, all his suffering, all his mundane humiliations. He was finally himself!

Around him sparkled a kind of light that resembled an opaline gleam. Above his head extended the immensity of the azure of the heavens. Beneath his feet the earth was retreating and the horizon slowly became more distinct. The rivers presented all their sinuosities simultaneously; the houses and villas seemed to spring from the bosom of the earth; the sea extended in the distance like a vast sheet of silk, stirred by the wind; the fields displayed their golden escutcheons, quartered in green and purple; the forests covered vast expanses with their somber mantle; people were no more than little dots moving hither and yon, vain and imperceptible dust! Then again, there was no sound and no movement around the aerial voyagers. A profound, absolute silence! Not the bleak and somber silence of human solitudes but a silence that was, so to speak, melodious. It seemed to them that the distant harmonies of the celestial worlds were about to reach their terrestrial ears.

While Ludwig concentrated on these new and sublime impressions, Bitorff, to whom they were familiar, managed the aerostat and devoted himself to various experiments whose program he had organized with his companion before leaving the earth. When his calculations informed him that they were at an altitude of six hundred meters, he told Ludwig; the latter shivered, for the aeronaut's voice burst forth with supernatural force, and had nothing human about it. Meanwhile, the atmosphere was beginning to get chilly. The ineffable wellbeing that Klopstock had experienced was succeeded by a period of icy cold. Bitorff's voice lost its marvelous vibration. A hum began to deafen their ears. They were at twelve hundred meters.

Ten minutes later, Ludwig thought he could make out an almost-unintelligible murmur. He tried to ask Bitorff whether it might originate from speech addressed to him. To his great surprise, he could not hear his own voice at all, and he had to make great efforts that wearied his lungs and throat to proffer his question.

"We're two thousand meters above the earth," Bitorff finally managed to make him understand. "The expansion of the hydrogen gas contained in the balloon, which has been increasing since we left the ground, has now reached such an extent that I'm obliged to open the valve. Otherwise, the envelope of our vehicle would burst under the strain."

Meanwhile, a thick veil, similar to one of the heavy mists that sometimes expand over the earth during a thaw, obscuring darkening entire cities with their noxious shroud, spread over the earth and ended up concealing everything from the voyagers' eyes. Soon, dull roaring sounds rumbled in the distance below the balloon. Terrible noises burst forth. Broad lighting-flashes hurled their fiery wings through the chaos. Flamboyant serpents of lightning launched forth in all directions. There was something terrifying about that revolution of the elements, seen and heard by two men who were only sustained in mid-air by a frail piece of taffeta inflated by a little hydrogen. Bitorff felt fear grip his heart, but Ludwig experienced a sort of savage joy. He laughed strangely; he clapped his hands; he jumped up and down. One might have thought him the spirit of tempests, in the midst of his accursed triumph.

The balloon was still rising, by virtue of a regular movement completely imperceptible to those it as lifting. The storm ended up by no longer being anything more than a mute black dot beneath their feet. That dot gradually dissipated and disappeared. The earth showed itself again, but confused. One could still distinguish, with great attention, roads like black threads and rivers like tresses of silver and gold. Above the aeronauts, the sky was resplendent with a serenity of which the earthbound can have no inkling, even on the highest mountains. Its azure took on a deep blue tint, which declined towards the lower regions into a greenish hue.

"Four thousand meters!" shouted Bitorff's voice, beginning to recover its strength, to his companion, who was numbed by a violent cold.

That voice burst forth in deafening vibrations a quarter of an hour later, when it announced: "Six thousand meters!"

Nothing was any longer visible on the earth but large masses. Bitorff threw into the air two birds that he had brought on the balloon. The poor creatures extended their wings to take flight, but they fell like leaden masses; their air, too rarefied, could no longer lend them support. Ludwig's respiration became more difficult; his chest was oppressed, chilled by the cold—and yet he felt excited by a feverish agitation. His heart was beating rapidly, his breathing accelerated. Two birds and a rabbit that still remained in the gondola began to choke, and were not long in dying for lack of viable air.

"Eight thousand meters," said Bitorff.[28]

---

[28] Berthoud was probably inspired to write this story by the fact that Charles Green and Spencer Rush had set a new altitude record of 7.9 kilometers in 1839, which was to remain unsurpassed until 1862. The description of Ludwig's experiences is presumably based on those reported by Green and Rush. The previous altitude record of 7.28 kilometers had been set in 1803, which might help to explain the date cited in the story's opening.

His voice had become dull again, and with a gesture he showed Ludwig that nothing any longer remained beneath their feet. The earth and the clouds had disappeared; the immensity of space surrounded the balloon in every direction. As for the cold, it was intolerable. Their shallow breath was scarcely sufficient for the conservation of animal warmth. Blood leaked from the eyes, nostrils and ears of the audacious duo; their words were inaudible. The balloon, the only object they could see, seemed about to expire, so impetuously was the hydrogen gas escaping. Beneath them, the blue of the sky; above, strange and unknown darkness, through which the stars projected a light deprived of scintillation, which had something funereal about it. There ended physical nature. There were located the impenetrable barriers imposed by God on human audacity.

The gas condensed, and the balloon ceased climbing.

"Master," said Bitorff to Klopstock, "if we don't want to die, let's make haste to descend to earth! You can see it: the divine hand has written in terrible letters: 'Thou shalt go no further.' But what are you doing? Have you lost your mind? What! You're throwing out our ballast! You're taking off your clothes!"

"Because I want to go further!" cried Ludwig, enthusiastically. "Yes, I want to cross the barriers imposed on humankind. Look! The balloon, free of all ballast, is still rising; let's break the gondola, hang on to the cords and reach the heavens!"

He began to put this plan into operation. Bitorff launched himself toward the valve and opened it, in spite of the despairing efforts of his companion. The balloon descended; the air gradually became less cold as they arrived in less elevated atmospheric layers. The earth reappeared beneath them, initially as an indistinct gray mass; then it gradually took on a more precise form. Its rivers and roads became visible, details reappeared, people and animals increased in size...and the balloon finally touched down about two leagues from Hamburg.

Bitorff exploded in transports of joy.

Ludwig Klopstock wept with rage and disappointment. "We could have gone into the darkness of infinity!" he repeated to his companion.

"We would have perished!" the latter replied.

Without paying the slightest attention to the delight of the crowd that surrounded the two courageous voyagers and lavished applause upon them, without replying to members of the Hamburg Academy, who were imploring him to write a memoir on what he had observed and experienced, without even shaking the hand of his companion in peril, Ludwig drew away silently, climbed back on his horse, and rode back to Altona without stopping.

There, he bought large quantities of gummed fabric, loaded his purchases on to the rump of his horse, and shut himself up in his little house in Oltenzen, from which he did not emerge for an entire month. No one was able to see him during that retreat—not the farm laborers, nor a deputation from the Academy of Hamburg, nor even the village pastor. He did not even deign to reply to them though the door, which he refused to open. Were it not for the walk he took with his wife toward nightfall, and a few purchases of food, he might have been thought to be lying dead in his house.

Needless to say, this mysterious retreat gave rise to many strange suppositions. Some favored the hypothesis that Ludwig had lost his reason during his aerial excursion, others that he was devoting himself to a work of magic. The latter belief was not entirely implausible, for it was eventually discovered that Klopstock was building a strangely-shaped machine, which resembled a fish armed with large oars similar to fins; they were moved by means of a mechanism of cogwheels that was both simple and admirable.

That judgment became possible one morning when the inhabitants of Oltenzen saw Ludwig in mid-air, seated on his huge fish, maneuvering it more easily than a horseman guides a docile horse. In spite of the violence of contrary winds, he steered it to the right and the left, forwards and backwards, up and down. He finished by descending into his courtyard, so tightly that the two ends of the machine almost touched the sides.

The pastor, a learned man, in his admiration and at the risk of being indiscreet, went to knock on Klopstock's door , and begged him so insistently to open it that the scientists gave in. He took the pastor into his courtyard. At the first glace it was easy to see that Ludwig had found the secret of steering balloons.

"Your name is immortal, my friend!" cried the minister. "The entire universe will repeat it with enthusiasm! What glory will be yours!"

"Earth! Glory!" Ludwig repeated, disdainfully. "What does that matter to me? It's the heavens I want! No one has been able to go higher than eight thousand meters; I shall go to twenty thousand! I shall go to two hundred thousand! I shall go into the realm of other worlds! I shall go to the other worlds! I shall go beyond! I shall study nature! The immensity and the unknown will belong to me. I've found the means of steering my aerostat. That was an easy problem to resolve. But I've done better. The hydrogen gas that my machine contains expands or contracts as I dictate, without loss. These canisters contain the means of procuring me vital air, even in places where it is impossible to breathe. Cold itself, I have vanquished; it will be unable to hurt me!"

The pastor stood there, astounded by so much genius and madness at the same time.

"Farewell," said Ludwig. "Here is my will. If I fail in my enterprise, or if I no longer deign to return to the Earth, I leave it to you to look after that poor woman. Farewell!"

Without paying any heed to the remonstrations of the worthy churchman, he climbed into his balloon. He was about to take off when Ebba suddenly ran toward him, gazing at him with haggard eyes, clung on to the machine and shouted: "Don't go! Don't go!"

"You're right," said the scientist, after a moment's reflection. "Come! You shall share my fortune and my joy."

He picked her up. He seated her next to him. He waved to the pastor, and flew off into the sky.

The minister watched him for some time, maneuvering his machine easily, which ended up rising rapidly, soon appearing as nothing more than a black dot that gradually melted away into the azure of the heavens.

The worthy cleric awaited Ludwig Klopstock's return with great anxiety.

Ludwig Klopstock never returned.

THE MASTER OF THE WEATHER

Scientists, like poets, tend to have a sweet tooth. One of the most illustrious members of the Académie des Sciences, when he comes out of the weekly meeting on Mondays, never fails to go into the pâtissier's shop on the Rue Guénégaud, where he comforts himself for the fatigues of the debate by devouring more gateaux than he has destroyed arguments. As for our celebrated poets, Félix and Rollet, those two rival glories are counted among the most assiduous clients of the patisserie.[29] Often, the galette-seller at the Gymnase has recognized, among the hands that extend mysteriously from the crowd toward his firm dough, the yellow glove of an Academician poet, and the opulent *coupe-toujours* in the Boulevard Saint-Martin salutes with a smile that is both discreet and conspiratorial the author of the most beautiful odes in modern literature.

Charles-Louis Knebel was both a poet and a scientist. I leave it to you to imagine how he faced up to a good meal, and whether he had an ineffable affection for the desserts that his wife loved to prepare with her dainty white hands with the pink fingernails.

One can cite Knebel as one of the privileged individuals for whom renown, fortune and happiness only have smiles. Born into a social position that did not impose upon him any of the rude proofs of poverty and isolation, he saw his first literary endeavors welcomed with enthusiasm by the Prince of Ehringen-Wallerstein, of whom his father was the chancellor. As soon as he had heard about young Charles brilliant debuts, the Margrave of Anspach recruited him as a privy councilor.

---

[29] The former reference might be the Romantic poet Félix Arvers (1806-1850); the latter remains enigmatic. Like some of the names on the list of Knebel's acquaintances, they are probably invented.

Finally, Prince Frederick of Prussia offered him a lieutenancy in the regiment of his guards.

The épée and the epaulette are charms for a young and ardent heart. Knebel accepted military life joyfully, but soon became disgusted with the idle servitude of his new position, and surrendered without reserve to his penchant for literature. For many years, he accumulated more renown than his poetry assuredly merited, not ungraceful as it was. Influential at court, the possessor of a large fortune, a friend of Jean Paul, Griesbach, Hegel, Fichte, Schutz, Woos, Wollmann and Jacob, he was the absolute sovereign arbiter of all literary questions; no success was possible unless he deigned to confirm it. The age of fifty-six arrived for him without old age having deadened the vivacity of his imagination or afflicted his unalterable youth; thus, he inspired a violent love in Mademoiselle Louise Richdorff, a young Pomeranian of great beauty, who married him and gave him two sons.

Initiated into the ineffable pleasures of family life, he retired from the agitations of literary life, renounced the court and settled into a delightful retreat in Ilmenau. There, entirely absorbed by the joys and ecstasies of fatherhood, he devoted himself entirely to the education of his sons, composed the freshest and most delightful of his verses (*Flowers of That Year*), wrote a tragedy (*Saul*) that obtained an unparalleled success at Weimar and devoted himself passionately to the study of geology and physics. Mineralogy and the history of fossils owed important discoveries to him; he produced papers on the weight of the air and published scientific experiments on the influence of electricity on atmospheric variations.

Every year, a family fête brought Knebel's intimate friends together at Ilmenau. The feast in question was held on the anniversary of his marriage, which was also, by a singular hazard, the anniversary of his own birth. In 1816, Weber, Hoffmann and Schuter were among the guests.

During the serious part of the meal—which is to say, during the first courses—the conversation was rarely occupied by anything other than marvels and secrets of natural history obtained from nature. Hoffmann, in particular, never wearied of hearing accounts of the amours and affinities of gases for one another; the description of fantastic animals that the ante-diluvian strata of the earth contained caused him to utter cries of joy. Knebel delighted in recounting marvels; his voice ex-pressed itself with warm enthusiasm, his eyes sparkled, a gen-erous flush animated his cheeks and colored his noble visage. He talked about his projects and his endeavors, his desires and his hopes.

"Oh," he said, "if only I could attach my name to some great discovery in science! What a joy, what a pride would cause my heart to beat faster, if it were given to me to reveal one of the great mysteries of nature, as Franklin has done for the lightning-conductor, Montgolfier for balloons, Papin and Fulton for the power of steam and the mechanical application of that force!" And he added; "Yes, yes, I'd exchange my re-nown as a poet, and even my happiness as the father of a fami-ly, for the glory of such fame, such endurance!"

"Bah!" exclaimed Louise. "Don't say such blasphemous things, Charles! What would become of you, poor scientist, if you were not able, every morning, to kiss the fresh cheeks of your two sons? If your wife were not there to surround you with tender concern and relieve you of all the cares of material life? Who, without me, would attend to your slightest whims? Here, ingrate, serve yourself this jam from France; I ordered it especially from Paris, from the Fidèle-Berger, because you expressed a desire for that treat the other day. Taste it, and then, if you still dare, say that you'd exchange your happiness for a little scientific renown—you, one of the greatest poets in Germany!"

The sight of the jar of jam and Louise's affectionate words had an immediate effect on Knebel's conversation. He fell back from the heights of ambition into the sweetness of reality, and no longer paid any heed to anything except taking the top off the jar of jam and savoring its delightful treasures. He examined the red color of the brilliant paste, which he compared, as a geologist, to rubies, and as a physicist to the luminous traces left in the sky by the aurora. When he had consumed it in the manner of a chemist, in small doses, and had analyzed the taste—an unparalleled mixture of redcurrant juice, the perfumes of quince, the savor of sugar and the aromas of vanilla—he verified the Parisian origin of the porcelain jar while interrogating the color and analyzing the texture, smooth and firm at the same time, not without a dissertation on the different nature of French and German flints. After which, he passed on to the printed label of the Fidèle-Berger, a certificate that attested the superiority of the jam, as the name of Michelangelo at the base of a statue attests the superiority of a work of art.

Suddenly, Knebel's friends saw him go red and pale at the same time. He was turning the enveloped of parchment that had covered the jar over and over in his fingers, moistening the label and scratching it with precaution in order to lift it off without tearing it, succeeding in discovering the characters inscribed on the piece of vellum. When he had reached the end his attention was redoubled; he had stopped listening to the questions that were addressed to him, and no longer replied to anyone. An imperious and absolute preoccupation had taken possession of him. Sweat was streaming on his brow; a convulsive movement agitated his hands; his lips were stammering inconsequential words; both ecstasy and despair were legible in his facial expression.

"Horses!" he cried, finally. "Horses! I need to leave for Weimar right away—for it's in Weimar that you bought this jam, isn't it, Louise?"

"I asked Schermaker the confectioner to order them from Paris."

"Go find me horses," he repeated to his manservant. "Hurry up. A moment's delay might cost me eternal regret." He looked at the precious parchment again. "Dear God! You wouldn't put me so close to the accomplishment of my most ardent desire, only to cause me a disappointment that would destroy my happiness forever?"

163

"What's the matter with you, Charles? Your agitation is frightening me, my love. What motive is so imperious as to make you desert your friends, who have come to celebrate your birthday, in this manner? And your family, for whom you want to change the celebration into a day of isolation and widowhood?"

"What's the matter with me?" he replied, excitedly. "What's the matter! I can't say, for I wouldn't confide this secret now to my own mother, if she were still alive. What's the matter! If you knew, perhaps you'd become traitors to me, you whose friendship is so tender, so faithful, so well-proven. Here's the horses—let's go! Adieu! See you soon!"

Without kissing his wife and children, without shaking his friends' hands, he launched himself into the post-chaise that had been harnessed in haste, and shouted to the postillion: "A triple tip! A gold piece if you hurry!"

The carriage departed with lightning rapidity, leaving Louise and her guests stupefied.

Rapidly as the caleche flew along the road, and in spite of the postillion's ardor in urging the horses on, Knebel was restless, as if to hasten, by his own movements, the agility of the wheels. He got up, he sat down, he pestered the driver, he despaired of the slowness of his progress. Several times, Frantz, the old manservant who had followed his mater without being ordered to do so, wondered whether the worthy scientist's reason had not been disturbed.

Finally, they arrived at Weimar. As soon as the walls of the city appeared on the horizon, Knebel shouted to the postillion: "Go straight to the confectioner Schermaker's shop and don't stop until you're at the door."

In fact, a few minutes later, the confectioner saw a post-chaise arrive impetuously outside his shop. The horses were covered in foam, and it was necessary to throw water over the wheels to prevent them from catching fire. With a single bound, Knebel launched himself into the shop with the sprightliness of a young man.

"Where are the jars of jam that you ordered from France?" he demanded, without any other preamble, and in a voice so troubled that the confectioner was disturbed, and wondered privately whether it might not be a matter of some misfortune.

"I sent for six, in addition to the three Madame ordered."

"Where are the jars?"

"Here are four of them. The other two have been sold."

Knebel looked at the four jars, tore off the parchment that covered them, and threw everything out into the street with an energetic surge of anger.

"Where are the other two?"

"I've already had the honor of informing the councilor that I've sold them."

"To whom?"

"To Herr Goethe."

"To Goethe?" cried Knebel, despairingly. "To my rival? To the man who disputes the throne of poetry and science with me? May God curse you and the Devil strangle you!"

He leapt into his carriage and ordered the postillion to drive to Goethe's house

Goethe and Knebel had fallen out a long time ago. You can imagine the surprise of the former when he saw the poet come into his house in extreme distress, and say to him, as soon as he saw him: "In the name of Heaven, my dear Goethe, you haven't opened the two jars of jam that you bought from Schermaker's, have you? If they're still intact, please let me have them, and you'll find in me a devoted friend and enthusiastic admirer."

"All the jam-jars in my pantry at are your disposal," Goethe replied, who did not know whether he was dealing with a sane man or a lunatic. "I'll summon my housekeeper; if it would be agreeable to you, she'll not only give you the jam she bought, but the jam she made herself."

Without thanking Goethe, and without even replying, Knebel ran to the pantry, searched for the two jars from the Fidèle-Berger in the midst of the old woman's provisions, found them, and tore off the envelopes as he had done at the confectioner's.

"Nothing," he murmured. "Nothing! To come so nearly within sight of the goal and not to reach it! Oh, that's frightful!"

He wiped away a tear that as running down his cheek, shook Goethe's hand and stood there, immobile, somber and pensive.

Suddenly, it was as if he woke up with a start.

"Two jars! My wife still has another two jars! Just as long as she hasn't served them to my guests! As long as she hasn't thrown away the envelopes! Quickly, fresh horses for the carriage, and let's get back to Ilmenau!"

At daybreak the following morning, Louise saw her husband arrive, pale and covered in mud. His carriage had broken down on the road.

"Are you hurt, my love?" the young woman asked, anxiously.

Where are the other two jars of jam you bought in Weimar?"

"Here, in this cupboard."

"Intact?"

"Intact."

"Intact—thank God!"

He ran to the cupboard, opened it and snatched up the jars; they no longer had any covers.

"What have you done with the parchment that as wrapped around these jars? Louise, I need that parchment! I need it right now, at any price!"

"I gave it to the children yesterday. They asked me for it in order to make puppets."

"Where are the children?" Knebel stammered, who had not given them a thought thus far. "I want to see them! They have to give me the puppets they've made. They have to bring me the slightest clippings. If the little wretches have lost even the smallest fragment, I'll wring their necks."

The children were woken up. Their father did not kiss them; he was unconcerned anything but finding the scraps of parchment, and finding them intact.

When they were brought to him, and he had looked at them one by one, he threw them away disdainfully, and collapsed into an armchair.

With his head in his hands, he meditated for a long time, despairing, overwhelmed by grief.

Louise came to kneel bedside him, gently uncovered the face that he was keeping hidden, and put her lips to her husband's cheeks. She found them bathed in tears.

"What's wrong, Charles? What anxiety, what chagrin, is causing you to suffer so? Are our fortune, our honor and the future of our children under threat? If you only knew how it affects me to see you in this state of agitation! This is the first mystery you've presented me with, my love, the first secret you've kept to yourself! I wouldn't complain if I weren't seeing you unhappy, but your suffering belongs to me, and I want my share of it."

"Louise," he replied, "I have to leave for France."

"Leave for France!"

"I have to, I tell you. It's the price of glory and fortune for me."

"What need do you have or fortune and glory? Hasn't God given you as much as any man could desire down here?"

"All that's nothing, Louise. It's the shadow compared with the light, the cloud over the face of the sun. If I attain the secret I'm pursuing, the secret that I've touched with my finger without being able to grip, I'll change the face of the world, take my place with Newton and Cuvier, those two great geniuses. What am I saying? I'll rise above them, for they only divined and understood one of the Creator's thoughts, while I'll almost become a creator myself. Yes, Louise, nature will obey my voice, like that of its divine master...

"Adieu—I'm leaving for France."

He took some gold and a few clothes, kissed his wife and children in haste, climbed into a carriage and set off for Paris, without offering any further explanation of the reasons for his journey, and, without paying any heed to the rigors of winter or the fatigue of the journey, and with no other traveling companion than his old domestic.

When he arrived in Paris, without even booking into a hotel, and even though he was dying of cold and hunger, he went directly to the Rue des Lombards, to the Fidèle-Berger.

Knebel spent about ten minutes in the shop of the famous confectioner. When he came out again to resume his place in the carriage, the old domestic Frantz did not observe, on his master's visage, the discouragement and despair that he habitually read there. He even seemed to be calmer.

"Rue de Cinq-Diamants!" he said to the postillion.

At the name of that street it was he domestic who displayed emotion. Now, emotion, on that aged face, which resembled a mask of polished bronze, was a phenomenon sufficiently extraordinary for his master, the naturalist, to notice it. He did not, however, pay the slightest heed to such a great marvel. As usual, one sole thought, one sole sensation preoccupied him: to arrive at the unknown goal that he was pursuing.

The Rue de Cinq-Diamants forms a long, narrow, airless corridor inhabited by poor manual workers, into which carriages cannot penetrate. Knebel leapt out of his post-chaise and ran to one of the house at the far end of the street. Frantz leaned out to follow him with his gaze, and seemed to be watching out or his return with a kind of troubled curiosity.

Alas, the calm and confidence that seemed to have dissipated Knebel's bleak misery a little while before when he came out of the Fidèle-Berger had disappeared, darkening his pale clean-shaven features more than ever.

"Go and find fresh horses while I get some food," he said to the postillion. "I have to leave for Berlin in two hours."

"For Berlin!" Frantz exclaimed, putting his hands together in surprise and raising his eyes to the heavens.

To hear Frantz speak was equivalent to the miracle of Balaam's ass, which worthy animal gave advice to prophets.

In spite of his chagrins and disappointments, Knebel took note of it. "If you're afraid of the fatigues of another journey—to which, I'm very much afraid, others might succeed—you're at liberty to stay in Paris, Frantz," he said, rudely.

"Oh, sir! Can you have such an idea of an old and faithful servant? Surprise extracted the words that you heard from me, not the fear of fatigue. If you'll permit me to tell you how and why..."

"I have no need of advice," Knebel interjected, who, reproaching himself bitterly for his obstinacy, imagined that Frantz was about to address observations to him in that regard. "You go into that restaurant; order dinner for me and for you, and leave me to my thoughts."

Twelve days later, the post-chaise arrived in Berlin, without Frantz having pronounced another syllable. However, when he heard his master indicate to the postillion a poor and solitary road in an outlying district, an involuntary "Mein Gott!" escaped his lips.

"What's the matter with you, Frantz?" Knebel demanded. "Are you ill? You're very pale and agitated."

"My dear master, it's necessary that I tell you the reason for this emotion. Surprise is the cause of it. For the two months we've been traveling, I've thought that I was dreaming. Yes, certainly, no dream ever had circumstances as strange. When you came out of the confectioner's in Paris you went to the Rue des Cinq-Diamants, where I lived for several years. Now, you've stopped the carriage in Berlin opposite the very house where I loved for a long time with my poor master, Dr. Cornelius."

"Dr. Cornelius?"

"Yes, a knowledgeable physicist."

"What are you telling me, Frantz? My God, can you be the person who sold a parchment manuscript to the Fidèle-Berger?"

"Yes, Monsieur."

"Into my arms, Frantz! Into my arms! It's you that I've been searching for since my departure from Ilmenau!"

"Me, who was by your side? Me, who has never left you?"

"Yes, you Frantz. Do you know what became of that precious manuscript?"

"As I've just told you, I sold part of it..."

"And the rest?"

"The rest, sir, wasn't written on parchment, because my poor master, reduced to poverty, was obliged to finish it on paper."

"And what have you done with that paper? Speak—you're holding my life and death in your hands."

"I used it one evening to light the fire."

"Wretch!" cried Knebel, beside himself. "Get out of my presence and never let me see you again! Go on! Get away! The sight of you is odious to me, unbearable! For having burned the library of Alexandria, Omar doesn't merit half the execration that you deserve!"

"If you knew the circumstances in which I burned the papers, sir, far from treating me so harshly, you'd forgive me—approve of me, even—I'm sure of it. It was a matter, alas, of warming up my poor master's death-bed. My master...or, rather, my friend, sir, because, for twenty years, I shared the poverty and the endeavors of the savant Cornelius..."

"You shared his endeavors! Do you know his secrets?" cried Knebel, throwing his arms around Frantz once again. "My good, my faithful servant, forgive me for the harsh words I spoke to you. I was wrong. Anger carried me away. Come, Frantz, we're going to the best hotel in Berlin; you're going to rest for a few hours. You mustn't expose your precious health to further fatigue so soon. And tell me, Frantz, do you know what the book written on both vellum and paper contained? You see, chance procured me a fragment of it, and it's to recover the rest that I've left my house, my wife, my children, everything that I love, everything that gives me joy and happiness."

"I can't tell you what the manuscript contained, because it was the only secret that my master kept from me; in order to prevent my knowing it, he even wrote in Greek. However, perhaps I can give you, with regard to what you want to know, some incomplete documentation."

"Speak," said Knebel, "speak, and if you enable me to recover Cornelius' secret, I'll reward you with the gift of a brilliant fortune, beyond all your hopes."

In the meantime, the post-chaise had arrived at the Black Eagle Hotel. The two travelers installed themselves by the fireplace and Frantz began to tell his story, like a man long condemned to silence who suddenly finds a listener eager to listen to him. He gave himself the innocent joy of talking to himself, and push munificence in his own regard so far as to place at the head of his narration a kind of exordium, or prolegomenon, as they say in German universities.

"Destiny has its strange caprices," he commenced. "My grandfather was a brave captain in the service of the Austrian government. Unfortunately, he was killed in battle and left his widow and son without resources. The latter had no other resource, to escape poverty, than the profession of artisan. Later, he married a seamstress, and had a dozen children, and left nothing by way of an inheritance to the youngest—me—but the compassion of an old scientist who was our neighbor. That was Dr. Cornelius.

"Dr. Cornelius was in great need of a faithful and intelligent servant to look after him incessantly. Always plunged in the abstractions of science, he had no time or thought to spare for material life. Although young, I understood the duties of my position and I introduced economy and order into my benefactor's household, into which they had never entered. Cornelius possessed a fortune that, if well-regulated, could have procured us an easy and comfortable life, but he ruined himself in the fabrication of strange and bizarrely-formed machines. He was always in pursuit of an obsession whose objective he hid with great mystery. He lived in a laboratory infected by the most deleterious gazes, composed and decomposed substances, experimented on chemical agents and took no rest by day or by night. I can still see him, with his tall stature, his thin face, his huge bald brow and his eyes, flamboyant with a supernatural gleam. One morning, after leaning over a retort, reminiscent of a magician, Cornelius came out of his laboratory and embraced me with transports of joy, like those you showed me a little while ago.

"'Frantz!' he cried, 'I've completed my work! I hold the secret that I wanted o steal from nature. The name of Cornelius will take its place among the most glorious names; it will endure as long as the world, and will be blessed by generations to come.'

"'And what is this secret, my worthy master?' I asked.

"He leaned close to my ear, after looking around to make sure that no one could hear. 'Swear to me,' he said, 'on your salvation, not to reveal a single word of this mystery before I permit you to. Swear that oath, and you shall know everything.'

"I swore the oath that he was demanding of me.

"'Well,' he said to me, 'I've found the means of making myself the master of the weather...'"

"That was the secret of which a part was written on the fragment of parchment!" Knebel interjected. "Speak, oh, speak!"

The best way to hear me would be not to interrupt me, Frantz thought—but he resumed his story nevertheless.

"'I'm the master of the weather,' Cornelius continued. 'At my command, the rain will fall. When I wish, it will fold up its black wings and go throw itself into the sea that gave birth to it. I'll be able to dissipate the clouds that veil the sun and prevent the crops from ripening. No more floods, no more famine, no more of those frightful disasters that bring desolation and destruction in their wake. I'm the master of the weather!'

"'My good master!' I exclaimed, "Such power only belongs to God. In the name of Heaven, don't mistake for reality
utopias that are perhaps realizable in theory, but which practice can't help but destroy.'

"He looked at me, smiling, and said: 'You doubt the
power that my science has conquered. Well, I'll give you
proof of it. Do you see that cloud advancing toward us rapidly? Plant those rods that you can see in the ground in the form
of a circle. Attach to the top of each of those supports these
straw ropes that I wove yesterday. Now, stand close to me,
inside the circle formed by the apparatus. Look! Here's the
cloud, which is breaking up, and the hail beginning to fall
around us. Not one of those hailstones is falling in the circle.
A mysterious force is drawing them outside the limits that I've
traced for the storm.'

"Indeed, Monsieur, the hail was obedient, following the
direction that my master had imposed on it."

"I'm familiar with that magnetic phenomenon," Knebel
said. "I've experimented several times myself, and there isn't
a peasant in Germany today who doesn't put it into practice—
but I didn't know that Cornelius was its inventor."

"After such a proof, I could no longer put my master's
power in doubt. I gave him ardent assistance in the construction of his machines, but it was necessary, in order to meet
those expenses, to sell some of the property he possessed.

"'What does it matter?' he said to me, when he saw my
reluctance to let him take that resolution. 'What does it matter? Should one hesitate to complete the seed that, when
sowed, will fructify a hundredfold?'

"After four years of sacrifices and hard work, Cornelius
found himself reduced to absolute poverty, but nature had surrendered to him the entirety of the secret for which he had
been searching for so long.

"For a month thereafter, the village to which we'd retired
in order to live more cheaply, and more especially so that
nothing would disturb the scientist's meditations, only experienced atmospheric variations at the command of the master of

173

the weather. A few minutes were sufficient for Dr. Cornelius to cover the purest sky with somber clouds. In even less time, he could restore all its serenity to the celestial vault.

"Storms rumbled with their thunder and lightning, the wind whistled and the snow fell in large white flakes—and then, all of a sudden, ardent sunlight succeeded rigorous cold. All the crops in the village were destroyed and all the peasants without exception, could only obtain from their fields the bare minimum to support their most imperious needs.

"When I mentioned these misfortunes to my master, he smiled and replied: 'I'll be rich, and compensate them so generously for these losses that they'll bless me instead of complaining, as they're doing today.'

"'But why are you delaying revealing your secret? Master, our situation is scarcely more reassuring than that of the peasants who surround us.'

"'Listen to me,' he said. "Napoléon will arrive in Schoenbrun in a few days' time. It's to Napoléon alone that I'll reveal my secret; as the master of the world he alone merits such a communication, and he alone can reward it worthily. But Napoléon didn't understand Fulton, because the latter explained steam navigation with written theories, not with proofs. While he's reviewing his troops, I'll make the atmosphere pass through all the changes that I can impose upon it at will. Convinced by such proofs, nothing will impede the admiration of the great genius. His imperial mouth will proclaim me to be a superior man, before the entire world; we'll deal with one another as equals.'

"When the day of the review arrived, the doctor gave me the responsibility of supervising the most important items of apparatus, disposed seven or eight hundred meters from Schoenbrun. Full of hope for a triumph, he went to position himself in the crowd, in such a way as to be able, nevertheless, to direct the experiment with certainty, to the success of which he'd sacrificed his fortune and twenty years of his life.

"Heart palpitating with anticipation ad emotion, sitting at the foot of a great machine that rose some four or five meters above the ground, I soon heard the acclamations of the army saluting Napoléon. At the same moment, the sky, which my master had maintained somber and melancholy until then, opened majestically and unleashed floods of sunlight.

"On tenterhooks, I expected further atmospheric changes, but not ensued.

"I began to far that my master's science might have deceived and disappointed his power when soldiers fell upon me, dragged me away and threw me into a cell.

"I spent three months there, interrogated about my complicity in a crime about which I knew nothing and bombarded with questions that I didn't understand. I was confronted with a young man that I'd never seen before, who declared that he had never met me. Finally, I was introduced into my master's presence. Alas, he was a prisoner like me, and his reason had not been able to bear the destruction of his hopes; he had succumbed to dolor and was no longer able to make Napoléon understand the supernatural power that his science had conquered. He saw me without recognizing me, stammered inconsequential words, and only responded to my caresses by raising his emaciated hands to the heavens.

"In the end, our innocence was recognized, and we were set free. It was only then that I discovered the crime of which we had been accused. The machines disposed by my master for his magnificent atmospheric experiments had been mistaken for telegraphic signals and means of correspondence between the accomplices of the assassin Friedrich Staps.[30]

"Poverty awaited us on our emergence from prison. My master had no resources left, and fate had left him without any mans of combating the most frightful deprivation. My efforts could not restore him to rationality. Crouched night and day in a corner of the hovel into which we had been welcomed out of

---

[30] Friedrich Staps attempted to assassinate Napoléon at Schönbrunn on 13 October 1809, was intercepted and he was executed by firing-squad four days later; he was acting alone and his plan to stab the emperor with a knife was recklessly ill-conceived.

pity, he kept his eyes fixed on the ground and repeated incessantly, in a quavering voice: 'To Paris, the master of the weather! To Paris, the master of the weather!'

"A physician in the neighborhood, who treated my master gratuitously, declared that if any hope remained of returning the invalid to sanity, that hope had to be placed in a journey to Paris. The accomplishment of an imperious desire, the movement of the journey, and the change of location and air, might bring about the prodigy. Without counting on the success of the prescribed means, I resolved to try them out. Anyway, poverty in Germany or poverty in France was all the same to me.

"One morning, therefore, I went to the master and said: 'We're leaving for Paris, Master.'

"At those words, the idiot who had not understood anything I had said to him for a long time got up resolutely and leaned on my arm, and we set forth.

"The journey was long, for we had to make it on foot, begging from door to door for bread and the straw on which we were sometimes permitted to obtain a little repose. My master didn't seem to be suffering from, or even to perceive, the fatigue and misery. He walked with the force and resolution of youth. Silent and plunged in meditation, if he saw me succumb to discouragement, he pointed at the sky, took me by the hand, and repeated enthusiastically the only words of which his mind retained the memory: 'To Paris, the master of the weather!'

"Finally, we arrived at the goal of our journey. We took up residence in a miserable attic in the Rue des Cinq-Diamants, and a manufacturer of playing-cards took me into his service. I toiled from morning till dusk in his workshop, and then took thirty sous back to our dwelling. Thank God, it was enough to prevent us from dying of starvation, and we weren't required to resort to the humiliating resource of alms.

"My master's reason, without recovering all of its original energy, seemed nevertheless to be less weak and confused. I surprised him one day tracing geometrical figures and mechanical diagrams on the wall of the room with a pencil. He erased it all as soon as he saw me come in, as if he were afraid that I might rob him some important discovery.

"One evening, to my great surprise, I didn't find him there when I got home. You can imagine my anxiety. I wanted up half the night; he didn't reappear until midnight, covered with mud, worn out with fatigue and hiding something in his bosom that he carefully concealed from my gaze. When I thought I was asleep he took out his mysterious object that he had furtively procured. It was a leaf of parchment. He wrote all night; when dawn broke, he put out the lamp, after carefully hiding his work.

"The next day, I perceived that my master, in order to obtain the parchment, had spent part of the money that we still had. I succeeded in taking possession of the mysterious manuscript surreptitiously while Cornelius was asleep, but only saw unknown characters that seemed to have been traced at random. My poverty was too great to satisfy the desires of futile scribbling, so I took all my money with me, and, after leaving some paper on the table I double-locked the door.

"An accident that happened that very day, justified that rigorous economy measure only too fully, alas. I was seriously injured in the leg, and it was necessary to renounce all work for several weeks.

"To tell you what frightful suffering then came to overwhelm our poverty would be beyond human words. Kept prisoner in my paltry bed, with no linen to bandage my wound, without any bread to prevent the poor old man from dying of starvation, I dragged myself desperately as far as the landing to call for help. Either no one heard me or no one wanted to come to our aid, and we remained alone in the face of hunger and abandonment.

"My master spent his days and night writing. He erased, recommenced and added, and only seemed to feel the need for nourishment at rare intervals. When hunger pressed him, he turned his pale face, withered by privation and suffering, toward me, and looked at me with a dolorous astonishment, putting his hands to his stomach. When the crisis passed, he returned placidly to work.

"One morning—it was the eighth day—I found the old man lying at my feet. He was holding his manuscript in his hand, and showed it to me with a solemn gesture. Then he tried to say something to me, but his lips were hardly able to stammer the only words that madness had left in his memory: 'The master of the weather to Paris!'

"Then he fell back, stiff and cold.

"Desperation gave me strength. I overcame the pain and reached the door. I let myself slide down the stairs and succeeded, by leaning on the walls, in getting as far as the Fidèle-Berger. There, out of pity, they bought the sheet of parchment you found for a few sous. I exchanged those alms for a little bread and wine, and carried those treasures back to the lodgings.

"It took several hours to do all that, and I fainted twice before being able to get up the staircase. Finally, I got back to Cornelius. He was still there, stiff and cold on the floor. I rubbed his lips with the wine, and tried to make him drink a few drops. Nothing reanimated him. Then I threw the rest of the manuscript into the fireplace, and set fire to it—and, with the aid of the fugitive flame the paper gave me, I made one last effort to warm the poor fellow up. Alas, my efforts were superfluous, for nothing can return warmth to a cadaver.

"There's no need to tell you the rest of the story, sir. My master was thrown into the communal grave in a cemetery, and I went back to Germany, where I had the good fortune to enter your service."

Knebel left Berlin the next day to return to Ilmenau, which he never left thereafter. Always shut up in his study, he scarcely seemed to remember that he had a wife and children. He spent his days and nights meditating over the piece of parchment written by Cornelius, striving to recover the doctor's secret. Only Frantz was allowed into the room, and was not allowed to leave it, for he had to be ready to reply at any moment to the questions that the scientist addressed to him about the form and function of the machines constructed by the master of the weather.

One morning, Knebel came down from his laboratory, his face radiant with joy. He threw himself into his wife's arms; he hugged his sons to his bosom and he covered all three with kisses.

Frantz shared in his master's joy.

"Fortune and glory for us! Happiness for us!" said Knebel. "I've finally received the recompense of my courage and perseverance. I've rediscovered Cornelius' sublime secret." He added: "I have to go to Weimar to reveal my discovery to the prince and to carry out an experiment in front of him. Tomorrow, my dear Louise, tomorrow, my children, I'll come back, and never again have to think about anything but your happiness and affection."

Alas, he returned sooner than he expected. An hour later, his corpse was brought back.

The post-chaise, overloaded with instruments and apparatus, had overturned, crushing Knebel and his faithful Frantz.

That is why the secret of the mastery of weather was lost for a second time, and perhaps forever.

THE MADMAN

One evening in the month of May 1828, a post-chaise harnessed to two horses came into the courtyard of a hostelry in Toulouse. No one was occupying the exterior seat, reserved for a domestic, behind the body of the carriage. There were only two travelers inside. One was an old man, seemingly a sexagenarian; the other was a young woman who could not have been more than twenty.

The young woman signaled to one of the servants posted on the threshold of the hostelry to open the carriage door. The old man remained placidly seated in the corner in which he was huddled.

The female traveler got down first; an observer would have noticed her pallor and beauty, while she invited the old man, by voice and gesture, to get out of the carriage. She spoke in English, and from time to time a dry cough interrupted her solicitations. The man she was addressing seemed utterly unmoved by the invitations or the unhealthy condition of the Englishwoman. His head inclined over his breast, his clasped hands resting on his knees, his legs extended nonchalantly, he remained plunged in a profound preoccupation.

His companion looked around anxiously and pronounced a few words addressed to the hostelry's servants. No one replied, and the proprietor, whom she appeared to be addressing in particular, replied in the most unmistakable Toulousian accent: "I don't speak English, Madame."

The expression on the worthy proprietor's face enabled the young woman understand the meaning of the reply. She seemed saddened by it, raised her eyes to the heavens, pointed to the old man and explained by means of a rapid and expressive pantomime that he was ill and that he needed help to get down from the vehicle.

Two domestics immediately set to work. They expected to find a paralytic whom it would be necessary to lift bodily like a child. To their great surprise, the traveler opposed a keen and robust resistance to their efforts. He recoiled, pushed them away, and uttered cried of distress that the voice of the young Englishwoman could not appease. It was necessary to employ violence to get him out of the chaise. As soon as his feet touched the ground, he fell silent. The convulsive trembling agitating all his limbs gradually eased; his vague blue eyes ceased to express fear, but not suspicion. He looked around anxiously drew the large peak of the cap covering his bald head down over his face, and went to take refuge in the darkest corner of the vestibule.

The young woman, after having paid the coachman, rejoined the old man, passed her arm gently under his, and led him, not without effort and difficulty, to the apartment that had just been prepared for them. It was then evident how much the poor child was suffering. No animation tempered the mat whiteness of her complexion, except for the cheeks, which were covered with the feverish redness particular to invalids suffering from consumption. Her large blue eyes were shining with the sinister brightness also characteristic of that malady. In order not to succumb to the oppression that was stifling her, she was obliged to stop two or three times while climbing the staircase.

Having arrived at the first of the two rooms that were reserved for them, she left herself fall dejectedly into an armchair, and a few tears ran silently down her cheeks. In the meantime, standing in the place where the servants had left him, the old man was trying ever harder to cover up his face.

"They recognized me! They recognized me!" he said, finally, in terror. "Yes, they recognized me. They'll tell everyone my name. They'll repeat it with disgust. The local people will come to shout under my windows. They'll break the glass, they'll throw stones, they'll curse me. Into the Thames! Into the Thames!"

"No, Uncle, those fears aren't real; stop giving into them. We've left England; we're in France; no one knows us in this foreign land."

"No one?" he repeated. "No one! How can you believe, Diana, that my name is unknown in France? It was pronounced there with terror for a long time, when France was England's enemy. Later, it was repeated with admiration, as in all of Europe, as in the whole world. Alas, that celebrity has changed to shame. France, Europe, the whole world believes and cries, like London: 'Shame on him! Into the Thames! Into the Thames!'"

"Uncle, calm these dire ideas. Cast them out..."

"While I was sitting in the dock, before the Court of Chancery, prey to attacks of calumny and hatred, while England, to which I had devoted so much—talent, sleepless nights, fortune—played ignobly with my honor and called it into question, do you think that France remained indifferent and inattentive? No, it followed with interest the phases of that extraordinary case."

"But you were found innocent, Uncle; the court rejected the accusation."

"Yes, but the calumny hasn't died. The lies and perfidious accusations persist in spreading everywhere, although the law forbids their loud repetition.

"Once, when I crossed the street in London, people stopped when they saw me and said: *There he is, the man who defended the cause of noble England so energetically. He alone was worth entire armies: Walcheren, Spain, Algeria, Waterloo are there to prove it.* Now, they turn away from me; my best friends pretend not to see me and, if anyone recognizes me, he nudges his neighbor with his elbow and says: *Shame! Shame on that old man! He's soiled his glory and his white hair for money!* Oh, Diana, Diana, my poor Diana!"

He hid his face in his hands and remained in that desolate attitude for a few moments; then, raising his head energetically, he started pacing back and forth, and said: "And yet, I'm innocent, God knows, and the Court of Chancery recognized hat loudly. I'm innocent. Rather than submit to dishonor, I'd have preferred poverty and death. My God, how cruelly you're making me expiate my renown, since a man who has done everything for is fatherland has been obliged to flee like a criminal, since a man who has conquered a glorious name must pay, at the price of his blood, for that name to be forgotten and erased!"

A slight sound was audible outside. He shivered and broke off.

"They're coming," he said, "they're coming. They want to see me. They want to say to my face: *Thief! Thief! Shame! Shame! Into the Thames!*"

He bowed his head, pulled the peak of his traveling-cap entirely over his face, and, walking on tiptoe, went to hide behind a curtain.

The young woman, who had not ceased weeping bitterly during this sad scene of dementia, was seized by a violent fit of coughing, accompanied by nervous and convulsive movements.

"My God!" she said. "My God, give me the strength to resist the disease that's consuming me, until my care is no longer indispensable to that poor old man. If I succumb before the letter I'm going to write reaches England, if I have to die before it brings my brother to France, what will become of him, deprived of his reason and abandoned to the care of strangers?"

She sat down at a table and wrote the following letter:

My brother, hurry up and leave England; leave immediately for Toulouse; don't lose a single day, nor a single hour. I sense that God will call me to him, perhaps tomorrow, perhaps in an instant. And without me, what will become of the unfortunate old man to whom I've devoted my life? Alas, that sacrifice was beyond the strength of a poor frail and sick girl. I didn't take long to succumb to it.

My brother, how cruel it is to see an old man suffer thus, whom one known to be as innocent and pure as anyone! God alone knows the dolors I have endured in the presence of that intelligence, once so brilliant and now extinct, that was once surrounded by all the honors possible on earth, and is now crushed by all imaginable evils! My uncle's terrors have only increased; his dementia is taking on an increasingly absolute character, without liberating him from the obsession that is devouring him. Only one thought still remains in his burning head: that of the infamous stain on his honor made by calumny.

Come George, and come quickly. I shall succumb sooner or later under the burden of so such suffering. My uncle will remain alone in a foreign land, and to complete the misfortune, an unexpected incident is cruelly complicating the difficulties of his situation. The domestic who accompanied us and served as our interpreter, John, has suddenly disappeared, taking most of our luggage and all the money I possessed. I only have two hundred francs left, fortunately contained in a purse that I was carrying on my person.

I repeat, my brother, leave immediately for Toulouse. Adieu, I dare not hope that God will grant me the mercy of letting me shake your hand before dying. If such is his will, so let it be. I shall implore his mercy in heaven for you, and above all for the noble and unfortunate old man that I shall be abandoning.

Your sister, Diana.

After having written that letter, she sealed it, rang, and handed it to a domestic in order that it should be put into the post immediately. Then she took out a little pocket dictionary of English and French, riffled through it, and found beside the word for which she was searching, its translation. The servant called the proprietor, who read: *médecin.*

He immediately sent for the local doctor. The latter, when he came into the Englishwoman's room, was almost frightened by the rapid and frightful ravages exercised by the malady on the young woman.

"Do you speak English?" she asked him, in her mother tongue, as soon as she saw him.

He replied to the question, whose meaning he deduced, with a negative shake of the head. Then he approached her in order to interrogate her, by means of sign language, about the suffering she was experiencing. The signs were almost superfluous, however, for the energetic symptoms of consumption spoke clearly enough for themselves. She pointed rapidly at her chest and the sky, as if to declare that she was not clinging to any hope of a cure, and that she knew how serious her condition was—after which she designated hr uncle with a gesture of despair.

The old man was still hiding behind the curtains, his ears pricked, his eyes fearful, in the attitude of a man fearful of some peril. When he saw the physician advancing toward him, he covered his face with his hands and murmured: "It wasn't me! It wasn't me! I'm not the man they've accused of such cowardice."

As the insane man was expressing himself in English, the physician did not understand what he said, but it was easy to see that the old man's reason was impaired. He went back to Diana; she started weeping bitterly. She could feel existence abandoning her, and could not even give the physician the instructions and clarifications necessary to ease the mental condition of the old man that she was perhaps about to leave alone in the world. He would die abandoned.

Several times she tried to make herself understood by recourse to pantomime, but her gestures were insufficient to express the delicate nuances of such a malady and the mental causes that had produced such a severe intellectual shock. It did not take her long to see that the physician did not understand. She wrung her hands in distress; a violent crisis became manifest and provoked horrible fits of coughing.

For ten minutes, the doctor, in spite to the care he lavished upon her, thought that she was about to die. Finally, he saw life gradually return—but he recognized that a further fit was inevitable and imminent, and that the first had left her too weak and exhausted for her to resist any further.

She read those sinister anticipations in the physician's physiognomy, and, as if to take advantage of the time remaining, tried to get up from the bed on which he had laid her down. She fell back.

A second effort allowed her to seize a pen and a piece of paper. She then began to trace a few notes, in a faltering hand. The glances that she dated incessantly at the madman told the physician that the notes concerned the old man. When she had finished—and it was not without painful efforts that she had succeeded in scribbling seven or eight lines—she leaned toward the doctor, addressed a supplicant gaze to him, and handed him the sheet of paper. After making him understand that it was necessary to find someone to translate the instructions she had just transcribed, she let herself fall back on the bed, put her hands together, and waited for death.

The old man, seeing her lying there motionless, seemed to become anxious. He overcame his terrors and, in spite of the presence of a stranger, he advanced slowly and hesitantly toward the young woman.

It was not without a thousand precautions, and not without continuing to hide his face that he approached the bed and knelt down beside Diana's pillow. She seemed to be reanimated on seeing the object of her devotion and her dolor so close. She reached out to her uncle, took the old man's hand and drew him toward her, murmuring a prayer to appeal for celestial protection for him. At that supreme moment, all her solicitude was for him.

Perhaps he understood, in spite of his troubled reason, the misfortune and abandonment that were threatening him, for he repeated, twice, in an emotional voice: "Don't go, Diana! Don't go!"

She raised her head painfully and tried to smile in order to reassure him.

"Don't go, Diana, don't go," he went on. "If you go, I'll have no one to tell them that I'm not the man they're heaping

186

with scorn. The people will pursue me again, they'll throw stones at me. The people who recognize me will turn away from my path. 'Into the Thames! Into the Thames!'"

"My God!" she cried. "My God, won't you take pity on me? Won't you return his reason to him before I die?"

In the meantime, the physician was trying to understand the notes that the young woman had written. He could deduce the significance of the occasional word here and there, but the general meaning escaped him. He went out to search for someone who could give him an accurate translation.

When he went back into the main room of the inn, he could not repress a start of joy; two travelers, recently arrived, were standing next to the fireplace. The accent of their pronunciation testified to an English origin. The physician handed them Diana's note and asked them to translate it. One of the foreigners nonchalantly cast his eyes over the piece of paper, but he had scarcely read the first line than he handed it back to the physician.

"A man obliged to flee his country is no compatriot of mine," he said, harshly.

"But what does it matter, Monsieur? You can't refuse to translate that note for me. It's a matter of an old man who needs care and a young woman who is dying. Not to tell me what this short letter means would make it impossible for me to give them help; it would prevent me from fulfilling the duties of my profession and of humanity. Perhaps it would be killing them!"

Without replying, and as if they had not even heard, the two Englishmen straightened up, moved away from the table and sat down at the table where their dinner had just been served. Full of anger and indignation, the physician returned to the sick woman's room.

The latter guessed that her note had not been read; a burning tear, the last she was to shed, shone beneath her eyelid. She indicated her uncle to the physician, commended him to his care with a solemn and imploring gesture, and put her thin arms around the old man. The madman let her do it without understanding what was happening. The light of intelligence of which he had given evidence before now seemed totally extinct. He gazed at the physician anxiously and murmured his habitual phrases.

"It wasn't me! I didn't do what they they're accusing me of! Innocent! I'm innocent! Hide me! The people will throw stones at me! 'Into the Thames! Into the Thames!'"

Suddenly, Diana shivered. She raised her head, and a surge of joy lit up her face. She had just heard a few English words pronounced in the room next to hers. She pointed to the paper and signaled to the physician to go and ask for a translation. He replied by making her understand that he had already tried and had been refused.

The young woman sat up on her bed with a painful effort. Although the doctor tried to dissuade her and hold her back, she put her feet on the floor. She tried to walk—or, rather to drag herself—to the room next door. Several times, her strength betrayed her, but she persisted in her aim nevertheless.

When she went into the room where the foreigners were, one might have thought her a phantom emerging from the tomb; even the Englishmen, in spite of their natural phlegm, their apathetic insouciance and their cruel refusal, could not avoid emotion at the sight of the dying woman, so young and so beautiful. She handed the piece of paper to them and begged them, with a supplicant gesture, to translate its contents for the physician.

One of them took the note and was about to do what she asked when he suddenly saw her totter and fall. The physician ran to catch her. She murmured a few unintelligible words, raised her eyes and extended her hand toward the room where the old man was, and exhaled a long sigh.

"God has taken pity on her suffering," the physician said, taking the poor child's pulse. "He has recalled her to him."

The disorder and trouble caused in the hostelry by the lugubrious event of a death occurring in such dire circumstances is easily imaginable. While the Englishmen and the women hastened to get away from the sad sight, the servants helped the doctor transport the corpse to the old man's apartment. The latter did not understand the sad reality of the scene that was unfolding before his eyes. On seeing so many people arrive in his presence, he took refuge in a corner, not without murmuring and repeating incessantly: "It wasn't me! It wasn't me! Don't throw stones at me! I'm innocent. 'Into the Thames! Into the Thames!'"

Habituated as the physician was to the sight of death and the lugubrious scenes accompanying it, he could not repress a sharp emotion on seeing the cadaver of the young woman, whose gaze still seemed to be searching for the old man, to protect him. Piously, he put a veil over her face, still beautiful in spite of death, and went to meet the hotelier to discuss with him what was to be done with the old man who had found himself suddenly abandoned in such a fatal manner.

The hotel proprietor was busy settling the account with the English travelers, who getting ready to leave immediately.

"What, Messieurs!" cried the doctor. "One of your compatriots has just died; an old man of your nation remains without protection; you could provide some information about him, and instead of doing so, you're in haste to quit Toulouse!"

The two foreigners, like men anticipating annoyance, fuss and perhaps delay, made no response, paid their bill, climbed into their carriage and gave the coachman the order to leave.

"What are you going to do with the old man?" the physician asked the landlord.

He shrugged his shoulders. "I'll send for the justice of the peace. He'll draw up the official report. He'll examine the man's papers and dispose of him as he thinks it appropriate. Do you think I can turn my hotel into a hospital? It's bad enough to have a death. Now two travelers have left because they don't want to stay under the same roof as a corpse. If other clients arrive and find out what lies in that room, they'll go away and lodge somewhere else. I hope to God that I can get rid of such guests very quickly!"

He did, indeed, go in search of the justice of the peace immediately; the latter did not take long to arrive. At first he wanted to seal the room, but the host judiciously observed that the formality in question would only apply to his own furniture, given that the foreigners had not brought any trunk. The only thing they possessed was the post-chaise in the courtyard that had brought them.

Indeed, no luggage as found in the apartment. A purse containing eight or ten gold coins was all that the foreigners had.

The justice of the peace then beckoned the old man forward. The latter had taken refuge in a corner, according to his insensate habit. It was almost necessary to use violence to bring him before the magistrate.

"What is your name?" the judge asked him, in English, being able to speak that language.

The old man hid his face in his hands and obstinately refused to reply.

"At least you won't refuse to tell me the name of the young woman who has just died," said the magistrate, hoping by that stratagem to get some enlightenment from the madman.

The old man shuddered. "Dead! He said dead! Diana's dead!"

He threw himself toward the bed, lifted up the veil covering the young woman's face and shivered from head to toe on seeing her motionless and marked with the fatal seal of death. They thought momentarily that the redoubtable spectacle was about to return him to reason, but he only stammered a few inconsequential words; sobs escaped his bosom, and he ended up kneeling beside the bed.

"Well?" said the magistrate. "What is the young woman's name?"

"Diana! Diana!" murmured the madman.

"Is she your child or a relative?"

"My child, yes, the child of my heart. For me, she has renounced her homeland, her family, her fiancé. She followed me into exile. She's dead!"

"Why have you left your homeland, then? What reasons forced you into exile?"

That question threw the old man's ideas, which had seemed to recover some clarity, into confusion again.

"The people!" he said. "The people! Stones, cries, curses! 'Into the Thames! Into the Thames!' Oh, how cruel the injustice of her country was to a noble heart! Why am I not dead? There's no rest, except in the tomb. Fortunate Diana, who can rest!"

"But in France, a foreign country, you have nothing to fear from our compatriots. Tell me your name, as I'm required to record it by the law."

"The law! The law! Oh, I know that, he law! Judges who interrogate with perfidious skill, who lay traps into which one falls. Black-hearted men who only say 'you're innocent' after telling the entire nation of what you were accused. And then the nation doesn't want to believe in that innocence! The people are there with shouts and stones…it's necessary to hide, like a shame, the glory of the name that one made illustrious by so much effort, at the price of such difficult labor. Leave me alone, leave me alone: I have no name; I don't have one anymore."

After making further and lengthy attempts, the magistrate had to give up trying to obtain enlightenment from the old man, which his flagrant state of dementia would, in any case, have deprived of any legal value. The justice of the peace drew up the death certificate of a young Englishwoman known only as Diana. As for the old man, he decided that everything belonging to him—which is to say, the post-chaise—should be sold on his behalf, and that he should be placed in a lunatic asylum until someone came to claim him, with further measures to be decided later, if no one presented himself to take charge of him.

The hotel proprietor asked the justice of the peace to take the old man away from his inn immediately.

"The presence of a madman in my establishment," he contended, "might lead to unfortunate incidents. If he becomes violent, I have no means of restraining him. He might start breaking my furniture and trying to flee."

The magistrate yielded to this judicious reasoning and ordered the two policemen he had brought with him to take the foreigner to a hospice that he designated to them. The two men immediately went to carry out the order they had received. They found the old man sitting by Diana's bed, plunged into a profound meditation. They gestured to him to go with them. He smiled, signaled to them to speak more quietly, and pointed at the corpse.

"Shh! She's asleep, don't wake her. I'll go with you as soon as she's had enough sleep. It would be a cruelty to wake her. She's had so much fatigue and chagrin to bear!"

The policemen conferred with a glance, slipped behind the foreigner, grabbed him abruptly and started to drag him away. Then he resisted, crying out, and gave evidence of a vigor that one would not have suspected from his paltry appearance. The struggle went on for a long time. Exasperated by several blows they had received, the policemen ended up throwing their adversary on to the bed. There they succeeded in tying him up. Then they loaded him on to their shoulders and carried him away.

During the frightful struggle, Diana's body had been tipped on to the floor and trampled underfoot. It was thus that it was found by the old woman charged by the justice of the peace with rendering the final duties to the foreigner's mortal remains. Alone, she wrapped her in a shroud and deposited her in a coffin, after having taken her jewelry and cut off her beautiful blonde hair, in order to sell it.

"The dead," she said, with a frightful smile, "have no need of hair."

The following evening, the coffin was taken to the cemetery without any religious ceremony, for they did not know whether the dead woman belonged to the Catholic religion or the Protestant faith. A grave awaited her in a corner reserved for paupers; she was put in it, and then it was filled with earth.

And it was all over.

Some time afterwards, a post-chaise arrived in the court-yard of the hotel where Diana had died. Two young men were in the carriage. They had scarcely exchanged a few words with the proprietor when the latter saw them go pale and give the most profound evidence of disturbance and dolor.

"My sister! My poor sister!" cried the younger of the two.

"Diana! My dear unfortunate fiancée!" murmured the other, who was visibly on the brink of fainting.

They immediately ordered that the Diana's brother be taken to the hospice where his uncle was detained, and his companion to the cemetery where Diana was buried.

At the cemetery, it was necessary for the gravedigger to search for a long time for the place where the requested body lay. So many young women had been buried in the course of a month!

At the hospice, no searching was necessary. A register was opened and the reply was made: "Number 3,623. An old man, assumed to be English, age and domicile unknown. Deceased 28 May 1828."

Two corpses! Of that beautiful and pure young woman, and that great and illustrious citizen, nothing remained but two cadavers! Alas! What malady, then, had struck the old man?

The attendant consulted his notes and read out: "Furious dementia. From the moment of his incarceration he never ceased to give evidence of extreme agitation. Violent fever. Refusal to take nourishment. Death. At autopsy, inflammation of the meninges of the brain; tubercules on the lungs."

The young Englishman withdrew in consternation. The attendant called him back.

"Monsieur, will you tell me the name of the deceased. It's important to record the name in the establishment's record of deaths."

"It's an illustrious name, Monsieur. The unfortunate who died in a lunatic asylum, struggling in the shackles of a strait-jacket, was one of the most celebrated citizens of Great Britain. Great Britain has killed him with its ingratitude and its injustice. Record the name of Sir William Congreve."

"The inventor of the terrible rockets that bear his name?"

"You are only citing one of his entitlements to renown, and not the most glorious, for, if it served to ensure the defense and military might of his country, it can only be regarded, after all, as a means of destruction. Thank God, I can cite with pride other inventions as admirable and more useful. Our whalers owe him a device that removes all the perils from whale-hunting and almost all the fatigue. He has given our powder-factories improvements that tend to the prodigious. He has created a motor in which water combined with air can produce a prodigious force. Thanks to him, the counterfeiting of banknotes has become impossible.

"Finally, he was completing studies that would have given the world an invention designed to allow ships to be maneuvered at sea without sails, without masts and without the resources of steam-power. A deadly and fatal blow, struck by calumny and ingratitude, has interrupted that endeavor abruptly, and permanently, and has annihilated them.

"Wretches accused Sir William Congreve of an odious and implausible fraud. Nevertheless, the superintendent of the Tower of London required the old man who had sat several times as a member of parliament, the great inventor admitted into the bosom of the Royal Society, to sit in the dock of the court of chancellery. That court, after long and dolorous debates, proclaimed my uncle's innocence, but public faith had been deceived and the opinion of the citizens perverted. At the end of the hearing, a blind and furious populace, determined to see Sir William's acquittal as an injustice and unworthy partiality for a powerful man, assailed him, insulted him, threw mud and stones at him, pursued him with odious clamors, and wanted to throw him into the Thames. He only escaped by a miracle.

"So much injustice troubled Sir William's reason; the light of that great genius darkened and vacillated, alas. Imagine my despair. Imagine the dolor that struck our entire family. It was decided, on the advice of several celebrated physicians, that my uncle should leave immediately for the continent. It was hoped that absence, the change of location and the distraction of traveling might lead to a fortunate amelioration of Sir William's mental condition, and might even bring about a complete cure. Imperious affairs, on which my honor and my fortune depended, retained me in London for some time. Diana, my sister, engaged to a young man she loved, ready to contract a marriage that one the prosecution brought against Sir William had delayed, did not hesitate to devote herself to her uncle, and departed with him.

"We saw them draw away, hearts full of hope, with the certainty that my uncle would soon return to continue his work, and my sister to receive her fiancé's pledge at the altar. A domestic attached to Sir William's service accompanied those two dear individuals and assured them—at least, we thought so—of loyal, intelligent and efficacious protection...

"Do you know how that wretch justified our trust? He abandoned Diana, dying, and Sir William, without resources. He robbed them. The lure of two or three hundred pounds sterling led him to commit the most cowardly and odious crime. It was tantamount to murder.

"That last blow finished poor Diana, who was exhausted by fatigue and grief. Vanquished by absence, always in the presence of the sad spectacle of madness, she could not resist, and succumbed. And no one was there to collect her last sigh, no friendly hand to hold her hand at the moment of the supreme adieu. Isolation, abandonment and despair were seated beside her death-bed. But at least it was not in a hospice, it was not bound in the ignoble folds of a straitjacket, it was not confounded with the insane that she rendered her last sigh. She had a coffin. Her remains were not, like my uncle's, thrown into a common ditch, where it will be impossible to recognize them in order to give them a tomb."

A week later—for the legal formalities could not be completed more rapidly—two coffins, one covered with a black cloth, the other with a white one, and placed in a hearse, left Toulouse in the midst of a crowd that had gathered to see the funeral cortege.

But that curiosity was nothing by comparison with the emotion that excited London in the middle of the month of May. The streets were overflowing with people dressed in mourning; even the poor had found the means of procuring scraps of crepe to put on their hats. Everyone headed urgently toward the shores of the Thames, on the bank of which, at the place most appropriate for a disembarkation, a large and plush catafalque had been established, draped with velvet with lavish silver embroideries.

On the part where the coffin would rest temporarily, a coat of arms surmounted with a baronial crown was visible. Beneath it was a depiction of Britannia, kneeling piously and seemingly shedding tears, while a statue of Gratitude, arms full of palms and civic crowns, advanced to cover the illustrious deceased with them. Members of the regiment of the Coldstream Guards, in ceremonial uniform, with crepes on their drums, surrounded the catafalque and protected it against the unprecedented flood of curiosity-seekers who were trying to get closer to it.

Suddenly, a cannon-shot was head in the distance. The artillery of the port replied with a salvo, and a steam-boat was seen on the waves, whose flag, flying at half-mast, trailed sadly in the Thames as a sign of mourning.

Then there was a tumultuous rumor among the crowd, soon succeeded by a profound and pious silence. Everyone bared their heads, and some knelt down. One poor devil, either by virtue of carelessness or because he had emptied, while awaiting the boat's arrival, more tankards of beer that was appropriate, kept his hat on; acts of violence were committed against him. The police had a great deal of difficulty preventing him from being thrown into the Thames. They only got him away by pretending to arrest him and promising to take him to prison as a punishment for his culpable irreverence.

In the meantime, the steamer reached the quay and disembarked beneath the catafalque. Immediately, the military band played the most lugubrious tunes, the drums beat a slow measure, and there was a moment when all eyes were filled with tears.

When these honors had been rendered to the mortal remains brought by the steamboat, a numerous deputation of important individuals, mostly bald-headed, advanced to the foot of the catafalque. There, the chairman, in a sonorous voice, pronounced Sir William Congreve's eulogy. He listed the numerous and illustrious services rendered by the deceased to science and the fatherland. He painted a picture of that celebrated man devoting his life and his fortune to his studies, to giving the means of victory to England. He spoke dolorously about the great invention on which Congreve had been working when death struck him.

"Without his premature death," he proclaimed, "perhaps England, already so powerful, would be marching even more proudly at the head of the nations of the world. Her redoubtable fleets might be tripled; the tempest would no longer be redoubtable for them; and steam, that great and sublime invention, that motive force that will be the admiration of future centuries, would find itself effaced and vanquished."

He wiped away a tear, and added: "Although God did not want to permit Congreve to realize his almost-divine idea, and he recalled him before his time, the fatherland knows nevertheless that the great engineer would have overcome all the difficulties of his project; only a few obstacles, of no real importance, still prevented it from being put into execution. Thus, although we do not enjoy the benefit with which he wanted to endow his country, we nevertheless owe an eternal and boundless gratitude to the great man who created it. Let us

197

engrave the name of Congreve on our public monuments, let us teach our children to repeat it with veneration."

Sobs interrupted the voice of the worthy chairman. Hurrahs replied to him from all directions, attesting to the great sympathy that the orator had encountered in his audience, and to the extent that the sentiments of regret and veneration for Congreve were shared—sentiments that he had just expressed with so much eloquence and sympathy.

Two or three more speeches followed, after which, various deputations placed wreaths on the coffin.

First there were the artillerymen, for whom Congreve had invented the pockets that bore his name and had won them so many victories.

Then came the whalers. For, if the fatigues and perils of their rude profession had diminished, that was because of Congreve, the illustrious Congreve.

Five or six bodies of workmen, who owed to Congreve important ameliorations in the machines and implements of which they made use, followed the whalers, but the individual who made the greatest impression on the witnesses of the scene was a mutilated old soldier whose life Congreve had saved on the battlefield in Spain, and ho had found in the engineer a constant and generous benefactor. He related how Congreve had carried him, dying, how he had fought the enemy for him, and the cares by which he had succeeded in curing him. He added the delicacy with which a generous pension had been paid to him every year, without its provider wishing to be identified.

"But I knew, myself," he added. "Although my benefactor tried to hide it, I read in his eyes the joy that my happiness caused him, and my heart told me that that happiness was his work. My God, who else would have taken an interest in an old invalid like me?"

Needless to say, that story caused tears to flow from those who heard it, and from all directions blessings were heaped on the name of Congreve, "the friend of the people, the benefactor of the country and the most generous and disinterested of men."

When the general emotion had clamped down somewhat, a hearse pulled by four richly-harnessed horses advanced to receive the coffin—but the people did not want to allow the horses to do their work. The reins were cut, and everyone began to pull the carriage, which traversed the principal streets of the city of London in that fashion; for, without taking account of the itinerary planned in advance to take the coffin to the house where a mail coach as waiting to transport it to Staffordshire, they proceeded to parade it through every district, in order that all the citizens could pay their regretful respects to the great man whose loss it was necessary to deplore.

While these tumultuous and enthusiastic scenes were unfolding, and Congreve's remains were subjected to an apotheosis on the part of the people who had driven him mad by dint of ingratitude and injustice, two young men clad in black had a second coffin disembarked in solitude. That coffin, covered in a black cloth, was Diana's.

The two young men had remained on the ship, sad, silent and almost indignant, during the ovation given to Congreve's coffin.

"They're making a god of the man they murdered," one said to the other.

"This poor victim also owes her death to them," added the other, on whose face the mortal ravages of malady and despair were visibly legible.

"It's the story of almost all great men," put in an old Protestant minister charge with saying the final prayers over the white coffin. "After the hemlock, the apotheosis."

"But this angel, this young woman they killed in killing her uncle..."

"Her recompense is there," the old man said, pointing to the sky.

The young man smiled, a celestial hope animating his visage.

"Yes," he said, "yes. Those whom humans separate down here..."

"God reunites in his bosom for eternity," added the minister, in a grave voice.

Translator's afterword

In England the name of Sir William Congreve (1772-1828) has been somewhat eclipsed by that of the famous dramatist who shared his name, but not his title. Few people know that it to Congreve the inventor that the "rocket's red glare" mentioned in the American national anthem, in relation to the siege of Fort Henry, was due to a device of his invention. In fact, his rockets were not every effective as weapons of war, although it could be argued that they were to first step on the long road to Apollo 11. His adaptation of rockets for the propulsion of whalers' harpoons was also limited in its applicability, although he did indeed help to make the production of gunpowder easier and safer, and his invention of a new kind of paper for banknotes was sufficiently effective as a safeguard against forgery that modern techniques have merely refined it. He obtained numerous other patents, and did, indeed, publish plans for a method of propelling ships without the employment of oars, sails or steam, but he also published plans for a perpetual motion machine, and both devices exhibited more optimism than practicality.

Congreve was the comptroller of the Royal Laboratory at Woolwich and the M.P. for Plymouth from 1814 until his death, and was also chairman of the Equitable Loam Bank and a director of several companies, one of which was responsible for a share issue that resulted in charges being brought against its directors in the Court of Chancery in 1826. It is conceivable that Congreve was not involved in or aware of the share issue, but he immediately fled to France, where he lived for two years before dying on 16 May 1828 in Toulouse. His young wife and three children went with him. The court took most of that time to reach a decision, but decided shortly before his death that the share issue was clearly fraudulent. Congreve was buried in Toulouse with military honors; he did not die in an asylum, and his body was not returned to England.

Everything in Berthoud's story is, therefore, a tissue of fantasies built around the name of a real individual and a few of his actual achievements. The endeavor is not, however, entirely out of keeping with the spirit of its era. Berthoud was acquainted with Paul Lacroix, alias Bibliophile Jacob, Edgar Quinet and Jules Michelet, the French Romantic Movement's three leading historians, two of whom also wrote significant works of fanciful fiction, while the third—Michelet—became notorious, occasioning the observation that "no historian ever cared less about accuracy." Berthoud was also familiar with the best-selling works of the Toulousian Étienne Lamothe-Langon, which mostly consisted of fake memoirs attributed to real historical individuals, which were extremely cavalier in their inventions.

THE CAULDRON OF BICÊTRE

In 1835 I went to Bicêtre regularly three times a week in order to follow the lecture course on mental alienation offered by one of our most intelligent and knowledgeable doctors, F .[31] The rest of the day was employed in anatomical studies and dissections, in which I was supervisee by an intern of the establishment, Dr. Émile D***, to whom the art of surgery owes one of the most remarkable books on pregnancy and childbirth.

To serve and assist us in the most difficult parts of our work we had an orderly at the hospital whom epilepsy had reduced, at least apparently, to a condition bordering on stupidity. He was a machine who received, with a remarkable facility, the impulsion one gave to him and carried it out with a mechanical perfection. He was never in default and never exceeded the orders he received. He did not understand anything but the literal meaning of what was said to him, but by way of compensation, he never fell into the more perilous inconvenience of subalterns who aim at intelligence. He did not interpret, and did not seek to understand. I can still see him, with his vacillating gait, his pale cheeks, his deep-set eyes with their scintillating irises, and his mouth, sometimes disfigured by horrible convulsions.

The faithful bearer of a copper cauldron from which he was never separated, he rarely spoke, and his voice resembled the broken sounds that emerge from an unhealthy larynx. In any case, attentive without slowness, dexterous without arrogance, humble without baseness, he resembled one of those genies that a talisman renders subject to the will of a magician and resigns himself to a power he knows to be invincible.

---

[31] Perhaps Jean-Pierre Falret (1794-1870), author of *De l'aliénation mentale* (1838).

More than once I suspected in Jean—that was his name—more intelligence than he consented to show: a word, a gesture or a glance betrayed it, but he would immediately resume is vulgar appearance, warily on is guard against my observations and ever ready to disconcert them.

One evening, however, I resolved to penetrate the mystery with which he surrounded himself—if, indeed, he did surround himself with mystery. Retained by bad weather and obliged to stay the night at Bicêtre, I left a bottle of champagne on the table after supper. Jean had a habit of appropriating our dessert; he therefore took possession, as usual, of everything that there was on the table.

When he reached the bottle of champagne, he picked it up with the conviction that he would find it empty, and was surprised when its weight informed him that it was almost full. A kind of convulsive tremor passed through all his limbs, tensed and knotted by his malady. His vitreous eyes became as resplendent as the eyes of a cat in the dark, and he replaced the bottle on the table—after which he examined the walls of the room slowly, and arrested his crazed gaze on the door of the study in which we were lurking. In that attitude, he waited attentively.

After a few seconds, he returned to the table, put the cork firmly in the bottle and went to put it with the silverware in the old oak dresser that formed, with two rickety chairs, the dining-room furniture.

That was not what I wanted.

"That bottle is for you, Jean!" I exclaimed.

He shivered, and I thought for a moment that he was about to suffer a fit of epilepsy; his face was covered by a lividity even more sepulchral than usual, and his knees wobbled beneath him. He succeeded in mastering his emotion, but he had to sit down and open a window in order to render an energetic respiration to his oppressed lungs.

Curious to see what would happen next, I resolved to study Jean without him knowing that he was being watched, I therefore closed the connecting door between the dining room and the study in which we normally sat—after which I extinguished he lamp and pretended to leave by another exit. Instead of going out, I applied my eye to the keyhole.

Jean was still there, emotional and sitting in front of the bottle.

Eventually, he got up, took the bottle and placed it between his eye and the candlelight, in such a fashion as to illuminate the liquid contained in the glass envelope. During that contemplation, a smile devoid of intelligence, in which the instinct of gluttony was clearly legible, parted the epileptic's lips to allow a glimpse of his long yellow teeth. One might have thought that he was studying each of the bubbles of air rising from the bottom of the bottle to burst at the surface of the liquid.

Gradually, Jean's face darkened, the intelligence reappeared, and effaced the material expression that I have described. A thousand memories full of bitterness and despair appeared to the poor man's imagination; a tear rolled down his cheek, hollowed out by misery.

Suddenly, he emerged from that bleak sadness by means of an abrupt and violent effort, gripped the bottle, tore out the cork, raised it to his lips and drank long draughts from it.

When he put the bottle back on the table it was more than half empty. Jean was no longer recognizable; a light redness covered his prominent cheekbones, his damp forehead seemed free of the grip of the malady and his gait took on a firm and solid appearance. To cap it all, his hands came together petulantly, and his chest heaved as he sucked in air avidly.

"Ah!" he exclaimed, with a gesture full of vigor and petulance, "I feel twenty years younger." He drank again and added: "I can almost see, as in the past, Gabrielle's white hand pouring me a glass. One might imagine that Désaugiers were about to present his glass to me once more, that we might clink them together cheerfully."

And he hummed one of those Bacchic refrains that the members of the Caveau once repeated to the clatter of bottles, in the midst of noisy choruses.[32]

I opened the door then and came in. Jean came toward me, held out his hand and accosted me with the manners of a gentleman. "Your wine is delicious!" he exclaimed.

Curious to return him abruptly from the height of his excitement to the humility of his real situation, I pretended to bump into his copper cauldron, and said, with false ill-humor: "What's you cauldron doing there, Jean?"

He gazed coldly at the utensil, from which, by virtue of a kind of monomania, he was never separated, and which he employed for the most bizarre purposes; then, pushing it away with his foot, he said: "To the Devil with the cauldron! I don't need it any more—for, after all, life is a good thing, and I want to live!"

As he concluded that Epicurean statement, he kicked the cauldron ten paces behind him, and extended a caressant hand toward the bottle again.

"Why are you treating your old friend and inseparable companion like that?"

"Because I want to live, I tell you."

"How can the presence of the cauldron be injurious to your health?"

"It's evident that you don't know your history. I was only carrying it with me in the hope of dying soon, because it brings bad luck to anyone who touches it. Anyway, in letting me live it wasn't giving the lie to its evil influence, for if you knew how ardently I've called up death to aid me...! A little while ago I would have received it as a blessing, but I was mad then. Well, in truth, life's a good thing, isn't it, my friend?"

---

[32] The Caveau was an early-19th century social club in Paris, whose members were mostly drawn from literary circles; the composer and dramatist Marc-Antoine Madeleine Désaugiers (1772-1827) was its president from 1808-15.

He tapped me on the thigh as he addressed that jovial question to me, and filled his glass to the brim.

"What's the story of your cauldron, then?"

"To begin with, the cauldron is a cooking-pot," he said, with a roguish expression, "only its lid is missing and its side-handles have been replaced by a single iron handle. That cooking-pot's been at Bicêtre for many years; it was brought here is the 17th century, and had never ceased, ever since, to play a dramatic role. Damn it, my dear chap, I'll tell you the story; I'm certain that you can make something good out of it; I'd be delighted to make you that little gift. Come on, let's move to the fireplace—go fetch your lamp, because this odor of tallow candles is odious to me. Stoke up the fire with a fresh log, and listen to me.

"Have you ever been to Rouen? Yes? Well, you'll doubtless have noticed an old house two hundred paces from the cathedral, whose pointed gable terminates in a gargoyle in the form of a dragon with a woman's head. A dealer in wall-hangings has lived in that house for the last twenty years. But in the 17th century, it was the laboratory of a apothecary who was reputed to be dabbling in alchemy. The fact is that he possessed, not only one of the best-stocked pharmacies, producing a considerable income, but a capital of twenty thousand écus. In those days, you know, twenty thousand écus was worth almost twice as much as it is today.

"Diane Daupats, the apothecary's daughter, was, in consequence, one of the richest catches in Rouen; a large number of suitors came to ask her father for her hand in marriage. He replied to them all, gently, that his daughter wasn't old enough yet to take a husband, and that, in any case, he thought that a little love wasn't a bad thing to put into a household, and, in consequence, that Diane would marry the young man for whom her heart felt a penchant.

"Diane was only sixteen and, although she was one of the prettiest girls in Rouen, thanks to the way her mother had brought her up, she wasn't a coquette. Her greatest joys were going to hear mass on Sunday and playing battledore and shuttlecock with one of her father's apprentices. The latter, the poor son of a peasant, used to being harshly treated by the other apprentices, nevertheless gave evidence on all occasions of a intelligence that Maître Daupats didn't take long to notice.

"The apothecary tried him out. Satisfied with the manner in which Salomon de Caus passed the various tests to which he was subjected, he appointed him his senor apprentice and gave him full authority over those who had previously crushed him under their domination.

"The young man didn't abuse that power, not subjecting the two fellows to the vexations that they had heaped on him, and ended up being almost forgiven for the favor he had enjoyed.

"That favor, I can tell you, wasn't limited to concocting, under his master's supervision, the complicated potions and medicaments of which medicine made lavish use in those days. Madame Daupats treated him benevolently, and Diane found that no one knew how to handle a racket and launch a shuttlecock like Salomon. Gradually, the apothecary and his wife became accustomed to regarding the young man as a member of the family. So, when they saw him gradually falling into a profound sadness, he experienced a veritable distress. Maître Daupats had recourse to all the elixirs most likely to triumph over that melancholy, which he attributed to peccant humors, and Madame Gertrude exhausted all her ruses and all her womanly perspicacity trying the penetrate the reason for that mysterious chagrin. The apothecary's drugs only served to render the invalid's complexion even paler, and the good woman's inquisition only drove Salomon into an even more absolute reserve.

"One morning, Salomon went to find his master and declared, stammering all the while, that it was his intention to leave Rouen and go seek his fortune in Paris. Maître Daupats looked at him with the cold and bitter gaze that the presence and bad behavior of an ingrate excites.

"'You're free to go whenever you please,' he replied to Salomon's request.

"Salomon wiped away a tear and went out without saying another word.

"When the rest of the household learned about the departure of everyone's favorite apprentice, everyone became emotional and shared Maître Daupats' sentiments regarding an apprentice who, with no apparent reason and for the hazardous lure of a risky fortune, was leaving the people who had treated and loved him like their own child.

"He supported the mute reproaches of the wounded family without trying to justify himself and without going back on his determination.

"However, Maître Daupats, ordinarily so just, began grumbling at his apprentices without any reason; Madame Gertrude let the roast burn that a maidservant was cooking under her direction; and finally, Diane wept and hid her tears by pretending to read prayers in her Book of Hours.

"When evening arrived in the desolate household, Madame Gertrude, going along the corridor where the apprentices' bedrooms were, heard sobs coming from one of the rooms and pricked up her ears. It was Salomon who as crying.

"Moved to pity, she opened the door and found the apprentice giving evidence of the most violent despair. At the sight of Madame Gertrude, he tried to suppress his dolor, but he couldn't do it, and his tears flowed in even greater abundance

"'My child,' she said. 'if you're regretting a moment of error, it's not necessary for a false shame to prevent you from going back on a resolution you regret. Youth merits indulgence, and we're ready to forget a foolish thought, quite natural at your age.'

"'I don't merit the happiness that you've heaped upon me,' he said. 'I have to go. By going, I'm giving you proof of my devotion and my gratitude.'

"'Then it's necessary to go,' replied Madame Gertrude, almost as emotional as the young man. 'Adieu, Salomon; may God watch over you and may his bounty protect you.'

"She left the apprentice and went to find her husband. She told him what Salomon had just said and added: 'Do you understand now, my love, why your apprentice wants to go?'

"'I only understand one thing, which is that he's being stupid as a result of the consciousness of his fault.'

"'I can see into all this more clearly than you,' Madame Gertrude told him, 'and if you let me take care of it, I don't think that anyone will be weeping in the house any longer—for Salomon isn't the only one who's shedding tears.'

"'Eh? Who else is weeping, then?'

"'Our daughter Diane,'

"The apothecary, absorbed by the preparation of the most difficult medicaments to concoct, raised his head and looked his wife in the face. Then he let slip one of those exclamations which cannot be translated, in any language, by any combination of the letters of the alphabet.

"'Do as you wish,' he added, after a moment's reflection, when he had recovered from his initial surprise.

"Madame Gertrude threw her arms around her husband's neck and went back up to Salomon's room. He was busy packing in clothes into a haversack. 'Salomon, she said, 'you'll have to postpone your journey for a week. My husband needs you here until then; you'll be free thereafter to leave, if you persist in your resolution and still think you ought to quit Rouen.'

"Salomon seemed both sad and glad to have to defer his departure. He took out the clothes and underclothes that he had put in his haversack and replaced the objects one by one, tidily, in the little cupboard of his room.

"Afterwards, he went downstairs to the pharmacy and resumed his customary station."

At this point, Jean interrupted his story and pointed at the bottle. I poured out everything it still contained for him; he sighed on seeing it empty, put his glass to his lips and slowly drank the foam-crowned wine. He drank it to the last drop, clicked his tongue against his palate in order to savor the aroma better, sighed again, and looked at me.

Jean looked once more at the emptiness of his glass, started to smile with the disdainful irony of a fashionable individual deigning to sit down at a poorly-served bourgeois table, and shrugged his shoulders slightly. Then, crossing his legs and moving closer to the fire, almost all of whose heat he appropriately casually for himself.

"Where the Devil was I up to?" he asked me, in a cavalier manner. "Oh, I remember now.

"I have no need to tell you what thoughts of every nature assailed and preoccupied Salomon during the rest of the day and that night. The next morning, the old apothecary summoned his apprentice and, after having carefully closed the door of his laboratory, so that no one could hear what he was about to say, he murmured in a sacredly audible voice: 'Salomon, a great misfortune has struck me. In the desire to increase my fortune considerably, I chartered a ship to go to the Indies to fetch a cargo of medicinal plants. Not only was all my fortune engaged in the enterprise, but I had to resort to loans. Well, the ship, on its return journey, has just sunk off the coast of Normandy; my ruination is complete; there's no more bread for my old age. As soon as my misfortune become known, my creditors will have me thrown into prison. It's not my own fate that I deplore; my imprudence has merited it— but what will become of my wife and my daughter?'

"Salomon looked at the old chemist with a mixture of surprise and suspicion. The old man hid his face in his hands and seemed to be shedding bitter tears. 'Master,' he replied, then, 'I'm only a poor apprentice who possesses nothing in the world. An interior voice, however, tells me that I shall be able to protect your wife and daughter against adversity. Let me make a confession that I had resolved to hide from you by my departure. I love Diane. Without the fatal blow that has struck you, the secret would never have escaped from my heart. Let me marry Diane.'

"'Alas, my friend, your generosity is deceiving you; you have no idea what suffering poverty brings to the father of a family. My boy, when people make fun of you, and laugh in your face, one bears those blows cheerfully, to which one can riposte with insouciance and courage—but one cannot be insouciant regarding the dolors of a wife and child! Don't waste your youth and your future in such an existence.'

"'I'm young and I feel strong," cried Salomon, enthusiastically. 'I'll be able to conquer my wife a fortune in exchange for the one that fate has stolen from her,'

"The old man reflected for a few moments. 'Your confidence in the future has won me over,' he said. 'Become my daughter's husband. A month will doubtless go by before anyone learns of my ruination; let's take advantage of it to complete your marriage; that space of time will also permit me to arrange my affairs in such a way as to be able to leave you my pharmacy. Undoubtedly it will be shackled by enormous mortgages that will absorb almost all the profits, but at least you won't remain in the grip of adversity and without arms with which the combat it.'

"He held out his hand to Salomon, who raised it respectfully to his lips. At the same moment, Madame Gertrude and Diane came into the laboratory. 'Daughter,' said the apothecary, 'I've just betrothed you to my apprentice Salomon de Caus.'

"Diane's charming face was covered by a blush; she lowered her eyes and made no reply. Madame Gertrude took her daughter's hand and placed it in that of the happy apprentice.

"He fell at the knees of his promised beauty. 'Won't you,' he asked, in a voice trembling with emotion, 'ratify my happiness with a word, or a sign?'

"She ran to take refuge in her mother's arms with a delicious shame. As Salomon seemed sad and anxious, she detached the blessed rosary that she wore suspended from her waist and slipped it into her mother's hand. Madame Gertrude took it to Salomon; Salomon would not have exchanged his happiness for that of the angels.

"He was, moreover, like all men whose foreheads are marked by the ardent seal true love in their youth, a serious fellow of great intelligence, who felt called to success by a superior organization, and full of energy. In making the resolution to marry a poor wife, he had not hidden the extent and the consequences of such an engagement from himself. He therefore set about studying the resources that he might create and organizing the means of remaining victorious in the struggle that he was about to undertake against fate. His passion for Diane raised him above all difficulties, and he was already glimpsing in the distance the fortune that was holding out a golden crown to him.

Meanwhile, the preparations for the marriage were made in the house as if nothing had changed in Maître Daupats' situation. Everyone in Rouen was astonished that the rich apothecary was giving his daughter to the son of a peasant with no money, when the most eligible suitors had offered themselves for Diane. A thousand suppositions were already being made, such as are always prodigal among townsfolk, especially the women, and even ladies of the highest rank.

"In spite of the respect he had for Madame Gertrude and her husband, Salomon could not help being secretly critical of their imprudent conduct; his bride's rich trousseau, the wedding feast that was to bring together a hundred guests, among the richest and most highly-reputed people in the town, seemed to him to be veritable extravagances. He did not understand how anyone could throw money around with open hands when conscious of imminent ruin and the scandal that would soon be produced by the public divulgence of such terrible news. He was afflicted by it, and tried on more than one occasion to talk about it to his father-in-law and Madame Gertrude.

"They were both obstinate in changing the topic of conversation, and continued in their prodigality.

"The exaggeration of a fault rarely fails to throw those who suffer from it into a contrary excess. A chatterbox renders people silent, a prodigal drives them to avarice. That is exactly what happened to Salomon. He started secretly organizing his future household, and did so with an economy so prudent as to be almost excessive. He had recourse to second-hand dealers to buy furniture, and thought he was concluding an excellent bargain when he paid a few sous less than it would have cost from the manufacturer for an object that had already been used. So, morning and evening, he roamed the poorest streets, hunting high and low for old items and haggling over every farthing.

"One day, Salomon perceived at the door of a copper-smith a copper cooking-pot in good condition, the dimensions of which seemed to him to be appropriate for a young house-hold. An old woman was holding it in her hands and examining it with minute attention. She felt it all over—inside, outside and round the sides—caused the copper to ring, and made sure that nothing impeded the movement of the lid, after which she offered the merchant a price.

"The merchant raised his eyes to the heavens as if he had heard a blasphemy uttered, swore that he would be losing more than half, and refused the old woman's proposition.

"The latter persisted, and made concessions.

"The coppersmith, for his part, dropped his price slightly, and was perhaps about to concede when he saw Salomon darting one of those covetous glances at the cooking-pot which merchants hardly ever misinterpret. Immediately, he became more demanding than ever; acrimony entered into the bargaining; the old woman moved away, discontented and as if to give up the game.

"Immediately, Salomon, who thought that a good thing, ran up to the merchant, gave him the last price that the latter had demanded from the woman, and was just about to carry off his acquisition when the old woman came back.

"On seeing the cooking-pot in someone else's hands she went pale with anger, and her eyes seemed to swell up with venom, like those of a poisonous animal. 'That cooking-pot's mine,' she said, in a hoarse and menacing voice. 'I was haggling over the price before you.'

"'Yes, but I bought it before you,' Salomon replied, sarcastically, irritated by his adversary's brutal tone.

"'I want it! I must have that cooking-pot!' she repeated, reaching for the object of her covetousness with two long stiff hands, which reminded Salomon involuntarily of the claws into Medieval sculptors formed the hands of the evil angel.

"Salomon retreated automatically, put the cooking-pot under his arm, covered it with his cloak and carried it away.

"The old woman followed him.

"'That cooking-pot is very fine,' she said, in a low voice, croaking like a crow tearing at a cadaver, 'but it isn't the first time I've seen it. Did you know that, my handsome young man?'

"Salomon made no reply.

"'I knew it; I saw it often in the hands of Catherine Lestoquoy. Catherine placed it at a crossroads at eleven o'clock at night, on pieces of wood that she'd taken from the remains of a coffin in a cemetery To set the wood alight she went to fetch fire from the lanterns on the gibbet, after which the flames emerged long and devouring—except that instead of raising their ardent tongues toward the heavens, they licked the earth and seemed to want to enter into it. You've got a fine cooking-pot there, my handsome young man.

"'When the wood was ablaze, Catherine threw water into it taken from a marsh covered with fire-follets, in which the corpse of an unbaptized child had been buried. After which she added many other things, which I won't name for you, profane, but of which I know the mysterious recipe. You've got a fine cooking-pot there, young man!

"Then plaintive voices came out of the cooking-pot, and other voices replied to them from the bosom of the earth, the gibbet and the cemetery itself. The moon was hidden by a bloody cloud, the signpost at the crossroads trembled on its stone base and phantoms flew through the air. You've got a fine cooking-pot there, young man!

"'Joyfully, Catherine took off one of her shoes, took a dead man's bone and stirred the water in the cooking-pot.

Midnight sounded then, and a circle of mysterious beings came to dance around the fire. When Catherine shouted three times: *To me, Master, to me!* they clapped their hands and stamped their feet, and the they all went away; everything disappeared; silence fell. You've got a fine cooking-pot there, young man!

"'A fine cooking-pot for a witch, for an old witch like me! It would have served me until the day when, put on a pyre like my Mistress Catherine Lestoquoy, I would have called Satan to my aid, and demanded a good place in Hell, among the Devils and their wives. You've got a fine cooking-pot there, young man!

"But for a fiancé, for a Christian who dreams of dying with his hands together on a bed with his eyes turned to Heaven, it's a fatal talisman. It summons demons, it attracts misfortune, it casts fatality everywhere. You'll weep more than once for possessing it; you'll struggle more than once under the vengeance of the witch from whom you've stolen it. You've got a fine cooking-pot there, young man!'

"Salomon hastened his steps in order to get away from the woman's pursuit and threats. The more he hurried, the more she increased her pace; nothing could free the apprentice from that sinister and pitiless murmur, every word of which struck his heart with an invisible whip.

"Several times, he felt that he was ready to hurl the cooking-pot she was claiming with such threats at the old woman. A sentiment of false shame always prevented him. He would have blushed to yield like that to puerile threats, unworthy of a man, a Christian and a scientist.

"Still talking, still cursing, the witch only stopped outside the apothecary's house. When she saw Salomon, with the cooking-pot, go through the low-set door ornamented with sculptures, she threw back the ragged cloak she was wearing, raised her arms to the sky, lowered them toward the ground, and seemed to trace a mysterious circle with one of her fingers. Salomon, under the influence of a kind of fascination, watched her through the window. He saw the hideous creature devoted herself to bizarre gestures, appealing by cabalistic signs to invisible beings and fulfilling all the reproved rites of a conjuration.

"Then she put her hands around her mouth, and shouted with all the might of her shrill and piercing voice: 'You've got a very fine cooking-pot there, young man!'

"At that moment, the watch patrol passed by. The officer in command had the old woman surrounded by his soldiers. 'I've been hunting for you for three days, you damned witch,' he said. 'Thank God I can finally arrest you and deliver you to the law—which will, it's necessary to hope, liberate the city of Rouen from your evil spells.'

"The old woman allowed herself to be tied up by the soldiers, not putting up any resistance. Except that, when the led her away toward the prison she turned to the window where Salomon was standing and let out a burst of laughter that chilled the apprentice with terror.

"Without hesitation, he picked up the cooking-pot and went to throw it into the Seine.

"The next day, Madame Gertrude came home with a copper cooking-pot under her arm. 'Look,' she said. 'I've just struck an excellent bargain. I bought this cooking-pot, just for the price of the copper, from some fishermen who had just found it in the Seine.'

"A month later, the witch was burned in the main square of Rouen. When she was led to the pyre, instead of repenting and thinking about the salvation of her soul, she proffered the most horrible blasphemies, and when the flames began to bite her limbs, she howled: 'That young man's got a fine cooking-pot!'

"Then she expired."

Jean interrupted himself again and said: "My lips are very dry. Nothing tires you out and gives you a thirst like talking next to the fire. Give me a drink, I beg you."

And he held out his glass to me.

I pretended not to see Jean, and yet, my eyes couldn't turn away from him. I could no longer find in that poor devil his habitual manners. His figure, previously curbed by humility, had now taken on an attitude full of pride, and he was carrying his head proudly, which had no lack of expression.

For the first time, I noticed the aquiline form of his Grecian nose, the sarcasm of his thin mouth, and the bitter smile of his lips, of a bright red that went marvelously with an energetically-tilted chin and a neck solidly planted on powerful shoulders. The light that fell vertically on his bald cranium rendered legible there, in the mysterious characters that Gall was the first to teach us to read, the projection of a keen intelligence, a powerful memory, a poetic imagination and an ardent love of the marvelous. In sum, there was nothing, from his hands, withered as they were by rude and abject labor, to his bare feet, emerging from the sabots that shod them, in which one did not observe, in an undeniable fashion, the particular characteristics of a man of pure race ad superior organization.

His soft voice, the elegant and well-chosen expressions of which he made use, the animation of his large blue eyes, and the singular energy of his gestures, full of distinction, added further to my surprise and caused me a sort of embarrassment. I sought in vain for the inferior that I was accustomed to treating as a kind of machine, appropriate at the most for carrying out, under an external impulsion, some elementary task. I found myself face to face with an equal, who was perhaps soon about to display before me a superiority of which he was conscious.

So, when the storyteller turned to me, and said to me with the cool and casual manner of a friend: "Send for some champagne, then!" I got up mechanically to order an attendant to go and find a second bottle and bring it to me. The worthy fellow hesitated for a few seconds, for the rain was falling heavily, and the tempest was roaring furiously. It was necessary to go across the courtyard and walk at least two hundred paces to reach the wine merchant's shop. Nevertheless, he armed himself with resolution, wrapped himself up in an old cloak, and left.

Satisfied, Jean resumed his story.

"At the sight of the fatal talisman that Madame Gertrude had brought back to the house, and learning of the strange manner in which it had been recovered, Salomon felt full of mortal anxiety. The witch's words on the pyre did not serve to reassure him, and he resolved to make a further attempt to get rid of such a deadly utensil. A few days before his wedding, he got out of bed in the middle of the night, took the cooking-pot and went to deposit it on the far side of the city, in a district inhabited by poor workers.

"*It's impossible*, he told himself, *that anyone would not be tempted to appropriate a copper cooking-pot and keep it for their own use; thank God, I'm rid of it now!*

"He had not yet reached home again when a frightful din caused him to turn his head and look behind him. A huge dog was running after him at a frantic pace, dragging behind it the fatal cooking-pot, which street-urchins had tied to its tail. The animal, exasperated by pain, impatience and rage, was howling, and its lips were flecked with bloody foam. A man tried to stop it, but the dog leapt at his throat and tore it out. Five or six other people made similar attempts, but had to give up after receiving serious bites that put the out of action.

Salomon, in despair at being the involuntary cause of such great misfortune, resolved t put an end to it, even at the risk of his life. He took out a little dagger that he then had the habit of carrying on his person, armed himself with a knotty stick, commended his soul to the Blessed Virgin, and ran straight toward the dog.

"Then a battle began between the two adversaries during which Salomon nearly succumbed several times. It required a great deal of composure and the most resolute courage to stand up to the monstrous hound, whose enormous mouth, armed with long fangs, broke the apprentice's enormous club like a frail stick.

In the end, determined to triumph or perish, the young man wrapped his first in a handkerchief and threw himself upon the dog, engaging it bodily, and struck it so fortunately in the heat that the redoubtable animal fell dead on the spot.

"Salomon got to his feet covered in blood, but safe and sound.

"Immediately, the acclamations of the crowd that had witnessed the rude combat saluted enthusiastically the athlete who had fought so well and triumphed so courageously. People pressed around him, shook his hands, embraced him, and ended up taking him back to his house with the greatest honor, amid resounding cheers.

"Insensible to these testaments of admiration rendered to his bravery, Salomon, his heart full of remorse, reproached himself bitterly for the evils caused by his imprudence. *Thank God*, he thought, *at the price of my blood and my remorse, at least I'm free of that infernal cooking-pot!*

"That wish seemed to have been granted, because, for an entire week, he heard no mention of anything. And that week ended with his wedding celebration.

"Finally, as he was about to extend his hand to conduct his fiancée to the altar, his father-in-law said to him: 'Salomon, forgive me for having tested you and made sure by means of a ruse of the honesty of your character and the sincerity of your love for Diane. I'm not ruined, as I told you, my son; far from it. You'll receive a dowry of ten thousand gold écus, and I'll also cede you the exploitation of my pharmacy, for I'm rich enough, my dear boy, to retire from commerce and live henceforth on the income from my investments.'

"At these soft and benevolent words, Salomon surrendered himself freely to the joy of his happiness. *The fatality that was pursuing me*, he told himself, *has finally ceased to harass me, thank God*. So, during the marriage ceremony, he prayed with fervor and gratitude.

"When they came out of the church, all the young people of the town, in their best clothes, were waiting for the married couple to honor them and escort them back home. They formed a cortege, with cries of 'Long live the beautiful Diane!' and 'Long live the courageous Salomon!' And arquebuses mingled their explosions joyfully with those affectionate clamors.

"It was necessary, to please the general enthusiasm, that the wedding-party, instead of returning directly to Maître Daupats' house, parade in pomp through the principal streets of the city. The most illustrious ladies were on their balconies, from which they threw bouquets to the newlyweds; poor people clapped their hands. Such a fête had never been seen before.

"That wasn't all. When the cortege arrived at the Hôtel-de-Ville, the aldermen in their robes were standing on the threshold, and two ushers came to ask the newlyweds to come before the magistrates. They obeyed urgently. When they had answered the demand, the Maire invited them to sit on crimson velvet armchairs that had been prepared for the ceremony, after which he made a long speech, in which he spoke, in savant and complimentary terms, about the courage of which Salomon had so nobly give proof a week before. He compared him to the demigod Hercules, the tamer of wild beasts, the conqueror of the Nemean Lion and the Lernean Hydra.

"'The city of Rouen,' he added, in conclusion, has charged its magistrate to give you a reward, bit what can we offer you, who are marrying a young woman as rich as she is beautiful? What can remunerate the service that you have rendered your compatriots? We therefore resolved to have the cooking-pot that was the cause of the misfortunes afflicting Rouen, to which you put an end by your intrepidity, gilded. The city wanted you engrave on it the following words:

THE ALDERMEN AND TOWNSPEOPLE OF ROUEN
TO SALOMON DE CAUS
XI MAI MDC...

"Look," said Jean, interrupting his story and showing me the cooking-pot. "One can still read that inscription clearly. Only the last figures of the date have been effaced.

"When the magistrate had finished his speech, trumpets set about sounding glorious fanfares, and the young people took possession of the cooking-pot, which they carried solemnly in front of Salomon. The Maire offered his hand to the bride, to the sound of bells, fanfares, arquebuses and acclamations.

"Maître Daupats and Madame Gertrude blessed God for having given them such a son-in-law. Diane looked at her husband with eyes full of tears of affection and pride.

"Salomon was the unhappiest of men. The fatal cooking-pot that was being carried before him seemed, like the sword of Damocles, to be disaster and death suspended above his head. He sensed that henceforth, no tranquility was possible for him in this world. The threats and vengeance of the witch were only too real. That diabolical talisman, of which there was no means of liberating oneself, was sufficient proof of that. The unfortunate fellow felt doomed to misfortune forever.

"When they arrived at Maître Daupats' house, the young people who were carrying the gilded cooking-pot hooked it to the ceiling in the hall of the nuptial feast. The guests took their places around the table, and the Maire and his aldermen were invited to the banquet, which went on, as was the custom in that good old epoch, long into the evening.

"During the meal, Salomon incessantly expected the cooking-pot to detach itself from the ceiling and fall on to his wife's head. Nothing happened, however, and calm finally returned to the young man's heart when it was permitted to him to leave the dining-room, in which he swore never to set for again.

"There is no impression so sharp that it does not end up eventually fading from our memory. Eight years later, not only did Salomon go back into the room whose door he had sworn never to open again, but he did not even think about the

221

witch's cooking-pot. It had been relegated to some forgotten corner of the house, where it lay covered with rust and dust. Salomon, a happy husband and an even happier father, was rich, honored and beloved by his fellow citizens, who had raised him to the dignity of an alderman. He had acquired a brilliant reputation by the publication of several scientific works.

"Heaped with honors, overwhelmed by business affairs, and charged in addition with the administration of Rouen, it was perfectly natural that Salomon de Caus should have forgotten the terrors and superstitions of his youth.

"Besides which, he had many other reasons more powerful than business, fortune and renown; there was his wife Diane, whose beauty time had only augmented; there was an only daughter nine years old, baptized with the sweet name of Marie, of an angelic grace, whom he loved madly. In order not to be separated from those two cherished females, he refused the seductive offers that were made to him on several occasions by kings and princes desirous of attaching such an eminent scientist to their households.

"He submitted to municipal honors because every citizen owes to his homeland the tribute of his experience and his enlightenment, but he would gladly have abdicated them in order to devote himself entirely to the ineffable joys of his tenderness and domestic bliss.

"One morning he came out of the Hôtel-de-Ville in Rouen and hastened his pace in order to get back to the house sooner and kiss his wife and daughter, whom he had not seen all day. He noticed at a distance an unusual agitation in his house. The apprentices were running back and forth fearfully in the pharmacy. His heart gripped by ominous presentiments, he broke into a run.

"The bewildered Diane was hugging little Marie to her bosom, and the child was crying: 'Mother! Mother! I can't see!'

"Full of terror, he asked Diane for explanations. She scarcely had the strength to give them to him. While playing in the kitchen, Marie had imprudently come close to a cooking-pot on the boil; a few drops of scalding water had splashed into the child's eyes, and she had been blinded.

"Salomon looked at the fireplace, and saw the witch's coking-pot there. 'Woe!' he cried, "woe! Why is use being made of that diabolical utensil?'

"'Today is the anniversary of the heroic deed that once earned you the gratitude of the entire city. I wanted to remind you of it, my love, by preparing the soup and having it served in that cooking-pot, which bears such a glorious inscription.

"Salomon took his daughter in his arms, and set about examining the poor little creature's eyes with minute care. He was trying to see whether any hope remained of curing her.

"At that moment, an explosion rang out. The cover of the cooking-pot, launched into the air by the force of the steam, had just struck the ceiling, and it came to land at the scientist's feet.

"At the sight of that phenomenon, he forgot everything—everything, including his wife's grief and his daughter's blindness. He fell into a profound reverie; the hands that were embracing Marie were detached from the child, and Diane spoke to him several times without him replying, or even having heard..."

"Here's the wine you asked for," said the attendant, opening the door and placing two bottles of champagne in front of Jean.

The latter gave an order to the astonished attendant—who nevertheless obeyed it mechanically—to bring a second glass. After which, he uncorked the bottle and did the honors himself, pouring me a glass. Then, refilling his own glass, he raised it to his lips with the slight salutation of the head, full of elegance and distinction that is commonplace among Englishmen and Germans.

Jean swilled another glass of champagne and continued his story.

"After the fatal days whose details I have just related, nothing could extract Salomon from the profound melancholy into which the accident suffered by his daughter had thrown him. As for the poor mother, she put all her faith in God; she spent almost every day at the church, invoking the Virgin on behalf of her child.

"Diane explained her husband's preoccupation to herself by the desire that was devouring him to cure little Marie and return her sight to her. *Salomon*, she said to herself, *is studying the causes of the evil in order to be able to combat it effectively and triumph over it.*

"It was not the same with Salomon's neighbors, for they accused him of madness—and, in fact, one could not abstain from sharing that supposition in the presence of the changes that overtook the behavior of Marie's father. Pale and thin, his complexion wan and his hair unkempt, dressed in a negligent fashion, there was a strange gaze in his distracted eye that only belongs to the insane. Six months had aged him ten years. Already, white hairs were mingled with the long curls that fell in disorder about his neck, and profound wrinkles were hollowed it on his once-cheerful and expansive forehead.

"Furthermore, in the midst of that absolute forgetfulness of real life and the gravest interests, an unprecedented activity devoured him. He did not have a minute to devote to the duties of his profession, the concerns of his business or the direction of the community of which he was an alderman. He scarcely remembered that he was a husband and father, but spent his days and nights consuming himself in meditation and study. He continually undertook long and distant journeys. He left for Germany, for England, for Italy, suddenly and without any apparent reason.

"Before separating himself from them, he scarcely fond time negligently to embrace his wife and his daughter—his daughter, who could no longer see him and held out her arms to him, weeping.

"When he quit his house and family like that he often forgot to take the necessary underwear; often, he even set off without any money—but he never neglected to take the witch's cooking-pot. It accompanied him on his slightest excursions; he was scarcely able to consent to be separated from it when he was only leaving the house for a few hours. Always hunched over that instrument of evil, he seemed to be attached to it by a magical power.

"The abandonment to which Salomon yielded his fortune did not take long to bear fruit. The neglected pharmacy gradually lost customers, and an accident soon discredited it.

"One day, when Diane's husband chance to be at his counter, a local resident brought in a prescription written by one of the city's most renowned physicians. Salomon prepared the medicament personally. An hour later, the invalid, who had previously only experienced a slight indisposition, died in the most frightful agony.

"The medical examiners summoned declared that a pharmaceutical error committed by Salomon had killed the unfortunate victim of culpable distraction. The guilty party was ordered to pay considerable compensation. Two months later, a similar error with a similar result occurred again.

"This time, a parliamentary warrant was issued, which prohibited Salomon from continuing to exercise the profession of apothecary and ordered him to sell his establishment within three months, on pain of seeing it confiscated by the government.

"Diane's tears and prayers were unable to persuade Salomon to take care of his business and comply with the parliamentary warrant. Three months later, the pharmacy was closed; government agents carried out the confiscation, and set about liquidating the assets in order to make compensation payments. Nothing extracted Salomon from his apathetic preoccupation. When the desolate Diane showed him the poverty that was advancing with rapid strides toad them and their child, he traced cabalistic figures on the wall, carried out geometrical operations in the sand with his foot, and, making no reply, went to shut himself away with the gilded cooking-pot in a little room that he had rented in order to establish a laboratory there.

"To begin with, the people of Rouen had thought that Salomon was mad, but a vague and perfidious rumor soon began to accuse him of being occupied with magic, of pursuing the Great Work, and of having recourse, for that purpose, more to the aid of the Demon than the enlightenment of science. So, when the magistrates, with common accord, took away his title of alderman, the measure received general assent. People exhibited no less satisfaction when it was learned with what rigor the parliament of Normandy as treating him. He expiated his former popularity by a general hatred. When he went out, fingers were pointed at him; children avoided his presence and his old friends turned away at the sight of him in order not to have to recognize and greet him.

"You can imagine Diane's despair; already her daughter was beginning to suffer the first afflictions of puerility. The little blind girl no longer had anyone to look after her but her mother; it had been necessary to dismiss the domestics, to take up residence in a mansard and reduce themselves to living on the income of a small pension bequeathed to Marie by her grandmother. The entire fortune that Diane had brought to Salomon as a dowry had been annihilated.

"Alas, other despairs and further opprobrium were still reserved for the unfortunate woman.

"One night, Diane, after having waited in vain for her husband all day, gazed sadly, by moonlight, in the direction of the laboratory that Salomon had rented about two hundred paces from the mansard that now served as lodging for those whose happiness had long been assured by their fortune. Suddenly, there was a horrible noise; it was the laboratory that had exploded. The debris launched by the unparalleled explosion fell back over a wide area, not without causing numerous accidents. Seven or eight passers-by were injured and a child whose skull was fractured by a large stone died.

"In the midst of the frightful disorder caused by such an event, Diane, distraught, ran to the scene of the disaster in order at least to receive the last sigh of her husband, whom she expected to find the first victim of the explosion. To her great surprise, she found him uninjured, occupied in collecting his scattered papers. Such composure exasperated the people who had witnessed the event; the words 'sorcerer' and 'a soul sold to the Devil' were circulating in the crowd, and did not take long to be shouted aloud, with rage. People armed themselves with stones and hurled hem at Salomon; he was attacked like a wild beast. The imminence of the peril returned his reason and presence of mind. He understood that flight alone could procure him a chance of salvation, and he therefore ran away before the furies that were pursuing him, crying: 'Death to the sorcerer! Death to the murderer!'

"He would not have escaped their range without Diane's help. She snatched the cloak that was covering her husband's shoulders, placed Salomon's hat on her own head and exposed herself, for more than ten minutes, to the risks of the stones that people thought they were throwing at the apothecary. When she supposed that she had allowed the fugitive time to get out of the city and find a safe refuge, she threw the cloak down at her feet and informed the people of their error.

"Even the most frantic were touched by such devotion, and permitted Diane to leave. Some, full of admiration and pity for the poor woman, even resolved to make sure of her husband's escape because of his wife's courage. Not only did they reunite her with Salomon, who had taken refuge with one of his relatives in a house on the outskirts of the city, but they even procured them horses in order to leave Rouen and go to Paris; for henceforth, the man who had been for such a long time the idol of the citizens of the former city could no longer expect to find there anything but the hatred of his compatriots and the rigors of the law.

"The exiles' journey was long and difficult. It was in the midst of the most bitter rigors of winter that Salomon reached Paris with his wife and daughter. Diane had taken off her warmest garments in order to wrap Marie in them; after which, she had placed her on the horse whose bridle she held, walking in the snow and icy mud of the road. Her husband traveled placidly on his horse, which he allowed to wander almost at will. His head slumped over his chest, entirely devoted to his habitual meditation, one might have thought that he had no traveling companions, and certainly not that those companions were his wife and daughter.

"Finally, they arrived in Paris; they went to lodge in one of the poorest houses in the Faubourg Saint-Antoine. There, Salomon resumed—or, rather, continued—the course of his unknown speculations, and Diane set to work to earn bread for her child and her husband, while waiting for a devoted friend, one of Salomon's former apprentices, to send them the few items of furniture and linen and a little money that they had left in Rouen.

"Almost a month when by before the interrupted navigation of the Seine permitted that consignment. Finally, it arrived to offer a little relief to the wretched family. Salomon was only attentive to and sensible of one thing: the possession of the copper cooking-pot. He took possession of it with transports of joy such as he had not shown for a long time, and went to shut himself away with the object, as if he had rediscovered a treasure.

"Poverty is like gangrene; it devours those it strikes. Hardly a year had gone by before Diane was obliged to sell her linen, her furniture and even her own bed. Exhausted by fatigue and by sleepless nights, she ended up falling ill. Salomon paid no heed to that, and did not discontinue his solitary studies.

"One evening, Marie came, groping her way, to call him and beg him to come to their mother, whose suffering was worse. He promised to do so, but did not keep his promise. The blind child made further pleas. In the end, he gave in, regretfully, left the loft that he had adopted as an abode, and went to Diane.

"She held out her hand to him. 'I'm dying, Salomon,' she said.

"Those terrible words returned Salomon to real life he gazed desperately at his wife. The unfortunate woman had spoken only too truly; she was dying; death had already marked her with its inexorable seal.

"'Salomon,' she went on, 'I'm dying; I've suffered a great deal these last five years, and I've suffered for you. Well, I shall die blessing you, if you'll promise me to renounce insensate projects to take care of your daughter, as the duties of a father ordain.'

"Salomon took Diane's hand and kissed it, sobbing.

"'Look at what you have done! You've destroyed our happiness and our livelihood, for the sake of dreams impossible of realization. You've expelled from our home fortune, love, the joys of paternity, and even honor. Starvation is threatening us, the law is pursuing us; our child, blind, will remain alone in the world, without anyone to guide her, although she can't walk without guidance. Blindness makes it impossible for her to do any kind of work, and she's devoid of bread to nourish her. She won't even be able to beg, for seduction and outrage would mercilessly afflict her youth and beauty. Salomon, in the name of the tenderness of old, in the name of our child, for the salvation of your soul, listen to me. Swear to me to devote the rest of your life and your thoughts to your daughter; don't trouble the last moments of a dying woman. Burn all those books that are troubling your reason, perverting your judgment and hardening your heart. Have pity on our child, Salomon! I implore you with my hands joined.'

"'Forgive me, forgive me!' Salomon cried, his voice punctuated by bitter sobs. 'Forgive me, Diane, for it's me who ought to be dying of shame. Curse me in the Heaven to which you will rise! Demand of the sovereign judge all the rigor of his vengeance, if my thought ever strays again, just once, toward the projects of glory and invention that only the Evil Spirit could have suggested to me. I only want to live from now on to expiate my sins and protect our child; I swear that to you on the salvation of my soul. May God deprive me of my share of paradise if I succumb again even once!'

"'God hears you and will give you the strength to keep your promises! God bless you!' Diane murmured, with her tremulous lips.

"She reached out to Marie, who was weeping at her bedside, took her hand and put it in Salomon's, and then stammered a few more confused words; they were prayers for her husband and her child.

"Gradually, her voice was extinguished; the murmur ceased, and nothing more was heard."

Throughout that part of his story, Jean had negligently refilled his glass several times; it was with the same negligence and without perceiving it, so to speak, that he had emptied it. I was not without anxiety, for the carbonic acid contained in the champagne might have aggravated the storyteller's unhealthy condition and thrown him into one of those terrible fits of which no description can give any but an incomplete idea. I therefore picked up the bottle that had not yet been opened and placed it close to me in order to put it out of Jean's range.

Jean darted a mocking glance at me; then, seizing a carafe half-full of water, he emptied it almost entirely into his glass. However, he only drank a small mouthful, which he spat out disdainfully, and contented himself thereafter with slightly moistening his lips.

"It's very late," he said then. "My head feels fatigued; good night, Monsieur."

"What about the end of your story?"

"It's in that bottle," he said, pointing to the champagne. "Do you think that my suffering brain, devoid of strength, can find any energy other than by artificial means? You're afraid of making me ill; don't worry—far from it; I think this little debauchery will be salutary for me."

He took possession of the last bottle of champagne; I did not have the courage to take it out of his hands.

Jean cut the brass wire circling the bottle; the cork popped out with explosive force and hit the ceiling.

At the same moment, a frightful storm burst; all of a sudden, lightning seared our eyes and a clap of thunder resounded so terribly that we felt the commotion in our breasts. I shall never forget the glance full of bravado and despair that the drinker darted at the heavens. A painter would have wanted to give a fallen demon that expression of simultaneous suffering and rage.

He remained silent for a few moments; I watched him fighting against the storm that was suffocating his lungs. Vertigo produced by the carbonic acid was spinning before his eyes, entwining its invisible grip around his forehead, where I could see large blue veins swelling. Several times he tried to speak, but his voice always expired in a murmur on his convulsive lips.

Finally, by a superhuman effort, he overcame the sensations to which he had initially succumbed, and resumed his story.

The words emerged with difficulty from his mouth, slowly and one by one, as Laubardemont describes those of the possessed of Loudun.[33]

"Salomon had sworn an oath at his wife's deathbed; he was determined to keep it no matter what the cost; that was his duty. While the corpse was still lying on the bed, where it had rendered its soul, Marie's father went to take from his laboratory all the papers that he found there; the threw them into the fireplace, which devoured them, and the flames of which

---

[33] Jean-Martin de Laubardemont (1590-1653), a state councillor appointed by Cardinal Richelieu, was the magistrate charged with the prosecution of the priest Urbain Grandier, who was charged with bewitching a county of nuns in the town of Loudun, convicted and burned. The French Romantics were fascinated by the affair; Alfred de Vigny incorporated an account of it into his novel *Cinq-Mars* (1826); Alexandre Dumas waxed lyrical about it in *Crimes célèbres* (1839-41); and Jules Michelet retold the story in *La Sorcière* (1862). It is now best known in England as the subject of Aldous Huxley's lay *The Devils of Loudun* (1953) and Ken Russell's film *The Devils* (1971).

threw their bright red radiance on to Diane's face. Then he passed his hands over his brow as if to rip out a thought entirely, wiped away a tear, and went to kneel next to the blind girl who was praying beside her mother's mortal remains.

"The next day, he gave the witch's cooking-pot to a carpenter in exchange for a coffin.

"A week later, Salomon was fulfilling the humble functions of an assistant laborer in the establishment of a local druggist. He spent entire days compressing pills and making up preparations too difficult and too fatiguing for the merchant.

"He had been reduced to that extremity because everywhere he went to ask for work, people had sent him away without even wanting to listen to him. A parliamentary clerk had agreed to give him a few copies to transcribe, but when he had seen is new clerk's poor handwriting, he had dismissed him immediately. Like the son of the king in the fable, Salomon, who possessed a superior intelligence and whose knowledge was immense, found himself reduced to working with his hands to earn his daily bread.

"Unfortunately, those hands were unskillful, and above all, weak. Not only had the unfortunate father gravely impaired his health, but the druggist did not take long to perceive that a robust domestic would be able to do his work better. One evening, he told the pale and sickly man, whom the lightest tasks caused to sweat blood and wear out his arms, that he could no longer employ him.

"Salmon begged him to revoke an order that would reduce his daughter to the most absolute deprivation. He begged him, implored him, threw himself at his feet. Moved, the man gave him a thirty-sou coin and said to him: 'I'd rather give you alms than have you spoil my merchandise with your clumsiness.'

"Misery had crushed Salomon's heart too thoroughly for it to rebound in revolt against that insulting charity. He picked the coin out of the mud, went to a local bakery, bought a loaf of bread and took it to his daughter.

"For a week, they both lived on the proceeds of that thirty-sou piece. On the last two days Salomon only pretended to eat; he hid his bread under his coat and gave it to his daughter the next day.

"Cold was then raging with extreme violence; a glacial draught blew relentlessly and pitilessly through the poorly-sealed attic in which the two unfortunates lived. One morning, alas, it was necessary to quit that miserable refuge; they were thrown out pitilessly, and with violence. The owner had wearied of lodging strangers who had not paid him two sous for a year.

"Salmon linked arms with his daughter and wandered at random through the streets of Paris. That night, Marie had shelter and bread because her father begged and was able to extract a few sous from the charity of passers-by.

"The next day, all those to whom they addressed themselves rejected them mercilessly. He was, in any case, a poor beggar; after the first refusal he jibbed and was unable to be importunate.

"Marie prayed to God and said in her prayers: 'Lord, won't you put an end to my agony? Won't you finally reunite me with my mother in paradise?'

"She interrupted her plaints when she heard her father coming, In spite of herself, however, her hands pressed her breast convulsively and her extinct eyes were raised toward the heavens.

"Salomon remained beside his child, silent and motionless, until nightfall.

"When night came, he got up, went into a bakery, took a loaf of bread from the counter, and brought it to Marie. 'Here's some bread, my child,' he said, 'take it.'

"Marie made no reply. He put the bread on the blind girl's knees. The little girl's hands did not move.

"He leaned over her. Her eyes were closed. He put his hand on her heart; it was no longer beating.

"He took the bread and went back to the bakery. 'Here,' he said. 'I stole a loaf of bread a little while ago. I'm bringing it back.'

"The baker took pity on him and told him to keep it, as alms.

"Salomon started to laugh bitterly. 'Alms! Alms for me! I've begged and I've stolen for my daughter; my daughter is dead; I no longer want anything from the shameful pity of men.'

"'Your daughter is dead,' said the baker, who was a compassionate man, and lived in accordance with the Gospel. "May God give you the strength to withstand such a rude blow."

"Salomon drew closer to him. 'Listen to me,' he said. 'If you will do what I ask, there will emerge from my lips, and my fear, full of maledictions, a word of blessing for you. Give the cadaver of my child a shroud and a coffin.'

"The baker, moved, hastened to go with the poor father to pick up the young girl's cadaver. That same evening, Salomon followed the coffin in which Diane's child as eternally asleep to the church and to the cemetery.

"When the funeral ceremony was over, he shook the hand of the charitable baker and went away. For a long time he wandered aimlessly, oppressed by dolor and making plans to demand shelter from death.

"Prey to those sinister thoughts, he sat down mechanically on a doorstep, and by virtue of an instinctive movement huddled himself up as best he could in order to keep the cold at bay. A kind of dolorous torpor gradually overcame him, until daybreak.

"When he woke up, he saw a housewife emerging from the house next door, with a copper coking-pot in her hand. It was the wife of the carpenter to whom he had given the utensil in exchange for a coffin for Diane. The sight of the diabolical object that had exercised such a fatal influence upon his life suddenly reanimated him.

"'I don't want to die!' he exclaimed. 'Glory, fortune and immortality await me! I can march toward them without shackles; today, I'm free.'

"He stood up, shook his rags, and drew away.

"To see him march with strength and confidence, as if he really were heading toward a goal that he was in haste to reach, no one would have recognized him as the father who had just buried his daughter and the wretch who was dying of starvation. He felt a vigor and a confidence that he had not experienced for a long time. His brain, freed from the iron hand that had been gripping it, formed thoughts full of energy. He had almost recovered the ardor and faith of his youth; one might have thought that a mysterious voice was repeating in his ear: 'Your time of trials is over.'

"He had only taken some two hundred strides when he found that a man had been thrown by his horse in the street and sustained a serious head-injury. Salomon cut through the crowd, reached the gentleman and set about dressing his wound with so much dexterity that everyone recognized his superiority and his expertise, and accorded him the deference that one shows on such occasions to a special individual. The apothecary prescribed the drugs necessary to complete the care he had just given, and offered to take the invalid, who had recovered consciousness, back to his home. That offer was accepted gratefully, and Salomon was accommodated, in the capacity of physician, in the house of the Marquis de Combalet,[34] for it was that nobleman, a favorite of Cardinal Richelieu, to whom Diane's husband had rendered such opportune assistance.

"The Marquis, surprised to discover so much knowledge and intelligence in the man he had found dressed in rags, did not take long to conceive a considerable affection for his

---

[34] Antoine de Beauvoir du Roure, Marquis de Combalet (died 1622), only receives a footnote in French history by virtue of having married Cardinal de Richelieu's niece, a lady-in-waiting to the queen mother, Marie de Medici.

nurse. He did not want to receive care from anyone but Salomon, and refused to give admittance to the physicians that his family summoned. He had no reason to regret that resolution, for two months after his fall he was completely cured.

"One morning, he went into the room that Salomon occupied in his house, close to his sick-room, and found him occupied in writing and drawing bizarre diagrams. 'Master Solomon,' he said, 'I owe you my life; I have to need to tell you how grateful I am and how much affection I have for you. Put a price on your services, therefore; if I cannot repay you in full, at least I can show you that I'm not an ingrate. Speak sincerely, and don't hesitate to open your heart to me. If you care to attach yourself to my household, you'll fulfill my dearest wish and will find in me, not a master, but a friend.'

"Salomon raised his head, cast an eye over his papers, as if he were reluctant to set them aside, and replied distractedly: 'Monseigneur, before long I shall possess fortune and glory. A few more days and I will have completed the design of a machine destined to change the face of the word. Deign, therefore, to grant me a refuge in our house until my work is completely finished, and then obtain me a audience with Monseigneur le Cardinal, and you will have fulfilled all my desires.'

"'I hope to do more for you, my dear Salomon,' the Marquis said. 'I shall see you soon.'

"He went down to the courtyard of the house and found the Marquise, who was waiting for him on the perron. 'Monseigneur,' she said to him, 'your squire tells me that you intend to ride the unruly horse that nearly cost you your life the other day; out of affection for me, don't do that.'

"'That would be weakness,' the Marquis replied. 'It's necessary that I prove to the malicious creature that I'm not afraid of him, and that I'm able to reckon with him. Have no fear, Madame.'

"So saying, he kissed the Marquise and leapt on to the horse. Scarcely had the impetuous beast felt a man on its back than it started kicking and bucking, and exhibiting the greatest fury. The Marquis held firm and true, used the whip and the spurs, struggled, resisted and manipulated the bridle skillfully. After a quarter of a hour, victory finally went to the rider, and the stallion, bathed with sweat, became pliant and docile to the bit, like the calmest of mares.

"Delighted with his triumph, the Marquis turned to the reassured Marquise with a smile, saluted her with his hand, and departed at a gallop.

"Just as he was about to go through the gate of the residence, a domestic, who was holding a cooking-pot, appeared at the end of the street. The sunlight, falling directly upon the copper vessel, was reflected resplendently, producing a dazzling light. At the sight of that glare, which suddenly hurt its eyes, the horse reared up, throwing its rider to the ground, fractured his skull with a kick, and killed him on the spot, before the eyes of the distressed Marquise.

"It did not take long to discover that the copper cauldron that had caused such a great misfortune belonged to Salomon, who had bought it back from the carpenter to whom he had previously sold it. The steward took advantage of that excuse to expel from the house a man whose credit with the Marquis had made him jealous so many times. Salomon did not put up any resistance, and headed for the Cardinal's palace, where he solicited an audience with the Minister, making use of the name of his former protector in attempting to reach the man who held the destiny of France in his hands.

"After long solicitations, he succeeded in obtaining that audience. The Cardinal, who was in pain, and whose struggles with the king had thrown him into one of the nervous commotions that afflicted him so frequently, received Salomon harshly.

"'You've been seeking an audience with me for a month now,' he said, in a low and bitter voice. 'What do you want?'

"'Monseigneur,' Salomon replied, 'I'm the possessor of a secret that might ensure His Very Christian Majesty power over the entire world. Henceforth, vessels will have no more need of sails, and the speed of navigation will be multiplied a hundredfold. Carriages will move without horses.'

"'And what means will you employ to bring about these marvels?'

"'The steam of boiling water.'

"The cardinal picked up a silver whistle from his waist and blew a shrill blast on it. An officer appeared.

"'Since when are madmen allowed access to me!' he exclaimed. 'Throw this man out!'

"'Monseigneur!' cried Salomon. 'In the name of Heaven, don't refuse to listen to me. However impossible they may seem to you, the marvels of which I speak can be executed before your eyes as soon as you wish. My life will answer for the success—take my head as a hostage! Steam is an energetic force.'

"The cardinal made a gesture with his head and Salomon was dragged away.

"Salomon drew his dagger to resist those who had seized him..."

Jean abruptly interrupted himself; his hand extended toward the bottle, but his strength failed him and he fell back into his chair. He tried to speak, but no voice emerged from his lips and he fell like an inert mass at my feet.

I cannot tell you what I experienced then. The thunder was rumbling, the lightning flashing, the rain lashing the windows. A mass of smoke and ashes, whipped up by the wind, suddenly erupted from the fireplace and extinguished my lamp.

I confess that at that moment, a veritable fear took hold of me, and I called for help.

Two attendants came running, and hastened to lavish care on poor Jean—who, in spite of their efforts, remained motionless, as if life had abandoned him.

The two men, realizing that their assistance remained powerless to reanimate the epileptic, carried him to the infirmary.

I spent all night in the most mortal anxiety. Several times I went out to ask the attendant whether the fatal crisis that had struck Jean had lost its violence, but I could not succeeded in gaining entry to the epileptics' section. The rules of Bicêtre expressly forbade any person not on the staff of the establishment to go into its wards by night.

I saw Jean again the next morning. He had resumed his silent and humble behavior.

"Well, Jean," I asked him, "are you feeling much better this morning?"

He hastened to take off his cap to salute, looked at me with a surprised expression, and replied in a voice that was even more respectful than usual: "It happens so often that it's not worth the trouble of talking about it."

"But wasn't last night's crisis more terrible than any other?"

"Last night? Is Monsieur not mistaken? It was in the evening, when I came back to the ward, that the illness struck...but perhaps Monsieur is right. I doubtless had two crises during the day. My poor head is so sick! I can scarcely remember what happened to me an hour ago."

He bent down in order to poke the fire, picked up a broom and set about his humble functions in silence. After which he advanced toward his cauldron and prepared to hoist it on to his shoulder, as usual.

"Couldn't you finish yesterday's story now, Jean?" I said. "I'm very impatient to know how it ends."

He looked at me as if I were speaking a foreign language, about something unknown. He did not seem to understand my question.

"A story?" he repeated.

"Yes—the story of your cauldron."

"Well, my God," he said, "that's a very simple story. The cauldron belonged to a poor madman who lived for fifty years imprisoned in a padded cell at Bicêtre, where he had been thrown on Cardinal Richelieu's orders. Like all madmen, he protested against the order that kept him captive, and claimed to be in possession of his reason. If he could be believed, he knew marvelous secrets that would enable carriages move without horses and give them the rapidity of a bird in flight. Unfortunately, he never failed to add that he was pursued by a curse, that a witch had cast a spell on the copper cauldron found in his home in Paris and brought to Bicêtre with the debris of his possessions, in which his nourishment was now served to him. He begged for someone to take the cauldron away from his cell, and flew into the most violent fits of anger at the refusal or the warders in that matter. Nothing was done about it. He was let alone, and during the fifty years he spent in the asylum, he had that utensil before his eyes.

"However, he had been heard to insist so often, during that half-century, on the deadly properties of the vessel, that after the old man's death, no one wanted to make use of it. Before I arrived here it stayed in a corner, where it did not fail to justify, by way of two or three accidents, its evil renown. Once it fell from a nail on which it had been hung and mortally wounded the head of a kitchen-boy. It was thrown into a cellar, and God known how long it remained there. One day, some children found it, and wanted to make use of it to cook some soup of their own making; four of the children died from verdigris poisoning. When I became an attendant, I saw that the cauldron was still in good condition, and that, in spite of its evil reputation, it could render some service. So I adopted it, half out of incredulity regarding its deadly properties, and half out of superstition. I no longer had anything to fear from death, I told myself, and far from dreading it, I desired it. Perhaps the diabolical cauldron would put an end to my suffering.

"Alas, Monsieur, as you can see, I'm not dead; my hope hasn't been realized and the fatal influence of the cauldron has no effect on me—unless it's responsible for the attacks of epilepsy from which I suffer so frequently, and of which I never showed any symptom before my arrival at Bicêtre. But Monsieur, if that malady has a cause, it's not necessary to accuse that poor piece of copper. Poverty, chagrin and abandonment explain the veritable causes of my suffering too adequately for there to be any need to look for others."

At that moment a bell rang; it was the signal for some service for which Jean was responsible. He picked up the cauldron and ran to his post.

Three or four months went by before I was able to return to Bicêtre. A journey to Flanders had taken me way from Paris for that entire time. On my return, I hastened to go to Bicêtre to shake the hand of my friend Doctor Émile.

I found him in the dissection room, with a cigar in his mouth and a scalpel in his hand, occupied in searching a cadaver for the characteristic signs of cholera, the first symptoms of which had just declared themselves at Bicêtre. He interrupted his lugubrious work to shake my hand; then, indicating the poor object on the marble table, he said: "This poor devil suffered a great deal; the cholera has not inflicted more frightful and crueler dolors on any of its victims." He continued, like a true physician: "There's one curious observation to make; perhaps it's necessary to seek its cause in the subject's epileptic condition."

Turning back to the unfortunate individual who furnished that scientific observation, he continued: "Poor Père Jean— and to think that the man played a brilliant role in the social order, than en entire audience rose to its feet to salute the name of the poet whose play, full of grace and intelligence it had just admired. To think that those hands, so often occupied in the humblest employments, once disposed of the destiny of a king. Napoléon honored that head with his hatred; at the height of his power he remembered the name of that old man in order to pursue him with his vengeance."

"What was that name, then?" I exclaimed.

"Jean Baudrais."

"Jean Baudrais!" I repeated.

"Yes," said Émile. "Yes, events pass so quickly in Paris that those who have been involved in them are soon forgotten, no matter how brightly they shone. Listen, then, and I'll tell you what one of the employees of my establishment told me a little while ago—for like you, I had no idea, until two hours ago that this man was Jean Baudrais.

"In 1769, there was a charming and intelligent young man in Paris, recently married to a young woman of sixteen, whom he loved passionately, and whose grace equaled her angelic sweetness. When that couple, as remarkable for their youth as for their beauty, were seen in public people pointed to them in admiration, and more than once they found themselves surrounded by a crowd; no one at court or in the city was talking about anything but the two beautiful Tourangeaux. Marie-Antoinette wanted to see them, and had them introduced to her; she thanked Jean Baudrais, in the most affable terms, for delightful comedy entitled *L'Allégresse villageoise*, which he had composed to celebrate the dauphin's birth, and did not dismiss them until she had taken off a diamond necklace, which she asked Madame Baudrais to accept.

"Not so many years later, Jean Baudrais was at the Temple. He presided over a dozen municipal functions there. It was the twenty-fourth of January. Having become a member of the commune, he had acquired a measure of popularity by the violence of his demagogic declamations, and no one more worthy that he had been found to supervise the preparations for the frightful drama that was about to take place. Jean Baudrais therefore received from the hand of King Louis XVI that prince's testament, and he countersigned it before handing it to the commune; thus, the name of this poor wretch, who will be thrown into the common grave of a hospital, is attached to one of those eternal monuments of which fearful history can only count two or three examples.

"It was Baudrais, again, who sent the twenty-five louis d'or found in Louis XVI's writing desk to the public treasury. In 1817 a lawsuit was brought against Baudrais by the heirs of Monsieur de Malesherbes, who claimed that sum. He demonstrated by means of irrefutable proofs that it had been handed to the secretarial clerk.

After the king's death, Baudrais, doubtless in recompense for the said functions that he had fulfilled at the Temple, became one of the administrators charged with the supervision of the police. He was denounced in that epoch for being 'too easy' on pretty female petitioners. The truth is that Baudrais always showed compassion to the numerous victims of the Terror; that more than one person owed their liberty to him, and that he often, to his credit, saved victims from the scaffold.

"That benevolence was assessed as weakness and lack of patriotic fervor. Robespierre rendered him destitute and had him thrown in prison. Preparations were being made for his transfer to the Conciergerie and submission to judgment when Robespierre as overthrown and send to the scaffold himself.

"Baudrais was set free, but, although he had nearly perished under the blows of the power that had just collapsed, he was nevertheless set aside. He accepted the obscurity to which he was condemned without overmuch chagrin and fulfilled for some time the humble functions of a justice of the peace in the Cornmarket district. Anxiety was generated nevertheless by his presence in Paris, and he was ordered to embark for Guadeloupe with the title of civil, criminal and appeal judge in commercial matters. He obeyed, resignedly, embarked and arrived at his post in 1797.

"Three years later, although he had not left the island and was uninvolved with any political movement, he received his destitution and an order to leave immediately for Cayenne. Napoléon, who nourished sentiments of hatred against him for reasons that remain unknown, had taken his revenge, like a true Corsican. On his orders, Baudrais had been included among the one hundred and seventy-three people accused of complicity in the affair of the infernal machine.[35]

---

[35] In December 1800, in the days of the Consulate, a Royalist plot was formed to blow up the First Consul Napoléon Bonaparte's carriage with a bomb manufactured by an Italian engineer. The blast killed a number of people, but an error of timing meant that it missed its intended target. Napoléon initially refused to believe that Royalists were responsible, blaming Jacobins instead, and had 130 "suspects" summarily departed, none of whom had anything to do with the plot; the truth was subsequently uncovered by the prefect of the Parisian police and the redoubtable minister of police Joseph Fouché, but

"In spite of the injustice of that condemnation, it was necessary to obey. Baudrais was deported to Cayenne. He remained there for several years, after which he found a means to escape and flee to the United States. There he lived for thirteen years, working with his hands. He fulfilled the functions of a cashier in a bank. He would have preferred to be employed as a clerk, but his handwriting, remarkably irregular and almost illegible, never permitted him to do so. He therefore spent his days relentlessly tramping the streets of New York, with a heavy bag on his shoulder, taking bonds whose due date had arrived from institution to institution. In the evening, when he returned to is mansard, he worked ardently on the composition of a very mediocre poem, to which he founded great hopes of fortune and renown.

"In 1817 he resolved to return to France, of which Napoléon's fall permitted him to dream, Regnaud de Saint-Jean-d'Angely and Réal,[36] exiled in their turn, who had found their old friend in America, clubbed together to give Baudrais the means to carry out this plan, and he arrived in Paris in the early months of 1818. The majority of his former colleagues were in government, and he had recourse to them, but all doors, including those of people who owed their lives to him, remained closed to a firmer member of the commune. Publishers showed their disdain for the poet's manuscript. That latter disappointment was perhaps even more dolorous than the former.

"Meanwhile, his resources were exhausted. Poverty had already arrived sand starvation was approaching. Madame Baudrais fell ill and had to go into the hospital. Then all courage abandoned the poor old man. Separated from the woman

Napoléon did not allow the ex-Jacobins he had deported to return when he realized that he had jumped to the wrong conclusion.

[36] Michael-Louis-Étiene Regnaud de Saint-Jean d'Angely (1761-1819) was one of Napoléon's most trusted aides, and was, in consequence, exiled under the Restoration. Pierre-François Réal (1757-1834) replaced Fouché as Napoléon's minister of police; he too was exiled under the Restoration.

who, for so many years, had courageously shared his ill fortune, he fell sick himself and was picked up one morning in a Paris street, at the foot of a boundary-marker, where he had fallen down, exhausted by need and fever. The minister of police had him sent to Bicêtre, among the charity cases. You know the rest, my friend. Jean Baudrais resigned himself courageously to fulfill the functions of a humble ward orderly, and did not recoil from any of the repugnant aspects of that employment. He could, at that price, earn a little money, which he could send to his wife, from whom he was separated, and whom he went to see every week at the Salpêtrière, where she had been placed."

The doctor extended his hand over the cadaver by way of an oratorical gesture, and added: "This is the denouement of the drama—a hospital amphitheater!"

At that moment, attendants came in with a coffin. They had come to remove the mortal remains of Jean Baudrais, in order to take them to the cemetery.

One of the men bumped his leg on the copper cauldron, which was on the ground next to the table. He put his hand to his foot with the most expressive evidence of pain.

A fortnight after that, Dr. Émile came to see me in Paris. I reproached him affectionately for having gone such a long time without visiting me.

"It's not my fault," he replied, shaking my hand. I had to look after a poor fellow on my staff. He had a wound on his leg, insignificant in appearance; the negligence he showed on caring for it led to an inflammation; the inflammation caused ulceration and gangrene. In brief, I had to amputate the leg the day before yesterday."

"Did it go well?"

"He's gone to join Jean Baudrais," he said, with a sigh.

"What strange fatality is attached to the cauldron!" I exclaimed.

Émile shrugged his shoulders. "There you go," he said. "You poets seek the extraordinary everywhere; do you think the cauldron is bewitched? My poor fellow, examine with a little attention all the events in the life of any man, and you'll see a similar chain of fatalities therein. Don't you know that King Gustave III of Sweden died because his secretary broke his spectacles and couldn't read his master a letter warning him about a conspiracy. Go back from cause to cause and you'll arrive..."

"At God," I interjected.

"That's the conclusion to which I wanted to lead you," the doctor replied, bowing respectfully before the august name that I had pronounced."

Translator's afterword

Salomon de Caus (1576-1626) was a Huguenot, and, in consequence, spent much of his life outside France, although he did work for Louis XIII as an engineer and architect; he never lived in Rouen. In a book published in 1615 Caus described a steam-driven pump, but it was not a new invention. The idea that it entitled him to be considered the true inventor of the steam engine was popularized by the 19th century scientist and statesman François Arago, but the contention is highly dubious. Thus the entire story-within-the-story told in "The Cauldron of Bicêtre" is a pure work of the imagination— as, indeed, the frame story ultimately represents it to be, although that narrative move might seem a trifle pusillanimous to some readers.

The biography of Jean Baudrais (1749-1832) summarized by "Dr. Émile" is broadly accurate, except for the details of his death. He did, indeed, die in Bicêtre, of cholera, but did so three years before the story is set; he was admitted to Bicêtre because of his advanced age and his identity was not unknown to the staff there. He did not suffer from epilepsy, and there is no evidence that Napoléon had anything more against him than he had against the other 129 former Jacobins that he banished after the affair of the infernal machine.

The witch's cauldron is, unsurprisingly, a pure invention.

THE SECOND SUN

If there is a charming place in the world to take the waters, it is surely Spa. One finds in combination there all the picturesque qualities of wild nature and all the comforts of the most exquisite research. One can be a poet in the morning and an epicure in the evening—and only a few hours on the railway separates Spa from Paris.

Here is the approximate genre of hygienic treatment followed by one of the so-called invalids who found himself at Spa fifteen years ago. A poor writer, pursued during the winter by balls, dramatic spectacles, study and the social whirlwind, in order to cure himself he needed pure air, verdant countryside, undemanding distractions and perhaps, strictly speaking, a little water extracted from a mineral spring.

Thus, waking up late in the morning, he roamed the countryside, visited the magnificent manor of Justenville, sat down in the shade of the ruins of the old Château de Franchement, and always came back from these artistic excursions fairly early, so as not to miss the pleasures of the evening.

Among the brilliant and joyful host that gathered at Spa, an old phantom of sorts was seen wandering, whose status as an invalid no one could conscientiously contest. Lazarus emerged from the tomb could surely not have displayed a more livid and emaciated face. Sometimes he followed fervently the prescriptions of the doctor who presides over the waters and seemed to be clinging to life with all his strength. At other times he threw himself into the most dangerous excesses, drinking like four Englishmen—not water, but wine—consuming his nights gambling, and passing disdainfully by the fuming waves of the fountain of Pouchon.

The irregularity of the hygienic habits of the stranger was reproduced in his social habits. Sometimes he stayed alone and apart, and scarcely replied to the servants who asked for his instructions. At other times he was gracious, assiduous, amiable and witty with everyone, and caused the strangeness of his appearance to be forgotten by means of the section of his speech and the melodious softness of his voice.

One day, when the Parisian *feuilletonist* was walking past the spring of Sauvenière, preoccupied by some novel or other whose idea he was developing, the stranger suddenly accosted him.

"Monsieur," he said, without any other preamble, "If you're looking for a subject to write about, I'll give you one that would, I think, lend itself to dramatic development in a singular fashion. Sit down here, if you please, and lend me your ear.

"The story opens in Copenhagen..."

The man of letters found the opening sufficiently original and unexpected for it to be worth the trouble of listening to the story. The old invalid, who expressed himself quite fluently in French, collected his thoughts for a few moments, placed his hands on his knees, and fixed the strange gaze of his large green-tinted eyes upon his auditor.

The story, as I have just told you, Monsieur, begins in Copenhagen. No city in Europe, especially if one considers its population, has a greater number of colleges than Copenhagen. In 1479, Christian I founded an *alma universitas* with statutes drawn up by the Archbishop of Uppsala, endowments of land and various privileges. Christian II enriched it with wealth confiscated from the clergy. Christian VII increased the number of professors and modified the statutes in such a way as to rejuvenate them and render them useful and practicable. Today, numerous royal or private foundations give bursaries to two hundred pupils; a cloister serves as lodging for a hundred others, who also receive free books and food.

The University of Copenhagen has a dozen extraordinary professors and sixteen ordinary ones; the rank and salary of the former correspond to the rank and salary of a major, without counting the four écus paid annually and personally by the majority of the pupils that they instruct.

Doctor Magnussen had been the Extraordinary Professor of Philosophy at the University of Copenhagen for nineteen years, eleven months and two days when he fell gravely ill and died.

The death of that man, one of the most knowledgeable in Denmark, whose modest and laborious life had been as honorable and pure before God as before men, left his widow and his daughter Stierna in a state verging on poverty. He bequeathed them nothing for a heritage by his library, a few scientific instruments, a little house in the suburbs and a sum of three or four hundred écus, which would give them an income of a hundred livres at the very most.

In order to live, the two women had been counting on the pension to which the widows of professors were entitled after twenty years service on the part of their husbands. Alas, those twenty years were twenty-eight days short of accomplishment, and the rector, after consulting the other professors and the minister himself, declared to Madame Magnussen with tears in his eyes that the letter of the law had to be rigorously observed, and that she would not be inscribed on the pension list.

The widow received this sad response to her application with more resignation that she had expected of herself. She accepted her fate courageously and resolved to live on her industry and handiwork.

This proved more difficult to do than she thought. In vain she asked everyone she knew for embroidery work, or even dressmaking, but no one wanted to entrust a lady with work that professional seamstresses would inevitably do better and at a lower price. The resource on which the widow and her daughter were counting was therefore lacking; they decided, as a last resort, to take advantage of their house, and to let the dead man's bedroom and library to two boarders.

It cost Madame Magnussen a great deal to introduce strangers into her home in this way, and to become, in a way, their servant, but she was able to put so much dignity and noble simplicity into the manner in which she carried out her humble duties, that she only seemed more worthy of consideration and respect. Her first guests were, in any case, persons attached to the University and thus, so to speak friends.

One of them was an old Extraordinary Professor who taught Theology, the other a young man appointed, by virtue of the modifications caused by the death of Dr. Magnussen, to the Ordinary chair of Medicine. His name was Bertel Granh, and did not take long to obtain pardon from the widow for his twenty-six years, thanks to his correct conduct, the mildness of his mores and his passionate love of study. He only came down from his room at meal-times, said a few kind words to Madame Magnussen, bowed timidly to Stierna, and, on leaving the table, returned to his scientific labor—unless it was a holiday, and he was invited to take tea in company with his old colleague and two or three friends of the professor's widow.

A year after her husband's death, Madame Magnussen fell dangerously ill. Dr. Bertel Granh lavished his care upon her, so devotedly and so expertly that he succeeded in warding off the fever that had put the poor woman's life in jeopardy. The recovery of the convalescent was celebrated by a family feast. Stierna embroidered a tobacco-pouch for Dr. Granh, and the latter resumed his solitary and laborious life as before.

In the meantime, the old Extraordinary Professor completed the twenty years that gave him the right to retire from the University, and he resolved to spend the days that remained to him in the village where he had been born. The loss of the boarder was a significant matter in Madame Magnussen's household, raising the serious question of how he might be replaced. Bertel, when consulted, proposed a new professor, a childhood friend, who had come to teach medicine in one of the University's three Ordinary Chairs. Ole Matthiesen thus came to occupy the room that had fallen vacant, and was not long delayed, like his friend, in gaining the affection of their hostess.

Good fortune seemed to have returned in full to the widow's house, and her prayers thanked God every day for the consolations he deigned to accord her; a mother would not have been happier and more contented in the midst of her children than she was in the company of the two young men. Stierna lived alongside them as if she were their sister; she supervised the bleaching of their linen, put her care and pride into keeping it in good condition, and the last thing in the world she would have wanted was to leave them the least concern regarding their material life. You should have seen her in the morning, in her little corset and a short skirt, with her lovely arms bare, putting the cravats and vests she had just bleached out to dry on the washing-line in the courtyard, and hastening to make breakfast as soon as the cathedral clock struck seven-thirty. The two professors never had to wait a minute for their first meal, and they set off for the University afterwards with their arms fraternally linked, not without having received a maternal greeting from Madame Magnussen and a smile from Stierna's rosy lips that said: "Au revoir!"

When they came back at midday, the young woman had replaced her pretty morning garb with a dress that was simple, but did justice to the suppleness of her figure and left the smooth contour of her swan-like neck all its grace and purity. Ordinarily, she knotted her blonde hair with ashy gleams on top of her head, which thus left uncovered a forehead as white as ivory, on which an angelic serenity was ensconced. The large near-black lashes that veiled her blue eyes gave her naïve and noble physiognomy an expression of ineffable candor that had nothing terrestrial about it. That glint of another world, moreover, was evident in her entire person; her feet did not seem to be made for trampling earthly dust; her hands, before which Thorwaldsen[37] would have knelt, retained a divine whiteness in spite of her domestic chores; finally, one could not hear her vibrant and melodious voice without being moved. Everything—including her name, Stierna, which

---

[37] The Danish sculptor Bertel Thorwaldsen (1779-1844).

means *star* in Danish—concurred in rendering that harmony of grace and celestial virginity more complete and irresistible.

To see the two young professors going to the University, arm in arm, knowing that they had been childhood friends and were living under the same roof, one would naturally have believed them to be united by the most tender amity and the most absolute confidence. That was not the case, however. Under the appearances of a cordial fraternity, they lived more isolated from one another than if they had been separated by a great distance. Always ready to exchange the little services of which they might mutually have need, to settle a bill, to lend a book or to explain the obscure meaning of a difficult passage, they had never felt the need to say an affectionate word or to deposit in one another's hearts the slightest intimate thought. Grave and melancholy during meals, scarcely raising their eyes toward Stierna, they only spoke to her in order to reply to her questions; Matthiesen never showed her more intimacy than Granh, and Granh made every effort never to cross the respectful limits at which Matthiesen stopped.

Madame Magnussen and Stierna put no difference into their affection and their conduct with regard to the two lodgers—but in each of them, that fashion of acting was natural, while in the two young men it resulted from real calculation, tacit convention and a set purpose that would have been evident to souls less naïve and confident than those of the professors widow and her daughter.

For two entire years, nothing changed, at least in appearance, in the relationships between these four individuals—except that Ole and Bertel became increasingly somber, and an amicable reproach from Madame Magnussen or an affectionate reprimand from Stierna could not always succeed in restoring a little serenity to their brows.

The young woman and her mother attributed this sadness to the fatigue of study. As for the two professors, neither of them was unaware of the true cause of their mutual and somber depression. Each of them had read his comrade's heart. However careful they were not to meet one another's eyes, hazard occasionally brought the glances of hatred that they darted at one another into collision.

One night, Ole Matthiesen, who could not sleep, had got out of bed and tried to distract himself with study, that opium which, perhaps better than any other, can numb the passions, suspend thought and daze the mind by means of intoxicating vertigo. Absorbed in his reading, he suddenly shivered, for the door opened abruptly and Berthel's pale and somber face appeared.

"We can't go on living like this," said the latter. "Don't you agree, Ole Matthiesen?"

"Yes, Berthel Granh," Ole replied, getting to his feet to take down two pistols that were hanging on the wall. What you've just said, I've been thinking for a long time. When you came in, I was wondering whether I ought to go find you. The death of one of us, that's what's required."

"Listen to me, Ole—a duel would put the whole city in turmoil. The survivor would be lost forever, forced to renounce his title of professor, obliged to flee Demark or submit to the rigor of the law. He would only be satisfied in his hatred—and we want more than that, don't we. Ole?"

"I understand you, Bertel. Yes, let the hazards of chance decide between us. The one who is not favored must die, but die in secret, without anyone knowing his fate, without anyone in the world being able to discover what has become of him."

"That's what I wanted to propose to you. Very well, pick up that Bible and that dagger I see in your belt. Here's mine, for we've been wearing daggers for a year. In a few seconds, the cathedral bells will chime midnight. At the moment when the last chime begins to sound, we'll each bury our blade in the pages of the book. The one who picks out the letter closest to the beginning of the alphabet will dispose of the destiny of the other."

They waited for a few moments in silence, their eyes lowered and their hearts pounding; then midnight began to chime. At the final stroke, they slid the daggers between the pages of the holy volume, profaned by their sanguinary pact.

Each one search avidly for the letter picked out by his adversary.

"A D!" cried Bertel.

"You have a B," Ole replied.

A mortal silence fell between the two enemies. Ole was the first to break it. "So be it," he murmured, in a low hoarse voice. "I will keep my word, and you shall never hear mention of me again. How much time will you give me?"

"Three days."

"That's more than I'll need." Ole added, with bitter irony: "You're generous, Bertel—let me be."

Bertel went back to his room, his heart gripped by an iron hand. He felt a thousand times more miserable hand before. Far from soothing the distress he was suffering, the loss of Ole added to its harsh violence. He wanted to go back to his old friend and release him from his fatal promise, but he found the other's door locked, and when he knocked and begged him to open it, not only did he receive no response, but Madame Magnussen, woken up by the unaccustomed noise came running, hastily clad in a dressing-gown, to ask anxiously whether Bertel felt ill. The latter, disconcerted, admitted an indisposition, and was obliged to resign himself to drinking strong herbal tea and submitting to the care of the worthy and obstinate woman until the moment when he could, without implausibility, assure her that he was no longer feeling poorly and that his illness had dissipated. Only then did Madame Magnussen go back to bed, congratulating herself on the success of her cure, and not without admiring more than ever the marvelous virtue of centaury[38] tea for curing stomach cramps and nervous spasms.

The next day, Ole and Bertel went to the University arm in arm, as usual. They did not exchange a single word, but that often happened, especially when one of them had an important lesson to prepare.

---

[38] *Centaurium erythraea*, an herb of the gentian family.

When Ole came back at midday, he found a letter; it had arrived during his absence. He opened it, and as soon as he had cast his eyes over is contents, he manifested an excessive joy.

"Good news!" he cried. "I'm rich now! A distant relative has left me a considerable fortune: a hundred thousand écus. I have to leave tomorrow morning for Holstein, where my new domains are located. I swear that I shall only have one regret in leaving Copenhagen—the pain of leaving friends like you, Madame Magnussen and Mademoiselle Stierna; you too, my dear Bertel—give me the pleasure of employing with you, before leaving, the language of a brother.

"I will write my resignation as professor, Bertel; you shall hand it to the Rector yourself, begging him to excuse me for the precipitation of my abrupt departure. You will inform him of the necessity that obliges me to leave Copenhagen immediately. I shall not take any luggage; that will permit me to go more quickly. Then I shall exchange a poor life for another—a life brilliant with pleasures, no doubt. I want to make legacies and write the testament of my agonizing poverty. Madame Magnussen will inherit my two sets of silver cutlery; Mademoiselle Stierna will accept this ring that my mother gave me; and Bertel shall have all my books, for which I shall henceforth have no further use!"

He said this with so much gaiety and frank folly, that even Bertel wondered whether Ole's supposed fortune might be real.

"To table!" Ole went on. "To table! Let Mademoiselle Stierna serve us her best preserves; let French wine be brought out of the cellar, as on high holidays! Is not the great news of my fortune and my liberty a celebration for us, my friends?"

They sat down at the table, and when the meal was over, and the two women had clinked glasses with the traveler, the latter offered a large glass of brandy to Bertel.

"How pale you are, friend," he said. "What? The one who is staying is sad, while the one who is going away rejoices? Away with tears and grief! Let us embrace, brother, and say farewell."

As he said that, he kissed Bertel on the cheeks, then hugged Madame Magnussen. Stierna, who was emotional, came forward and presented her forehead to Ole's lips. All the young man's false gaiety collapsed then; tears filled his eyes, sobs punctuated his voice and he almost fainted. He struggled visibly against that cruel emotion, but he soon mastered it, brushed the beautiful child's hair with his lips, and went away precipitately.

Having arrived at the extremity of the suburb of Copenhagen, he stopped, waved his handkerchief in a gesture of farewell, and disappeared.

He had been out of sight for a long time, but Bertel was still standing on the doorstep, motionless, pale and exhausted.

"What a nice young man!" murmured Madame Magnussen. "And to think that we'll never see him again!"

"We'll see him again!" cried Bertel. "I'll run after him; I want to stop him from carrying his fatal journey to its conclusion."

He had already set forth when he heard Stierna sobbing, and saw that the young woman's cheeks were streaming with tears.

"It's too late!" he said, stopping. "The carriage is carrying him away along the Holstein road."

Either by virtue of fatigue or emotion, the old man interrupted his narrative momentarily, but he resumed it in these terms.

After Ole's departure, Madame Magnussen's house was overtaken by a profound sadness. Be it understood that the house did not lose its gaiety, for it had been very rare for the four people previously inhabiting it to have emerged from the melancholy habits that two of them owed to the loss of a father and a husband, and the others to the passions that were tormenting them, but it lost its movement and its life. Bertel proposed to the widow that he should take over, for his own use, the room left empty by Matthiesen's absence; he offered as a pretext the impossibility of devoting himself, in his small cell, to the studies in physics that he intended to undertake. In reality, his sole objective was to prevent any other person from coming to live under the same roof as Stierna.

By virtue of a seemingly-inexplicable contradiction, however, he had never been less inclined to seek the young woman's company. He even seemed to be avoiding her, and let entire days go by without addressing a word to her. Sometimes, nevertheless, the naïve young woman would catch sight of Granh's gaze furtively attached to her, without her being able to explain or understand what motives brightened that gaze with a dark and almost sinister fire. At times she wondered anxiously whether the departure of his friend might have disturbed the young man's mind, for he was subject to strange fits that seemed not far from madness. At table, he forgot to put the food into his mouth; he let his pale head slump on to his breast, and it was necessary for Madame Magnussen to call him by name three or four times before extracting him from that waking sleep. At night, he was heard wandering around his room, and opening the window to spend entire hours gazing at the sky. He often wept, yielding to fits of despair, and Ole's name escaped his lips convulsively.

One morning, he came down so pale and disfigured that Stierna's heart was moved to profound compassion. She went straight up to the young man, and stopped him when he tried to go around her and go outside.

"Don't run away from me like that, Dr. Bertel," the gentle creature said, in her ineffable voice. "I need to talk to you. For a long time now, you no longer talk to me; you seem to be avoiding me. Have I offended you unwittingly? If so, tell me, in order that I can avoid committing the same fault again. Above all, forgive me, for I deeply regret having injured you."

"You haven't offended me at all, Stierna. If I no longer speak to you, if I avoid you, it's because I feel unworthy to address you, ashamed to soil you with my presence."

"What do you mean, Monsieur Bertel? For the sake of the friendship that my mother and I have for you, put an end to this sad mystery—explain it."

"When you know, Stierna, it will be you who turns away from my presence, you who will no longer want to see or hear me."

"Me, Bertel? The person who has lived close to you for so many years? The person who loves you like a brother?"

"Like a brother, you say? Well, if that brother had committed a crime, would you not expel him from your presence forever?"

"A crime! Oh, that's not possible!"

"And yet I have committed a crime! Blood soils my hands! I'm a murderer."

"Oh, be quiet! Be quiet! I'm afraid. Let me go away."

"You shall hear me out now, Stierna. Now that you've forced me to open the abyss, your gaze shall penetrate its depths. Listen, then! I loved a young woman; another also loved her…I staked my life against that of my rival. I won; he has killed himself."

"Horror! Horror!"

"Don't you want to know who that young woman is, Stierna?"

"Oh no! Don't tell me. Let me go!"

"That young woman is named Stierna Magnussen."

"Take back those fatal words, Bertel—take them back, I beg you on my knees. See my anxiety, my despair! Tell me that you're playing with me, that all this is nothing but a cruel game! I'd be your accomplice. For me, someone would shed blood! For me, someone would commit murder! Oh, something more frightful still! An unfortunate has been reduced to suicide! He has lost his body and soul at the same time! Tell me that it isn't true!"

"It's true."

"It's true, and you haven't yet fled this place? Father, in the Heaven where you reside, your gaze must be turned away from me that such shame should afflict your house and soil your child! Back, Bertel! Back, murderer! Can't you see that you horrify me?"

Obstinately, Bertel remained standing before the poor desperate girl. "Before repeating the order to go away and never see you again, before telling me again that you're horrified, Stierna, listen to what I have I say: if I leave this house, it will be to die."

"To die?"

"Yes. You've already damned one soul; you will damn another."

"My God! My God! What have I done that you should subject me to such cruel ordeals?"

"Can you believe that I have struggled against my remorse, that I have repelled the thoughts of suicide that pursue me, for any other motive than the love I feel for you? In the midst of the inferno of my heart, a joy sometimes gleams that suspends its suffering. That joy is seeing you, hearing your soft voice. You're sending me away; perhaps you're doing the right thing, and being charitable—I shall now have the courage to die."

"You're right, Monsieur—stay. You must. Since I am the involuntary cause of your crime, I must submit to its expiation, and accept my share of your remorse. Stay, and may God grant you repentance, as he has given me eternal despair."

"Repentance! Remorse! Oh, God did not wait for our prayer to give me that. You don't know, then, that the nights are sleepless for me, that a slow fever is devouring me incessantly, that a name sounds incessantly in my ears? That that name is constantly on my lips, ready to escape with the confession of my crime? Remorse! If you could understand the remorse that I suffer, instead of the horror I inspire in you, you would take pity on me; you would hold out your hand to console me, and you would mingle my name in the prayers you address to God. You would cry out, saying: 'Lord, have mercy on him!'"

Compassion was indeed the sentiment that Stierna did not take long to experience for Bertel. After the initial moments of horror and fright, she reflected that he was unhappy, and unhappy because of her. From then on, a dangerous pity preoccupied her keenly, and kept her thoughts relentlessly fixed on the young man, day and night—for sleep had quit the maiden's room henceforth. She was distressed by Bertel's sin and remorse, asked God for forgiveness on his behalf, and sought by a thousand affectionate means to give the guilty man some hope in divine mercy. She lavished interest and indulgence upon him. To render his sin less burdensome, she generously took half of it upon herself, and tried to bear it with him.

That community of secrecy and repentance, the sublime and voluntary complicity, did not take long to become a sentiment more tender than Stierna herself believed, against which she did not protect herself. No tender word ever emerged from their lips, but whenever Stierna saw Bertel paler than usual and prey to spasms of despair, she furtively took his hand and fixed her large blue eyes upon him, shining with celestial compassion.

In the meantime, Bertel's mother fell dangerously ill. He was obliged to leave abruptly in order to see her one last time before death separated her from her son forever. He wept so bitterly, and suffered so keenly, that Stierna promised of her own accord to write to him for as long as his absence lasted, and kept her promise. She only talked, in her letters about the dying woman, God, hope and Heaven's forgiveness, but she nevertheless wrote every day, and, so to speak, devoted the entirety of every day to Bertel.

When the professor returned, his mother was dead; there was no longer a single wretched person in this world to love him. Stierna tried to render that isolation less cruel—so successfully that one day, sitting next to the large fireplace in which a fire of pine-logs was blazing, forgetful of the past, with their clasped hands, they found themselves talking hopefully of happiness and the future.

Many trials and years separated them, alas, from the day when they would be able to realize the beautiful dreams they

260

forged. They were both too poor to be able to marry for some time to come. Bertel possessed no other fortune than his professorial salary, and he still had to pay off, with the same revenue, the rather considerable debts that his mother had left in dying. But what did time and trials matter to those in whose hearts hope had succeeded despair, and who could at least glimpse, however distantly, future felicity? The memory of Ole sometimes returned to trouble them, like a reproach, but it seemed to them nevertheless that forgiveness descended on them from the heavens, drop by drop. Before the magnificent splendor of love, the somber glow of remorse faded away.

A year went by in that fashion, for Stierna and for Bertel, in the ecstasy of a powerful and chaste tenderness. Madame Magnussen knew and approved of the secret engagement of the two young people, although they had never taken her into their confidence. It was thus that she had loved her husband for a long time before marriage became possible. Such mystical unions are common in the North, where poverty reigns so harshly. With a noble pact of love in the heart, a young man struggles courageously against the difficulties of life, and conquers, if not a fortune, at least a measure of ease. Then he comes to kneel at the feet of the one who is waiting for him without mistrust, even when time and distance separate them.

Uncomplainingly, Stierna and Bertel lived under the same roof, beside one another, and although they never exchanged a kiss, they looked forward desirously, but not impatiently, to the distant epoch that would bring about their marriage.

This situation, which would seem impossible and perilous in our French mores, became quite simple and full of charm in Copenhagen. The two lovers spent their life in a sweet and mild intoxication; the body slept, only the soul lived.

In any case, they saw one another only a little more frequently than in that past. Only meal times and the occasional family occasion brought them together.

Bertel devoted a large part of his evenings to studies in physics—an interest inspired in him by the instruments left behind by Stierna's father and long forgotten in a little room where things the family did not use were stored. He loved to talk about the phenomena of the science to which he was passionately devoted, and he initiated the young woman into the mysteries of that fantastic new world and that unknown nature.

All of that was marvelous to Stierna, whom her father's prudence had wisely left in a charming ignorance, and who only went out of the house twice a year, and even then with her mother. The past, the present, the future—real life, in sum—consisted for her of Bertel, her mother, her little house and the memory of Ole, the last of which became vaguer and more distant every day.

The sweeter such an existence is, the more painfully the blow that overturns it strikes. Madame Magnussen fell gravely ill, and there was soon no more hope of a recovery. According to the Gospel, a strong woman who has long been prepared for a holy death by a life of virtue only feels anxiety, in that redoubtable moment, for the child she leaves behind on Earth. That anxiety was consoled by the thought of the love she knew Bertel to have for Stierna. One morning, she summoned them to the bed in which she would soon die, and took them both by the hand.

"Bertel Granh," she said, in a faint but distinct voice, "you love Stierna, and Stierna loves you. I therefore leave her a protector down here, and can quit the Earth without dread. I know that you have tried to conceal many mysteries from me, my children, but I know that secrets, even the most innocent, love to remain in the darkness. May God bless you as I bless you, my son…Stierna!"

They fell to their knees, for it was before a cadaver that they were praying and weeping.

The day after the day on which Madame Magnussen's mortal remains were buried in the cemetery, Stierna, leaning on Bertel's arm, went in tears to the house of an aged female relative, to spend the period of her mourning there and await the moment when she might marry her fiancé. That moment need not be far away, for Bertel hoped to pay off all his mother's debts within the year, and it would then only remain for him to amass the small sum necessary for him to establish a household. The lovers therefore separated on the old aunt's threshold.

It was agreed, before the separation, that the professor could make occasional visits to his intended. Admittedly, Bertel also promised to pass beneath Stierna's window every day, while travelling to and from the University, and that Stierna added that she would always be at the window.

The fiancés, therefore, saw one another twice a day, at eleven o'clock in the morning, when the professor came back from the University, and at two o'clock, when he returned for the afternoon classes. During his first departure and his second return, darkness pitilessly deprived them of that happiness.

Stierna was able to invent ingenious pretexts to be leaning on her windowsill when one of these sweet moments of the day, so keenly anticipated, drew near. From some way off she watched Bertel approaching, only walking slowly in order to allow is eyes to linger on the young woman for longer. When he arrived before her, they exchanged a long, tender gaze; then, hearts beating, one of them continued his route while the other, smiling and excited, pretended to work fervently at some dressmaking project, while actually following the sound of footsteps drawing away with her ears.

For six months, the life of the lovers was entirely encapsulated in these two daily rendezvous and in the visits that Bertel made about once a fortnight. They liked their rapid but free encounters at the window much better than the solemn visits, during which it was necessary carefully to lock their love away in the depths of their hearts, in order that the secret of their souls did not fall into the power of a bourgeois and meddlesome curiosity. Stierna therefore counted down with the charming anguish of expectation to the moment when Bertel would bring her happiness all day long. Bertel forgot the fatigue and annoyances of his laborious profession beneath the consoling and tender gaze that he received in passing beneath the balcony.

Monsieur Magnussen's widow had died in the autumn. At the end of summer, Stierna felt herself becoming vaguely anxious and sad, for several times, Bertel, in going to the university, had arrived several minutes late, and had passed under his fiancée's window almost at a run, in order not to arrive after the beginning of classes that was being signaled by the last strokes of the bell. Another day, she felt her eyes fill with tears on remarking the preoccupation of the young man, who only remembered to look up at her window after leaving it five or six paces behind him.

These evidences of distraction and lack of enthusiasm were repeated several times. The guilty party seemed only to be carrying out a duty or following a habit in coming to receive the tender greeting of his fiancée. Stierna struggled for a long time against her own conviction before accepting that painful thought, but in the end, she could not mistake the fatal reality, for Bertel passed by without raising his head on two consecutive days.

While she sought despairingly to explain the cause of this deadly change, a few friends of the aged relative came to dinner in the old lady's home at Christmas. The majority of the guests were at the University.

In the evening, when they had left the table to surround the fireplace, the conversation turned to an Extraordinary Professor's chair that had become vacant. They talked about the competitors who had applied for it, but no one mentioned Bertel's name. Now, if he had acquired that position, the young man's honoraria would have been doubled, and nothing would any longer have opposed their marriage.

"I thought that Dr. Bertel Granh had more right than any other to apply for that chair?" objected the blushing Stierna, who could not master her emotions, and could not bear the crushing weight of doubt any longer.

"You're quite right, my pretty maid," replied one of the old professors, "but since Dr. Granh has come into a considerable inheritance, he is not longer concerned to occupy a chair that would necessitate new and laborious studies. He is even disposed to enjoy his fortune more freely, for he came to ask for an unlimited leave of absence yesterday, while I was with the rector. It's my nephew Christian who will take over Dr. Granh's chair in medicine in the interim."

"Doctor Granh has only received news of this inheritance in the last few days, then?" asked Stierna, who could not yet believe in such ingratitude and treason.

"All of Copenhagen has been talking about it for four months. It's not at all astonishing that you don't know anything about the news. You live in such a profound and reclusive solitude."

Pale, beside herself and bewildered, the young woman hurtled out of the apartment and ran, mad with despair, to the house where she had once spent so many happy moments, and where Bertel now lived alone.

She knocked, but no one opened the door. She called out, but no one replied.

In the end, a neighbor put her head out of a widow and shouted: "There's no longer anyone in the house. Dr. Bertel Granh left a little while ago by mail coach, for a long journey."

Stierna collapsed in a faint.

The old man interrupted himself, but did not notice that he had stopped speaking. His gaze wandered vaguely through empty space, and seemed to be pursuing memories full of bitterness and despair. Sweat was streaming down his forehead, laden with profound wrinkles; his green-tinted pupils burned with the sinister flame that the accursed angel emanates. Several minutes went by.

Suddenly, he woke with a start from that sleepless dream, and looked around in astonishment, as if he were surprised to find himself in Spa, beside a stranger. He needed some further time to get his ideas in order and reconnect the present with the past that had earlier come to live before him. A smile, full of sarcasm for the weakness of the human organism and for himself, creased his lips, while an impulse of shame and anger made him shrug his shoulders.

"Do you know Stockholm?" he asked the Frenchman, abruptly, with the evident intention of extracting himself, by means of a violent effort, from the dolorous thoughts that were assailing him.

"No," replied the man to whom the question was addressed.

If I were a poet, like you, I could make a brilliant description of the Capital of Sweden. I'm not a poet, and I shall only tell you that there is, on a hill in Stockholm, a quarter inhabited by the city's poorest inhabitants, named Mosebacke. Steep, muddy, narrow, plunging paths, sometimes mere wooden stairways—such are the roads of Mosebacke. I leave you to imagine the houses. In particular, there was one there more wretched and hideous than the rest, but in exchange, it had the advantage of standing in the most isolated spot, and the only inhabitants it sheltered were workmen who go out at daybreak and return after nightfall. At the summit of the hovel, like black eyes, were two round windows. They served to provide air and light—my God! what air and what light!—to two miserable lofts. No one in the quarter knew who lived there, and no one wanted to know.

An old woman, a kind of cretin, half-sorceress and half-idiot, was the only living creature who had any relations with the tenants of the mansards. Every morning, she deposited food at the thresholds of their doors and received a coin in exchange.

One evening, a terrible explosion burst forth in one of the lofts, and a huge flame escaped through the window, in a manner that threw the entire Mosebacke quarter into alarm. People came running, broke down the door, and found a young man lying motionless in the midst of strangely formed instruments, some of which had been smashed by the explosion.

The occupant of the next room had not been disturbed by the frightful shock that had nearly caused the old house to collapse. Partly out of anxiety for him, and partly to seek help for the dying man, the rescuers knocked on his door; he did not open it and they called out without obtaining any response. Common people do not usually exhibit great patience, so they had begun to break the door down with an axe when it finally turned on its hinges and revealed a face in which nothing human remained. Terrible scars streaked it in every direction, scarcely leaving anything intact but the eyes and mouth.

This being—for no one dared give him the name of man—went into the room where his neighbor as lying, and at the sight of him uttered a cry that resembled the sinister call of a hyena. He went to the dying man, revived him, bathed his face with fresh water and leaned over him to make certain of his awakening.

When the other, having emerged from unconsciousness, got to his feet and suddenly found himself face to face with the individual who had brought him back to life, he turned his head away, put his hands together and cried: "My God, have pity on me! Do not bring your just anger down on me! Do not deliver me to the eternity of Hell!"

"You're still alive, Bertel Granh," said the hideous unknown. "It's not face to face with Satan that you find yourself, but face to face with Ole Matthiesen. Pull yourself together! In exchange for a frivolous amour, you have given me genius— and soon, I hope, a glory without rival. I forgive you everything, including the hideous scars inflicted by the pistol-shot that I fired at my head to keep the promise I had sworn to you. Someone lifted me up, dying, as I lifted you up just now, and saved my life as I am saving yours, and since then, a sublime obsession has preoccupied me and cause me to renounce, joyfully, all the ridiculous passions of human beings. I shall be the benefactor of the entire universe. Statues of me will be erected; the face of the world will be renewed, and it is Ole

Matthiesen who will work the miracle. The work is complete! The light will not be long delayed in shining."

All this was said rapidly in Latin. Ole then turned toward the people the explosion had attracted.

"We thank you, Masters," he said to them in Swedish. Your care is not longer necessary. I have rediscovered one of my old friends in the man you have come to rescue, and if he needs help, he will obtain the most active and prompt assistance from me. As you see, though, he is standing up, recovered from the shock caused by the explosion that alarmed you."

Everyone withdrew. Ole and Bertel remained alone. Ole silently paraded his gaze over the broken objects that lay in the loft. They were apparatus used in chemistry and instruments used in physics. The explosion had been caused by a flask of hydrogen gas that had suddenly ignited.

Mathiessen remained plunged in a mute and bleak reverie for some time. Finally, he broke the silence.

"Listen to me, Bertel!" he said. "Because of you I attempted suicide. If you're still alive, it me to whom you owe your life!"

"Yes, Ole—and I ask your forgiveness on my knees. I would like to be able to prove my gratitude, even at the price of my own existence."

"Well, you can."

"How?"

"By making once again the pact that we made before in Copenhagen."

"Stierna is free, Ole, "Bertel interjected, with a sight. "You can marry her."

"Stierna!" said Mathiessen, violently. "Stierna! Is it really a matter of a woman? Tell me why, Bertel Granh, you have trampled underfoot that insensate passion that drove you to stake your life against that of a friend? You say nothing? I know why! It's for love of science and thirst for glory."

"Yes, I admit it."

"An idea—a great idea—is preoccupying you."

268

"Yes! Like the one you mentioned to me just now, it will regenerate the universe and make the name of the man who realizes it eternal."

"Do you know, Bertel, the thought that has occurred to me in the presence of all this debris of scientific instruments? It's that we're pursuing the same idea. A secret and accursed voice is murmuring in my ear that, once having been rivals in love, we are now rivals in glory. If that's the case, Bertel, one of us has to die!"

"You're right," Bertel replied, unhesitatingly. "Listen to me. Haven't you groaned sometimes, on thinking about the long nights that desolate Denmark? Haven't you thought that the man who could create a second sun with take a place second only to God in the admiration and gratitude of men?"

"That's your idea?" jeered Matthiesen, shrugging his shoulders. "I feel reassured—it's ridiculous and impossible, that's all."

"Impossible!" cried Bertel, picking up two jars that the explosion had spared. "One of these two vessels, each of which terminates in a narrow tube, contains oxygen, the other hydrogen. The two flames, combining in combustion, only give a bluish light, but let me bring in a refractory body—this piece of chalk, for instance—and watch!"

Immediately, a resplendent light sprang forth, at which the eye could not look directly, even furtively. Dazzled, Ole turned his head away. Bertel was exultant.

"You see, my second sun already appears to you to be more than a hollow dream! But this is only a rough and imperfect work. The light does not reproduce itself; the gases are exhausted; the refractory body loses its properties. It requires a man versed in science to watch over the apparatus incessantly, to prevent an explosion. I shall create a sun that will be, in approximate proportion, as bright and as durable as God's sun. Listen closely, Ole.

"The solar fluid behaves like the electrical fluid. It produces the phenomena of light and heat when it strikes objects and finds any obstacle whatsoever in its rapid movement.

269

Thus, the sun is an opaque body which surrounds an atmosphere of luminous electricity.

"Starting from this principle, I have discovered that bodies become phosphorescent by virtue of the effect of heat and electrical discharges. I recognized, too, that bodies nonconductive of electrical fluid retain that phosphorescence longer than others.

"Given that—mark me well, Ole! This time, follow my operation with all the attention of which you are capable, for a prodigy will become manifest. I place a morsel of carbon, a refractory body, in the middle of this glass globe. I attach to that carbon two platinum wires, which are connected to the poles of a dry Voltaic pile.

"Take note: these metal wires are secured to the mysterious columns of the pile—columns enclosed in a cylinder of sulfur and made up of alternate leaves of zinc, silver and paper.

"I obtain a vacuum in the globe with the aid of a pneumatic pump. On your knees, Ole—here is a sun!"[39]

Ole could not suppress a cry of admiration. It was a sun, a true sun.

"You see," Bertel continued, "that I am approaching the completion of my work. It's no more than a matter of applying my sublime discovery on a vast scale. This is the means of ensuring that execution.

"I shall construct, in sheets of copper, a balloon five hundred feet in diameter. The balloon will be filled with hy-

---

[39] What Berthoud has in mind is a carbon arc lamp, although his description is faulty, partly because his theory of solar light-production is mistaken. The principle of the carbon arc lamp had been demonstrated by Humphry Davy in the first decade of the century, but all attempts to produce a viable version of any sustained electrical light-source had been frustrated before Berthoud wrote this story. It was not until the 1870s that the first viable carbon arc lamp—the so-called "Yablochkov candle"—was developed, and not until 1878 that Joseph Swan patented the first electric light-bulb with a carbon filament.

drogen gas, purified with extreme care, and purged, as far as possible, of all foreign bodies.

"Beneath the balloon I shall attach an apparatus similar—in with gigantic proportions—to the one you see, in which a small sun with shine. A veritable sun, moreover, like the sun in the sky, since it is similarly composed of an opaque body and an envelope of luminous electricity.

"The Voltaic piles will be alimented easily; the Earth is nothing but a vast reservoir of electricity. Do not two eternal magnetic currents pass from one pole to the other? And has not our great Oersted demonstrated that magnetism is nothing other than electricity in one of its transformations?[40]

"My balloon has nothing to fear from external agents, since it is constructed of solid metal, rendered unalterable and indestructible by a chemical preparation that is easy to compose. I shall coat it with this preparation, which will protect it against the slightest oxidation.

"The hydrogen will not be able to escape from the interior, because the envelope that keeps it prisoner remains impenetrable from the inside as from the outside, even for the most subtle gas.

"Finally, a metal cable, which will also serve as a conductor to the galvanic piles, will suffice to hold my apparatus anchored in the atmosphere.

"You see, Ole, these theories are certain. I have created a sun! Soon, there will be no more nights for Denmark. Liberated henceforth from obscurity, Denmark will have almost nothing to fear from the rigors of winter. What do you say, Ole?"

"I say that your invention seems beautiful, great and useful to me, and that it will astonish Europe—but that it's nothing compared with mine."

"What's yours, then?" Bertel demanded, feeling jealousy bite into his heart as he saw the serenity with which Ole had listened to him.

---

[40] Hans Christian Oersted (1777-1851) discovered that electric currents create magnetic fields in 1820.

"It will distress you, for my discovery will render yours almost useless."

"Speak."

"I've found a means of living without eating."

"Without eating?"

"Yes, I've discovered that nourishment is a prejudice."

"And with what are you going to replace alimentation?"

"With nothing. For a long time I've been meditating on this problem. Finally, I tried not to eat, that's all—and I succeeded. As the Greek philosopher did to prove movement, I walk. For twelve days already nothing has approached my lips. I feel a little corporeal weakness, it's true, but in compensation, my intelligence has never been more brilliant and richer! Freed from physical shackles, the soul acts in all its powerful liberty."

"But your idea is extravagant, Ole! You'll die of starvation."

"I haven't eaten for twelve days, and I'm doing admirably."

"It's an insane idea."

"No more insane than your sun."

"But my sun exists, and I've given you proof of it."

"And have I give you none? I, who am speaking, thinking, reasoning and acting, liberated from the inconvenience of nourishment for twelve days? Farewell, Bertel."

"No," cried the latter. "No, I won't let you complete an insane suicide, Ole. I won't leave you until I've made sure that you're taking some nourishment."

Ole took out a dagger. "Do you recognize this weapon?" he asked, with a sinister smile. I held it in my hand the night when you came to find me in my room on Madame Magnusson's house. You want to destroy my glory now, as you wanted to destroy my life then. If you take a step, I'll strike you. I'll kill you."

As he said this, the unfortunate madman left Bertel, went back into his loft, locked himself in and barricaded his door from the inside, with the aid of some enormous wooden beams.

For two days Bertel heard the noise of Ole's voice and footsteps through the wall that separated them. When that time had elapsed, he heard nothing more. Full of alarm, he had warned a magistrate of his anxieties. The door was broken down and Ole Matthiesen was found dead on his paltry bed. A manuscript was lying at his feet, entitled: *On the Prejudice of Nourishment*.

When Bertel went back to his cell, he fell on to the pallet that served him as a bed, devoid of strength. A frightful doubt had gripped his heart, his thought, his entire being.

In the presence of Ole's insane conviction, and the obstinate perseverance with which the unfortunate had believed in his absurd theory until his final death-throes, Bertel wondered whether he too might not be pursuing a lie, a demented utopia. That doubt—and what torture is more rightful than doubt, Monsieur?—squeezed him in its execrable claws, choked him and ended up disturbing his reason.

His torment was horrible.

Suddenly, he threw himself furiously once again into the culpable dream to which he had immolated his duty, his conscience, his happiness, his entire existence. He clung to it; he wanted to sacrifice everything to it, to the last faculty of his life, the last thought of his soul. A moment later, he cursed his mad obsession, and, laughing bitterly, he repeated: "Insane! Insane!"

In that struggle, that doubt, that fever, he actually felt his mental strength weaken and his reason lose its lucidity. Inconsequential words escaped his lips involuntarily: truncated, aborted, incomplete, incoherent ideas were passing through his brain and filling it with tumult and disorder.

The peril was deadly and immense. If he did not put an end, by a prompt and energetic resolution, to that redoubtable crisis, his life and intelligence would succumb! Then, Monsieur, by a superhuman effort, Bertel desperately trampled his ideas of science and glory underfoot. He swore, by the salvation of his soul and on Ole's corpse, to renounce them forever, to turn his head every time the demon evoked them before him! But those ideas, more obstinate than ever, pursued him, harassed him, surrounded him with an infernal circle, and whirled around him, repeating:

"The second sun! The second sun!"

In the hope of feeing himself from that torture, Bethel departed in all haste for Copenhagen. There, he knew, he would find a celestial creature, the one who had already protected him against remorse! He wanted to renounce his prideful errors at her feet, to ask for a forgiveness that he would obtain, and shelter from despair and madness beneath the wings of an angel...

Alas, Stierna was dead. She had died praying to God for Bertel.

Since then, Monsieur, many years have gone by without Bertel having found a moment of peace and rest. Hunted by a horde of invisible demons, he still marches on without stopping, like Ahasuerus. To his right and his left stand two equally fatal ideas: the memory of Stierna, full of remorse; and the crazy conviction that the creation of a second sun was a great, wise, sublime work! In vain, Monsieur, since the day when he renounced that ridiculous folly, has he refused to open a book of physics; in vain has he carefully avoided contact with the scientists he has met on his travels; everywhere a voice repeats to him:

You could have created a second sun!

And that voice is right, Monsieur—at least, I think so. Do we not live in a century in which physics is progressing with great strides and working miracles? Electricity and its study have opened up a new world. With the aid of electricity, Monsieur Becquerel,[41] that illustrious scientist, has created

---

[41] The reference is to Antoine César Becquerel (1788-1878), the grandfather of the more famous Henri. Initially a mineralogist, his investigation of the application of electricity to chemical analysis and synthesis, following in the footsteps of Humphry Davy, allowed him to produce tiny precious stones in 1823.

veritable precious stones. I have seen little sapphires that have emerged from his laboratories; even for the most expert and experienced lapidary, they do not differ and any respect from the precious stones that nature produces. Monsieur Jacobi[42] has made veritable statues by means of electricity, which bear the imprint of the most delicate work with a precision impossible for a skillful sculptor. Finally, Monsieur, Bertel's sun itself, while the Danish professor rejected it as an absurd dream, was invented by Humphry Davy and perfected by Faraday. Those two celebrated physicists have used means very similar to Bertel's methods, and arrived at the same results.

As for the copper balloon, it has been imagined and proven possible by one of the most skillful physicists of our time, Monsieur Prechtel,[43] the director of the Polytechnic Institute of Vienna. That scientist has even drawn up plans for the balloon's construction; in order to realize it, it would be necessary to expend the cost of a frigate.

If Stierna's lover had not been discouraged, you see—if he had repelled his doubts, if he had not given in to fear, if he had had an unbreakable faith in himself, and if, finally, Ole's madness had not disturbed him—given the time, the patience and the will, he would certainly have immortalized his name and created a second sun.

The stranger, who had let his head fall into his hands and was holding it hidden therein, finally raised it again, displaying features more deeply scored, more downcast and more livid than ever.

---

[42] Moritz von Jacobi (1801-1874) invented electrotyping, or "galvanoplastic sculpture," in 1838; the technique was rapidly adapted for relief printing, which remains its primary application.

[43] Johann Joseph Prechtel (1778-1854) made numerous contributions to electrical physics and technology in the 1820s and 1830s, but the idea of making balloons from copper sheets had first been proposed before the end of the eighteenth century and several experimental models were constructed in France in the 1840s, although none proved practicable.

"Bertel, such as he is," he said, in a sepulchral voice, "accepts his discomfiture with resignation, in expiation of his treason in regard to Stierna. If his sin was great, its punishment is terrible!"

As he finished these words, he got to his feet, turning away to hide the tears that were running from his lifeless eyes over his sun-bronzed cheeks, and hurriedly walked away.

The French journalist searched for him in vain that evening during the seven o'clock walk, at the ball, in the gaming halls, and the theater—in sum, everywhere. He did not find the unknown anywhere; no one could give him any information about him.

The next morning, it transpired that the old man had left the waters of Spa, not only without telling anyone, but also leaving all his luggage and a considerable sum of money behind in the room that he had occupied in the inn where he had been staying.

SCIENTIFIC FANTASIES

THE STAR-EATERS

During the Crimean War, while Colonel de Saint-A***, married scarcely six months before, was fighting under the walls of Sebastopol, his wide, Comtesse Blanche, was living on the banks of the Loire in a Medieval château, transformed into a comfortable habitation by virtue of determination and money.

The bedroom, in particular, offered a truly singular mixture if the severe luxury of the 14th century and the elegant research of the nineteenth. However, the dressers, in sculpted black oak-wood, the big bed with spiral columns and tapestried canopies, the armchair with fantastically damascened arms, and the fireplace with the Saint-A*** coat of arms, as high as an attic in the Rue de Helder, harmonized in a charming fashion with the brocade draperies, the lace curtains, the Boule furniture and a piano, a masterpiece by Érard.

A decoratively-woven carpet had replaced the sheaves of reeds that had covered the worn floor of the room four centuries earlier, although it is true that the floorboards had given way to a parquet of exotic wood, which embellished itself in summer with incrustations, arabesques and designs as precious as the marvels of the carpet that covered and hid it in winter.

At present, the carpet was still covering the parquet, for April had only just begun to blazon the escutcheon of the zodiac with the bull of Taurus; belated snow veiled the pathways and the flower-beds of the garden and dusted the branches, scarcely in bud, of a stand of squat trees that grew directly beneath the Comtesse's windows. These tall bushes occupied the location of a profound ditch that had been full of water in Feudal times, but was dry today and partly filled in by the rubble of collapses, invasions of vegetation and the patient and indefatigable leveler called time.

One morning, when the pretty chatelaine had received good news from the Crimea, and she was dreaming simultaneously of the past and future, with her forehead leaning against one of the large windows of her room, she noticed a very busy bird. It was building its nest at the top of an old pollarded oak. From the window, the comtesse could look down on the work, which was approaching completion, only lacking a few twigs to form a neat little construction, composed of moss and roots bound together by reeds. A soft bed of linen, feathers, down, silk and cotton carpeted the nest's interior.

The female bird was working alone, seizing a blade of grass or a dry stem, stopping, running, looking, plaiting and weaving. The male, perched on a nearby branch, was whistling his most beautiful song, like a savage of the Rocky Mountains, leaving the housework to his companion—but he was hunting on her behalf, also like the Sioux. While singing, he kept a keen lookout all around. At the slightest movement in the grass or under the snow, he launched himself forward, skimmed the soil, brought back to his female and placed in her beak—without keeping any for himself—the entire produce of his swoop, always provided that, by hazard, the swoop in question had been productive. I say *by hazard* because, alas, more times than not, he returned disappointed, with his beak empty, to resume the place he had quit and recommence his fruitlessly-interrupted song.

The Comtesse did not take long to sympathize with the young household. She appropriated beetle-larvae destined for the nourishment of the pheasants, and threw a handful to the two blackbirds.

The latter, without the slightest apprehension, raced to pick up the meal-worms and then flew to the window to see where that living manna had come from. The Comtesse resumed her distribution.

278

The blackbirds found the process so much to their taste that, a week hence, they were taping the window with their beaks, casually coming into the room and taking their nourishment from the young woman's slender white fingers, and, if necessary, cleverly tracking down the porcelain vase containing the larvae for which they showed themselves so gluttonous. A large cork sealed the vase, but with two thrusts of the beak, the blackbird and his mate caused the cork to leap out, and the pillage commenced.

The Comtesse, whose isolation was cheered up by the society of these winged friends, let them do as they wished, and even encouraged them—all the more so when five blue-green eggs, specked confusedly with rust, laid by the female in the nest, were succeeded, after twenty days of incubation, by five little yellow beaks, always chirping, always open and always insatiable.

The chicks, introduced by their parents, soon exhibited the same free-and-easy attitude toward the Comtesse. More than once they woke her up at daybreak, so forcefully were they tapping at the windows and so shrilly were they crying out with impatience and hunger. It was necessary to see them when she finally gave in to their desire—it was, I insist, necessary to see them flying on to her arms, breast and head, pecking her, caressing her, and then, having paid their tribute of affection, darting and ferreting everywhere. They took no account of the protests of the chambermaid, nor of the thrusts of the beak of the large grey parrot, which were more brutal than well-aimed. The residence was theirs; I can guarantee that they made more than ample use of it!

A few months later, toward the end of September, the Comte had returned to his château, with seven wounds, fortunately scarring over, with the rank of brigadier-general and the sash of the Légion d'honneur. Sprawled in a large armchair, still pale and weak, he was savoring the ineffable benefits of convalescence. The Comtesse, seated at the piano, had just finished playing one of those old melodies of Northern France, the naïve grace and simple motifs of which reminded the general of his love-affair with Blanche and the good times when, without her having yet confessed that she loved him, she had played the songs of her homeland for him, as she did that evening.

When she had quit the piano and taken the convalescent's hands in hers once again, airborne voices, which had nothing human about them, suddenly repeated the last phrases of the tune that the Comtesse had played.

"Are there other fairies than you here, then?" the general asked, smiling, without understanding what he had heard.

"Fairies, no—but goblins, yes," she replied, opening the window and uttering a light cry of summons.

Seven little stars became visible in the air then, which were flying, wheeling, rising up and descending, spiraling outside the window.

Then the seven stars went out, and a flock of blackbirds—not counting the general's moustache—boldly invaded the drawing-room and settled on Blanche's arms and head—after which the birds resumed their flight in the garden via the window.

"Which explains the singers," said the general. "In fact, they're not the first musicians of that sort I've heard. In the Rue du Petit-Musc, in the Celestines' barracks, the blackbirds that nest in the trees in the courtyard repeat my regiment's trumpet-fanfares...but the stars! What of the stars?"

"They intrigue me as much as you, my friend. Never have I seen that phosphorescence shining in the beaks of my protégés." Laughing, she added: "Perhaps it's an light-show they've put on to celebrate the return of their liege lord to his domains."

"By God!" replied the Comte. "I'm not the friend and pupil of General Levaillant[44] for nothing. One day, under Arab

---

[44] This might be either of two sons of the naturalist François Levaillant (1753-1824), Jean and Charles, both of whom became generals and fought in African campaigns.

fire, while crossing a ditch in order to reckon with those clowns, he perceived a rare insect in the grass of the verge, stopped his horse dead, dismounted, picked up the beetle, stuffed it into the finger of one of his gloves, got back in the saddle, and then chased after the Bedouins so furiously that two hours later, their leader surrendered and led forth the horse of submission. Give me your arm, Blanche, and let's go into the garden to see what's going on."

They headed into the grounds, approached the raised bank, and found the blackbirds occupied in pecking amid a veritable sea of light. At every instant, one of the birds took flight, holding in its beak a sort of little star, which shone for a few seconds and then went out, never to light up again—after which the blackbird returned to the quarry and repeated the operation.

The general leaned over, plunged his hand into the heatless flame that was undulating over the surface of the ground, and picked up a handful of earth, in which he saw five or six of the myriapod insects that entomologists call *Scolopendra*, and which popular parlance, with its picturesque energy, calls centipedes. These *Scolopendra* belonged to the smallest species, which is designated by the epithet *electrica*.[45]

For some times, the Comtesse and the general contemplated the strange spectacle of a flame fifty centimeters long and broad, which bore no resemblance to any other flame, and in which hundreds of *Scolopendra* were swarming. On the general's orders, a gardener dug in the soil around the phosphorescent mass, and the displaced soil was literally covered with droplets of fire. One might have thought that an invisible sprinkler wielded by a fairy had distributed a luminous rain

---

[45] *Scolopendra electrica*, the electric centipede, enjoyed a certain celebrity in the latter part of the 19th century, when various scientists were studying it in association with the attempt to determine the chemistry by means of which luminous insects generated their light. The physicist William Crookes was one of several who kept specimens in his lab. Once the problem was solved, the species became less interesting; poets have always preferred fireflies.

everywhere the spade had touched the earth. If one crushed a little of that soil in one's hands, it left shiny streaks there.

"You see, dear Blanche," the general said, "how nature is pleased to dress the most humble and seemingly obscure of creatures with her splendors. Do you know why *Scolopendra* not only shine with a mysterious gleam but also spread so much light over everything that surrounds them? Nature has gratified them with such beacons in order that they might send one another signals of love, like Hero and Leander."

"And so that they might reveal their hiding-place to my little star-eaters! Here they are, all seven of them, coming back to the *Scolopendra* hunt! Let's leave them to it. All the more so because the night is cool and I don't think that humidity is exactly a remedy effective against chills and incompletely-scarred wounds."

"She's right!" sighed the general. "To seek to understand the ultimate causes of creation is one of the insensate dreams of humankind. As we were informed by the almoner who cared for us in the Crimea, the *Imitation* has all too much reason to say: *Falluntur saepe hominum sensus in judicando*.[46]

"Yes!" the Comtesse interjected, laughing. "We should not take so much pride in appearances. See how our beautiful and mysterious stars of a little while ago have become no more than worms, and our star-eaters no more than black-birds."

"Alas, that's the story of all human things. *From far away it's something, but at close range, nothing*."[47]

"A century ago, La Fontaine voiced the truths that we are discovering at present...I even think that they were already past their first freshness in his time..."

---

[46] This quotation from Thomas à Kempis' *De Imitatione Christi* (1418; tr. as *On the Imitation of Christ*) translates roughly as "Suffer us not to judge with the sight of our outward eyes."

[47] This quotation is the concluding line of Jean de La Fontaine's verse fable "Le Chameau et les Bâtons flottant" [The Camel and the Floating Sticks].

"You're right, we repeat things continually," the general replied. Placing his lips on Blanche's forehead, he murmured: "There's nothing true and lasting but love!"

"Yes, when it lasts," she replied, laughing.

"Since when do angels speak ill of God?" asked the general, leaning with even more tenderness on his wife's arm.

And they went back indoors on that beautiful Autumn night, forgetting the star-eaters—forgetting everything, except their tenderness.

LUMINOUS FLOWERS

The Chinese truly are a singular people! All the discoveries of European science and industry are recorded in their books, especially in their popular legends. One might think them miners who exploit diamond mines according to their whim but have no idea how to extract the precious stone from its matrix.

In the Chinese encyclopedia entitled *Fayuan-Zhulin*, book LII, there is the story of a princess named Me-Chi, with whom Racmi, the king of the land of Djambouli, was greatly enamored. Mei-Chi could not consent to give her hand to Racmi, because the prince offered her gifts that were magnificent but vulgar, and she only wanted to marry a monarch who could create unknown marvels for her.

One evening, after sunset, Racmi arrived at Mei-Chi's house. Mounted on a meek and well-dressed elephant, he was preceded by a thousand lantern-bearers and followed by a cortege of bayaderes, who were dancing and causing the air to resound with their songs.

From her window, the young woman shouted to the king; "Do you think that I've never seen a richly-clad elephant or heard bayaderes singing before?"

"Divine beauty," Racmi replied, "deign to climb on to this elephant; allow yourself to be conducted by the choir of bayaderes to my palace, and, if you do not see there that which you have never seen before, I swear an oath never to mention the word *love* in your presence again."

Mei-Chi shrugged her shoulders, and replied that, not believing a word of what he had said, she would go to his palace in order to rid herself of his obsessive love once and for all.

So she climbed up on to the elephant, and allowed herself to be taken to the king's home. Racmi showed her into a gallery full of plants, especially nasturtiums, the favorite flowers of the Chinese. Scarcely had Mei-Chi come in than the thousands of torches lighting in the gallery were extinguished. All the flowers began to glow, and two red birds sang the following verses:

You do not wish, O Mei-Chi,
Charming but pitiless tiger.
You do not wish all hearts
To light up for your beauty

How can they not burn
Since all inanimate things light up
And burn in your presence
With a celestial and supernatural flame.

Mei-Chi wiped away a tear and allowed her hand to fall into the hand of the happy Racmi. Then, suddenly excited, she cried: "It wasn't you, Prince, who had the idea of giving me this fête; it was suggested to you by someone else."

"Yes," he replied, "first by love, and then by the Buddha."

Mei-Chi sighed. "I have given you my hand," she said. "Keep it. Nevertheless, it's to the Buddha that I should have accorded it."

She said that to torment the prince, adds the satirical story-teller of Peking, for she knew full well that princes can purchase ideas, but hardly ever have any of their own.

There is no lack of talking birds in Europe, beginning with the blackbirds of the Celestine barracks, which, from the treetops where they perch freely, repeat the fanfares of the municipal guards' trumpets on a daily basis.

As for flowers that glow, they exist, and I have seen then, no less recently than yesterday.

Outside the official society of science there is in Paris a small group of individuals who modestly and silently devote to persistent studies the scarce leisure time left to them by the labors from which they wearily obtain their daily bread. Some have just entered into life and are beginning to trace the furrow of their future there; others, grown old beneath the harness of industry or administration, are reaching the end of their career. All, without exception, can only covertly, often at the expense of their sleep and always at the cost of sacrifices exorbitant for their slender purses, deliver themselves to a passion that is imperious and despotic, as all passions that one is able freely to satisfy.

And yet, from this unknown and poverty-stricken congregation, great discoveries sometimes emerge, some of which have already seen the light of day and attained their rank, but most of which remain in obscurity. Patents cost so much! And the Académie des Sciences is so good at burying, for good or ill, everything that is submitted to its consideration! It appoints a committee to make a report, it's true, but the committee never makes its report. I can give you too long a list, alas, of inventions and discoveries accepted and applied universally today, but which have been waiting for ten years for a report from the committee nominated by the Institut.

At the home of one of the pioneers of science I mentioned just now, when the weather outside was freezing, in a little greenhouse heated by means of new and ingenious apparatus in which electricity plays a role, it was given to me to see created, almost at will, the luminous phenomena that certain plants present, which would have amazed Linné and Goethe.

In the month of July 1762, Elizabeth-Christine Linné, the daughter of the famous naturalist, while taking an evening stroll in a garden, noticed—not without a shock of surprise-little flashes of light springing from the flowers of a clump of *Tropoelum majus*. Now, are you familiar with the flower that botanists call *Tropoelum*? It's the nasturtium—that popular climbing plant, so commonplace that its flower has given its name to a color.

Elizabeth immediately ran in search of her father and a few friends, who accompanied her and became witnesses, in their turn, to the phenomenon that had astonished her. Shortly afterwards, she published a note on the subject in the *Memoirs* of the Stockholm Academy.

It's not only in the nasturtium, but also in the pot marigold (*Calendula officinalis*), the tiger lily (*Lilium bulbiferum*), the African marigold (*Tagetes erecta*), the Mexican marigold (*Tagetes patula*), the annual sunflower, a relative of the topinambour, and the oriental poppy, that I and a dozen friends were able to observe such a charming phenomenon.[48]

The most complete darkness enveloped the greenhouse. We were sitting facing a large flower-bed in which the plants I've just named were assembled, which had been obtained by artificial culture.

After ten minutes' wait, an oriental poppy was the first to begin emitting flashes of sufficient magnitude to allow us, not only to see the flower that produced them but also to distinguish its neighbors quite clearly.

These flashes were repeated several times, and were soon confused with those that the other plants were not long delayed in emitting in their turn, albeit with a lesser density.

These flashes were sometimes bright, sometimes faint. Pale, almost white, and about eight to ten centimeters long, there is nothing better to compare them to than daylight. On raising the temperature of the greenhouse, and passing a slight electric current through it, the fantastic illumination acquired greater celerity, vivacity and force.

I think that until now, no one, except for Linné's daughter and M. Friès,[49] the director of the botanical garden in Uppsala, has been witness, as I have been, to a phenomenon still considered dubious by a large number of naturalists. I do not think, above all, that they have seen it produced, in the month of November, almost at will, in an enclosed space.

---

[48] The three plants for which Berthoud only gives partial details are *Helianthus annuus, Helianthus tuberosus* (also known as the Jerusalem artichoke) and *Papaver orientale*.

[49] Elias Fries (1794-1878)

Botanists have not admitted these phosphorescent plants at present, and have denied the vegetable kingdom the singular property of spontaneously producing authentic electric sparks—or at least contested the privilege.

Gesner[50] admits that he has seen nothing of this sort in his very rare text entitled *De raris et admirandis herbis, sive quod nocte luceant, sive alias ob causas lunariae nominantur*. (On a few rare and admirable herbs which, either because they shine by night or for other reasons, are called *lunar*.) The best-known instance is that presented by rotting wood; the phosphorescence manifested by that material was initially attributed to the presence of *Byssus phosphorea*, but the observations of Retzius and Humboldt and the more recent ones of M. Bartig (*Bot. Zeit.*, 1855, no.2) have proved that it resides in the ligneous substance itself.[51]

Other fragments of vegetation in the process of decomposition can similarly cover themselves with phosphorus. Meyen has seen mushrooms in various stages of decay become luminous in the dark. M. Tulasne, for his part, has studied and carefully described the phosphorescence of dead oak leaves. M. de Martius, in his *Voyage au Brésil*, has described the vivid light that the milky sap of *Euphorbia phosphorea* emits at the moment when one squeezes the sap out of the stem. Finally, an analogous observation has been made in Brazil by Mornay, in a liana.[52]

---

[50] Konrad von Genser (1516-1565)

[51] The fungus that Linnaeus classified as *Byssus phosphorea* was subsequently reclassified as *Thelephora caerulea*. Anders Jehan Retzius (1742-1821) and Alexander von Humboldt (1769-1859) are the next two scientists cited, but Bartig seems to be unknown except for his contributions to the *Botanische Zeitung*, in which he is sometimes cited as Th. Bartig.

[52] The first three scientists cited here are Franz Meyen (1804-1840), Louis René Tulasne (1815-1885) and Carl von Martius (1794-1868); the expedition to Brazil undertaken by the last-named was in 1817-20. The Mornay cited is probably Charles-Edgar, Comte de Mornay,

Phosphorescence similarly occurs in a few living and fully intact vegetables. The best known example, and the one most frequently studied, is that of *Rhizomorpha subterranea*, a fungus that develops in the wood of mine-shafts; the extremities of its filaments emit a glow so bright that, according to Meyen, Candolle[53] and Humboldt, one can read a book by its light.

Another fungus remarkable in this respect is the *Agaricus crepidotus* of southern Europe. Other species from the tropical regions possess the same faculty of becoming luminous in the dark; they include *Agaricus gardneri, igneus and noctilucens.*[54]

A moss, *Schistostega osmundacea,*[55] which grows in grottoes and caverns, emits by day, in certain circumstances, a beautiful emerald-green light. Bridel[56] has shown than this light originates from the reflection and refraction of diurnal light by little confervoid[57] filaments found under the moss.

How many marvels equally unknown and equally uninteresting remain to be discovered, with the aid of chance? For human genius consists in drawing certain deductions that drive from facts that hazard presents—facts perhaps observed a thousand times by vulgar minds.

Since I began with a Chinese story, I shall finish this chronicle with an apologue of the same origin. It is entitled "Of those who only see the surfaces of things" and is part of the Book of a Hundred Parables by Pe-yu-King.

---

one of whose expeditions is commemorated by a painting of his tent made by Eugène Delacroix.

[53] Augustin-Pyramus Candolle (1778-1841).

[54] Linnaeus identified *Crepidotus* as a "tribe" within the genus *Agaricus*, but it is now considered to be a separate genus, and *A. gardneri* has also been shifted to the genus *Lysurus*.

[55] *Schistostega pennata*, commonly known as "goblin's gold" is the species that Berthoud means to indicate.

[56] Samuel-Elisée Bridel-Brideri (1761-1828)

[57] "Confervoid" derives from *Conferva*, a type of filamentous aquatic alga.

"There was a Richi[58] who had retired to a mountain to try to acquire intelligence (Bodhi). He had obtained the six supernatural faculties and was endowed with a divine sight that penetrated everywhere. He could clearly see all the precious things that were hidden in the bosom of the earth.

"When the king had been informed of this, he was ravished with delight and said to his minister: 'How can we make sure that this man remains constantly in my kingdom, going nowhere else, and that my treasure is enriched by a multitude of precious things?'

"One of the ministers, whose mind was very limited, immediately went to the Richi and plucked out his eyes. He brought them to the king and said: 'As I have plucked out his eyes, he will not be able to go anywhere, and will remain constantly in this kingdom.'

"The king said to him: 'If I desired keenly that the Richi should remain in my kingdom, it was because he could see all the treasures hidden in the depths of the earth. Now that you have plucked out his eyes, what further need have I to make him stay?'"

Alas, many scientists in Europe—I mean official scientists—willingly treat their young rivals in the same fashion that the courtier treated the Richi.

---

[58] I have left this term as it is given by Berthoud, although it would not normally be applied to a person, usually being employed to designate a subcategory of *koans*. Most French and English writers contemporary with Berthoud would have called the individual in question a Yogi.

WHICH SHOULD NOT BE READ BY ANYONE AFRAID OF NIGHTMARES

There are men in Paris who have conquered, by force of merit and hard work, the four honors most envied down here: knowledge, consideration, renown and fortune. Almost all of them were only able to arrive at that goal after having traversed the first phases of maturity. You will doubtless believe that they enjoy those victorious means of wellbeing peacefully, and that, having arrived at the summit of human desire, they have paused there to rest.

Listen to me carefully: I know one of those men—and it is the same story with almost all of them—who has to get up at four o'clock in the morning in order to find two hours during which he can wrote down the bold and powerful ideas amassed in his brain. If he did not encroach so courageously upon his sleep, on the day when death comes knocking nothing would remain of his science but a name; his immense works would remain lost to his glory; every day people reap the benefits of it without knowing what they owe him. Those two hours, others dispute with him, and most of the time, it is necessary for him to give them up.

Before dawn, often in the middle of the night, people run to his home, wake him up, summon him with loud cries, in tears and in despair. Then he abandons everything, repose and work alike, for where he is summoned there is suffering to soothe and good to be done. So he hurls himself into his carriage, which speeds at the fastest gallop of his admirable horses, to carry relief to the bedside of a dying man. While, with the marvelous diagnostic ability that he owes even more to his superior intellect than to his studies, he is identifying the cause of the illness and indicating means of combating it, several more people come to interrupt and summon him. Other individuals who are suffering require his help. He cannot take a step without everyone knowing where he is coming from and where he is going; he is pursued and demanded everywhere.

The morning passes thus; when the hour comes for him to go to the hospital of which he is in charge, he has often not yet taken any nourishment. The knowledgeable doctor, who prescribes admirable rules of hygiene, neglects them for himself. No matter! He mops his brow and eats standing up and in haste. While he goes from bed to bed, his pupils follow him, respectfully collecting his slightest words, forever one of them throws a powerful light on surgical science. A Spartan would be astonished by his laconism, which says everything in the fewest words possible. When the round is over he teaches a brief lesson, and, surrounded by people who have come to ask for his help for the sick, he goes across the hospital courtyard followed by a veritable crowd.

He listens, understands, responds, promises, prescribes, launches himself into his carriage and goes home, where his antechamber, his drawing room and his dining room are overflowing with people anxiously waiting for him. He receives his clients one by one in his study, and, in spite of the strange, diverse, contrasted maladies that arrive in succession to present their multiple and mysterious symptoms to him, his attention never wearies, the clarity of his gaze is never obscured. And yet, here come more people from every direction, asking for him and pulling him away from his consultation.

He is undisturbed; he is unafraid; he remains calm, patient, serene and lucid. Finally, at four o'clock, he climbs back into his carriage. The team harnessed to the carriage is the third he has worn out since the morning. He begins running all over Paris again. I have never been able to discover when and how he dines; a family, affections and the joy of an evening by the fireside are impossible for him. He is always on the go, incessantly, a Wandering Jew driven by the pitiless hands of science and charity. Midnight is often chiming when he returns home, and he is glad if no one is waiting at the door to say to him: "If you don't come, Monsieur, my mother will die."

Then he feels tears moistening his eyes, for the generosity of his heart equals his immense knowledge. He leaves again with the poor tearful girl and only comes back a long time afterwards, dying of fatigue, worn out, starved of rest and sleep. And as I have told you, his manservant has orders to wake him up at four o'clock in the morning, no matter what time he went to bed, and no matter what complaints the poor sleeper utters. The manservant cannot leave until he has seen the physician out of bed and wrapped in his dressing-gown, before sitting down at his desk opposite the lighted lamp. Then the victim of science recommences his routine, as he did the day before and will do the following day.

He has friends who love him dearly, who bear him a truly fraternal affection, but he only sees them when they are ill. One day, one of them had recourse to the innocent ruse of a supposed malady in order to spend a quarter of an hour with him. The excellent man laughed at the joke, enjoyed it, had a hasty breakfast during which he amused himself like a child, and said as he left: "Don't do that again. Give me your word, for if you were to have recourse to it again, doubt would ensure that I wouldn't be able to come to see you anymore. I belong entirely to those who are suffering." And he left at the gallop.

Since that morning—which is to say, for a year—the two friends have not seen one another.

The other day, the writer was strolling peacefully along the boulevard, dreaming in the sunshine, stopping at shop windows, waxing ecstatic at the charming young women, so elegantly dressed, who were passing by, and mulling over an idea for an article fermenting in his brain, when he suddenly saw a fast-moving carriage coming toward him. He made out its form, its livery, its magnificent horses, and signaled to the coachman to stop. The coachman, recognizing one of his master's patients, obeyed. The door opened; he climbed in; and the two friends, after shaking hands, sat side by side, exchanging friendly words and cheerfully told one another the thousand trivial things that two people who like one another have to relate when they have not seen one another for a long time.

The carriage kept going, however, and the writer, astonished that it had covered such a long distance without stopping in front of the house of some invalid, finally asked where he was being taken. "To the Faubourg Saint-Germain, to the lodgings of an American doctor who arrived in Paris a few days ago, who has witnessed some curious experiments on human life carried out in Lancaster. It should interest you. Come along and see."

The carriage finally stopped. They went up one of those broad 18th century staircases that one only finds nowadays on the far side of the river, and were introduced into an apartment furnished with exquisite taste. An exceedingly handsome young man with very distinguished manners came to met them; he expressed himself fluently in French, and briefly expressed the enthusiasm that the illustrious physician inspired in him. The latter, however, was impatient to broach the topic of conversation that had caused him to abandon his patients for an hour, and said, with the naïve and brusque curiosity typical of him: "You've carried out curious experiments on a condemned man?"

The American passed his white hand, which a woman would have envied, through the gilded curls of his blond hair, smiled graciously and blushed slightly, but only because of the timidity he experienced in the presence of a glorious master of medical science.

"Yes, Doctor," he replied. "The condemned man was named Henry Cobler.[59] He was a kind of savage, half redskin and half European. He'd committed sixteen murders, and

---

[59] This name is abridged; the details dramatized by Berthoud are derived from Washington L. Attlee's pamphlet *Report on a series of experiments made by the medical faculty of Lancaster on the body of Henry Cobler Moselmann, executed in the jail yard of Lancaster County, Pa., on the 20th of December, 1839*. Philadelphia: T. K. & P. G. Collins, 1840.

talked about his crimes with the ease and almost with the satisfaction of a hunter recounting his exploits. Habituated for twenty years to gambling with his own life and those of others, he envisaged death calmly. One couldn't find a more suitable subject for the studies we had in mind, don't you think?"

My friend replied to that rather un-American question with a nod of the head and a monosyllabic murmur.

The foreigner went on: "It was decided that the execution would take place inside the prison. The sheriff declared that he would give his agreement to any dispositions that were not prohibited by law. A new voltaic battery was brought from the University of Pennsylvania, formed of two hundred plates organized in accordance with the Wollaston method.[60] Finally, a committee of twenty-two people was selected, of whom I was one, in order to carry out and supervise the operations.

"Cobler did not yet know, however, the date of his execution. When the day came I accompanied the chairman of the committee to the condemned man's cell, and we had a conversation with him regarding trivial matters. He seemed quite placid, and agreed with a good grace to fill a bottle that the chairman gave him with air from his lungs. The chairman sealed the bottle hermetically. Cobler's pulse, which I took while pretending to give the unfortunate man a handshake, was eighty-four per minute. He complained of a slight headache.

"'It's the lack of exercise in the open air,' he said, with a forced smile. 'I'll be getting some air soon.'

"When that thought came to mind I felt his pulse-rate rise to a hundred and seventeen. His heart was beating so violently that one could have counted the movements through the fabric of his waistcoat.

"At that moment, the warder came in, and read Henry Cobler the sheriff's warrant that fixed his execution for the

---

[60] William Hyde Wollaston (1766-1828) invented a battery in which the zinc plates could be raised out of the acid to slow down their erosion.

following day. The condemned man went pale; his features lost their composure; a convulsive frisson that he tried to repress ran through his limbs; his feet twitched so violently that one of the canvas shoes he was wearing split. All through the night, which he spent in prayer with the minister, an ardent fever devoured him. The next morning, when he appeared on the scaffold, he had aged ten years. The fatal platform fell on the twentieth of December at two seventeen a.m. A few movements resembling efforts were manifest; at two-twenty, Cobler's soul was before his Creator."

The American physician then reported various observations regarding the manner in which the blood congeals in a cadaver that has suffered a violent death. Three minutes after the execution, the pulse was a hundred and forty; then it beat at two hundred and forty for two minutes; in the fifth and sixth minute it reached three hundred; by the seventh it was only a hundred and fifty, and by the eighth it had ceased entirely.

The American doctor's two listeners looked at one another fearfully and asked one another with a mute glance how it came about that there were men sufficiently devoted to science to carry out such studies.

After a brief pause, and with the same composure as if he were speaking of the previous evening's opera, the foreigner continued: "As for the heart, over four minutes, its sound became muted, but nothing disturbed their rhythm. Then they were heard to recover their force; there was no more appreciable noise by the twelfth minute."

It is necessary to apologize to readers to whom this already seems too horrible, but the title has warned them as to what they would find in this chapter; let them be warned, furthermore, that what follows is no less hideous.

"When the body was taken down from the scaffold, forty-seven minutes after the execution, it was taken into a neighboring room and placed on a table insulated with wax, the spinal cord was cut. By means of a perforation of the trachea, an artificial respiration as established, and the two poles of the electrical battery were placed, the positive on the left of the neck and the negative on the seventh rib on the left side. I shivered with horror, monsieur, for all the organs of respiration quivered: the nose dilated, he chest swelled, the lips opened and stirred. I distinctly heard air going in and out of the lungs.

"The position of the negative pole was changed; when it was placed beneath the navel, he cadaver seemed to have recovered a complete existence. A candle presented to the nostrils was blown out by the force of the respiration; the arms stirred; the legs and thighs trembled; the eyelids parted to allow a glimpse of vitreous eyes. Finally, all of a sudden, Cobler propped himself up on his elbow, extended his arm and raised his head. The operator who was moving the negative pole over the subject recoiled in horror. One might have thought that the cadaver had been resuscitated."

I will spare you the scientific details of the experiments that the Lancaster committee continued to make. Of considerable interest to professionals, they would have none for those who demand excitement or distraction from these informal pieces. After two hours of conversation, the doctor and his companion took their leave of the English physician, who recounted such frightful thing with his imperturbable self-composure, his white hands, his pink cheeks and his blond hair, who had gone up on to the scaffold during an execution in order to study a man's final convulsions at close range, to place his hand on the dying man's heart, to count its pulsations and feel their gradual extinction.

"You look pale, my friend," said the doctor, as we left.

"Anyone would. What purpose do these atrocious experiments serve?"

"The discovery of a few traces of the great secret of life," he replied. "God only delivers the faintest fragments of his divine secrets to perseverance, courage and hard work. Science makes people cruel. If you knew how many animals' lives the study of the slightest organic phenomena costs every day...there are poor dogs that die of starvation, others that expire half-dissected. In a book that my celebrate colleague

Dr. Amussat has published on the introduction of air into the veins,[61] he recounts ingenuously that his experiments have inflicted cruel tortures on and killed thousands of rabbits, whole packs of dogs, herds of horses and flocks of sheep.

"It's true that, unlike the Americans, we haven't yet gone as far as to deliver humans to the executioners; we content ourselves with carrying out amputations in crowded amphitheaters and teaching at the bedsides of the dying. But I repeat, that is the price of knowledge; it's take it or leave it; there's no other choice. The end sanctifies the means.

"In any case, believe me, however habituated one becomes to such things, the heart is never blasé about them. It requires more courage than one might think to draw a scalpel over a poor creature struck by illness, and whose existence often depends on the composure with which one operates. So the profession of surgeon, noble as its objective is, demands an abnegation and a devotion that the world at large does not suspect, and to which it which its shows itself too unjust.

"Here we are back on the boulevard. Resume your walk and your pleasant idling. Me, I'm going to visit the sick, to listen to complaints and make ingrates."

---

[61] Jean Zuléma Amussat (1796-1856) was most celebrated for his pioneering work on urogenital surgery, but Berthoud refrained fro popularizng his account of how to contrive an artificial anus in a new-born child. The work cited here is *Recherches sur l'introduction accidentelle de l'air dans les veines* (1839), which reports his investigations of the question of whether embolisms introduced during surgery could kill patients.

THE STORY OF A TREE IN THE CHAMPS-ÉLYSÉES

In the Champs-Élysées, not far from the crossroads, there is an elm tree that I thought in my youth the most beautiful tree in the row; on its own, it shaded almost everything around.

Originating from the Trianon nursery, that tree was uprooted from its native soil in 1759 and transplanted to the location it occupies today. It was about ten years old then, and its slender form was somewhat reminiscent, I must admit, of a beanpole. With its roots laid bare, mutilated and stripped of their native soil, with its trunk jolted on a rickety cart, and its bark bruised and damaged, the poor thing arrived at its destination.

A hole was dug in the ground, which was both sticky with clay and full of stones, as well as could be contrived, and it was planted there as it was, abandoned to the grace of God.

It was under the direction of the famous botanist Thouin[62] that the plantation was accomplished; his methods seem rather crude today, but they were sincerely admired in the epoch when he put them to work.

In such poor conditions, the elm languished for some time, without anyone worrying about it unduly. In the early years, it only bore a yellow, meager and belated foliage that did not last long. Over time, nevertheless, with the aid of the vigor of youth, it ended up getting the upper hand. It plunged some of its roots into the utmost depths of the terrain, while it extended others near the surface, horizontal, gnarly and branching, organized like stems and endowed with marvelous powers of suction. It was seen to grow tall and stout, to be-

---

[62] André Thouin (1746-1824).

come verdant, and take on proportions both elegant and robust.

Unfortunately, when that salutary crisis occurred, political events were subject to great upheavals; royalty was unsteady, the Marquis de La Fayette had already made his appearance.[63] A street-urchin, who much preferred patriotic ovations to the endeavors of his workshop, tore off the elm's most beautiful branches in order to throw them under the feet of the white horse of the hero of two worlds.

The poor tree, bruised and broken, covered with gaping wounds that let its sap flow out, almost died for a second time—but good times soon followed. Throughout the Revolution, and even during the Consulate and the early years of the Empire, it lived peacefully in a profound solitude and forgetfulness, without anyone even thinking of pruning its lush branches, which grew at their whim, here and there, high up and low down, in every direction, and ended up forming a dense and inextricable vault of verdure in which flocks of sparrows, finches and wood-pigeons nested. It even flowered. A scientist, who doubtless had nothing better to do, amused himself by counting its seeds, and found three hundred and twenty-nine thousand of them. Let us admit, however, that not a single one of those seeds grew, and that they served as pasture for all the birds resident in the branches.

No one passed close to the elm, except for the aforementioned scientist, and, occasionally, the infamous inhabitants of the Allée des Veuves and the infamous dens of vice that surrounded the ill-reputed quarter. One day, in fact, an old man was found at the foot of the tree, bathed in his own blood, riddled with stab-wounds and robbed of his watch and his purse; it was the unfortunate botanist. But no one paid any heed to him or gave any thought to delivering his murderers to the

---

[63] The "appearance" in question is presumably the Edict of Versailles that the Marquis de Lafayette, having returned briefly to France after his distinguished service in the American War of Independence, persuaded Louis XVI to issue in 1787.

law. In those days, similar crimes were committed frequently, and with impunity, in that corner of Paris, where the Moulin Rouge, the Jardin Mabille, innumerable restaurants and countless gas-lamps flourish today. The gaiety of a certain society has chosen and adopted, in order to expand thereinto, places long haunted by vice, crime and darkness, which have nowadays become the busiest and best illuminated in the capital. There, where brigands once demanded our money or your life with dagger in hand, prostitutes now deploy their seductions—just as dangerous, of course; they rob more dupes in a season than all the thieves in the Allée des Veuves did in twenty years.

In 1814 and 1815, the elm saw hordes of Cossacks camping under its branches. They hung the produce of their pillage there; their horses, as savage as them, browsed its bark; finally, the hideous children of the Don lit their bivouac fires against its trunk, which burned it in an outrageous fashion and stigmatized it with ineradicable wounds.

During the Restoration, the elm recovered somewhat. The Restoration had other things to occupy its thoughts than the trees in the Champs-Élysées. It ordered street-lights to be attached to them at intervals, but those street-lights only served, as Dante put it, to render the darkness visible.

The July Revolution arrived, and that put a permanent end to the repose and health of our elm.

The new king wanted to embellish Paris, and commenced with the quays and the Champs-Élysées. To the former he gave trees, to the latter, gaslight!

Gas! It requires subterranean channels and cast-iron conduits that seek out the roots under the ground, mutilating them, crushing them, severing them, tearing them and preventing them from extending. There are leaks that infect them with hydrocarbons and literally poison them. There is a glare the renders it impossible for the poor tree to rest and sleep. The products of that fatal light infect the foliage, cover it with fumes, grill it and deprive it of the nocturnal slumber of which vegetables have just as much need as the creatures of the animal kingdom; finally, they pervert the economy of its natural functions and asphyxiate it by preventing it from aspiring and expiring carbon dioxide and oxygen.

After that came the asphalt sidewalks, which no longer permitted the rain to penetrate the earth and evaporate therefrom; they poisoned the atmosphere with their vapor and fumes. How, in those deadly conditions, could an elm conserve its robust constitution, resist abrupt changes of temperature, supporting alternations of hot and cold in the same day, and suffer the fury of the winds that broke its branches, hollowing out crevices and gutters in the gaping wounds they made, along which bleeding sap ran with the rain?

Take note that I still have not mentioned illuminations, the most redoubtable of all scourges. Woe betide the roots that the poles required by those illuminations seek out in the depths of the earth! Woe betide the leaves and branches deluged with fume and roasted, for an entire evening, by the fetid exhalations of lanterns. A sticky sweat covered them with a corrosive coating, in which accumulated, additionally, the formidable dust raised up by the tramping of the crowds.

Thus, our elm and many of its companions were beginning to perish in 1848. They shed their withered foliage before time and strewed the streets with formless and nameless debris. Even the most indifferent pedestrians observed their languor, their pitiful condition and their dry rough, cracked bark, peeling off in various places.

One spring evening, a little beetle landed on the hero of this story, and slid insidiously between the sinuosities of its bark. Over an extent of at least two and a half leagues, with its the reddish-brown wing-cases and feet, its head ornamented with two long antennae, and its black body bristling with little spikes, it set about ferreting here and there until it encountered a location appropriate to its perfidious designs. It stopped at a part of the bark that formed a sort of microscopic valley, protected on both sides by high protrusions, like hills. In the middle of that valley was a soft, damp substance that had partly decomposed as a result of time, bad weather, and the miseries and sufferings of the tree.

In that substance, the insect that entomologists call *Scolytus multistriatus*,[64] did not delay, assisting itself with its feet and mandible, to open the entrance to a naturally-formed fissure in the elevated bark. Once it had penetrated between the bark and the living wood, it began to hollow out a tunnel parallel to the cortical fibers in the vertical dimension. It did not work straight ahead but contrived curves and serpentine lines, seemingly capricious but occasioned by insurmountable obstacles opposed by the hardness of certain parts of the wood.

The scolytus in question was a female. When she had drilled and perforated sufficiently she laid her eggs, covered them with the vegetal debris that her inroads had produced, retraced her steps to her entry-point, paused at the opening, sealed it hermetically with the aid of her body, and died, making sure by that final act of affection of the conservation of her eggs.

The eggs of the scolytus gave rise to a hundred larvae equipped with robust mandibles, which, scarcely hatched, began to inflict frightful damage, shredding the wood and hollowing out tunnels in all directions. When they were sated to bursting-point, they metamorphosed into pupae and became, a fortnight later, adult scolytes that flew off, mated and returned to lay eggs in their turn.

That race of diggers multiplied in a fashion so rapid and frightful that, a year later, there was not a single intact tree in the entire Champs-Élysées.

No invasion ever takes place without bringing in its wake a population of enemies and parasites. Once the scolytes were masters of the trees in the Champs-Élysées, ichneumon flies converged from all directions, which slipped under the bark in

---

[64] Berthoud has "*scolyte destructeur*," but obviously means the European elm bark beetle responsible for "Dutch elm disease," so I have substituted the standard specific designation.

order to lay eggs there destined to produced larvae avid for scolytus larvae; then came the millipedes, the woodlice, the ants and the earwigs, all contributing, each according to its strength and habits, to the general work of destruction. So, the bark of the elm, once so beautiful, was seen to blister, to peel and to fall off in large plaques, leaving the moist and delicate tissues of the living wood bare and defenseless.

Monsieur le Comte de Rambuteau,[65] the memory of whom the city of Paris conserves with gratitude, was moved to compassion by so many trees threatened by death. He looked for a physician for them, and ended up finding one. He was, let it be said in passing, a veritable doctor of medicine.

Under the direction of that physician, the bark that served as a repair of scolytes was attacked mercilessly; millions of insects were destroyed; the gaps were tarred; grooves were cut at the feet of the trees, disposed in rows, designed to allow water and air to reach the rots. The roots of the tree were backed vertically with drainage tubes, the openings of which were covered with broken tiles; bark that was thoroughly diseased was scraped away or removed; finally, the decorticated trees were literally enameled. Today, you can still see them, like invalids in their hospital casts. Furthermore, you will smile at the sight of the upper parts their trunks, circled by a kind of tin-plate funnel simultaneously reminiscent of a teapot

---

[65] The Comte de Rambuteau (1781-1869) was the Prefect of the Seine from 1833-1848, and in that capacity he began the methodical transformation of Paris that was eventually taken over and completed under the Second Empire by Baron Haussmann. His principal motivation was hygienic, inspired by the terrible cholera epidemic on 1832, which he blamed on the cramped and insanitary streets. A passionate horticulturalist, he was insistent on establishing plantations of trees alone the new avenues he constructed. He also introduced the characteristic public urinals that were long characteristic of the capital.

and the instrument that Molière did not hesitate to place in the hands of his matassins.[66]

Among the most melancholy, the sickest, the most extensively plastered with compresses and the most circled with grooves is the elm whose historiographer we have elected to be. Will it escape death? Will it recover its former vigor and verdure? God alone knows, and the future will inform us. As in all real romances—as Balzac said—its story lacks a denouement.

In the meantime, a former minister, Monsieur le Comte Jaubert,[67] had devoted to these great botanical invalids a charming notice in which he lavishes both science and compassion. That example has emboldened the author of these notes to tell the story of an elm in his turn; and then, as a final excuse, he recalls this legend of his dear and pleasant native land. There was once, on the summit of a rock, an impregnable château where a Baron lived who devastated the entire region for ten leagues around by his exactions, his pillages and his murders. One night, the Baron dreamed that his supreme hour had sounded and that he found himself confronted by God, at the fatal moment when as the church says in its terrible song of *Dies irae*, the just sense their punishment assured: *Cum vix Justus sit securus.*

The angel Raphael was holding a golden balance; Satan was accumulating on the left all the Baron's mortal sins, represented by the demons that had inspired them. Seven could be counted, who were circling and holding hands around a group of ten others; finally, six were clinging on to the extremity of the beam and trying to force it down on their side.

---

[66] Matassins were comical dancers dressed in silly costume and armed with wooden swords or pigs' bladders mounted on sticks like those employed in English Morris dancers. Berthoud presumably has the latter devices in mind.

[67] Hippolyte-François Jaubert (1798-1874). The catalogue of the Bibliothèque Nationale lists numerous treatises on botany published by him in the 1850s, several relating to Paris, but it is not obvious from the titles which one Berthoud has in mind.

The first were saying: "Prideful! Avaricious! Lustful! Envious! Gluttonous! Wrathful! Idler!"

The second were howling: "Impious! Blasphemer! Church-burner! Bad son! Murderer! Liar! Lecher! Adulterer!"

The third were screeching, with triumphant laughter: "He fought and pillaged on Sundays! He never set foot in a church! He never went near a confessional! He profaned sacred vessels! Instead of fasting, he gorged himself on meat, even on Good Friday!"

On the right-hand pan, nothing was visible but one very tiny angel. Alone, he was counterbalancing the weight of the gigantic and hideous horde of the Spirit of Evil.

"Who, then, are you, gentle protector, who are saving me from the eternity of Hell?" asked the Baron. "Before I descend into purgatory, tell me your name. For, alas, in my sad and culpable life, I do not recall ever having done a single god deed."

"On the eve of your death," the angel replied, "you found a flower in your garden partly desiccated by the ardor of the sun. It lay wilting on the ground; you raised it up with your hands; you braced it with the aid of a stick that you had cut with your dagger; finally to irrigate it, you fetched water in your helmet from a nearby well. That is what has saved you from damnation."

The legend adds that the Baron woke up with a start, and that, softened and touched by the immensity of divine mercy, he converted, distributed his wealth to the poor, made his château into a convent, took the cloth and died in an odor of sanctity. He must be stationed in paradise beside Saint Fiacre, the patron saint of gardeners.[68]

---

[68] The 7th century Irish ascetic Fiachra went to France in search of solitude and became a hermit in the province of Brie, where he cultivated his garden. He is also the patron saint of victims of venereal disease and cab drivers. (But French cabs were called *fiacres* because the Hôtel de Saint-Fiacre in Paris was one of the first institutions to hire out carriages, not because they contributed to the spread of venereal disease.)

THE DIABOLICAL COAL-MERCHANT

On one of the autumn evenings that fog renders so lugubrious in northern France, a farmer already past his prime was passing through a forest that did not enjoy, it must be said, a very edifying reputation in those days.

Tiot Watremetz—that was the man's name—was walking, with some difficulty, along paths that were hidden from his gaze by the white and fetid vapors that were increasingly rising from the ground. Sometimes he stubbed his toe on a stone, sometimes he sank knee-deep into earth soaked by the rain; sometimes, even though he was testing the ground in front of him with his staff, he found himself face to face with a tree whose already-leafless branches were tearing at his face, or a thorny bush in which his legs became caught.

After three full hours of walking through the forest, he ended up getting completely disorientated, and no longer knew whether he ought to go forwards or backwards, steer to the right or turn left—with the result that, his brow bathed with sweat and harassed by fatigue and exasperated, he let a horrible oath escape from his lips that was singularly tinged with blasphemy.

As the same instant that he committed the sin in question, he heard a little dry cough behind him. He turned round swiftly and found himself face to face with a tall, thin individual dressed entirely in black, save for a red velvet hood that enveloped his face.

"Well," said the unknown man, wrapping himself even more tightly in the folds of an ample cloak lined with a fine and rich sable fur, "it seems that you've gone astray in the forest. An unfortunate thing, believe me! The fog doesn't allow a man to see two paces ahead of him, night's falling, the wolves are howling and you have no weapons."

"Yes I have," replied Tiot Watremetz, testily and almost angrily. "Yes I have—I have this holly-wood staff. So long as I hold it in my hand, so long as it's connected to my wrist by its leather cord, I fear no wolf, nor man, nor devil."

"Well," replied the unknown man, "the wolves are beginning to get hungry, thieves haunt the woods, and the Devil might well be here, lurking in some corner. I'm told that he likes this crossroads well enough."

"Where are we, then?"

"At the Sabbat crossroads."

"The Sabbat crossroads!" the farmer repeated, going pale.

"A pretty spot—but not at this hour, and even less so at midnight."

"You're right," Tiot Watremetz replied. "Thank you for having informed me as to my path. I'll be home in an hour."

"Unless something unfortunate happens—which I hope it won't. *Au revoir*."

"God bless you," replied Tony Watremetz, who set out again with his firmest stride. He was not sorry to quit the man, for whom he felt, without any reason, a profound and invincible aversion.

On hearing the farmer's last words, the unknown individual, struck by a sudden indisposition, nearly fainted. Pale and trembling, scarcely able to stand up, he would have fallen but for a tree, against which he leaned. At any rate, the indisposition in question disappeared as quickly as it had arrived, and five minutes had not gone by when a strident voice called Tiot Watremetz back.

"Hey, friend!" the voice cried. "You've forgotten something. Wait for me—I'll return it to you."

Tiot Watremetz turned round and found himself face to face for a second time with the singular individual whose voice he had just heard coming from more than two mencaudees away.[69]

"Are you very rich, then, to strew bags of coins around forests like this?" the other asked him, presenting him with a bulging leather bag.

"That bag isn't mine."

"Whose can it be, then? Aren't you curious to see what it contains? There must be at least two hundred écus in it."

"I feel sorry for the man who lost it, and I urge you to take it to the burgomaster of the nearest hamlet."

"Oh yes! If you'd found the bag, would you take it to the burgomaster of the nearest hamlet?

"Wouldn't you do as much yourself?"

"Me? Well, perhaps I'd return it to its owner, if I knew who he was—but the burgomaster! The burgomaster would simply put it in his own strong-box, and neither I nor the owner would ever here mention of it again. Then again, look at the bag—it's been lying for a devil of a long time in the corner where I just changed to unearth it with the tip of my stick. Shall I give you some good advice? Let's split it."

"Take what doesn't belong to me?"

"Pick up what belongs to anyone, that's all."

The bag seemed to grow and triple in size in the unknown man's hand. "Well," he murmured, "I said two hundred écus—it's a thousand, two thousand, four thousand gold coins that the purse contains. Oh! Rich gems, admirable diamonds hidden at the very bottom, underneath that beautiful round sum. Have you ever seen so much gold in all your life?"

"No," replied Tiot Watremetz, almost angrily, darting a covetous glance at the treasure in spite of himself. "Go to the Devil and leave me in peace!"

He started walking again.

"To the Devil!" sniggered the other. "One could do worse. I've heard it said that the Devil isn't always a bad

---

[69] A mencaudee was actually an ancient measure of area rather than distance, so the use of the term here might be a mistake.

companion. Since you're refusing to share with me, I'll keep it all."

He ran after Tiot Watremetz then, who was just entering a large field in which more pebbles grew that wheat. It was known as the Field of Stones because of the druidic monuments that loomed up on all sides. Catherine, the farmer's wife, had brought it to him as a dowry.

The nocturnal tempter casually linked arms with the farmer, who was not at all pleased by that familiarity.

"Look," he said, "you understand, don't you, that all this is a joke? The purse is mine, and I only showed it to you for a bit of fun. But come on, be frank. If you found a bag like mine on your path, wouldn't you pick it up?"

"No."

"And if you found ten?"

"I wouldn't steal them, I tell you."

"And if they contained millions? Enough to become a great lord? To do anything you might wish? To see others at your feet, as submissive as serfs, as slaves? To swim in opulence instead of crouching in poverty! To rest instead of working! To command instead of obeying! Well, what do you say?"

"What's the point of replying, since all those treasures aren't here?"

"They are here! Here they are!" said the unknown man, who, clapping him on the shoulder, bumped into one of those druidic monuments that one encounters so frequently in certain parts of France, where they litter the fields.

The stone fell over with a formidable sound, and revealed, at the bottom of a gaping hole, such a mass of gold that a king could not have spent it in a year.

"You're Satan in person, then? " said Tiot Watremetz, raising his hand to make the sign of the cross.

"I am, as they say, an old devil—and nothing more!" he retorted, laughing—for he was always laughing, and his laughter made Tiot Watremetz feel ill. "Once, twice, you don't want to have anything to do with me? Done."

Giving the farmer a clap on the shoulder, he replaced the stone and vanished.

Tiot Watremetz went home, so pensive that his wife asked him what was the matter with him. He told her, sighing, what had happened to him.

It was his wife's turn to become pensive. That hardly ever happened, for there was no housewife for ten leagues around more lively, more good-humored and, above all, so determined. Needless to say, the two spouses spent a sleepless night. At daybreak, Catherine got up, got dressed, told her husband to do likewise, and to put a pickaxe over his shoulder, picked up another herself, and marched straight to the Field of Stones.

Tony Watremetz showed Catherine the block of sandstone that the unknown man had moved so briskly the day before. They noticed, fearfully, three black holes in the middle of the block that looked as if they had been hollowed out by fingers of red hot iron. Their terror increased further on seeing, in the wet grass, footprints that had not only burned the grass but charred the soil. There could no longer be any doubt about it; Tiot Watremetz had been dealing with the Devil.

Catherine made the sigh of the cross, and her pick-axe struck the ground first. "God help us," she said, "this sterile field belongs to us. Let's dig and take possession of the treasure!"

They worked thus for nearly a month, hollowing out a wide ditch, but only arrived, after so much labor and effort, at a layer of shiny black rock, so friable that it broke effortlessly beneath the pick. You can imagine their disappointment.

"You wanted to enter into a contest with the Devil," sighted Tiot Watremetz, piteously. "You see what so much trouble has got us."

A burst of laughter relied to those words, and a mysterious individual appeared, sitting on a druidic stone, without them having been able to see where he had come from or how he had got there. Tiot Watremetz recognized the traveler he had met a month before.

"Well, he who plays with fire burns his fingers!" he sniggered, in his shrill voice. "You wanted to match wits with a spirit and you're nothing but imbeciles! Here, look!"

He picked up three or four pieces of the black stone that the ditch contained, arranged them in a heap, put some wooden branches underneath and rubbed the end of his finger against the ground. Immediately, a lively flame emerged from his fingertip, with the aid of which he lit the little bundle of twigs. The black stones caught fire in their turn, and produced a blazing fire.

"If there's no gold there, isn't this just as good?" he asked. "There's a shortage of wood in the region, and the neighboring forest, devastated by incessant felling, will soon contained nothing but saplings. This ditch, whose seams of coal extend for more than a league underground, contains enough to heat ten whole provinces for a century. Exploit it, and you'll become richer than the gentleman who refused Lazarus the crumbs from his table."

"What are you asking in exchange for the mine? For once you've gone, we won't find anything there any longer. The coal it contains will go the same way as the gold it enclosed the other day."

"I like your pretty little wife's common sense!" he riposted, sitting down more comfortably on the stone on top of which he was perched. "Let's see! For ten years I'll guarantee you health proof against anything, and a fortune to make the jealous people in your village die of jealousy—which is to say, all the inhabitants except one."

"Ten years!" said Catherine disdainfully. "You're hardly generous."

"Damn! One doesn't dicker with you very easily, or very cheaply. Well, let's make it twelve years."

"No—fifteen."

"Twelve! I won't be beaten down by a minute."

"And after that twelve years?"

"I'll come and offer you a hand, to guide you to another mine much richer than this one. Go on—sign and let's get it over with. The *Angelus* won't be long in sounding, and I have urgent business that doesn't permit me to linger, or to hear the sound of that annoying bell."

"I accept," said Catherine, "but alone. My husband, you understand, doesn't enter into the bargain at all."

"I'd rather have one woman that thirty thousand simpletons like him. Sign this little parchment for me."

"I don't know how to write. I'll put my cross."

Satan trembled more than Tiot Watremetz was trembling, who was nevertheless on the brink of fainting.

"Put your finger in the mud and press it on the paper. Good! *Au revoir*!"

The earth opened up beneath his feet and he vanished.

"What have you done, Catherine? What have you done?" groaned Tiot Watremetz.

"Continue to live in peace like the good Christian you are," she replied. "Satan's reputed to be very clever, but however smart he is, women don't lose out to him in comparison."

For eleven years, eleven months and thirty days, nothing troubled the ever-increasing prosperity of Tiot Watremetz and his wife. Six thousand workers employed in the coal mine revealed by Satan and nine others located not far away were not sufficient to meet the demands of the various customers who came to buy the coal.

Gold flooded into Messire Watremetz's house—or, rather, château, for Catherine had acquired noble titles for him. Furthermore, the fashion in which she spent her vast fortune won her the affection and respect of everyone. She founded hospitals, built churches, endowed poor girls, lent money to the needy and gave to the indigent, and attracted more blessings than the archbishop himself, even though he was universally deemed to be a very charitable prelate.

On the evening of the thirty-first day of the twelfth month of the twelfth year, Satan came into Catherine's room. He bowed to her in a sprightly fashion, and, with the air of a well-bred gentleman, told her in fine words that he was at her disposal to undertake the journey promised in the terms of their agreement.

"I was expecting you," she replied, graciously, with one of her finest curtsies. "Just grant me the time to give a few orders."

"To have more hospitals and churches built, I suppose? My word, no! The use you've made of the fortune you owe to my munificence has been too silly for me to let you continue with such a scandal. Good works, as you call them, displease me royally."

"You'll permit me, at least, to say goodbye to my husband?"

"Never mind that! Petty people's manners, my dear. Let's go!"

"An honest woman keeps her word. When midnight chimes, I'll go with you." She stood up and put on her mantle. "How cold it is!" she said. "I'm shivering from head to toe. Outside, I feel sure, it's cold enough to crack stones. I need to bring a little heat with me. Hold on, I'll just throw this bundle of carnation stems on the fire. Promise me you won't take me until they're consumed—it'll only take a quarter of a minute."

"By my pitchfork!" cries Satan, impatiently. "There's never an end to it with women. You won't be cold where I'm taking you. Come on!"

"If you don't grant my request," she said, laughing, "if you don't swear to me not to take me until this bundle is burned, I warn you, I'll make a fuss. I'll resist and call for help—beware of the curé and his exorcisms!"

"I swear to you, then!" he cried, irritably. "But hurry up, or I'll use violence."

Instead of throwing the handful of carnation stems into the fire, she plunged them into a font full of holy water hidden behind her.

Satan uttered a howl of range that was audible a league away. Catherine started laughing so loudly that she had to hold her sides.

"Get away, simpleton!" she said, when the stifling laughter permitted her to speak. "Get away with your scant shame, presumptuous as you've been to match wits with a woman. Get away, I tell you, or I'll sprinkle you with this holy water from your horns to your cloven feet. Return alone to your eternal furnace, and may my endless prayers, when God admits me to his paradise, add to your chagrin and your despair!" As she finished speaking she brandished an aspergillum, which put the accursed angel to flight.

Don't believe, however, that the Demon did not avenge himself for his disappointment. The next day, water flooded Tiot Watremetz's coal mines; there were terrible collapses; fire-damp caused terrible ravages there, and the edifice of the two spouses' immense fortune did not take long to crumble. They scarcely retained enough to live on, and that humbly.

But, as Dame Catherine observed, maliciously, the poverty that Satan inflicted upon them only served to ease their road Heaven, since it is specifically written in the gospel: "Blessed art the poor, for theirs is the kingdom of Heaven."

Such is the legend that was recounted to me in my infancy by a sexagenarian maidservant, the daughter of a foreman in the mines of Anzin. At present, who knows whether anyone except me still knows the tale, three or four hundred years old, transmitted from mouth to mouth, which is perhaps being written down for the first time today? The humblest engineer knows better than the Medieval Satan how to discover coal mines; pumps powered by steam intercept and expel subterranean waters; scaffolding simply and expertly disposed reduce collapses, and fire-damp, which has simply become carbonated hydrogen, is stopped, impotently, by the metallic sheath with which Davy has enveloped the lamps that bar his name. Science arrives and legend, alas, goes away.

Jean-Jacques Rousseau, who, in the *Nouvelle Héloïse*, shows us with so much aplomb the imaginary art of manufacturing fine vintages with simple wines of any kind, said nevertheless: "I will only believe in chemistry on the day when chemistry can recombine what it breaks down."

Thank God, twenty years later, chemistry has realized and exceeded the program of the author of *Émile*. Like it or not, it is necessary today to believe in chemistry. There is no lack of convincing facts, and they are becoming more numerous every day.

Monsieur Barouilhet,[70] for example, has just provided the solution of one of the gravest problems of geology. He has produced artificial coal.

To obtain this result, which the 16th century would have regarded as sorcery, and the eighteenth as a endeavor akin to the conjuring tricks of the Comte Saint-Germain, he interposes layers of ligneous matter between layers of marl and encloses them in a vessel that without being completely sealed, is nevertheless disposed in such a fashion that the gases disengaged can remain for a determined time in contact with the wood and marl.

He then submits that preparation to a temperature that scarcely surpasses two hundred degrees, and he obtains products that completely resemble coal; we might even say that they are identical to it.

The coal modifies its nature in accordance with the wood employed and the more or less powerful effect of the temperature. A few leaves placed between the layers have left their imprint on the artificial coal—literally, as one sees in natural blocks extracted from mines.

It results from this experiment that of all the theories made on the formation of coal, one alone is true: the one that attributes it to masses of vegetation assembled by waters, rather like peat-bogs, and then submitted to the effects of the central fire of the globe, then much more powerful than in our day.

---

[70] This result was reported in the scientific journal *Cosmos* in 1858, where Berthoud, who repeats sections of it almost word for word, evidently found it, but Monsieur Barouilhet is otherwise untraceable.

How much there is in a sonnet! said the fine minds of Louis XIV's court, although they had other reasons for admiration around them, including Molière and Bossuet. Can the 19th century not cry, with more reason, and a more legitimate pride: How much there is in a lump of coal!

Even Louis XIV and his court would recognize today that a lump of coal and its products are worth more than a faultless sonnet, which, according to Boileau, was itself worth as much as a long poem.

There is everything in oil, even essences for confectionery.

When one distils coal, one obtains three substances: one solid, coke; the second liquid, tar; and the third gaseous, carbonated hydrogen. One can also harvest waters from it from which one can extract, in abundance and cheaply, ammonia, widely used in industry, which, at the end of the last century, was bought from Orientals at a high price, it being claimed that it could only be obtained from camel dung.

You are familiar with the immediate employments of coke and hydrogen; one lights, the other heats.

As for the tar, such as it emerges from the retort, its employment is less immediate. People have tried to substitute it for asphalt in road-building but it lacks solidity and resistance; the feet sink into the black layers, almost as they do in mud, except that one does not get them out so easily.

To take advantage of coal tar, it is necessary to distil it further.

Chemistry first, and then industry, obtain from this substance, previously useless, liquids infinitely variable in density and properties, for a light oil scarcely weighing as much as alcohol to the heavy, nacreous solid naphthalene, which plays an often-efficacious role in curing skin diseases.

The hydrocarbons produced by the distillation of coal tar form a family of substances appropriate to remove stains from fabrics, such as etherene, carburene and benzene.[71] The last-named enjoys great popularity; everyone in Paris possesses a bottle, and every cleaning shop displays bottles of it in its windows.

The second distillation of coal tar gives rise to another family, that of gazogenes. Mixed with alcohol they can replace fuel oil to a certain extent, and are known by the name of liquid gas. Almost alone, they possess the property of dissolving rubber; they cause the noxious odor emitted by garments coated in that substance. Finally, submitted to certain reactions, distilled again and combined with ether, they become essences with a delightful perfume, which Parisian confectionery, the best in the world, employs to give its bonbons the taste of strawberry or pineapple. Rum and cognac often receive their bouquet from a few drops of the least of these essences.

One also obtains from coal tar a pigment analogous to one of the precious colors obtained from madder.

Various properties of coal products, observed and studied, will doubtless not be long in giving further progress to industry. Tanning, among others, will one day achieve results in a matter of hours that can presently only be obtained after months of work. The principle on which these future methods rests exists in theory, but its application still remains insufficient. One finds oneself blocked by one of those invincible obstacles that hazard often ends up removing when human genius, thinking itself vanquished, gives up.

But let's get back to the bonbons.

Sugary confections with the flavor of apple, pear, quince, melon and many others, the English sweets that have become popular and are sold by grocers, owe their aroma to combinations of butyric ether with vinegar, valerianic acid or coccinic acid, extracted from coconuts. Butyric ether is itself merely a

---

[71] Berthoud's versions of these terms are taken from primitive classification of hydrocarbons drawn up in 1836 by the French chemist Auguste Laurent (1807-1853); some have become obsolete but I have retained Anglicizations of the terms he uses rather than substituting the modern terms for the compounds in question.

compound produced from butyric acid. Now, that acid is obtained by the distillation of decomposing organic matter, such as cheese or meat. Let us add, to reassure the disgusted, that one can also prepare it by the metamorphosis that sugar, starch and other analogous substances undergo on contact with nitrogenated substances capable of acting as fermenting agents.

And besides, does not chemistry, like fire, purify everything?

A HAUNTED ROOM

Most of us shrug our shoulders and laugh pityingly when someone mentions those mysterious rooms, once so common in old châteaux, where no one could sleep easy, because they were haunted by spirits. Nevertheless, the most courageous and the less credulous emerged from those sinister places, and sometimes still emerge today, in a state of irremediable unease, pale, frightened by strange visions and disinclined to undergo such a rude ordeal again.

In the Middle Ages, such phenomena were explained either by the visitation of a soul in pain soliciting prayers that would extract it from purgatory, or by the presence of some demon put in possession of a part of the château thanks to some crime committed between its old walls.

In the 18th century, strong minds denied these stories, ridiculous in their opinion, and treated as imbeciles those who did not share their incredulity relative to the subject.

Now the 19th century has come, which, in its maturity, not only observes but also explains the reality of phantasmagorias that frightened our ancestors, in which philosophers of the Voltairean school did not believe and which, at present, many people mock.

It is from English and French medical journals that the facts you are about to read are taken.

Last year—which is to say, in 1858—a young lord inherited an ancient manor house in the mountains of Scotland, in which there was a "Green Room" in which no one dared to spend the night. It was said that two or three audacious individuals who had attempted to sleep there had only emerged from it dead or in a pitiful state, even the most fortunate needing weeks to get over it.

On the very day that he took possession of his manor house, Lord MacM*** ordered that the Green Room be made ready for him and announced his intention of residing in it for the entire duration of his stay. By acting thus, the new inheritor wanted to show the domestics and tenants that he was not to be duped by some crude trick doubtless invented to keep a master to whose surveillance they did not want to submit away from his estate.

At first he slept peacefully in the Green Room, which was rather small, and in which, as its name indicated, everything was green: the wallpaper, the curtains, the ceiling, the woodwork and the carpet. After a few hours of sleep he experienced a violent nausea, intolerable stomach aches, vertigo and hallucinations, which only dissipated after several days when he was relocated to another room.

He attributed that serious indisposition either to the natural dampness of a room uninhabited for more than half a century or to the neighborhood of a small pond situated a short distance from the windows, whose stagnant waters might be producing the symptoms that he had suffered by their pestilential miasmas. The pond was drained, the room disinfected by means of a large peat fire maintained there day and night, and two months later the young lord, sticking to his guns, went to bed again in the Green Room.

He had not been asleep for an hour when he heard groans. No one would have dared to come in, and he had taken precautions, for the door was bolted. He had forbidden his staff to enter, but the next morning, when he did not come out, the door was forced and Lord MacM*** was found dying in his bed.

By a fortunate chance, Dr. S. Taylor,[72] a professor of medical jurisprudence at Guy's Hospital, was in Scotland, not far from the manor. He was summoned in haste, and found the young lord sufficiently ill to inspire serious anxieties.

---

[72] The reference must be to Alfred Swaine Taylor (1806-1880), the great pioneer of British forensic medicine, who was appointed Lecturer in Medical Jurisprudence at Guy's in 1831, who campaigned against the sale of arsenic products for domestic use in the 1850s, although the case described id fictitious.

It was only by changing residence and returning to another of his properties near Edinburgh that Lord MacM*** was able to recover. Even then, he was not completely cured, and suffered several months of palpebral conjunctivitis, a painful and tenacious kind of ophthalmia.

The owner of the Scottish manor told Taylor that after falling asleep peacefully, he had suddenly seen, either in that strange state of torpor that is neither wakefulness not slumber, a green monster loom up before him that had gazed at him in a sinister fashion. Then the phantom had leapt on to the bed, dug its claws deep into the young man's breast and dug around there for a long time, causing him intolerable agonies. Finally, it had disappeared, after having passed a red hot iron fork that it was holding in one of its hands through his eyes.

"My lord," said Dr. Taylor, "if you wish, I can exorcise the demon that has twice cause you to feel its power so cruelly within a month."

"Doctor, I'll write to my steward telling him to carry out any instructions that you give him."

"The orders will be quite simple," said the Doctor. "You've been poisoned by copper arsenate."

"Who has dared to make an attempt on my life? Tell me the murderer's name, so that I can denounce him to the law."

"The criminal won't appear at the Court of Assizes. It's quite simply the painted paper in your room, which has been prepared with Scheele green. Before bringing you back to Edinburgh, I shook the books that had been in the accursed room for many years and collected the dust that covered them; finally I tore off a section of the paper stuck to the walls, and I submitted the dust and the paper to Reinsch's process. The paper alone yielded 450 grains, which is 22 grams, of a substance containing enough arsenic to cover a copper plate ten feet square. Subsequently treated with heat, the material formed octahedral crystals of arsenic.

"By going to reside in the Green Room, you stirred up the poisoned dust that had been covering the furniture, the books, the wallpaper, the parquet and the bed-curtains for a long time. It penetrated your nose, eyes and throat, as far as the lungs, and put your life in danger. As for the demon, the suffocation of your lungs and your feverish brain gave birth to it. Have everything that is green in the bewitched room torn out and burned, and you can then inhabit that room with as much impunity as the beautiful white and gold room that we're conversing in at present.

The Green Room did, indeed, become a Yellow Room, and since then, one can spend the night there without being subjected to nightmares, or poisoning, or palpebral conjunctivitis.

Let us also say that in the heart of Paris, in our own apartments, similar accidents can happen, and often do. It is not even necessary that the apartments in question have green paint and wallpaper; the essence of terebinthine,[73] frequently in use, is sufficient to produce dreams, headaches vomiting and dangerous symptom—even death.

Some time ago, a young seamstress ignorant or imprudent enough to sleep in a mansard that she had painted herself that evening, and from which she had not removed the pot containing the paint, was found dead in her bed.

Dr. Marchal de Calvi[74] has published a remarkable work on poisoning produced by essence of terebinthine.

An actress at the Théâtre des Variétés almost fell victim to her imprudence in moving into a newly-painted apartment too soon. At night she woke up suffocating, and could hardly find the strength to pull the bell-cord; in spite of the care lavished upon her she remained plunged in the most alarming absolute prostration for five or six days. One of the senior employees of the Palais des Tuileries has recently suffered ordeals of the same kind.

---

[73] Nowadays known as turpentine.

[74] Charles-Jacob Marchal de Calvi (1815-1873) held the chair of anatomy and physiology at the Val-de-Grâce hospital. The work cited is *Mémoire sur l'empoisonnement par la vapeur d'essence de térébanthine* (1856).

Madame A***, who lives in the Rue Neuve-Coquenard, has been afflicted even more cruelly; in consequence of inhaling terebinthine vapors she has lost her reason and required, to be cured, a sojourn of eight months in a lunatic asylum.

Dr. Maffei, a physician in the Tuileries quarter, was fulfilling his duties one day, giving a consultation in the imperial château, when he was suddenly overcome by a strange stupor. His thoughts became confused and, so to speak, extinguished. He sought the most commonplace words without being able to find them.

He felt his pulse; its beat was slow and weak; a kind of paralysis overtook al his limbs, and it was with a superhuman effort of will that he succeeded in getting up from his armchair and dragging himself to a window, the opening of which he demanded by gestures.

The external air rendered him a little of his strength, of which he took advantage to remove his cravat and coat. He felt life and intelligence gradually return. However, it was nearly two hours before the last traces of the mysterious illness disappeared, whose like he had never experienced before. When he tried to put his coat on again, the strong odor of terebinthine that it gave off gave him the key to an enigma that had almost proved fatal. Monsieur Maffei's valet had cleaned the collar of the garment with the essence and, unfortunately, had not used it sparingly.

Will this enumeration of accidents do any good? We fear not. Alas, no one resembles more than a journalist the poor Greek girl who spent her life making true predictions that that no one wanted to believe.

When he was only the Comte d'Artois, King Charles X, in his youth, stopped one morning during the carnival in the middle of the Pont Neuf, climbed on top of his carriage and, taking out of his pocket a purse that was heavy and bulging with coin, as Rabelais puts it, started shouting: "Who wants to buy six-livre coins for thirty sous?"

More than a thousand people went past the prince without doing anything but laugh, shrug their shoulders and repeat, knowingly: "What kind of idiot does he take us for?"

Only one woman—a market trader—approached the Comte d'Artois and said: "I'll risk it! You're too handsome a chap to cheat an old lady; if I were young I'd have less confidence. Here's fifteen thirty-sou coins; give me fifteen of your six-livre pieces."

There were jeers in the crowd then. Soon, however, the cheers took on a different character when the brave fishwife stuck her fists on her hips and said to them, in the language of the market: "If you weren't stupid, you'd have recognized that charming charlatan, as I did, as the king's brother."

Everyone then precipitated themselves toward the caleche, but the prince whipped his horses, departed at a gallop and disappeared.

How many six-livre coins do science and publicity offer every day to the masses without their wanting to accept them, I don't even say for thirty sous, but gratis.

If you want to know about other dangerous effects produced by the employment of verdigris, listen to another story.

Paris is overflowing with unknown dramas.

Nowhere, as Montaigne says, "does the inconstancy of the various oscillations of fortune, present a greater range of visages." Nothing is certain there, neither wealth nor poverty, obscurity or renown, popularity or unpopularity, or even power. Yesterday, I saw a man coming out of a two-franc restaurant who had been a minister and had left the most honorable memories in the administration. On the other hand, I have encountered in a two-horse caleche the son of one of my former porters, who, aided by hazard and the Bourse, now has a town house and distributes gold by the handful. God grant that he does not end up exercising a profession less worthy than that of his father. There is one of my good Flemish proverbs that says: "The plant that grows on the compost heap will return to the compost heap."

I also know a young woman, brought up in the midst of luxury, with a dowry of eight hundred thousand francs, who came home the day after a ball to find that a seizure by bailiffs had left her with nothing: no house, no carriage, no wellbeing, not even the certainty of daily bread. As cowardly in adversity as he had been presumptuous and insensate in prosperity, her husband had committed suicide. She, by contrast, who had been gentle, charitable and sober in the bosom of luxury, took her two children by the hand, looked poverty in the face without apprehension, rented a small ground-floor apartment in a distant quarter, and became her florist's apprentice. In a matter of months Madame X*** became more skillful than her mistress, set up in business for herself, and did not take long to become advantageously known to fashionable milliners, who marveled at the perfection of the products that emerged from her hands.

Commerce in artificial flowers forms one of the largest and most lucrative industries making up what traders call "Parisian goods." Not only do the capital and the départements consume considerable quantities, but the rest of Europe and all of America obtain provisions from our market.

So, Madame X*** could not keep up with the orders that were arriving from every direction. Often, her work and that of her former chambermaid, a faithful Bretonne who had not wanted to be separated from her in the evil days, continued long into the night; however, four apprentices, young women saved from poverty and perhaps misconduct, lent her ardent support.

Need had disappeared in the early days, and ease had arrived—the pleasant and noble ease that one feels so glad and so proud to owe to hard work—when all of a sudden, a mysterious illness, a kind of epidemic, struck the tiny factory. The complexion of all the young women took on a livid aspect; they experienced frissons; cold sweat and nervous tremors became manifest, complicated by body vomiting, with atrocious aching in the head and all the limbs. Finally, the slightest prick made by a needle or brass wire caused ulcers on the fingers of the six florists that refused stubbornly to heal.

A local practitioner was consulted and could not understand the strange phenomenon. Nevertheless, he put the blame on the dampness of the ground floor. Madame X*** moved out the next day and established herself on the fifth floor. The mysterious illness, which disappeared at first, came back a week later more violently than ever.

This time, the physician attributed it to the unhealthiness of the neighborhood.

Madame X*** relocated her workshop to Neuilly, in the heart of the countryside. A week had not gone by before the six florists experienced the fatal symptoms yet again.

The Breton chambermaid thought the scourge as the work of a demon or spell-caster, and commenced a novena.

The doctor ran out of explanations.

Fortunately, Madame X***'s old doctor, having learned by chance about the alarming state of his former client, came running, and understood at the first glance at the so-called epidemic that was desolating the workshop was caused by the very industry practiced therein.

In fact, the charming profession of florist, such a near relative of art, is surrounded by perils. All those who exercise it or manufacture the materials that it employs are exposed to the risk of poisoning. That is because arsenic forms the base of each of those materials.

To begin with, many natural herbs and employed, which are sprinkled with arsenous greens after being covered in gum. Then, when the florists assemble bouquets, the dangerous powder is detached and fills the air with venomous dust. Furthermore, the fabrics from which the leaves are made are coated with a paste whose base in Schwenfurt green—fabrics that have to be cut up into little pieces, stuck together, manipulated and often applied to the lips. With such handling, the near-impossibility of avoiding accidents is understandable.

When Dr. J*** had enlightened Madame X*** about the dangers of her profession, the poor woman dissolved in tears.

"So it's necessary," she cried, "to renounce the profession that has given me the means of vanquishing poverty and obtaining an honorable existence!"

The doctor lowered his head sadly and went out, broken-hearted. A few days later, however, he came back full of joy.

"Don't worry, Madame," he said. "A means exists of removing all the unhealthiness from the profession of florist. That means consists of incorporating into the coloring material employed in the manufacture of greens a special collodion—a mixture of ether and cotton prepared with sulfuric acid, known as cotton powder—which, far from harming industrial manipulations, renders them easier as well as completely inoffensive.

Thus, today, Madame X*** and her workers, completely cured, can fabricate flowers with impunity, without compromising their health.

A SCIENTIST'S CRUELTIES

If one wanted to list all the bizarreries and all the cruelties that science inspires and scientists commit, for immense newspaper pages would not be sufficient. Animals furnish innumerable victims to these men, insatiable in the discovery of a few of nature's secrets. There is an anatomist who, in the name of society, consents to spend his life in an attic and to live in a condition bordering on indigence in order to dissect animals at his ease and to examine the most microscopic parts of their nervous apparatus, the digestive system, the circulation, the respiration and all the marvels of their organization. That man, that Decius of natural history, has his works printed at his own expense, which no one in France reads, and, more especially, no one buys, but which generate astonishment and admiration among foreign scientists. Mention his name to the qualified scientists of our public establishments and they will shrug their shoulders disdainfully.

It is true that that eccentric—as he has been called for forty years, and perhaps more—has dedicated all his time, his fortune, his health and his life to the study of just two animal species: cockchafers and cats, but let us add that these studies provide the key to the entire system of organization of insects and mammals. What does it matter that the unfortunate fellow does not have the smallest pension, is nothing at the Natural History Museum, and leaves others to take possession of his discoveries or claim credit for them. One cannot show oneself to be more authentically eccentric!

We knew, a few years ago, at the Collège de France, a young man of great talent, whose name now enjoys a just scientific celebrity and who has won a Prix Monthyon for having exercised, for I don't know how long, the profession of torturer of animals. He had collected the largest possible quantity of stray dogs, and submitted them to tortures that would cause the imagination of the least sensitive person in the world to quiver. Some he inoculated with frightful diseases, on others he carried out dangerous operations, allowed his victims to recover, and then killed the in order to study the results of those operations. He starved them or fattened them at will; sometimes he fed them nothing but egg-white for months on end, and sometimes gelatin. He did not let a single day pass without poisoning or detoxifying several of his prisoners. He amputated their limbs, bled them only to inject various substances into their veins thereafter.

Finally, I shall retain as long as I live the memory of an unfortunate swan that lived for a fortnight in Monsieur Magendie's[75] operating theater with its breast open in order that he could more easily study the movements of the unfortunate bird's heart and the circulation of its blood.

These dramas do not only take place at the Collège de France but at the Jardin des Plantes and everywhere else that there are naturalists. God only knows the number of jackals, foxes and dogs that Monsieur Flourens[76] has immolated, not to mention the pigs that he fed on madder and then killed in order to observe the manner in which layers of bones are formed and superimposed in living beings.

Take note, however, that if I have cited the names of members of the Institut, and listed the scientific murders to which they devote themselves, it is not without reason, for I have to tell you about one of the most odious examples of cruelty that the fanaticism of science has ever committed.

---

[75] François Magendie (1783-1855), an important pioneer of experimental physiology, became notorious as a vivisector, and drew sharp criticism from numerous British scientists, including Charles Darwin. His exploits lent considerable impetus to the anti-vivisectionist movement.

[76] Gustave Flourens (1794-1867) conducted expensive research into brain function by means of lesions deliberately inflicted on animal brains. His work on embryology and the work on bone formation cited here (published in *Théorie expérimentale de la formation des os*, 1847), is less famous, as is his work on anesthesia.

I find myself, alas, united to the guilty party by a long and proven friendship; now, I ask you, how many friendships exist that have not been broken, or at least deteriorated, by time and sad proofs?

It was in 1848, when the terrible June riots were threatening Paris, and one awoke to the general clamor and waited with anxiety for the fatal raising of the curtain on a drama that had, alas, been anticipated for a long time.

One morning, I received a note that said: *come to see me; I have a curious experiment to carry out, and I'd like you to witness it.*

The man who wrote to me thus lived three or four leagues from Paris, in a kind of small country house, half-cottage and half-château. The revolution had given men of letters leisure which, if by no means comfortable, was nonetheless complete. I respond to my friend's invitation.

I found him sitting on the threshold of his house, built amid the ruins of an ancient château; he came to meet me with a smile on his lips, and seemed quite astonished when, with a perfectly natural preoccupation, I talked to him about the troubles agitating Paris.

"Bah!" he said. "Do as I do, and don't read a single newspaper; follow my example in turning away from your door all hawkers of news, and let the good God, who is great and merciful, do as he will."

With that, he took me by the hand and took me into an immense cellar, which bore a strong resemblance to a dungeon, and whose door, broken twenty years before, permitted reptiles and bats to establish their domicile there freely.

"Here, look," he said, he said, lifting up a hooded lantern after opening it, "see how many bats there are living in this crypt. Have you ever seen a finer collection of *Vespertilionidae*?"

Indeed, I saw a rather vast quantity of bats in the cracks that time had chiseled in the upper part of the vault, suspended by their hind feet, heads down, enveloped in their wings as if by a cloak.

"For three months," he continued, closing the hood of the lantern again, "I've been befriending these animals, in order to be able make a success of the experiment I'm planning. Every day, I release an immense quantity of insects in the cellar, which I collect from the surroundings. Several bats even take the insects from my hand, including a little rearmouse, *Vespertilio murinus*, which certainly recognizes me, and perhaps even has some affection for me. It's a female and she has established her domicile over there, at the far end of the cavern."

He took me by the hand and led me further into a profound obscurity, all the way to the back of the cellar, where he reopened his lantern.

Indeed, I then saw a bat suspended from the vault like the others; on seeing my friend, she did not seem in the least frightened, opened her mouth and uttered a little cry, displaying a double row of sharp white teeth.

He took a tin-plate container from his pocket full of peppered months and presented one of the night-flyers to the bat, which snatched it and chewed it with the finest appetite in the world.

"That's not all—look, she comes when I call."

He whistled, and this time the rearmouse, detaching itself from the vault, circled around the naturalist and seized on the wing, several times and with remarkable skill, the moth that he held up to her in his fingers.

While she devoted herself to this exercise, I could not help remembering the admirable accuracy of expression and observation with which Buffon describes the bizarre flight of bats, which he calls a kind of "uncertain fluttering" executed with effort, in an awkward manner. In fact, they only take off from the ground with difficulty, never rise to a great height, and can only accelerate, slow down or even steer their flight, which is neither rapid nor direct, imperfectly. They proceed by mean of abrupt vibrations, following an oblique and tortuous course. In spite of all these difficulties imposed on her by nature, the rearmouse nevertheless seized all the moths that my companion offered her, without ever having to come back for a second attempt.

When the animal was sated, it hung itself from the vaults by its hind feet again. Then, the naturalist took from his pocket a piece of iron wire embedded at one end in an iron handle, and asked me to heat it up in the lantern-flame.

"You know," he said to me, while I carried out the task he had confided to me, "that bats can steer in the midst of the most profound darkness. In caves completely deprived of light, they negotiate in flight the numerous corners of their dwelling without hesitation, without every colliding with projecting rocks or the walls of vaults. A bird could not act with as much security and precision even in broad daylight. How do they do that? You might tell me that nocturnal animals have the faculty of concentrating the faintest beams of light their extremely dilatable pupils, and succeeded in distinguishing objects clearly enough to guide themselves, to see their prey and seize it—but in total, absolute darkness their pupils can dilate to any extent; they cannot perceive beams that don't exist, and in such circumstances a bat would be just as blind as any other animal. Nevertheless, it acts as if it can see there perfectly."

"Georges Cuvier, the great genius of natural history, observed that phenomenon," I replied. "If my memory isn't mistaken, he explained it by saying that the ears of bats, almost always very large, form and enormous membranous surface along with its wings, almost bare and so sensitive that the animals can probably navigate in the dark holes in which they live purely by mans of changes in air pressure."[77]

"Isn't it rather a sixth sense with which nature endows bats?" he said. "Isn't it one of those organs without analogy

---

[77] The Italian scientist Lazzaro Spallanzani (1729-1799) had conducted experiments that led him to conclude that bats navigate using the sense of hearing rather than sight, so Cuvier was simply endorsing his conclusion. It was not until the late 1930s, however, that the method of echo-location employed by bats was conclusively demonstrated by David Griffin and Robert Galambos.

333

with human senses, and which, in consequence, escapes the anatomical research of our naturalists? We shall see! Is your iron wire red hot?"

"Yes," I replied.

He raised his hand toward the vault, picked off the little bat, which allowed itself to be taken without resistance, yielding with confident abandon to a person she considered, and perhaps loved, as a friend.

The torturer seized the red hot iron wire that I was holding, drew it over the bat's eyes, blinding her, and set her on the ground.

At first, the poor little beast utter cries of pain, and writhed on the ground for a few minutes; her entire body trembled convulsively and her wings opened and closed with unequivocal signs of pain.

With one knee on the ground he watched her do it with impassive attention.

Eventually, the bat calmed down. She extended her ears to the left and right, righted herself, dragged herself toward a wall, climbed it slowly but surely, raised herself up to a height of two or three feet, let herself fall, extended her wings, took flight, and without hesitation, as if she could see perfectly, regained the spot that she had occupied when the naturalist had taken hold of her in order to treat her with the cruelty to which little King Arthur had once been the victim in the Scottish legend.[78]

"Let's leave her there to rest," he said. "We'll come back this evening to continue our experiment."

We went back up to his residence.

All day long he seemed preoccupied, paying mediocre attention to what I said to him, and while we were eating dinner he suddenly pushed away his plate, took out his watch and exclaimed: "She must be getting hungry. The time is ripe."

---

[78] This reference is rather cryptic, as there does not appear to be any reference to the legendary king falling victim to such a misfortune.

As he finished speaking he got up from the table and, whether I liked it or not, I had to follow him down to the cellar again.

Having arrived before the blind bat, he emitted the summoning whistle to which he had accustomed the bat. She trembled visibly, shook her ears and extended her wings slightly.

Then the naturalist took a moth in his fingers, which he held by one wing, and began buzzing in the attempt to escape the hand that was holding it.

Then the bat detached herself from the vault, described two or three circles around us, went past my friend's hand like an arrow and seized the nocturnal insect with as much surety as if she still had the use of her eyes.

"Cuvier was right!" I exclaimed.

"Perhaps," he replied, repeating the experiment that had cost the poor bat her sight five or six times. "Perhaps, also, it's the sixth sense I mentioned."

We separated. I came back to Paris. It was the twenty-first of June 1848.

On the twenty-second, Paris fell prey to the horrors of civil war; barricades desolated all our streets; cannon fired grapeshot at the insurgents; blood flowed everywhere; our most illustrious general fell to French bullets, and the Archbishop of Paris paid with his life for the courageous attempt that he made to save stray or guilty sheep.

The first letter I received after those fateful days was from my friend the naturalist. It made no mention of anything except the anatomical studies that he had undertaken to try to grasp the secret of the sixth sense given by nature to bats.

Yesterday, I went to visit him, and found him still poring over his studies. More than five hundred bats have fallen victim to his scientific investigations; the cellar has been entirely depopulated of its nocturnal guests, and only one single bat remains: the blind rearmouse.

"At least," I said to the fanatic, "you've spared her, in memory of the cruel torture to which you rendered her victim."

"Oh!" he replied, with a sigh, "If she wasn't serving my study of the instincts that blindness creates in *Vespertiliones*, I'd have dissected her a long time ago, like the rest. You can't have any idea how difficult it is for me to find bats nowadays. There isn't a single one for five leagues around."

You see, the love of science is a fanaticism, if not a monomania, as Esquirol[79] said, who spent his life dissecting, not bats, but human brains.

---

[79] The psychiatrist Étienne Esquirol (1772-1840) worked for many years of the Salpêtrière, where he played a significant role in modernizing the care and treatment of mental illness. He popularized the diagnosis of "monomania"; unlike Flourens, he did not dissect brains, so Berthoud presumably means that observation metaphorically.

STORIES FOR CHILDREN

HEIDENLOCH CASTLE

Some twenty years ago, there was a small country house a few leagues from Heidelberg, inhabited by the Baron von Heidenloch and his only daughter, the lovely Notburga.

Although the Baron was the only descendant of a family of burgraves that had once been powerful, redoubtable masters of the entire region, he was nonetheless a modest landowner, cultivating his fields as best he could. His ancestors had given up living in Heidenloch Castle seven or eight generations before.

The castle, after having been the terror of the country for three centuries, was now merely a mass of ruins. Those ruins, moreover, still justified their sinister name, which signifies "pagan tower" in German, for it was claimed that specters of the dead and hideous demons still wandered by night among the fallen towers, and especially in the subterranean workings.

One night, it was asserted, a peasant passing close to those subterranean chambers had noticed that an impetuous air current was escaping from them, and that moans and groans were mingled with the strange wind. He ran away and returned to his lodgings half-dead.

In spite of that fear, however, he could not banish the idea from his imagination that he had to visit those subterranean excavations, and one Quasimodo Sunday he went into them resolutely, after having armed himself with a crucifix and placing a scapular and relics around his neck.

First he went into a straight narrow tunnel hollowed out in the rock, and headed toward a bizarre vacillating light that was shining in the distance. He arrived at a closed door in which there was a carbuncle that was producing the strange light.

His heart palpitating and his forehead bathed with cold sweat, he knocked three times on the door. It opened of its own accord, and the peasant found himself face to face with four tall men sitting around a round table on which there was a book bound in black velvet and ornamented with gold. The four men, as pale and thin as cadavers, wore ancient German costume; they seemed nonplussed by the sight of the peasant, and began to tremble.

"*Pax vobis!* Peace by with you!" the peasant said to them by way of a greeting, feeling no less emotional than them.

"*Hic nulla pax!*" they replied, meaning "there is no peace here."

"*Pax vobis in nomine Domine!*"—the peace of the Lord be with you—the peasant added.

For their part, they repeated in faint voices the lamentable words "*Hic nulla pax!*"

He approached the table then and said, a third time: "*Pax vobiscum!*"

They pointed silently to the book, on which was written, in large golden letters: *Dies irae*. Day of wrath!

"Who are you?" he asked them.

"We don't know ourselves."

"What are you doing here?"

"We're awaiting the last judgment, fearfully."

"Are you alive or dead?"

"Neither alive or dead."

"Have mortals anything to fear from you?"

"We are the guardians of this place, and woe betide those who come like you to disturb our mysteries."

It would have needed far less to make the peasant turn on his heels; he did not need to be told twice to go away, and he ran all the way back to the farm. He found it on fire, and while he was trying to rescue his wife and children a beam fell on his head and blinded him.

He therefore paid with his earthly happiness for his fatal visit to the subterranean workings of Heidenloch; henceforth without a family, reduced to poverty and deprived of sight, almost an idiot, he vegetated for several years, begging at the side of the high road and repeating in a voice that made anyone who heard it shiver: "Don't go into the cellars of Heidenloch."

So, the Baron paid little heed to the old castle, which was, in any case, a quarter of an hour's walk away from his house, produced nothing but weeds and was haunted by spirits. He only paid attention to his daughter and his garden, going to Heidelberg regularly four times a year in order to buy a dress for the former and shrubs and rare flowers for the latter.

In spite of the strange name she bore, like all the women in her family since time immemorial, Notburga as a charming young woman, pale and rosy-cheeked, mild-mannered and reputed to be the best housekeeper for ten leagues around. She knew how to produce triple value from her father's meager income, by virtue of the way she administered it; the house was spick and span from the attic to the cellar; the table recommended itself by an abundance and an expertise that even a gastronome would have admired, and there was still, when the need arose, clothing in the house for poor children, bread for the needy and a glass of wine for convalescent old people. As for the sick, Notburga visited them in their homes, and always came out heaped with their blessings.

One day, as the Baron was finishing his dinner and his daughter was pouring him an excellent glass of distilled cherry liqueur, someone rang the bell at the gate, and Notburga's little dog started barking and running toward a stranger who was coming along the avenue toward the house.

The Baron hastened to drink the rest of his cherry brandy, put his glass down on the table and got up to greet the stranger, who, after having bowed and sat down in the chair that Notburga offered him, abruptly said to the Baron: "Will you sell me Heidenloch Castle, sir?"

The Baron, amazed by this proposition, which he had scarcely expected, looked the stranger up and down. He was still a young man, short, with an agreeable physiognomy, although he wore a full beard, which was very rare in Germany at that time, and his eyes darted a singular gleam through the large blue-tinted lenses of his spectacles.

"I'm waiting for your reply," the unknown man said, smiling.

"In truth," said the Baron, "I'm not at all sure what to say. The old castle is no use to me at all, but it's the heritage that my ancestors have left me, and I'm wondering whether it might not be disrespectful to them to sell it to a stranger."

"Is that all that's stopping you? Then lease it to me for ninety-nine years and three hundred and sixty-four days."

"That's an excellent means of settling the matter," said the Baron, rubbing his hands.

"And how much rent do you want for Heidenloch?"

"What do you think of a hundred florins a year?"

"I'd rather pay for the whole ninety-nine years and three hundred and sixty-four days at once. I'll offer you eighty thousand florins."

The Baron had great difficulty in repressing a cry of joy, and his broad face was covered with a sudden red flush.

"Eighty thousand florins," repeated the unknown man.

"I accept, gladly."

"Wait—that's not all. If I find the buried treasures in the uncultivated grounds of the castle that I suspect to be buried there, or precious objects of any kind whatsoever, I'll give a fifth share to your daughter."

The Baron's face darkened. "I very much doubt that you'll find any treasure at Heidenloch. If that's the reason you're buying the castle, I fear that you're making a bad bargain."

The young man smiled again. "That's my concern. Would you care to come to Heidelberg tomorrow, to the office of the notary Kalisch. You'll find your eighty thousand florins and the contract all ready to sign."

With that, the singular individual bowed, and, without adding another word, departed with such promptitude that the Baron could neither escort him nor return his bow. So the Baron let himself fall back into his chair, drank a second glass of cherry liqueur to steady his mind, and looked at his daughter.

"Well, Notburga," he said, shaking his head, "what do you think of that?"

"I think, Father, that it's an excellent arrangement, which will triple our income."

"And will serve you as a dowry, my love. Ha ha! Now you can marry whomever you wish—even a councilor. Eight thousand florins! What worries me is the buried treasures he mentioned. Is there, in fact, anything hidden under the ruins of the castle?"

"Don't worry about that, Father. Since the young man's paying you ten thousand times what you estimated that the wretched rubble to be worth, let's wish him the best of luck finding heaps of gold and diamonds."

"You're right, as always, my girl. Right—I'll go sign the document in Heidelberg tomorrow." Suddenly, he jumped out of his chair. "His name! He didn't tell me his name! Am I the victim of some kind of trick? Is someone playing games with me?"

"Who would think of playing tricks on poor folk like us?" the young woman replied. "The young man's honest and genial face ought to drive away any such idea. Come on, Father, go and water your flowers, as usual, before we go to bed. Then, after having thanked God for the unexpected blessing he's given us, let's sleep peacefully until tomorrow."

Sleep peacefully! That was easy to say, but not so easy to do, alas. Needless to say, the Baron did not sleep a wink all night, and he left for Heidelberg earlier than was necessary.

He went straight to the notary's office. He had scarcely given his name than the latter started to laugh. That laughter chilled the Baron, who thought once again that he might be the victim of a practical joke.

"Ha ha!" said the notary—a short man who seemed to have the ambition of one day rivaling the famous Great Tun of Heidelberg, which contained I don't know how many liters.[80] "Doesn't this affair seem to you like a dream?"

"Indeed it does," relied the Baron. With a forced smile he added: "Is it one? I don't even know my would-be tenant's name."

"In truth, I didn't know it myself yesterday evening, and I scarcely know it today. He came to see me looking exactly as you saw him, and deposited two enormous sums of gold on my desk. 'I'm renting Heidelberg Castle on a long lease,' he said, 'for eighty thousand florins. Here they are. Here's a rough draft of the lease. The Baron will come to sign it tomorrow morning. Pay him and take these two hundred florins for the expenses of the document and your honorarium.' With that, he disappeared without waiting for my reply.

"When I had recovered somewhat from my surprise, I read the document. The most skillful man of law in Germany couldn't have drafted it with more care, except for one condition that made me burst out laughing—the one that grants Fraulein Notburga, your daughter, a fifth of any buried treasures discovered in the castle's dependencies. Buried treasures! That's a joke! Buried treasures! An excellent joke!"

"But in sum, what's my tenant's name?"

"Fritz Saal. Councilor Fritz Saal."

"Does he live in Heidelberg?"

"Who knows? Does he know himself? According to the information I've been able to glean, as best I could, since yesterday evening, although he's still young he's already traveled the five continents of the world. Sometimes here, sometimes there, he nevertheless possesses, at the gates of the city, bequeathed to him by his uncle, Councilor Gewartius, a house

---

[80] A little over 200,000, to judge by the present one (the fourth in the sequence).

full from top to bottom with bones of every sort, and stones collected from a thousand different places. My head clerk affirms that he saw him, last night, stop at every one of the pebbles on a path, pick them up one after another, and sometimes put them in his pocket. According to the same clerk, when he can't procure certain stones, he has molds made of them, and he went all the way to Leipzig just to bring back a cast of the famous sandstone found near the Oxen Tower in Köthen, one which the imprint of a six-fingered hand can be seen—not to mention those from the village of Hohentregel, on the gray surface of which imprints of hands and feet can be seen.[81] I'd blush to tell you the prices it's rumored that he pays for these things, for which you or I wouldn't give a kreutzer."

While the notary was speaking, the Baron plunged his hand mechanically into the bags that had become his property, making the beautiful gold coins that they contained clink."

"No matter where the good fortune come from, it's welcome!" he said. "Would you care to buy me, with this capital, some good and reliable bonds, or find me some excellent mortgage that won't require too much difficulty in administering the income, whose returns I can obtain regularly on a weekly basis?" Having completed this request, he started out on his return journey, not without buying two silk dresses for his daughter and a good quality outfit for his old maidservant.

When he returned to Notburga and the young woman and the maidservant had admired the presents the Baron had brought them, the latter told them all the strange and mysterious things he had learned about his bizarre tenant, who took on the proportions of a legendary figure in the eyes of the two women.

---

[81] These references remain untraceable, although the German town of Köthen (which Berthoud renders as Kuhthurn, apparently having borrowed the reference to the "*tour des vaches*" [oxen tower] from a military memoir by Guillaume de Vauldroncourt published in 1840, which refers to the town as Kuhturn) was renowned at the time for archeological discoveries of relics of Stone Age humans.

It was a full week later when the councilor came to take possession of the old castle, accompanied by a veritable army of workmen. There were at least four hundred of them. The councilor began by giving them orders so lucid and so easily understood, and having them carried out with so much precision, that the ruins of the castle were seen to be transformed, as if by magic, but without losing their picturesque physiognomy, into a habitable dwelling.

The councilor arranged things in such a manner that not a minute of time could be wasted by any of his workers, and that they never made a superfluous thrust with a pick or a shovel. Thus, the work of several months was completed in a week.

When the masons and locksmiths left, upholsterers who were almost as numerous arrived with immense carriages. They decorated the interior of the castle, and, still guided by the councilor, always under his piercing eye, they improvised an endeavor that seemed like the work of magicians, it was simultaneously so sumptuous and severe.

It was common gossip in the village, and even in the Baron's house, that immense galleries lit by high widows had been constructed, which enclosed a library of more than a hundred thousand volumes, and, which seemed even more serious, a collection of bizarre or gigantic bones careful by arranged on cushions, as if they were made of solid gold—not to mention the minerals marbles, petrifications, animals in bottles full of alcohol, drawers overflowing with seashells, and display cases full of exotic butterflies, animals, birds and reptiles so expertly stuffed that one might think they were alive.

No necromancer had ever had a laboratory more extraordinary and more frightful to behold.

Abruptly, that great agitation of four hundred incessantly active workmen coming and going, hammering and sawing, carrying and arranging, was succeeded by absolute silence and solitude. From one day to the next no one was any longer to be heard or seen, and if the castle had not been lit up from top to bottom every evening, to the remotest corners, one might have thought that it was uninhabited.

In spite of custom, Councilor Fritz Saal, when he had settled into his new home, did not pay any neighborly visits to the local landowners. He did not even go to see his landlord, the Baron. When, by chance, he emerged from his abode, he strolled at a leisurely pace strictly within the boundaries of the old castle. A large Newfoundland dog and two men equipped with long implements reminiscent of lances followed him. From time to time, the dog barked; at times, too, the councilor was seen to make a gesture with his hand, and immediately, the men that were following him would drive their implements into the ground, and pull them out against after having driven them in very deeply. The councilor carefully examined the earth that clung to the ends of the lances, which were turned back in a kind of cross, doubtless designed for that purpose, and took specimens of it. Then he resumed his walk, to repeat the same procedure a few steps further on.

The peasants, who saw all that from afar, ended up taking their new neighbor for a sorcerer looking for treasure, all the more so when other extraordinary things were said about him.

For instance, he had taken into his service a village girl who knew how to cook fairly well but, on the other hand, had very little understanding of order and forethought. Katt possessed a charming and lively face, which went very well with her blue eyes, blonde hair, youthful complexion and slight turned-up nose, as befits a pretty German country girl. However, she devoted a good deal of time to coquetry and as much to placing an embroidered velvet bonnet as pertly as possible on top of her head as to remembering her master's orders. So, on several occasions she forgot to go shopping in town, and one evening, when the councilor wanted to take his habitual cup of tea, he found that there was no sugar in the house.

Now, as I said, Katt was as coquettish as she was negligent, and if she forgot to make sure that nothing as lacking in her master's house, she never forgot to buy ornamentations of every sorts with the good wages she received.

Her master said to her: "Katt, since, in spite of my instructions, I've run out of sugar this evening, I'll make some with your clothes."

Katt smiled at that threat, which seemed to her to be a joke. But the councilor abruptly tore away Kat's apron, took off a very pretty colored headscarf she was wearing over her shoulders and her tulle bonnet—a bonnet bought the day before, if you please—threw the lot into an earthenware pot, poured over it the contents of a big bottle of oil of vitriol, which was used to clean the copper and brass, added some water, and put it on the fire.

After which he had her fetch some chalk, which he mixed with that fantastic stew and let it boil for some time.

When that singular preparation was cooked to perfection, he fashioned a filter out of paper, made use of it to strain the contents, allowed them to cool and said: "There's some excellent sugar for this evening."

With that he went out, after having drunk a glass of the preparation, the rest of which he had carefully transported into the pantry, which he locked, taking away the key.

Indeed, a few days later, the liquor had been transformed into crystallized sugar of dazzling whiteness.

"You see, Katt, how I make sugar," said the councilor, sugaring his tea with his apron sugar. Next time you forget something, your entire wardrobe will go the same way."

Needless to say, from then on, the councilor never ran out of sugar again, and Katt told everyone who cared to listen what a sorcerer she had for a master. When she was asked why she did not leave the service of the reprobate, she cited the fear that he inspired in her and her dread of being bewitched by him if she ever handed in her notice. The worthy girl did not add that her master also paid her excellent wages, and that with him, one could filch a little from the household budget with impunity.

It is said that one eventually gets used to things that seem very awkward and strange at first. However, after eighteen months or two years of residence in the old castle, Fritz found himself the focal point of the curiosity of his neighbors, and even the townspeople of Heidelberg, more than ever.

God alone knew how many more-or-less absurd rumors were put about on his account. If he had been seen astride a broomstick flying to the sabbat he could not have been more earnestly accused of acquaintance with the Devil and being his henchman.

It must be admitted that the singular individual did nothing as other people did, and was quite content to surround himself with mysteries calculated to provoke curiosity. Thus, for example, one morning, he laid waste pitilessly to a market garden and an orchard in order to take away the soil, which was a fine clay. Workmen then enclosed that clay in large containers, carefully sealed, and sent off a hundred thousand kilograms, then two hundred thousand, then five hundred thousand, and then a million. But where was he sending it? That was the question. The councilor escorted each consignment personally to the nearest railway depot, and it was only in the depot that he wrote the destination on the cases in pencil.

While these consignments were in progress the councilor, with the celerity for which he was well-known, had an entire village built two hundred meters from the castle, on a part of the soil where the famous clay was not found; nothing was lacking: neither a chapel, nor a school, nor a butcher's shop, nor a bakery. One morning, a veritable army of miners arrived, speaking a German dialect that was difficult to understand even in Heidelberg. Come from God only knew where, they were immediately housed in the newly-constructed village, and, as they found lodging, meat, bread and all the necessities of life there at a good price, and their children received free education, and physicians paid by the councilor treated the sick, they naturally kept apart from the peasants of the neighborhood, of whom they had no need and whose language they could scarcely understand or speak.

Besides which, those rude workers spent their days and nights digging immense ditches at the bottom of which they were soon spending twelve hours a day, to such good effect that the councilor as soon exporting even more coal than he had exported of the famous clay, and he had to construct a branch railway-line two or three kilometers long at his own expense, which linked the castle to the nearest depot.

Now, a kilometer of railway line costs a million.

His small army of workmen, his manner of doing things his own way, the famous story of Katt's apron, recounted, repeated, commented upon, exaggerated, disfigured, and most of all the isolation in which the councilor enabled his workers to live, and lived himself, justified only too well the rumors of sorcery that were running around on his account.

Thus, it was not without emotion that one day, Fraulein Notburga, who was alone in the house, saw the councilor come in, to whom she had not spoken since the day he had come to ask to lease the old castle.

He bowed profoundly to the young woman, inquired as to the Baron's health, and, while expressing his regret and not being able to say hello him, added that it was Fraulein Notburga that he had come to see.

The latter blushed to the whites of her eyes, and offered the councilor an armchair. He sat down in it and took off his blue spectacles in order to wipe away the dust that the journey had deposited on them. Notburga had difficulty suppressing an exclamation of surprise, for the councilor's face, deprived of the villainous lenses that hid his eyes, became truly charming. The councilor then seemed to be scarcely thirty years old, and his physiognomy possessed as much distinction as intelligence and mildness.

"Fraulein," he said, smiling at the expression of surprise that Notburga could not hide, "I have simply come to acquit myself of a debt. I owe you a fifth of the hidden treasures that I've been able to discover in the grounds of the old castle, and this is the total amount due, which I have the honor of bringing you."

Expressing himself thus, he deposited a small sandal-wood box on Notburga's work table, got to his feet, respectfully took his leave of the young woman, and returned to Heidenloch.

A few moments later, he Baron came home and found his daughter supporting her chin in her hand, having not yet thought about opening the box.

While she was telling him about the councilor's visit, the Baron turned the key and found in the box a bond for forty thousand florins, payable on presentation at the richest bank in Heidelberg.

"So that devil of a councilor really is a sorcerer, as they say!" exclaimed the Baron.

"Perhaps," replied a voice that caused the worthy man to turn pale.

He turned round abruptly, and found himself face to face with the councilor.

"Baron," he said, laughing, "I've retraced my steps because it seems to me that a chatelaine ought to know her domain. Now, as Fraulein Notburga owns a fifth of my subterranean treasures, is it not her duty, and in her interest, to visit the places where they are found and the men who exploit them on her behalf?"

The Baron nodded his head, and Notburga allowed a movement of joy to show.

"With your permission," the councilor continued, "I'll have the honor of welcoming you tomorrow at Heidenloch Castle. You'll spend the day there, I hope, and before we part we can talk about a new project that I have in mind. So I'll expect you tomorrow at midday."

And he disappeared as he had come, without the Baron and his daughter, stunned by the councilor's point-blank invitation, having seen him go, any more than they had seen him arrive.

The councilor's invitation was astonishing, in that it was the first time that the mysterious individual had allowed anyone to enter his home. Thus, the news traveled rapidly in the village; some people criticized the Baron for not refusing an invitation made by a man of such dubious reputation as the councilor's; others asserted that he was exposing himself to great dangers in going into a place where God alone—and perhaps, alas, also the Devil—knew what was going on. At any rate, the next day, the Baron found outside his windows and along his route all the inhabitants of the neighborhood, who had come to watch him and his daughter as they headed for the old castle and crossed the threshold.

The councilor was waiting for his guests at the boundary of the land that he had rented. Notburga noted gladly that he was not hiding his eyes behind ugly blue lenses, and the Baron wondered whether the young man who shook his hand, distinguished in his manners and appearance, was really the singular individual who seemed to be trying with all his might to justify the reputation for sinister strangeness that had acquired for twenty leagues around.

While the Baron ruminated that thought, the councilor offered his arm to Fraulein Notburga, and escorted her to his residence.

Nothing bore less resemblance to ruins, and even the castle, the ancient building once so desolate, might have thought to be a palace built by fairies. Royal luxury was combined there with artistic elegance, and the Baron's eyes could not open wide enough to admire so many marvels. As for Notburga, however much admiration she felt, she experienced more astonishment at the councilor's conversation, which was both witty and grave.

After an exquisite lunch, which did not last long, in spite of the German custom of remaining at table for a long time and emptying numerous bottles, the councilor—who only drank water and had only sampled two or three dishes—rose to his feet and proposed to Notburga that they begin the planned visit to the subterranean treasures.

First he led her into the garden, where the extraction of masses of clay was continuing.

"This," he said, picking up a handful of clay that was almost at ground level, "is a veritable treasure, Fraulein; it's kaolin, a substance that your castle possesses in abundance. Look! Kaolin in an earthen substance, very soft and pale, composed of silica, aluminum, potassium, magnesium, calcium and iron oxides, and water.

"Kaolin serves to manufacture porcelain, an industry whose discovery in China appeared to go back more than two thousand years before the Christian Era, and was only imported into Europe by the Portuguese in the 15th century.

"In the last two hundred years, rare deposits of kaolin have been found in France, Russia and Germany. Now, you can judge the importance and value of the almost inexhaustible supply of this material on which your castle is build. There's enough for a thousand years of exploitation.

"Below that are coal-mines of incalculable richness and exquisite quality. You were able to judge that during lunch, since the fruit essences with which the creams and compotes were made came from that coal."

The Baron looked at the councilor fearfully.

"My God, yes, replied the latter. "I can make sugar with my cook's apron and delicious liqueurs with coal. If you like, at dinner I'll make ice in a red hot crucible."

The Baron was an excellent man, an intelligent agriculturalist and very fond of growing flowers, but his education had been somewhat neglected in relation to the natural sciences. In addition, brought up by an old nurse who had muddied his brain in early childhood with tales of magicians, and living in the midst of a population for whom witches and their spells were articles of faith, he fell prey, in the councilor's presence, to a suspicion mixed with fear.

To begin with, it did not seem natural to him that a man could discover, in a matter of months, on land previously reckoned sterile, a layer of kaolin and coal mines. After that, the apron turned to sugar, the coal transformed into the essence of pears and pineapples, and the ice that could be manu-

351

factured in a hot crucible, made his head spin—and perhaps, at that moment, he would have given anything to be placidly cultivating his dahlias and tulips in his garden instead of wandering in that diabolical castle in the company of his bizarre tenant.

Notburga, on the other hand, had never felt so happy in her life.

Leaning on the arm of Herr Fritz—for she was beginning to call him by that amicable name in her thoughts, rather than using his title of councilor—she was taking pleasure in walking with him, the objects that he showed her and the things he said to her. She did not want the day to end. So, when she saw the Baron taking out his watch repeatedly to interrogate the hands, she felt herself becoming sad.

"Why, Baron, do you imagine that you'll escape my claws so soon?" demanded the councilor, laughing. "You and Fraulein Notburga are my prisoners until nightfall, and even beyond. Prepare yourselves in consequence, and bear your unease patiently."

"The roads aren't very good," said the Baron, "and there's a risk in the dark..."

"Does darkness exist if I don't wish it? I can't stop the sun like Joshua, but I'll create another sun, and if you can't see when you go home at midnight as clearly as in broad daylight, I don't want to see you or your daughter ever again— which would be the greatest chagrin I can feel! I like you so much—both of you—that I'd rather never be separated from you. Let's eat, Baron; we'll resume this conversation later."

In spite of the excellent meal that was served and the exquisite wines that overloaded the table, the Baron felt increasingly ill at ease.

"The moment has come to make the ice," said the councilor. "Have an incandescent vessel brought up from the foundry, Katt." And as Katt just looked at him fearfully, he went out, and came back shortly afterwards with two blacksmiths carrying a furnace full of fire, and red hot itself.

He then poured into a platinum vessel, submitted to all the violence of heat, a substance that spread a strong odor of sulfur through the dining room, threw water over that substance from a carafe, withdrew the crucible from above the furnace and emptied it on to a tray. A magnificent block of ice fell on to the tray.

"We can now have a drink as cold as we wish, he said, surrounding a bottle of champagne with that singular ice.

The Baron felt even more ill at ease. It was even worse when, as he got up from the table, the councilor said in his vibrant voice: "Baron, you already know what I've made of the domain of your ancestors at ground level; now it's necessary for you to see what I've made of it underground. To begin with, we'll go down about a hundred meters."

The Baron made a fearful gesture, but before he had pronounced a single word he saw the table vanish, as if by magic, and he felt the floor beneath his feet tremble slightly. The light of the sky and its stars, which could be glimpsed through the curtains at the windows, gave way to a profound darkness; a slight coolness succeeded the warm atmosphere that had enveloped the councilor and his guests, and a slight shock caused the room to shake.

"We've arrived!" said the councilor, opening a door that revealed the entrance to a black tunnel. "You're now a hundred meters below ground—a ground composed entirely of sandstone. Here, take a look!"

The Baron paraded his anxious gaze around.

"It's here, Baron, in the very bosom of the earth, that we're going to see the strange beings that in habited our globe before the creation of humankind.

"With regard to the different layers of which the earth's crust is made up, you can observe in my geology galley, and will be able to observe again, as much as you wish, specimens placed in order of their formation.

"This gallery is an abridgement of the history of the globe's formation. First you see here the primitive terrain of the crystallization of pure granite, granitic rocks, mica- and talc-bearing schists, and amphibolous rocks. These layers form the skeleton on the earth, produced by cooling after the original fusion. They contain seams of precious stones, statuary marble, rock crystal, copper and gold.

"Next come the intermediary or metamorphic terrains, forming an intermediary between the igneous rocks and the stratified terrains; they enclose kaolin, glass quartz and siliceous marls. The plutonic rocks, powerful eruptions of the central fire, terminate the first epoch of the terrestrial globe.

"The transitional terrains, with their schists, limestone and various sandstones, open the second epoch. The earth, considerably cooled, was then covered with vegetables, which produced the carbonaceous terrain. The masses of coal that one finds in the depths of the ground testify to the richness of the primitive vegetation.

"Anthracite, independent coals, mingled with sandstone and black schists, make up the bulk of the transitional terrains, where one finds formations of sulfur, mercury and a few metallic seams.

"When the earth's atmosphere was purified, the gases that composed it were partly liquefied, water flowed over the surface of the terrestrial crust and the sedimentary layers were able to form. The first of the secondary terrains, the Pencean,[82] is made up of pale red calcareous rocks tinted with white, which yield excellent chalk and beautiful marble.

"During the second period, volcanoes, still endowed with enormous power, vomited the ancient volcanic rocks; these rocks are distinguished from plutonic rocks by the numerous cavities that inflate and pierce them, as in our modern lavas.

"The third epoch commences with the formation of secondary terrains—Cambrian, Silurian, Devonian and Jurassic—in which exclusively nautical fossils appear for the first time, particularly crustaceans, polyps, fish and birds—or, rather, flying reptiles. No trace is found of terrestrial animals, which

---

[82] I can find no evidence of this term ever being employed in geological parlance.

proves that marine animals were created first. The Cirque de Gavarnie and the towers of Le Marboré in France are magnificent limestone formations of that sort.

"The Lower and Upper Cretaceous, with its gypsums, its lithographic stones, its lignites and its sandstones encrusted with shells close the third epoch. Then the terrestrial animals appear, which mark the fourth epoch of the history of the globe. One finds them in the Tertiary terrain, and science observes among the fossils the remains of giant primitive mammals. It's at the end of the Tertiary period that the *diluvium* is formed, evidence of the universal deluge.

"The post-diluvial and modern alluvia are represented in my museum by their principal rocks, the galets, stalactites and travertines.

"Let's begin by examining the skeletons of animals. As you can see, I've arranged them in galleries hollowed out in the very midst of the natural terrains in which one finds these creatures, the species of which have disappeared forever from the earth. All of them are gigantic, because, before God created humans, it was necessary for the inhabitants of our globe to be robust in order to live in the bosom of the rude nature that surrounded them.

"This collection has given me a great deal of difficulty in its compilation, but, thank God, it's as complete as possible; neither gold, nor voyages, nor fatigue have been spared in assembling it. Finally, skilful molds reproduce faithfully, so far as possible, all the originals that I have not been able to procure.

"Now, with a wave of my magic wand, I'm going to resuscitate these monsters. You'll see them, not lying there like inert skeletons, but as the Creator produced them, with their forms, their colors and their movements. I promised you their visit, and here they are."

So saying, he made as if to readjust the chalk wick that was giving such a beautiful light, but he extinguished it, and a profound darkness, an authentic pitch darkness, suddenly surrounded the Baron and his daughter.

Immediately, however, a soft light gradually appeared, like a dot, and at the far end of the tunnel, which might have been twenty meters long, objects appeared, confusedly at first, in the middle of a luminous circle, and gradually took on form and substance. There were strange trees, such as the earth no longer produces, and red sandstone rocks that loomed up on the shore of an immense sea.

Notburga could not suppress a scream of terror. A monster, half serpent and half fish, had suddenly emerged from the water, and seemed to be advancing menacingly toward her. It measured at least ten meters, and was dragging itself awkwardly over the mud with the aid of four short stout limbs. On reaching the shore, it seemed to catch sight of the councilor and his guests; it brandished a neck four or five meters long, like a serpent, in their direction, and opened an immense mouth garnished with sharp teeth as long as a human hand.

The Baron would rather have been anywhere else; his daughter leaned on her father's arm, trembling.

"Don't be afraid, Fraulein," said the councilor. "This monster, which is called a plesiosaur, will not occupy us for long, for I perceive a labyrinthodon, which will make short work of it."

Indeed, on the far side of the strand, a toad of a size to rival the plesiosaur, as tall as an elephant, was crawling along. It opened and enormous maw. The plesiosaur tried to flee but could not; the giant batrachian fascinated it by means of a mysterious magnetic power, and drew it invincibly toward it.

"Let's take advantage of their combat to get away, and climb up rapidly toward a more elevated terrain," said the councilor, bringing Notburga and her father back into the little room, whose door the closed.

The Baron fell into an armchair, rather than merely sitting down, and wiped his brow, which was bathed in cold sweat.

Notburga was pale too, and a little tremulous.

Fritz, who pretended not to see their emotion, opened the door again.

"Now we're in the terrains of the third epoch of the fourth period of creation," he said. "Many creatures, various in nature, lived then; their fossil skeletons are numerous, as you'll see. Nevertheless the proportions of their stature are sensibly diminished. There are even petrified bones of aquatic birds, some with webbed feet like our ducks, others equipped with long legs like our waders. Those remains, which form an animal half-lizard and half-fish, belong to the ichthyosaur, of which I shall evoke the specter, as well as those of the megalosaurs, or giant crocodiles, which then pullulated on the earth. But let's see our ichthyosaur first.

The light went out and, as before, a landscape appeared at the far end of the tunnel, this time composed of giant cycads, horsetails and ferns; those plants, so small today, were bigger than or largest modern oaks.

An ichthyosaur seemed to be asleep on the sand; its back, on which the sun's rays were falling, was shining with the most brilliant colors and sparkling like an immense precious stone.

Suddenly, a formidable whistle, reminiscent of one escaping from a steam engine, resounded in the air. The ichthyosaur opened its eyes wide and tried to get back into the water, but before it could do so a dragon, whose wingspan measured at least five or six meters, fell upon it and resumed its flight, lifting its prey in its redoubtable claws, while striking at it and lacerating it with its beak.

"Well, Baron, what do you think of that hunt?" asked the councilor. "Isn't that flight as good as that of a falcon or a heron? What a beautiful bird of prey that pterodactyl is, whose beak is between two and three meters long, whose iridescent body is so richly colored, whose robust neck had the force and flexibility of a boa constrictor, and whose pointed teeth are equivalent, in proportion and strength, to the bayonet of an Austrian grenadier guard! Look how the fellow is eating that ichthyosaur seven or eight meters long!"

"All this is quite marvelous, but quite horrible!" murmured Notburga, who was feeling faint.

"Then let's go back up to the surface right away," said the councilor, giving a signal. He went on: "Another time, we'll see the rest of the fossil animals that I have the art of resuscitating; among them there are moles as big as elephants, elephants as big as hills, covered in long furry fleeces like sheep, and dogs and tigers as big as horses, and a thousand other things that disconcert both human imagination and reason."

He had scarcely finished speaking when the little room reached the level of the castle again.

Pale and weak, Notburga ran to the window in order not to faint.

"Now, now, my dear Fraulein," said the councilor, with paternal solicitude. "Don't take my innocent jokes so seriously. I can explain everything to you with a few words, and make you smile at your terrors.

"The rising and falling room that you're in is made in imitation of those found in New York hotels. Nothing is simpler than their mechanism, invented in order that one can live on upper floors with no more fatigue than if one were lodged on the ground floor.

"As for the apparitions of resuscitated fossils, they're nothing but phantasmagoria slides improved by a friend of mine, an optician."

"And what about the sugar you made from your cook's clothes, and the ice made in a crucible?" demanded the Baron, who did not believe a word of those explanations.

"Child's play—the tricks of a student of chemistry. I could just as easily turn sugar into sawdust or paper; I can even make alcohol, ether or vinegar from it; it would be sufficient for me to have recourse to distillation. The French chemist Bracconot[83] was the first to carry out those marvels. He got there on seeing that the apron, where it had been splashed by

---

[83] Henri Bracconot (1780-1855) described the conversion of wood, straw and cotton into sugar by means of sulphuric acid in a paper published in 1819.

sulfuric acid, presented the characteristics of a burn without charring.

"*The cloth*, he thought, *has been eaten away by sulfuric acid without catching fore. What caused that?* And with that, he took the rag of the fabric and steeped it in the sulfuric acid. To begin with he obtained a sticky substance, soluble in water. He saturated it with chalk, submitted it to evaporation and then obtained a sugary gum analogous to gum Arabic. Twenty-one grams of dry fabric gave him twenty-six grams of that gum, free of sulfuric acid—which is to say, more gum than cloth.

"If, instead of saturating the mucilaginous solution of wood, straw or cloth in sulfuric acid with chalk, one dilutes it with several times its own weight of water and boils it for ten hours or so, one can then ensure that all the gummy substance is converted into sugar; it's then only a matter of separating the sugar from the acid and neutralizing the latter with chalk. The liquid, filtered and evaporated, has the consistence of syrup, and after twenty-four hours it all solidifies into a single mass of passably pure sugar.

"After that, one presses it forcefully in linen, and makes it crystallizes a second time. It only becomes dazzling white, however, after being treated with animal charcoal."

"And the cream from coal?"

"There's everything in coal, even essences for making confectionery. When one distils coal, one obtains three substances: one solid, coke; one liquid, tar; and one gaseous, carbonated hydrogen. One can also harvest solutions from which one can extract ammonia in abundance and at low cost, which in general use in industry, and was bought from Orient very expensively at the end of the last century, when it was supposedly only obtainable from camel-dung.[84]

---

[84] The reader will recognize this passage as one reproduced virtually word-for-word from the newspaper article previously incorporated into the item in *Fantaisies scientifiques de Sam* here translated as "The Diabolical Coal-Merchant."

"You know how coke and hydrogen are employed, in lighting and hating. As for the tar, as it comes out of the retort its employment is less immediate. People tried to substitute it for asphalt in road-building, but it lacked the solidity and resistance; feet sink into its black layers, almost as they do today in mud except that they don't come out so easily. To take advantage of coal-tar, it's therefore necessary to distil it further.

"First chemistry, and then industry, obtained from that hitherto-useless substance liquids possessing infinitely various densities and properties, from a light oil scarcely weighing as much as alcohol to napthalene, a heavy, nacreous solid that is often efficacious in treating skin diseases.

"The hydrocarbons produced by the distillation of coal-tar form another family, that of gazogenes. Mixed with alcohol, gazogenes replace fuel oil, up to a point; they're known by the name of liquid gas. Almost uniquely, at present, they possess the property of dissolving rubber; note, in passing, that they cause the noxious odor exhaled by garments coated in that substance. Finally, submitted to certain reactions, further distilled, and combined with ether, they become essence with delightful perfumes, which Parisian confectionery is the first in the world to employ to give bonbons flavors of strawberry and pineapple. Rum and cognac often acquire their bouquet from a few drops of one of these essences. One also obtains from coal-tar a tinctural substance analogous to one of the precious colors that is extracted from madder.

"Various properties of coal products, observed and studied, will doubtless not be long delayed in giving further progress to industry. Tanneries, among others, will one day be able to obtain results in a matter of hours that presently require months of hard work. The principle on which these future methods rests exists in theory, but its application still remains insufficient. One finds oneself blocked by one of those invincible obstacles that hazard often ends up removing when human genius, thinking itself vanquished, gives up.

"But let's get back to the bonbons.

"Sugary confections with the flavor of apple, pear, quince, melon and many others, the English sweets that have become popular and are sold by grocers, owe their aroma to combinations of butyric ether with vinegar, valerianic acid or coccinic acid, extracted from coconuts. Butyric ether is itself merely a compound produced from butyric acid. Now, that acid is obtained by the distillation of decomposing organic matter, such as cheese or meat. Let us ad, to reassure the disgusted, that one can also prepare it by the metamorphosis that sugar, starch and other analogous substances undergo on contact with nitrogenated substances capable of acting as fermenting agents.

"Let's now come to the ice made in an incandescent furnace. Nothing is simpler. Into a red-hot platinum capsule one pours a few grams of anhydrous—which is to say, water-free—sulfuric acid. That acid, which melts at ten degrees below zero, passes into the *spheroidal state* and maintains itself at a temperature of eleven degrees. If one projects water on to the spheroid formed by the sulfuric acid, the water, put in contact with a body at such a low temperature, freezes instantly, as you have seen."

"What is this *spheroidal state*, then?"

"When you project a liquid on to an incandescent surface, the liquid, no matter from what height it falls, doesn't wet that surface—which is to say that it doesn't come into contact with it, does not touch it. It takes on a globular form and remains at a constant temperature, inferior to its boiling point, no matter how high the surrounding temperature is."

"Thank God, you're not a sorcerer but a scientist," said the Baron. "I prefer that. And the famous light that competes with the sun, which will soon allow us to see clearly at midnight?"

"You've seen it during our subterranean excursion. A simple apparatus produces it with the aid of two gases, hydrogen and oxygen, which illuminate over a simple piece of chalk."

"Come on, my girl, get ready to leave; I'm in all the more haste to set out for home and see this splendid light now that midnight's about to chime, and all this excitement has made me singularly weary."

"Soon, Baron," said Fritz, gallantly placing Notburga's mantle over the young woman's shoulders, "I hope you'll no longer have to leave the old castle when you feel tired."

"And when will that be, councilor?"

"When, my dear Baron? When you're my father-in-law. In a month!"

This time, Notburga nearly fainted completely. Fritz caught her in his arms, and after she had recovered her senses, he said: "Don't you know that I've been in love with you for a long time, Fraulein Notburga? Don't you know that I came to take over the ruins of the old castle in order to be close to you?"

"I've realized that, Herr Fritz," she replied, letting her hand fall into the young man's.

"I see that nothing remains but for me to say amen," the Baron concluded. "I'm happy for her to become your wife my friend, but I warn you that I don't intended to be parted from my daughter, and you'll have to give me accommodation in the castle."

"You shall have the finest apartment," the councilor replied. "Fraulein Notburga, lean on my arm and permit me to escort you back to your father's house, until the same of can gather all three of us together."

They set off on the road to the little house, and when they arrived at the door, the Baron said: "You haven't kept your word, Fritz. I haven't seen the slightest ray of your famous lighting, and but for the kindness of the moon, I might have put my foot in a rut."

Fritz and Notburga must have been saying very interesting things to one another, because neither of them heard a word of the Baron's ironic reproach.

THE FIRST INHABITANTS OF PARIS

Four thousand years ago, immense forests covered the region occupied today by the city of Paris and the surrounding districts of Bondy, Ville-d'Avray, Marly, Bellevue, Meudon and Chaville.

In the epoch in which my story begins, those forests, all the more sinister in their appearance because winter had stripped them of their leaves, were composed primarily of oak-trees, elm-trees, ash-trees, willows, pines and firs, whose gigantic trunks, sometimes sturdy and powerful, sometimes thinned by the years, rose up into the sky or strewed the ground with their debris in the midst of an inextricable mass of bushes, brambles and wild plants. To cap it all, snow extended its white shroud everywhere.

As for the river that traversed those woods, a chill of seven or eight degrees consolidated its surface and added further, by virtue of its immobility, to the lugubrious aspect of the country.

Only bears, lions, tigers, hyenas, badgers, oxen, aurochs, sheep, reindeer, fallow deer, antelopes, wild dogs, wolves, wild boar, horses, hares and rabbits troubled the silence that reigned everywhere. Some were fleeing before bands of enemies; others were pursuing or devouring their victims; above them, birds of prey circled in the air, in order to take their part in the carnage.

The semi-darkness that still enveloped nature gradually dissipated, and the sun was beginning to show on the horizon when a troop of about a hundred humans appeared on the bank of the Seine, facing the island that now bear the name of the Île de la Cité.

The humans had been following the course of the river for more than a month; they stopped in response to an order given by an old man who seemed to be their chief.

While the women and children collected dead branches and built a pyre—which they lit by vigorously rubbing a piece of soft wood in a hole in a hollow piece of hard wood, which each of them carried suspended around the neck by a cord of animal-hide—the old man gathered his companions around him and addressed a few words to them in a rude and guttural language.

That council of humans, most of whom were of small stature, to be sure, but robust and thickset, clad in crudely tanned bearskins or reindeer pelts, was a strange spectacle, although it did not lack a certain savage majesty. Their reddish hair fell over their shoulders in its full length; their beards covered their chests; in their hands they held either clubs, lassos made of large punctured stones attached with long leather thongs, spears with flint heads embedded in cleft sticks, or axes whose stone heads were fixed into a bone or an antler with the aid of leather strips, applied moist and then dried in the sun, like those the indigenes still fabricate in certain parts of North America.

The women, similarly clad in hides, but more supple ones, similarly allowed their gilded hair to fall over their shoulders. Necklaces of petrified marine sponges and the teeth of wolves or oxen, arranged with an esthetic sensibility of sorts, were reminiscent of the ornaments still found today among the daughters of Africa, Polynesia and the New World. They wore crude fur shoes tied around their slender legs, and their feet were remarkably small. Finally, the melancholy gaze of their big blue eyes tempered the savage character given to their symmetrical oval faces by suntan, privation and fatigue.

The chief of the tribe, handing a flint ax embedded in a bull's horn to one of the men who were surrounding him, turned to the women and gave them orders; they rose to their feet respectfully to listen to them, and immediately hastened to carry them out. In a few minutes, they quit the fire around which they had previously been grouped, and while some of them placed their children on their shoulders, others grouped together either to carry canoes made of tree-barks sewn together or crudely hollowed out from a single tree-trunk, or large baskets woven with willow-branches, which contained frozen meat, acorns and variously-formed utensils in wood or stone.

They immediately set out to cross the river over the ice. The men marched at the head, the women and children came after them; finally, a few warriors, spears in hand, formed a rear-guard.

Having arrived on the Île de la Cité, the women stopped and set up a sort of camp there, while their menfolk explored the surroundings. They soon came back to announce to their leader that they had found a grotto, but that it served as a den for wolves or bears, to judge by the bones strewn around outside. Immediately, they picked up their weapons; tree branches were ignited, and the assault on the grotto began.

Some threw brands through a narrow hole that opened almost at ground level, while other climbed up above the cavern to see whether there might be a crack that would permit them to continue the attack from that direction. They did not take long to discover a broad fissure, through which they also threw firebrands.

Scarcely had the double siege begun than howls emerged from the lair, and a gigantic bear showed its enormous head through the basal opening, which only permitted it to emerge by crawling. A heavy stone, launched by one of the assailants, struck its forehead, and before it could retreat, wounded and bloody, twenty spears pierced it and rendered it incapable of further fight. With the aid of one of the lassos mentioned above, the roaring animal was hauled out of the grotto and they finished killing it.

Its female and four cubs, chased from their refuge by the fire, were subjected to the same fate.

The victory won, cries of triumph summoned the women; the latter carried the six cadavers to the fire that had been lit when they installed themselves on the island, and set about butchering them with as much skill as promptitude, aided by flint knives of all sizes. Some removed the skins and others detached the quarters of meat, while their companions broke the bones and took them to the warriors in order that they could eat the marrow while it was still warm.

In the meantime, the most succulent parts of the bears were pierced with sticks and roasted in the fire, while the remainder was attached to neighboring trees in order that the frost might harden and conserve it.

While all that was done, the flames, alimented by further bundles of wood, continued to crackle inside the cavern and send forth long sprays of sparks and black columns of smoke through the crack open at its summit; after which the formidable fire was allowed to go out.

Later, one of the warriors tried several times, without success, to get inside the cave; scarcely had he introduced his head through the narrow opening that served as a passage than he backed out again, half-suffocated by the smoke.

In the meantime, it was beginning to get dark and they had to make the arrangements necessary for camping in the open. They placed the boats on stakes planted in the ground, surrounded them with branches that were covered with the skins of the bears, still fresh, and the warriors crouched down with their lances beside them near these improvised huts, in which the women and children huddled.

These preparations terminated, night fell: a winter night with its profound darkness, the roaring of the wind and biting cold. Soon, the cries of ferocious beasts attracted by the odor of fresh pelts began to rise up in all directions; kept at a distance by the fires lit around the little camp, they testified to their disappointment with sinister clamors. The wild dogs, whose eyes could be seen gleaming in the shadows, uttered lugubrious baying sounds, such as their domesticated descendants sometimes utter in our countryside, which cause peasants to make the sign of the cross when they hear them— because it is, they say, an omen of death. The wolves howled, the hyenas sobbed, the lions roared, and the foxes yapped.

Sometimes, a tiger, more cunning, crept silently to the edge of the camp and sought by sliding its paws through the branches to seize a sleeping child. Then the mothers uttered screams of fear, and the warriors on watch seized their weapons and came to drive the redoubtable enemy away. If an injured tiger fled, more than one of its adversaries also fell to the icy ground, its torso labored by powerful thrusts of claws or a limb broken by formidable jaws.

The women, doubtless familiar with such scenes, hastened to attend to the wounded, and in accordance with the others give by one of them, who, although still young, exercised an absolute authority; they surrounded the wounds with strips of fresh leather or covered them with clay softened with warm water.

Finally, day began to dawn. The ferocious beats gradually retreated into the depths of the forest, and silence was reestablished around the camp.

As soon as the sun appeared over the horizon through the black clouds that enveloped the sky, the old man and his warriors gathered together, prostrated themselves before the star and addressed a long prayer to it. Then they got up again and, at a sign from their chief, headed for the cavern. A little smoke was still emerging from the upper opening, but even so, one of the warriors was able to get inside; a few minutes later, he came out again, and the old man and his companions entered in their turn.

The grotto, illuminated by torches made from resinous tree branches, resembled the majority of the abandoned quarries that one discovers, so to speak, at every step in the environs of Paris and in Paris itself. It owed its formation to one of those collapses so frequent in quaternary terrains, produced by the retreat of the waters. Elevated nearly four or five meters, and about sixty meters in circumference, it only presented a few cracks in places, of varying depth. There were no traces indicative of damp on its gray walls, now almost entirely blacked by the smoke of the fire lit inside the previous day.

Before taking possession of the primitive dwelling, the old man gave the order not to broaden but, on the contrary, to elongate the fissure that opened at the summit of the grotto.

Immediately, they set to work, and with the aid of large stones collected from the bank of the Seine, and powerful tools of half-carved flint, they did not take long to bring that work to a successful conclusion. In spite of the crudity of the instruments of which they made use, each of the humans employed in such rude work showed the skill that the hand acquires with practice, no matter how imperfect the tools it employs might be.

As the fissure grew, other warriors arranged stones across its width, which, without intercepting air and light, would conceal the mysterious opening from an enemy gaze.

Those precautions taken, the women crawled into the cavern. Some of them took away the plants and branches with which the bears had made a den for their cubs, brought a considerable quantity of dried wood, chosen preferentially from among resinous species, and lit a big fire in the middle of the cave, directly underneath the fissure in the vault, the smoke of which escaped and was lost through that natural issue, transformed into a chimney.

While some of their companions occupied themselves in this way with sanitizing the air and warming the glacial walls of the underground dwelling, other women made up beds of moss for the children in the cavities, attached nets and other fishing implements, animal skins of every species, and large wicker baskets to the wall, which they pieces with pointed bones. Afterwards, they all sat down in a circle around the fire, and by the bright but vacillating light they set about giving a further preparation to the skins of the bears and cubs killed the previous day. They carried out this work with extreme skill, making use of flint scrapers of all the sizes and shapes most appropriate to their various purposes. They removed all the pieces of flesh that they found attached to the inside of the skins, thus diminishing their thickness. They then soaked them in molten grease, rubbed them between their hands, twisted them, beat them with heavy stones like washerwomen beating soapy linen, and ended up, by dint of perseverance, rendering them extremely supple.

The oldest, having recourse to the invincible patience peculiar to savages, who take no account of time or difficulty, were piercing the bears' teeth in order to make necklaces of them; as a preliminary, by means of extremely thin pointed flints wedged in bones and repeated blows with stones, they were scraping out and excavating the roots of the teeth, detached from the broken jaw, with minute precaution. By dint of skill and time, they ended up obtaining a hole in each tooth, which they then enlarged and rounded.

A few young women, directed by the companion who had given them orders a short while before, with an authority respected by all, were devoting themselves to work that was even more delicate. With the aid of fragments of bone forming needles of all dimensions, polished and pointed at one end, and terminated at the other by a narrow opening through which an eye hollowed out in a narrow groove permitted the introduction of a fiber detached from the fresh tendons of an animal, they were sewing.

Thanks to their long sojourn in a bed of grease, those fibers—like ones still fabricated in America and Africa— became a veritable thread with which hides could be stitched into garments, and various component parts assembled.

The women were also responsible for polishing the wood of bows, arrows and spears, and of fitting flint points to the arrows and spears. The men reserved the task of fabricating the points.

In order to understand the nature of that work more fully, it is necessary to say that flint, especially when fresh and when the action of the air has not hardened and partly decomposed it, possesses a particular and little-known property. If its plane surface is struck with a sharp blow, a fissure is produced in its depth, which is prolonged for some distance and which isolates and separates a rounded cone. Mineralogists call this phenomenon the "conoid fracture." When the sharp blow is delivered to the edge of the flint, the fracture is merely "demi-conoid." In accordance with this property, which is well-known to manufacturers of rifle-flints, they have discovered how prehistoric savages manufactured their scrapers, knives and spear-points, as the savages that populate America, Oceania and Africa still do.

When splitting a flint, the warrior of the Île de la Cité began by producing two parallel and opposite faces destined to become the bases of prisms. Then they struck a sharp blow on one of those bases and detached a splinter extending from one to the other. By turning the fragment obtained symmetrically, the faces were formed one by one, resulting in a prism with several faces, which, according to its thickness, might have been eight and twenty-four faces. By striking a sharp bow between two of these faces, a fragment with three or four angles could invariably be detached. That operation continued until the nucleus became too small to be handled. On the majority of points fabricated in this fashion a curvature is observable at the extremity of the conoid fracture, because the flint normally produces slightly arched splinters.

The women imitated this kind of work to obtain the knives and scrapers designed for the preparation of hides.

Toward evening the hunters who had set forth in the morning returned to the cavern, bringing back wild boar, reindeer and hares. When they were all inside, the entrance to the grotto was closed with an enormous stone detached from the interior wall and roughly carved, in such a way as to seal it tightly, so as not to allow the penetration of cold draughts or wild animals. After that, the fire was revived by throwing dry wood on to it, and everyone sat down around the blaze, which provided both light and heat.

To cook the most delicate pieces of the prey that had been brought back, a hole was dug in the ground; three stones heated in the fire were placed in it, and the feet, head or certain sections of the intestine placed in the middle. That primitive oven was closed with a forth stone heated like the other three, and it was covered with hot ashes. Half an hour later, the delicate meats reserved for the chief and the principal warriors were removed, perfectly cooked. The latter sat down at a large stone that served as their table, and each of the cavern's residents, following their example, subsequently took part in the feast.

When everyone was seated, work recommenced. The women sowed, playing their bone needles and tendon thread; the men repaired or maintained their stone weapons and fashioned reindeer antlers into the hilts of daggers or hammers; they sometimes decorated them with carvings that were not lacking in a certain skill. Most of the time they took advantage of accidents and curves in the antlers to provide faces that they sculpted into the form of an animal.

Those figures are still easily recognizable today, after so many centuries, when archaeologists are fortunate enough to discover a few of them in caves occupied by the primitive inhabitants of Europe. One can see wild boar, red deer and, most commonly, reindeer. They do not have the stiff and immobile attitudes of Egyptian art. Depicted in motion, the legs of the reindeer are bent beneath them and their heads extended, as if they were gathering impetus; the boar are rushing forward, with their fur bristling and their formidable tusks extended; the red deer and the horses, by contrast, are grazing placidly.

Other carvings seem to be dedicated to religious symbols. The sun expands in a crown of rays, the moon is rounded and strange faces grimace from it. Sometimes there are whimsical designs, sometimes traced in relief, sometimes hollowed out, representing pearls, knots, stars, squares and diamonds.

The tines of red deer antlers served for the fabrication of a multitude of small objects, both utilitarian and ornamental, such as barbed arrow-tips and punches for piercing holes in pelts through which the women's crude bone needles could introduce threads.

Gradually, the incandescence of the fire died down and the cavern became darker. Then the old man stood up, and everyone imitated him silently. He made a gesture. Immediately, the women went to lie down next to their children on beds of moss and dry leaves; the men wrapped themselves up in their cloaks, and silence and sleep soon reigned in the cavern, where a profound obscurity did not take long to fall.

The next morning everyone woke up at the sound of the chief's voice and got up. The women hastened to relight the fire, and placed what remained of the half-consumed embers on masses of wood that crackled and caught fire. A long, thick column of smoke emerged through the fissure in the vault, and the warriors picked up their weapons. With great efforts, the stone sealing the entrance was rolled back inside the cave, and everyone went out through the narrow gap that led outside.

While most of the hunters headed for the forest that covered the opposite bank of the Seine, five or six others struck the ice on the river with large pointed stones fashioned for that purpose, opening a vast hole therein into which they threw pieces of thinly-sliced fresh meat.

When they supposed that the fish were biting—as fishermen still say today—they kept a close watch on their arrival, and set about harpooning the imprudent individuals that came up to the opening to eat and breathe.

The harpoons that they used consisted of a long shaft fitted with a barbed piece of antler or bone, and they rarely missed their thrust. Almost invariably, the fisherman, having struck his prey swiftly with a sure thrust, brought it back no less swiftly by an abrupt movement and threw it on to the ice, palpitating, where it was finished off by striking it with a stone hammer.

Women who were stationed close by placed the produce of the fishing in their wicker baskets, which they handed to their companions for transportation to the cavern.

Their abundant harvest of fish terminated, the fishermen came back to the bank and, following the edge of the forest, carefully examined the soil making it up. They did not take long to happen upon a vein of clay, whose icy surface they broke up and from which they succeeded in extracting a mass of compact and malleable matter, which they loaded onto their shoulders and brought back to the communal habitation. They kneaded that earth for a long time and, without any other instrument than their hands, formed primitive bowls, like those of which fragments are sometimes found, especially at Meudon.

Once the bowls were fashioned, they covered them with hot ashes, placed over the ashes a mass of incandescent embers, and then set about other work, leaving fire and time the care of baking their pottery.

At dusk, shortly before the return of the hunters, they gently cleared away the embers and ashes covering the bowls, and examined them scrupulously. Some, having failed to resist the action of the fire, were found to be either broken or furrowed with cracks that rendered their use impossible; others, by contrast, had acquired a real hardness and solidity, and were reliable, with a few precautions. They were filled with water, gradually exposed to the action of the fire, and eventually surrounded with flaming wood. When that proof was terminated, they were handed over to the women, who made use of them for the fish caught that morning.

Such was, for a few months and until spring, the existence of those savages who had moved slowly, step by step, through Gaul and the fringes of the Dordogne all the way to the banks of the Seine.

What motive had forced them to make that long and difficult emigration during the most rigorous season of the year?

Alas, it was a scourge that still desolates Europe today, and was already desolating that epoch so distant from our 19th century: war.

The tribe had occupied comfortable caves on the fringes of the Dordogne, laboriously fitted out by its efforts. Prey of every species was abundant in the nearby forests, which supplied them with wood in abundance, and the lakes and rivers were full of fish.

One day, a horde, doubtless chased from its own possessions by a more numerous horde, and in search of a favorable place in which to settle, found what they desired in the caves of Eyzies. Others were living there, but the unfortunates had too few warriors to resist a powerful enemy. The newcomers immediately took possession of the caves, massacring the in-habitants, and the few who remained of those unfortunates were obliged to go into exile and search for some deserted region far away, in order to live there in peace, sheltered from further spoliations.

Always searching, and finding redoubtable enemies eve-rywhere on their path, or tribes too strong for them to attack and drive them out in their turn, the band, composed of scarce-ly a hundred individuals, eventually stopped at the island, where they finally found a cave that was large, solid and easy to defend. No human foot had ever left an imprint on the sand of that shore, known only to wild animals. What more favora-ble spot could the emigrants hope to discover?

So, when winter disappeared and spring began to melt the ice of the river, to bring back a more clement temperature and to open buds on the trees, the exiles set about taking the measures necessary to settle securely and permanently in their new homeland.

Before proceeding with that endeavor, however, the old man, accompanied by two warriors, explored the surrounding region to make sure that there was no spot more favorable for the establishment of the tribe of which he was the chief. He reached, not without peril and fatigue, the heights of Mont-martre, which he had perceived across the marshes of the Île de la Cité. From the top of the hill he could survey the entire region: the woods of Saint-Cloud, Ville-d'Avray and Marly. Those places, then nameless, formed an island separated from another by the strait of Versailles, the valley of Sèvres and the valley of the park of Versailles.

Another island comprised Bellevue, Meudon, Verrières and Chaville, detached from the continent by the strait that followed the valley of the Bièvre and the hills of Jouy. Finally, there was another group of islands, now disappeared, covered with forests—for there was nothing to be seen anywhere but woods and water.

In spite of the proximity of two other islands—the Île Louviers and the Île Saint-Louis—the old man said to his companions: "The place where we're living seems to me to be the best-situated and the safest. We can't, therefore, establish ourselves in better conditions and more securely. To work, then! And may the Sun, our god, protect us."

When the old man had expressed that opinion—or, rather made that decision, approved by the other two leaders—he went back with them to the Île de la Cité, through the immense marshes that extended in those days between the banks of the Seine and the heights of Montmartre.

Sometimes it was necessary for them to climb into a small boat made from oak barks sewn together with strips of hide, like those the indigenes of Canada fabricate today, and which the chief's companions took turns to carry on their robust shoulders. Sometimes, leaning on long staffs with which they tested the terrain, it was necessary for them to walk over terrain that undulated beneath their feet and covered profound abysses, like some that still existed in the Pas-de-Calais near Clairmarais at the beginning of the 19th century, which recent works of canalization and drainage have caused to disappear. Reptiles, myriads of toads, frogs, salamanders and newts pullulated everywhere in the long grass; reeds, willows, poplars and tree-trunks felled by time and lying half-rotted in the water formed a perilous labyrinth and exhaled a noxious odor.

Finally, they succeeded in getting back to the Île de la Cité. The old man announced to the tribe, whose members had grouped around him as soon as he returned, that, the following day, they would begin to construct habitations on the banks of the island, and found a village that would permit each family to have its own dwelling and cease living communally in the cave.

Indeed, at daybreak the next day, all the men went into the forest and felled a large number of medium-sized trees, sometimes with blows of flint axes, sometimes having recourse to fire to consume the trunks at their base and oblige them to topple.

Most frequently, they made gashes in the trunks between twenty and twenty-five centimeters long, and threw a lasso

375

into the branches, which they attached firmly by powerful ropes of twisted hide. Then five of six men, combining their strength, pulled repeatedly on the rope, and caused the tree to fall at their feet.

Then, with the aid of levers, similarly made from long branches, they placed the trees on round logs stripped of their bark and fashioned into rollers, and thus brought them, laboriously, to the banks of the island. There they charred one of the extremities, which they placed in a blazing fire, and afterwards, with the aid of hide ropes and the association of numerous arms, they embedded that extremity in the mud, raised the pole upright and drove them in vertically with blows of flint hammers.

After that operation, to consolidate the piles, they heaped around them large stones collected from the bank and threw sand and clay on top of the masses. Many of those barbaric constructions can still be found in the lakes of Neuchâtel and Morat, where they have been given the names of *steinbergs* and *tenevières*, which mean "mounds inundated by water."

A month later, four hundred of these beams, at a distance of seven or eight meters from the island, without communicating with it other than by wooden drawbridges, formed a kind of fortification of piles on which cabins were constructed.

It was more trunks and branches that formed these squat houses, dressed with a daub of clay mixed with sliced vegetables. They were roofed with long reeds fixed by pickets and cords of bark-fiber previously macerated in water. Finally, an opening was contrived in the middle of each roof, beneath which a fireplace was set, consisting of five large stones, from which swirls of smoke were not long delayed in emerging.

After that, the life of the tribe established on the Île de la Cité took on a character of tranquility and order quite different from the one they had led in the cave. The men hunted all day, it is true, as before, but the women, during their absence, applied themselves to giving their dwellings a more cheerful appearance, and creating all possible wellbeing there. They ornamented the walls every day with tree-branches, renewed as soon as they faded; they covered the earthen floor with reeds and fashioned clay vessels, which they baked in the fire. They did not forget their clothing and all possible means of making themselves more beautiful in the eyes of their spouses. Sometimes they collected petrified marine sponges on the shore and took advantage of those little stones' natural holes to pass plant-fiber thread or animal tendons through them to make bracelets. Sometimes, they detached little pearls from blocks of chalk that were naturally pierced with holes, which today's naturalists call "globular tragos,"[85] and fashioned necklaces.

Every morning they bathed their children and themselves in the river, and swam gaily in the midst of all those hardy little savages, who competed in skill in the water. When they returned to the bank, they smoothed their long blonde hair with combs made from carved sea-shells and put on short dressed, such are still sometimes found in certain Swiss peat-bogs, among weapons made of flint and bone. The dresses in question left the arms free and naked, and a part of the breast, and only came down to the knees.

Having completed their toilette, they devoted themselves to household chores, preparing their spouses' meals, and in the evening, when the latter returned, plunged into the Seine again.

One still finds that passion for bathing and that quest for neatness in a large number of populations of America and Oceania, and it is common to almost all savage races. Untidiness is a relatively modern daughter of civilization and its sisters, poverty and carelessness.

---

[85] This term was indeed used by some archeologists to describe what they interpreted as items of Stone Age jewelry found in various European sites. Berthoud's text includes a drawing of a bracelet allegedly made from "fossil sponges." Fossil coral is a more likely material, and was still in use by some Native American tribes at the time, which encouraged analogical speculations of a dubious nature, in keeping with much the highly speculative reconstruction ventured in this story.

Sometimes, too, like the same savage peoples, with the aid of a needle made of the bone of a hare, terminated by a fine flint point securely embedded in the bone, and the antler of a fallow deer hollowed out in the form of a pot, they were able to mix a red dye and make use of it to inscribe bizarre tattoos on their foreheads, breast or arms. Monsieur Meillet[86] has found a similar item in the caves of Chaffaud; the deer-antler was still half-full of very pure and finely-powdered iron oxide. It is well-known that the ancient Scots, the Picts, did not disdain to paint their faces by analogous means.

In the evening, the warriors, laden with game, returned to their canoes of bark and wood, which they had carefully con-cealed in the reeds on their departure, and took to the water to regain the island. When their return was signaled by a trumpet or a kind of pipe made with the bone of a wild horse, the women and children ran to the bank and welcomed them with cries of joy, hurrying to relieve them of their burdens. The children took them by the hand and led them to the threshold of the tribal chief.

The old man listened silently to what the warriors told him about the incidents and produce of their hunting, ad-dressed a few brief observations to them, if necessary, and then went back into his hut, where he was soon brought the most delicate morsels of the day's haul.

Every household was then enclosed in its dwelling, with the exception of five or six warriors charged with keeping watch all night long on the security of the island. They made rounds, spears and bows in hand, and were ready, at the slightest hint of danger, to sound the alarm and rose all the men of the tribe. For that purpose they carried whistles hung around their necks on thin cords, made from the hollowed-out phalanges of a reindeer's foot, holed at the base of its stronger

---

[86] Alexandre-Alphonse Meillet of Poitiers made numerous relics of Stone Age humans at Chaffaud and elsewhere. He also appears to have taken out several patents for inventions, but Meillet was a very common name and one has to beware of confusing his name with numerous near-namesakes.

extremity. Such whistles, of which several examples have been found in the caves of the Dordogne, rendered a clear shrill note audible throughout the island, especially in the silence of the night.

Eight years went by without anything justifying these precautionary measures, and the prosperity of the tribe made further progress every day.

The warriors possessed a large number of axes, solidly embedded and obtained by a method that demanded no less than five years. In fact, the method consisted of making a fissure in a young tree, into which a flint blade as forcibly introduced, maintained by strips of hide tightly knotted and wound around the tree. The rest was left to the sap and time. When the former had fixed the stone ax unshakably, the tree was cut at its base, the top as removed and one found oneself in possession of a weapon whose solidity was proof against anything.

In addition, provisions of dried meat, acorns, fruits and roots ensured and abundance of food for the winter. Every day, new and ingenious ameliorations discovered by the women added to the comfort of the households; every day, children were born; the children, raised by their mothers, became adolescents, and the adolescents became men and warriors.

In the morning, the old man prostrated himself in the midst of his numerous subjects before the Sun, the only deity that they worshiped, blessed the star for the peace and happiness that it dispensed to those whose defeat and exile had previously tried them so cruelly.

To ensure that happiness and give it further duration, everyone wore on the breast a talisman formed by a bone on which an image of the Sun was engraved. That image consisted, as we have already said, of a neatly-drawn circle surrounded by radii depicting its rays.

Sometimes, beside the star, the moon was placed, with the eyes and nose that our almanacs give it; sometimes, they added depictions or snakes, or even crocodiles, with their open mouths ornamented with teeth. Does that mean that the exiles from the Dordogne were familiar with the crocodile, that child of hot countries? Whence came, similarly, those little axes made of syenite, sardonyx or jade, kinds of stone that are not found in Europe, which come from India, but of which one encounters rare specimens in archeological digs, in stages all the way from the Orient to the middle of Europe? Is there not a considerable probability that the races of the North originate from emigrations of eastern races? A circumstance no less strange is that the Chinese still call jade the Yu stone, or "stone of the Sun."

One day, the old man assembled around him the principal warriors of the tribe and held a long council, after which two of them crossed the Seine and went into the forest that covered the other bank. That same evening, the warriors came back, went to find the chief in great haste, and the following day, the latter summoned all the men of the tribe, in order to construct, from the shore of the island to the opposite shore, with enormous tree-trunks, a bridge of great solidity. The surface of the bridge was subsequently covered with a thick layer of stones, cemented in place with moist clay.

While the bridge was being built, other workers dug a trench on the opposite bank, in the middle of which they established a rather steep slope. They slid down that slope three enormous blocks of sandstone, which rebounded and came to rest, one by one, at the end of the bridge. They were pushed on to the bridge, across which they were guided by wooden levers, and finally brought to the middle of the island, after which the bridge was demolished.

That initial labor lasted nearly two months.

One of the ends of the two less massive rocks was then buried in the ground. Once they had been planted, a kind of earthen terrace was built with a gentle slope, which rose from ground level to the top of the two rocks. After that, the third stone, which was flat and about three meters long, two meters large and forty centimeters thick, was slid up that slope and solidly established on the other two, in such a way as to fashion a kind of table. When the work was finished the job of clearing away the terrace that had served to raise the flat stone was entrusted to the children. The procedure was imitated four thousand years later by Monsieur Lebas[87] to raise the Luxor obelisk on to its pedestal in the Place de la Concorde.

While it lasted, the erection of that monument, constructed at the coast of such much long and hard labor, preoccupied the tribe keenly. It was the object of all conversations, and even the children gazed from afar, with a kind of fearful respect, at the three heavy rocks with which an enormous stone table had been formed.

One morning, before the Sun appeared, the old man came out of his hut and, surrounded by warriors, undertook a kind of bizarre consecration of the table. After having remained prostrate before the star for a long time, he took dry aromatic herbs, which he ignited and allowed to burn in the midst of the swirls of smoke they produced. With their ashes, still warm, he traced a long gray line in the middle of the stone. Immediately, the warriors, guided by that line and with the aid of flint tools, hollowed out a groove five or six centimeters deep, and carefully threw the debris produced by that work into the Seine.

When the strange ceremony was over, the chief and his warriors went back to their dwellings and resumed their ordinary routines.

From then on, every morning, when the sun rose, the old man burned thyme and other plants in the gutter on the stone table—in which, no doubt, you have recognized one of those dolmens that are encountered in such large numbers in Brittany, and which are found in various other parts of France, Europe and Asia.

He examined the capricious swirls of the smoke attentively, and, according to whether they developed peacefully or the wind interrupted their vaporous evolutions, the old man, who fulfilled the functions of chief and pontiff, went away serene or preoccupied.

---

[87] The engineer Jean-Baptiste-Apollinaire Lebas (1797-1873)

Toward the end of autumn, when the nights were already drawing in and getting cold, the old man became increasingly somber after having studied the spirals of the sacred smoke. One evening, the hunters came back earlier than usual. Scarcely had they got out of the bark canoes that had brought them to the island from the other shore than they ran to the old man and told him with great agitation that another tribe had just established itself on the heights where Meudon now stands. They had occupied three caves and were beginning to hunt game in the forest, led by their chief, a grim-faced warrior who was still young and endowed with a prodigious strength—for he disdained, in order to do battle with a wild bull, to make use of a lasso. He faced up to it, griped it by the horns and dropped it at his feet. Even more astonishing, he as followed by six enormous dogs, which, tamed and submissive, obeyed his slightest gesture, indicating game trails and attacking wild beasts with him, including wolves, wild boar and aurochs.

The old man listened to this story silently, while a profound sadness spread over his face.

"May the day star protect us," he said, finally, "for peace and happiness are perhaps going to desert us. Let us redouble our vigilance. Let no fires be lit between now and tomorrow, in order that their smoke will not reveal our dwellings at a distance. Tomorrow we will deliberate as to what we ought to do. In the meantime, let the warriors charged with watching over the security of the island keep their ears pricked and let everyone have his weapons ready."

While the old man was speaking thus, a man accompanied by two huge dogs was sliding and crawling through the long grass that grew along the river bank. That dense mass extended alongside the Île de la Cité, and by means of the moonlight the stranger was able to count the number of huts raised on piles. Like their master, the dogs lay down on their bellies in the reeds, attaching their gazes to him, and, obedient to a signal that he gave, followed him without making a sound when he drew away carefully, still hugging the ground.

Once in the forest, the warrior got up again, and headed back to Meudon with large strides. Completely naked, his body tattooed with bizarre signs, he walked rapidly, guided by his dogs which indicated the easiest passages to follow through the trees and the brambles.

When he arrived at Meudon he uttered a shrill cry that assembled all the warriors of the tribe around him.

"You are in search of a favorable place to settle," he said. "Hidden in the reeds this evening, I was able to study the situation and the means of defense of the people living on an island on the river's edge over there. You will find what you need there. You lack provisions, they have plenty! The enemy is more numerous than we are, but they do not suspect our arrival and have no fear of our attack. Let's take advantage of their sense of security. Tonight, as you see, the moon favors us; she is hiding behind clouds while the rain falls. Let's go!"

Immediately, the warriors took up their weapons and attached flint daggers solidly encased in deer-antlers to their waists. Each one loaded a bark canoe on to his shoulders, and they set out.

A number of women followed them, carrying baskets attached to their backs, some containing embers divided into little pieces, and hollow balls of friable earth, similar to those still found in such large numbers in Switzerland, in the debris of lacustrian dwellings on Lake Zurich. The dogs went on ahead.

The small army, which advanced silently, did not take long to arrive opposite the island. There it halted, while the women, after taking off their garments, filled the balls of earth they were carrying with lighted embers that they stimulated with their breath.

When these preliminaries were terminated, each of the warriors took one of the women in a bark canoe that had been put into the water, and came as close as possible to the island. Immediately, the women launched their fiery weapons of war on to the roofs of the huts, covered with dry reeds.

The reeds caught fire; the blaze took hold and the warriors charged on to the island, uttering cries, while the women dived into the water and swam back to the other bank.

The attackers found themselves facing all the warriors of the tribe, with the chief at their head, who greeted them with spear-thrusts and blows from stone hammers and clubs, while the women, suddenly bringing flaming torches of resinous wood to the battlefield, allowed the small number of enemies to be seen and rendered the thrusts of their spouse and fathers more reliable.

Thus, in spite of their fervor and their bravery, the men who were expecting an easy victory did not take long to succumb. One of them fell dying at every moment. Even their chief, struck on the head by a blow from a club, was removed from the battle. Those who remained beat a retreat. They ran into a living wall that blocked their passage, and after a desperate struggle, they were massacred, along with the dogs, which showed themselves no less valiant or any less ardent in a battle that lasted more than an hour.

Some of the women, certain of their menfolk's victory, had left their torches behind in order to go put out the fires stated by the fireballs thrown at the huts. Friable as the crude bombs were, only a few had caused serious damage when they broke on impact with the roofs, spreading the incandescent embers they contained; in addition, many of them had fallen from the rooftops into the water, which had put them out and swallowed them up in the mud.

When not one of their enemies remained standing, the island's warriors, several of whom had been killed and the majority of whom had been wounded, finished off the dying and threw their cadavers into the Seine. They only spared one of the wounded, the young chief; the women, on the old man's orders, dressed his wounds as they did for their own wounded, except that they tied up his feet with strong leather thongs to make sure that he did not escape.

While their companions carried out these tasks, others, torches in hand, went over the battlefield silently picking up the dead, whose corpses they arranged around the stone table. There were daughters, wives and mothers there who recognized the bodies of fathers, husbands or sons, but not one betrayed her grief other than by silent tears that ran down her pale cheeks.

In the meantime, a small number of warriors had gone silently over to the other bank in order to surround and trap the enemy women hiding in the forest. After a brief and desperate resistance, using no weapons other than lassos, which they threw at them, the women were all taken prisoner, tied up and taken to the island. The warriors then went to Meudon, where they similarly rounded up the children and old men.

When they got back, it was broad daylight. The women of the tribe were weeping over the cadavers, and the prisoner chief, unconscious until then, began to come round thanks to the care lavished on him.

Then the old man came out of his hut and prostrated himself before the Sun.

"You have made us victors," he said. "Receive your part of the booty and the victory."

He gave the orders to stand the enemy chief up, who was supported so that he would not fall over, for his wounds and the consequent loss of blood had robbed him of all his strength.

"Look!" the old man said to him. "You have attacked us treacherously and have been defeated. Look! The women of your tribe are our women's slaves. Look! The old men and male infants of your tribe, like yourself, will be sacrificed to the Sun."

The horrible sacrifice began immediately. Each of the victims was laid on the stone altar, and the old man plunged a trenchant flint knife into their throats. The enemy chief was the last to submit to that fate, and the gutter excavated in the table of the dolmen spread out so much blood that it covered the ground with a large and horrible red sheet and ran all the way to the Seine, the waters of which it tainted for some distance.

Slavery, among the barbarian hordes that first took possession of Paris, was exercised with much less harshness than one might be tempted to believe. It was somewhat similar to the manner in which it is still practiced today in the Orient, in which it consists of a sort of inferior degree of the family. It bore no resemblance to the miserable fate of black people, always under the overseer's whip and treated like beasts of burden. In order for it to become that, and for there to be abuse of force, it requires an ignorant race to be dealing with a civilized one; outside of that circumstance one scarcely ever finds oppressed individuals or, more particularly, oppressors.

The slight difference in condition, mores and habits that separated the first inhabitants of Paris and their prisoners was too scantly visible not to be gradually effaced. Initially treated rigorously during the early days in which the pride of triumph and the excitement of victory lasted, the women and female children of the vanquished soon saw their lot ease and gradually began to occupy a rank almost equal to that of their mistresses. They lived under the same roof, shared in the same work and led the same life.

More industrious that their new companions, they made themselves useful by means of a host of petty services and ameliorations that they brought to communal existence; they understood a great many things more thoroughly and taught others the way to practice them. It was not long before the tribe owed them more supple fabrics more easily prepared, the secrets of dyeing furs in various colors with the aid of vegetable or mineral substances, better-fashioned and more convenient baskets, less fragile pottery, elegant forms of dress and, most especially, the art of arranging the hair of women into silky sheets, interlaced in such a fashion as to give a new charm to beautiful faces, fine features, pale complexions and fresh cheeks of the island women.

Two months had not gone by before it was impossible to distinguish the mistresses from the slaves.

The latter, for their part, submitted with resignation to their new condition; insensibly, they felt their resentment of the massacre on the dolmen lessening. It was, after all, an in-exorable consequence of the customs of war in ancient times, and they had seen it committed many times by their own men-folk. If the inhabitants of the Cité had been defeated, they would have been similarly put to death by the victors. So the eyes of the slaves, which moistened with tears to begin with, and their brows, which furrowed with hatred at the mere glimpse of the bloody altar, ended up getting used to the terri-ble sight; the impression they experienced faded and weak-ened, and they ended up passing the dolmen without a sigh, almost without any memory.

In any case, among primitive races the manner of feeling bears no resemblance to our excited and nervous sensitivity—which, however, is no less subject to the effects of time and forgetfulness. Confronted by austere labor and manual tasks at every instant, thought is not very active, especially in a robust race struggling incessantly against necessity.

Meanwhile, the greatest calm reigned in the vicinity of the island. Nothing troubled the hunters in their long excur-sions through the forests, and they came back so laden down with game that one day, the old chief of the tribe wanted to accompany them himself, in order to give his still-valiant hands the pleasure of unleashing his arrow upon some fero-cious beast one last time, or piercing a wild boar with his flint-tipped spear.

So he went forth, followed by ten young men whose skill and strength were proof against anything. His face reddened with joy and his heart beat with emotion when he suddenly found himself face to face with a lion, when his arrow struck it full in the chest and when the monster collapsed on the sand in the throes of death. It was not long before a wild boar and an aurochs were subjected to the same fate. After that last victo-ry, and as the sun had already traveled more than half of its course, the young warriors, on the order given to them by the happy hunter, loaded the three dead monsters on to the shafts of their spears, enlaced so as to make stretchers. To shorten their return journey, they headed toward the island through a part of the forest that they had not explored thus far, but which seemed bound to take them more directly to the bank of the Seine.

Suddenly, two enormous dogs barred their way and were getting ready to charge them when a voice ordered them to stop; they obeyed, quivering with rage, and without recoiling before the weapons that the hunters had hastily brought to bear.

At the same time, a young woman appeared, standing on a rock, holding a child in her arms.

"Sacred Chief," she said, addressing the old man, "swear to me in the name of the Sun that you will spare this child and not make him a slave, and I will bring to your tribe secrets of happiness and power that it does not have. I can teach you to tame wild oxen, the females of which give an abundance of delicious milk; I can teach you to make a dog into a friend, a defender and a vigilant guardian of your herds; I can inform you as to herb that alleviate the pain of wounds and balms that cure them. The daughter of a tribal chief, a prisoner of those you vanquished, I have been roaming this forest since their defeat, fighting wild animals for my son, thanks to these two faithful animals. If you heed my prayer, I will become your servant; if you refuse, I shall hurl myself and my son from the top of this rock, for I would rather he were dead than a slave."

The old man replied: "You are not of the race of our enemies, so we cannot treat you as an enemy. Come! Henceforth , you are my daughter, and your child is my son."

At these words, the young woman came down from the rock and prostrated herself before the chief, who brought her to her feet and took the child in his arms,

The little troop then headed silently for the island; the dogs followed, walking at their mistress' heels and keeping their intelligent eyes fixed upon her.

When they came close to the bank the old man invited the young woman and her child to take their places beside him in the bark canoe that took them to the Cité. On his order, the young men accompanying him sounded a kind of primitive fanfare with the horns they were carrying at their waists. The entire tribe—men, women and children—immediately assembled.

"This is my daughter and this is my son," said the old man, with a solemn simplicity. Take them to my dwelling."

People hastened to obey the order, but before accompanying her new companion, the young woman extracted a shrill sound from a bone whistle attached to her waist. At that appeal, the two dogs launched themselves into the water from the bank where they had remained, and ran to heir mistress, to the great astonishment and near alarm of the spectators.

She showed the chief to the dogs and placed the old man's hands on their heads.

"This is your master," she told them.

The two hounds, which were reminiscent of the strong race of Pyrenean dogs, licked the old man's hands and raised their eyes to look at his as if to ask for his orders. He gave them a sign to follow their mistress; they accompanied her to the threshold of the cabin to which she was conducted, and lay down there like vigilant and faithful guardians.

Twenty years later, the increase in the population of the Cité had obliged the tribe to take possession of the two neighboring islands, and even to establish colonies on the banks of the Seine.

Every day, the men separated into two bands, pastors and hunters; the former led to pasture the immense herds of cattle that furnished milk in abundance every morning and evening to the women, who had been taught the art of milking by the chief's adoptive daughter. Other flocks, comprised of sheep, added to the tribe's wellbeing; an abundance reigned therein, the possibility of which they had never suspected when they first settled on the banks of the Seine.

Thanks to the woman to whom they owed so much wealth, they now knew how to cultivate several plants, which furnished them with aliments or contributed to curing diseases. With hops and elderberries they concocted a beverage that was both bitter and tonic, which, after fermentation, acquired the property of rendering strength to hunters wearied by long excursions. Hazel-trees grew everywhere; cabbages acquired a more succulent flesh in carefully-dug ground; bedstraw served to transform milk into solid nutriment; even wheat was beginning to cover fields labored with a flint ploughshare and a plough formed of naturally-curved tree-trunks. Finally, everyone had a dog—which is to say, a friend and devoted servant.

Thus, the tribe became so powerful that no enemy any longer dared think of attacking it, and when the old chief died and had been buried under the dolmen, the child of his adopted daughter was elected to replace him.

She was regarded as a kind of divinity, for she revealed and taught the virtues of plants on a daily basis. The marsh mallow served her to calm the coughs that the dampness of the neighborhood and the north winds caused the majority of children to suffer, the dried roots of the arum to procure invalids a light aliment, and St. John's wort to make a balm to cure bruises and scar wounds.

She also informed her companions of the way to give meats a perfumed savor by associating the odorous stems of thyme and hyssop with their cooking.

Her son, docile to her advice, showed himself to be as intelligent as he was courageous; he fortified the islands and made them safe from any invasion; he equipped a flotilla of boats that permitted excursions to be undertaken to any part of the country through which the river flowed; he even attempted to tame wild horses, and succeeded in taking them prisoner with the aid of a lasso and then dominating them by audacity and energy, as is done today on the American pampas.

Such is the probable story of the first inhabitants of Paris, fantasy playing much less part in the story you have just read than you might think.

For want of any other merit, I have consciously reproduced the physiognomy of the Stone Age in France, in accordance with the archeological works and publications of Édouard Lartet, Henry Christy, Constant Troyon, Ferdinand

Keller, Johann Uhlmann, Otto Jahn, Colonel Friedrich Schwab, François Alphonse Forel, Maximilien Rey, Édouard Desor and Adolphe Pictet. I have seen and studied the majority of flint and bone weapons and implements of the Stone Age, in the collections of Messieurs Lartet and Christy, and in my own collection.

THE YEAR 2865

I left Dr. Evrard and returned to the Chaussée-d'Antin as midnight was chiming. I was exhausted by fatigue, so I did not take long to go to sleep as I mentally reviewed all that my old friend had told me, revisiting in dreams the epochs that he had evoked.

The next morning, my head a trifle heavy, I tried to get down to work.

Sometimes, when one is sitting at one's desk and one takes up the pen, Phoebus is deaf and Pegasus mulish, as Boileau puts it. In other, less poetic and less classical terms, some days, in spite of the perseverance one puts into it, one cannot find the opening words of the idea one wants to express. Those first words resemble the end of a confused and tangled thread that one wants to unravel. Once the end of the thread is discovered and seized, everything will wrong and the Gordian knots of the tangle will come undone easily—but the difficulty is getting a grip on it.

The physiologists, who are not always as fortunate in their explanations, suggest that the reason for that contest between the will and the idea is a lack of equilibrium between the imagination and the body. The former desires but the latter, which is not enslaved to it, jibs; "the husband orders, the wife resists," as Balzac says. It is necessary, therefore, to bring them into accord, to the same rhythm.

The best thing to do, in that circumstance, is to leave the desk, the pen, the ink and the paper and to devoted oneself to a completely different occupation. Some writers, including Casimir Delavigne, take their hat and go for a walk; others—Balzac, for example—wear out the soles of their slippers of the parquet of their study. Ampère played with his wig; Ludovic Halévy, that golden heart, taking generosity to the extent of weakness, sought to pick a German quarrel with those around him, especially his two sisters, in which he was not long delayed in being the first to laugh, as soon as he sensed enough movement in his nerves to write his beautiful pages of music. Walter Scott took up a hammer and nails and set the hands that had written *The Antiquary* and *Ivanhoe* to rearranging the trophies that ornamented his study.

As for me, if I dare to place my name humbly in the wake of so many illustrious ones, I have recourse to the example of the Scottish romancer; when I cannot find the diabolical end of the thread that I mentioned just now. I take off my jacket, I rearrange my books, I modify the disposition of my collections, and I tidy or untidy the cupboards that contain them.

Now, that is precisely what happened to me on the day after my visit to Dr. Evrard. With my head still full of all that he had told and read to me, I could not contrive to write those crucial first lines that I have just been talking about.

After having scribbled and torn up a dozen pages, therefore, I brought a ladder, climbed up on to the top step and started exploring and charging the position of some bottles, which, forgotten and covered in dust, had been placidly sat on top of a large Flemish dresser for years.

While I looked at those glass vessels and picked them up, trying to decipher the dusty and partly-effaced characters of their labels, the ineptly-closed door of my study came open, my little dog Flock starting barked with all his might and Mademoiselle Mine, my charming quadrumane from Madagascar, leapt on to my shoulder with a single bound. That sudden noise and the unexpected shock caused me to drop the bottle that I was holding. It fell to the floor, smashed, and a strong smell of sulfuric ether expanded to fill the room.

Immediately, a kind of vertigo took possession of me, and I only just had time to climb down the ladder and open the two windows precipitately, for the sake of the causes of the accident; my little dog, Master Flock, was already panting, and Mademoiselle Mine's large golden eyes were beginning to take to on an expression of languor, while her little hands, ordinarily so agile and nervous, were falling inert upon the thick fur of her flanks.

As you know, ether, which has such powerful anesthetic properties, evaporates quickly. Soon, however—at least, I thought so—thanks to a vigorous current of air established between the doors and the windows, no other traces of the accident remained but a large damp stain on the carpet. I picked up the glass debris scattered here and there, and re-closed the windows, while Mademoiselle Mine engaged Flock in an animated game of tag. As the emotions provoked by the accident, by strongly exciting my nerves, had doubtless re-stored my mental and physical equilibrium sufficiently for me to work, I sat down at my desk again, and, supporting my forehead in my left hand, I took up my pen in the right and dipped it in the ink.

I sensed that inspiration had finally deigned to arrive, and I was about to write the first words of my piece when ma-jestic songs became audible outside and captured the attention of my ears. Voices of a character previously unknown to me, of a immense power and a sweetness that seemed prodigious, combined with a melodious accompaniment of brass instru-ments similar, so far as I could judge, to those that my friend Sax has invented.[88]

The voices were singing distinctly, without a syllable be-ing lost, the words of the Gospel that the church has intro-duced into the All Saints' Day mass: *Venite ad me omnes qui laboratis et orenati estis; et ego reficiam vos. Amen.* Come to me, you who labor and are burdened, and I will comfort you. Praise God.

Then, suddenly, that song of hope was succeeded by a funereal song: *Absolve, Domine, animas omnium fidelim defunctorum ab omni vinculo delictorum.* Lord, deign to ab-

---

[88] Adolphe Sax (1814-1894), the inventor of the family of saxhorns and numerous other instruments, including the saxophone, was resi-dent in Paris from 1841 onwards and was teaching at the Conserva-toire when this story was written.

solve the souls of the dead and deliver them from the bonds of their sins.

"What does all this mean?" I wondered.

Suddenly, my door opened and a person I did not know came in, who sat down unceremoniously in an armchair near the fireplace.

Now, without my being able to explain it, that fireplace was no longer in the location it had previously occupied against the wall; it was in the middle of the room and had become a sort of item of furniture of extreme elegance, which was burning a gas of extreme purity.

I said that I did not know the person who had come into my study abruptly and was nonchalantly warming her feet, and yet it seemed to me that a close amity linked me to the young man in question, for I instinctively addressed him as "tu."

"What do you think, Azrael?" I asked him. "Isn't that beautiful music?"

"Yes," he replied, "you're right. The steam organs on the picturesque thousand-meter tower at the highest point of Montmartre are doing their work very well today. The words of the songs are emerging clearly against the accompaniment, which makes the stand out. But bah! That's only the infancy of the art."

"The infancy of the art, you say? Organs that sing, pronouncing words that can be heard distinctly all over Paris!"

Azrael looked at me, smiling. "One might think you were a thousand years behind the times and contemporary with Adolphe Sax, the first man to conceive and formulate the idea of those gigantic instruments. Thank God that his great-grandson continued and perfected his work so singularly. But what were you doing yesterday? I didn't see you all day. Myself, I went to the Hôtel-Dieu on the heights of Romainville to see an operation on a poor boy in whom I have an interest, and who broke his leg during a hunting-party in Berlin in the morning."

"He was in Berlin yesterday morning and had an operation in Paris yesterday evening?"

"The atmospheric highway was working poorly again—we took six hours instead of five to cover that short distance. It seems that the condensed carbon dioxide that powers the machine had suffered some evaporation. It's unpardonable! We manipulate that material easily today, so redoubtable for our ancestors that it killed a considerable number of the first people who attempted to apply it to the needs of locomotion and industry."

"And how is your invalid?"

"Everything went well. With the aid of the electricity that burns and cuts at the same time, the wound was opened, the splinters of broken bone removed and the periosteum—the delicate membrane enveloping the bones, which reproduces and regenerates them—conserved. It will take the patient a month at the most, to regain complete possession of his broken leg. Anyway, being ill is an inviting prospect, in order to stay in the new Hôtel-Dieu, two minutes from the center of Paris by aerial highway, with eight hundred private rooms. Every patient there is isolated, unable to hear the groans of his companions in distress, with no fear of the deadly miasmas of epidemic diseases, cared for by a Sister of Charity and visited eight or ten times a day by eminent surgeons."

"The operation must have been long and painful."

"What are you saying? Don't you know that chloroform, which can be obtained with irreproachable purity, has caused suffering to disappear from the surface of the globe? They boy I'm talking about had scarcely received his wound when I chloroformized him. I maintained him under anesthesia throughout the journey and only allowed him to wake up after the operation had been successfully concluded. At the slightest access of fever the same means will be used, and he will, so to speak, have been injured, operated on and healed without being conscious of it. But aren't you going out? There's an odor of ether in here that's suffocating."

"You're right," I said. "Let's go out."

I summoned my valet and asked him to bring my hat. He brought me a light, elegant and comfortable article that had nothing in common with the frightful stove-pipes with which fashion obliges us to cover our heads. I went to a mirror to see how the coiffure in question suited me; it harmonized perfectly with the clothes I was wearing, which bore no more resemblance to my customary frock-cost and trousers than my headgear did to my silk hat.

"Just a moment!" the young man said. "Before going out I have to send word to Berlin to reassure the injured boy's friends."

Azrael sat down at my desk and wrote a few lines on a small apparatus placed beside my writing-pad. Two seconds later, a note appeared on the apparatus in handwriting that was a trifle hasty but whose characters were clear and distinct.

The note said:

Thanks for the good news you've given us. We'll go to dinner with you soon. Be at the Café Carême-Duglére[89] at six precisely. It's the only one where the healthy traditions of the two creators of French cuisine are still maintained.
Berlin, 1 November 2865. 12.01 p.m.

I confess that I was confused.

"Which way shall we go? What if we go to see the Artillery Museum at Vincennes? I'd like to visit those monuments to a barbarity that has disappeared forever from the globe. How can one imagine nowadays that war ever existed, and that the reasoning of might, the massacre of hundreds of thousands of men, decided the destiny of nations? Thank God that the means of destroying armies, fleets and cities became so

---

[89] Marie-Antoine Carême (1783-1833) was a pioneering practitioner of *grande cuisine*, the height of French culinary art in the 19th century. The chef Adolphe Dugléré (1805-1884) was one of his pupils; at the time this story was written he was the manager of Les Frères Provençaux at the Palais-Royal, but became head chef at the Café Anglais not long afterwards.

infallible that it was necessary to renounce them. The electric machine that blew up the entire city of Kronstadt in 2859, and all its fortifications, instantaneously, was the last and ultimate effort of military science. Since then, permanent peace has reigned in Europe It's necessary to admit that our ancestors were great barbarians. Come on, let's go to Vincennes."

"I'll ask Jean to bring round a carriage."

"Why not a fiacre hitched to a horse—if there were still horses? We'll take a locomobile via the atmospheric highway. We'll be disembarking at Saint Louis' old château in ten seconds."

He opened the door and escorted me into a cabinet that had replaced the stair-head. A machine moving smoothly and almost insensibly took us from the fourth floor to the ground floor.

"And to think that a thousand years ago," my companion observed, "people preferred living on the first floor, where they lacked air and a view, to the fourth, where one enjoys those precious advantages. It's true that the architects of that era didn't understand that one could go up to one's residence by other means than that of a staircase. I saw one of those primitive machines the other day, at the Musée de Cluny. Can you imagine that one had to climb a hundred narrow and slippery steps, which also formed a kind of spiral rotating about an axis, capable of giving vertigo to the most solid head.

A harmonious bell, which struck a perfect musical chord, informed us that we had reached the ground. We opened a door and found ourselves in the street. Sidewalks garnished with paving stones of various colors, forming exquisite mosaics, bordered a street planted with trees, wider than the widest boulevards of the present day. The causeway no longer consisted of macadam or cobblestones, but of a kind of parquet, whose cleanliness was worthy of a Dutch housewife, on which the foot, far from slipping, posed securely.

My mysterious friend made a gesture, and an elegant vehicle immediately emerged from a garage and moved toward us with lightning rapidity. I stepped back immediately in order not to be crushed, but it came to an abrupt halt fifty centimeters away from me, without any hesitation or the slightest oscillation. Not daring to give evidence of my surprise, I took my place beside me friend on a comfortable and elastic seat, and a young mechanic with an intelligent face placed himself behind us.

"Where can I take you, Messieurs?" he asked.

"To Vincennes," I replied.

He touched a switch lightly, and we drew away. The vehicle moved so rapidly that I could hardly see the road along which we were traveling. By paying close attention, however, I was able to make out thousands of vehicles similar to ours, speeding in every direction along immense roads bordered by houses reminiscent of palaces.

"Aren't you afraid of some accident?" I said

"What accident? Are accidents possible? Can't you see the mastery the mechanics have of their locomobiles? The pedestrians walk on the sidewalks or cross the road with the aid of all these footbridges, which carry them up and across without them having the trouble of walking, by means of a kind of endless ribbon, always moving. One might think that you were seeing all this for the first time."

"We've arrived, Messieurs," the mechanic put in.

My friend gave him a gold coin and we got down.

I confess that the price of the journey seemed high, but I dared not make that reflection for fear of exposing myself once again to the mockery of the man who had already been so amused by my astonishment. Internally, however, I thought: *My God! Has the value of gold been so depreciated that one has to pay twenty francs for a cab-ride lasting a few seconds?*

"Let's go in," said my friend, linking arms with me.

The Château de Vincennes stood in the middle of an immense park in which exotic plants of every species were growing in the open air, among which, in the midst of a vigorously-growing field of sugar-cane I noticed in passing flowers of the most distant and various provenance, and the hottest climates.

On the bank of a stream Azrael picked a pitcher-plant of the species *Nepenthes rafflesiana*, discovered in 1828 in Singapore by Stamford Raffles, the urn of which contained exquisitely flavored fresh water. I imitated Azrael, detaching two similar flowers from their stems in order to study at leisure the urn, the male flower and the fruit.

Among these fields, so new to me, animals from all over the world were wandering, in a more-or-less wild natural state, for Vincennes had replaced the Natural History Museum, the Botanical Gardens and the Artillery Museum at the same time. Tigers, lions, panthers and jaguars were no longer pacing sadly back and forth in cages eight or ten feet square, and no longer eating spoiled meat declared unfit for human consumption but judged by scientists to be good enough for animals used to nourishing themselves at liberty on live prey. They were in vast enclosures surrounded by railings, it's true, but which were so well adapted to their habits that they ended up forgetting their captivity. One therefore encountered them in all their beauty and all their instincts.

As for the fortress itself, which loomed up behind the arbors of the menagerie and the fields of sugar cane, an immense roof of glass covered its completely, like a precious jewel of the architecture of the 13th century, in order to shelter it from the insults of the weather, and also to adapt it to its present purpose.

In fact, Vincennes was no longer either a royal residence, a fortified military station or a state prison, but an immense museum in which all the instruments of the past centuries were collected—instruments that had become useless by virtue of their terrible perfection and fatal infallibility.

When we went into the principal hall, showed around by an old man who seemed to me to be almost a centenarian, I expected to see cannons, rifles and sabers, but I only perceive gigantic electric machines; at first glance they resembled Ruhmkorff coils, and were based on the principle of that apparatus, but modified by the improvements that ten centuries of progress had naturally given them.

"Monsieur," said the director of the Museum, showing me a coil the size of a house, "this is the last word in the art of war. I operated this machine myself in my youth, for I was one of the last soldiers to fight in Europe. This machine produced, in a single second, twenty-four thousand electrical sparks four hundred meters long and two hundred broad. A single one of those sparks was sufficient to destroy an army and blast a town, as it proved only too well by razing Kronstadt in twenty-two seconds. That siege, which would have seemed utterly fantastic in 1865, ten centuries earlier, was, however, accused of dragging on too long. Indeed, as you know, in America, previously, where the civil war over the separation of the southern states was still going on, two armies had destroyed one another mutually in six seconds. Of the eight hundred thousand combatants present, only eight hundred escaped the electric thunderbolts, thanks to a lightning-conductor invented by the great-grandson of a French scientist of the 19th century, Auguste Bertsch, who left behind a justly-celebrated name."[90]

"Azrael and I," I said to the old man, would like to visit the part of your collection devoted to firearms, the usage of which preceded that of electric weapons."

"Since those childish machines interest you," the old man replied, obligingly, "would you care to accompany me to that part of my museum."

---

[90] In fact, Auguste Bertsch (1813-1870) is almost forgotten today, although he was famous when the story was written, at least in Paris, as a pioneer of photography; he invented a new collodion that made more rapid image-fixation possible, and followed it up with a mechanical shutter. Both technologies were improved so considerably after his death that his endeavors were eclipsed. Working in collaboration with Camille d'Arnaud, he made considerable strides in astronomical photography and also in photomicrography, the field in which his achievements most impressed Berthoud. He might well have achieved more had he not been a casualty of the Franco-Prussian War.

As he said that, he opened a door and introduced us into an immense gallery in which picturesque trophies were disposed, not only of ten-shot rifles similar to our revolvers, but also of cannons of every form and dimensions. I noticed, among others, a bomb a thousand meters in diameter, filled with gun-cotton and other fulminating materials, long since substituted for powder. One seemingly-frail machine could launch that bomb four thousand meters, which burst at an altitude of a kilometer and whose debris was sufficient to ravage an entire city the size of Paris.

"Haven't you had enough of these barbaric and brutal engines of destruction?" said Azrael. "Let's leave all these implements of the infancy of the art of killing people behind."

We took our leave of the director of the Vincennes museum and headed toward an immense hall illuminated by the full force of the midday sun. We found a professor there, still young, who was entertaining is pupils with the marvels of the microscopic world that remained so long invisible to the human eye.

"Would you believe, Messieurs," he said, "that until the middle of the 20th century, science did not possess either the means of weighing, or even of seeing, the emanations that bodies produce? Yes, the odor of a rose struck the sense of smell, the bitter perfumes of camphor gave people headaches, and mortal miasmas, carried from distant regions by the wind, caused epidemics, but chemistry, to which they had exclusive recourse for analysis, showed nothing and indicated nothing. The arrival of the microscope finally changed all that, bringing an end to so much ignorance and setting people on the path to the truth and demonstration.

"Here, for instance, is a morsel of musk, over which I place this objective, which magnifies the surface of objects forty million times. See what a series of jets of vegetable matter are escaping the camphor! See how they're dispersing! See how the spikes with which they're bristling cling on to the nervous papillae in the nose, titillating them energetically and penetrating all the way to the brain, where they determine slight congestions. Although also vegetal, the molecules of these violet flowers are of a completely different nature: supple, covered with a kind of oil, they insinuate themselves and slide into the olfactory apparatus to produce an agreeable sensation there. Well, our ancestors hadn't the slightest notion of all that!"

Then he showed, magnified twenty-five million times, the infusoria of the air and water, with their eggs, their three or four metamorphoses, and their strange ways of life. After that, he caused the mysterious products of the decomposition of organic bodies to appear, which once brought cholera from India to Europe. He similarly displayed those that produce epidemics of typhoid fever, puerperal fever and erysipelas in hospitals, and s many other maladies that could not be cured, prevented or stopped from spreading in the 19th century. Today, carbolic acid, spread by exhalations in the air whenever those miasmas appear, destroys them in a matter of minutes."

"All this is undoubtedly not lacking in a certain interest," Azrael murmured in my ear, "but as no one except a schoolboy of sixteen is unaware of these elementary notions, which I studied in my youth and doubtless you did too, let's not waste our time and let's continue our walk."

A false shame caused me to follow Azrael—much to my regret, I confess, for the professor had just announced to his pupils a series of experiments on the Entomozoaria, the strange worms that once infected meat destined for human nourishment, resistant to cooking in boiling water and poisoning with their living germs those who had recourse without precaution to such deadly aliments.[91]

---

[91] The principal members of the obsolete zoological class of *Entomozoaria* were leeches, but it also included a number of intestinal worms to which Berthoud makes reference here, which could indeed survive moderate cooking and were indeed dangerous to human health. His reference to *germes vivant* [living germs] is slightly misleading to the modern eye because he is unaware of the existence of bacteria; the infectious agents in question would be eggs or spores.

We went outside, therefore, and before long we found ourselves on one of the immense sidewalks that bordered the vast boulevards forming the most minor of Parisian streets. In the midst of an innumerable crowd, every step offered women of remarkable beauty to my gaze, who did justice to costumes that were simultaneously elegant and charming in their simplicity. Needless to say, the crinoline and the iron-hooped skirt were not featured at all in their styles.

"Oh, look!" I exclaimed, pointing one of them out to Azrael. "What an adorable creature! What a shame not to be able to keep an image of that beautiful individual as souvenir!"

"In truth," Azrael replied, "there are moments when you remind me of one of those émigrés of ten centuries ago, of whom it was said that they had learned nothing and forgotten nothing. Are you from the year 1865 rather than 2865? Don't you have your photographic apparatus in your pocket, as I do?"

So saying, he took a little box of a particular form out of his waistcoat pocket, directed it toward the lovely woman who had excited my admiration and moved one of its levers. Then he moved a second lever and deposited a portrait in a hand, of such finesse and exactitude that only the most charming miniatures of Isabey and Madame Oberlin[92] can give any idea of it. Resemblance, delicacy of tone, accuracy of hue, living expression—nothing was lacking.

I was careful not to let my surprise show, and silently placed the improvised painting in my wallet.

"I believe," Azrael said, sniggering, "that we have resolved the problem that Niépce de Saint-Victor was pursuing

---

[92] Jean-Baptiste Isabey (1767-1855) was a noted painter; "Madame Oberlin" was Salomé-Madeleine the wife of the Alsatian pastor Jean-Frédéric Oberlin (1740-1826), an enthusiastic advocate of social and tehnological progress whose innovations includes silhouette miniatures, whose endeavors in that line included a famous depiction of his wife and children.

404

in 1864.[93] But bah! It's nothing, after all, but an insignificant plaything. Everyone has one and it only costs forty francs—the price of a good cigar."

As he finished that sentence he presented his case to me and offered me one of the forty-franc cigars in question, which, I must admit, appeared to me to be very fine. I needed to remind myself, nevertheless, that gold must have lost its value, in order that I should not find puffs of tobacco that cost five francs apiece a trifle dear.

While I abandoned myself to these reflections, I noticed that immense umbrellas were being extended over the streets everywhere, moved by a mechanism that was both ingenious and simple, and that they had been substituted for the light and brightly-colored parasols that had once moderated the sun's excessively warm rays.

"That's right!" said Azrael. "I'd forgotten that, three days ago, the meteorologists charged by the State for monitoring the direction of the winds had forecast rain for today at four twenty-two and thirty seconds. I get angry when I think that our ancestors, in their ignorance, left their fields of wheat, their vineyards and even their gardens exposed without defense to the caprices of wind, frost, hail and the fury of the winds. Should they not have had meteorology at their disposal, as we do, to anticipate ill-timed downpours, and electricity, with the aid of which all those sinister phenomena have been mastered and vanquished forever?"

---

[93] Abel Niepce de Saint-Victor (1805-1870), the inventor of the photomechanical printing process known as heliogravure, was one of several people in Paris attempting to solve the problem of color photography when this story was written, and evidently seemed to Berthoud to be the one most likely to succeed. He had, in fact, already made his most significant discovery, having observed in 1857 that uranium salts produced a radiation capable of fogging photographic plates, but he could not persuade anyone—including Berthoud—to take the discovery seriously, and it had to be made all over again in 1895 by Wilhelm Röntgen

We continued our stroll through Paris, and I cannot describe all the dazzling sights that I experienced at every step. Everything seemed new to me, and I was watching dusk fall with disappointment when suddenly, with lightning rapidity, more quickly than I can say, the entirety of Paris was illuminated.

"What! Why are you trembling?" Azrael asked me. "Aren't you accustomed to seeing the fifty million gas jets that illuminate Paris light up simultaneously every evening, with the aid of a powerful electrical apparatus? Nothing is simpler, and it goes back to the remotest antiquity—1862 or 1865. A thin platinum wire that terminates at each gas jet conducts an electric spark produced by a Ruhmkorff coil to it. Our ancestors four generations ago went to admire the phenomenon, as they called it, at the Sorbonne, and even in shops selling silk clothing on the boulevards. That, at least, is what it says in the *Petites Chroniques de la Science*, by a certain S. Henry Berthoud, written a thousand years ago, which I found the other day, by the remotest of chances, in a corner of the Imperial Library.[94]

Chatting in that fashion, we were heading, as best I could judge toward the Champ de Mars. It did not take me long to hear the sound of waves, and I saw emerging before me mot merely a harbor full of ships, but an immense sea on the horizon. Azrael, without noticing my amazement, signaled to a small launch powered by condensed carbon dioxide to come and pick us up and take us aboard a ship that was getting ready to leave for China.

"My friend," he said to the captain when we had boarded the vessel, a thousand meters long and proportionately wide, "I have some small business matters to attend to in Paris that prevent me from accompanying you to Peking. I therefore

---

[94] The suggestion that the Second Empire might last a thousand years is presumably not intended any more seriously than the suggestion that the American Civil War might go one for almost as long, although Berthoud had no way of anticipating its collapse within a mere five.

request that you be kind enough o bring me back—alive, of course—eight or ten unicornfish, and a hundred fresh swifts'-nests. I've only been able to get ones of mediocre quality in Paris for some time. I intend those I'm requesting of your courtesy for a dinner-party I'm giving for a few friends in a fortnight, and I hope you won't refuse my invitation to join us that evening."

"Gladly," said the captain. "Do you need anything else?"

"I don't want to abuse your kindness—otherwise I'd ask you to administer a severe reprimand to the negligent sculptor Sang-Po, who hasn't finished the nephrite jade vases for which I sent him the designs personally more than two months ago."

"Very good!" said the captain. "Your commissions will be carried out, my dear friend; I'm only waiting for my provision of condensed carbon dioxide to leave. Ah. here it is! *Au revoir*!"

A container was carried aboard, assuredly not as big as one of the trunks of which Parisian ladies make use to transport dresses and hats when they go to spend a week in the country. We went back down into our small boat and the ship departed with the speed of an arrow.

"May God spare her from shipwrecks and tempests!" I exclaimed.

Azrael emitted a burst of laughter that caused my face to turn red. "Idiot!" she said. "What shipwrecks and what tempests can there be today, with the electric currents that control and deflect the winds and regulate submarine currents? Instead of saying and making me hear such silly things, let's go back to the harbor and visit the fish-parks established there—in accordance, admittedly, with the very elementary ideas of Coste, a member of the Institut in the year of grace 1865, but to whom belongs, nevertheless, the honor of having conceived and realized the beginnings of pisciculture in France.[95]

We returned to the shore and Azrael showed me immense parks formed by rocks cleverly arranged in such a fashion as to form vast compartments whose water was continually renewed by the sea without permitting the innumerable fish bred therein to escape.

"Monsieur Carême-Dugléré," said my friend to a young man with excellent manners who came toward us, "would you kindly do us the honors of these piscicultural basins. We're expecting friends from Berlin imminently for dinner, who left that capital at noon, and we'll choose, in the meantime, the fish that you'll be kind enough to serve us."

"I'm at your disposal, Messieurs," replied the young man. This is the lobster-park hollowed out under the rocks—for the animals in question like darkness and isolation. By contrast, the crayfish need air and light, so you'll see them all in the middle of their compartment, even at the surface of the water, so numerous that their antennae resemble millions of blades of sea-grass. Alongside live the turbots, the conger eels, the soles, the dabs, the rays and a few new species imported from Oceania, which the Chinese have taught us to appreciate and to serve their delicate flesh at our tables. I mean the holothuria, those exquisite echinoderms with which trepang is made, and which people hesitated to eat a century ago because they were said to resemble leeches. Unicornfish, the immense American oysters that measure no less than twenty-five centimeters in circumference, clams, another great species of the Venus family, and oysters of every sort, and finally mussels, pullulate in the other parks you can see further away. As for the artificial grottoes overlooking the bank over there and surrounded on all sides by the sea, they've been constructed to acclimate the birds knows as salangana, to which bird's-nest

---

[95] Victor Coste (1807-1873) published *Instructions pratiques sue la pisciculture* in two volumes in 1853 and 1856, and had some success in developing trout-farms and artificial oyster-beds.

soup is owed; we harvest an average of a hundred and fifty thousand nests a year, which is barely enough for Parisian consumption."

"Not to mention that they're not as high-quality, for a true gourmet, as the choice nests that come from Java and Sumatra," Azrael interjected, taking a small watch from his pocket.

Not only did that watch indicate hours, minutes and seconds, but it was also a thermometer, a barometer and a compass, although it was only as big as a twenty-franc coin.

"In half an hour our Prussian friends will be arriving, famished," he went on. "Come on, Monsieur Carême-Dugléré, let's pay attention to the menu for our dinner."

"Would the Messieurs like caviar, clam pâté and Chinese shrimp canapés for hors-d'oeuvre?"

"All that's a trifle vulgar, but exquisite," observed Azrael. "Accepted. Let's pass on to the soup."

"Bird's-nest soup?"

"So be it."

"For the next course, I propose offering you a Yangtze unicornfish and an elephant's trunk, Hong Kong style. Four young elephants fed on wild thyme and aromatic plants have just arrived from India."

"And what will you give us for an entrée?"

"Lophophore palates and a fish of your choice. As a roast, would the Messieurs like a Madagascar monkey with truffles, or a pheasant?"

"The monkey's more delicate, provided that it's a black-fronted Maki; its relative, the mococo, is bitter.[96] Let's see—it only remains to decide on the fish. What are you going to serve us? I'm tired of the vulgar fish reared in your parks; I'd like something less commonplace —a mackerel, for example,

---

[96] "Madagascar monkeys" would now be known as lemurs. The black-fronted lemur's allegedly less appetizing relative is better known as the ring-tailed lemur—that is presumably the species to which Mademoiselle Mine belonged.

brought to the table alive in the Roman manner and cooked before the eyes of the guests, so that they can enjoy the metamorphoses to which its beautiful colors are subjected."

"Nothing simpler. I'll go down in the diving-bell myself; if the Messieurs will deign to accompany me, they can choose the item that suits them."

"Gladly."

Without giving me time to hesitate, Azrael and Carême-Dugléré led me toward a kind of small square building that was at the edge of the sea. We went into it through an elegant door that was carefully closed and sat down in armchairs. Carême-Dugléré pulled a cord and we immediately descended to the sea bed. An electric lamp illuminated in the water in front of a large window of thick glass did not take long, thanks to its dazzling glare, to attract thousands of fish of a hundred species. Azrael pointed at a gigantic mackerel, and an ingeniously-disposed net moved by a simple electric mechanism immediately fell upon the poor fish and captured it.

"Let's go back up now," said Azrael. Before he had finished speaking he opened the door of the diving bell and we found ourselves back on the quay.

"The fish we've just caught will only come out of the sea to be transferred to our table," said Azrael, "and will thus furnish us with delicious meat. But we still have twenty-five minutes to spare before we go take our seats. Would you like to go fishing ourselves in the meantime, in the Seine?"

That's a singular idea! I thought, privately, while Azrael signaled to a locomobile to come and pick us up. I have never been able to understand the stupid pleasure of throwing a hooked line into the water, on which nothing ever comes to bite except a bleak or a gudgeon, and I thought it very bourgeois of my friend Azrael to propose such a vulgar means of killing time.

In two and a half seconds the locomobile took us to the Pont-Neuf—which did not prevent Azrael from chiding the mechanic for his slowness.

I was scarcely listening to that reprimand, which would have seemed excessive at any other time, because the sight presented to me by the Seine made me squint in amazement.

In fact, the Seine was covered with boats, which served as both habitations and boutiques for thousands of fishermen clad in the most picturesque fashion.

"Let's see," said Azrael. "Where's Master Nicolas, who looks after my flock of herons and pelicans? Good! He's seen me—here he comes."

In fact, an elegant yawl, moved by an internal mechanism, came flying over the water, landed at the foot of the statue of Henri IV, took us aboard and ferried us to a boat moored under the Pont des Saints-Pères. We had scarcely stepped down when thirty herons and pelicans ran toward Azrael, surrounded him and lavished their caresses on him, as dogs might have done.

"Master Nicolas," asked me friend, while returning the birds' caresses, "I can't see my pelican Flock."

"Flock isn't very well," Nicolas replied. "Yesterday, the gold ring that I'd attached to his neck so that he wouldn't swallow the fish he caught and kept in the pouch of his beak came loose. Instead of bringing back the fish, the glutton swallowed them all, with as much slyness as greed. I hope his indigestion isn't serious, though; I wouldn't want to see it prolonged, for all the world, for I don't know another pelican in Paris that can fish like him."

"Here, Rosamonde, here my beauty!" shouted Azrael to a magnificent female heron, which hastened to run to him. "You're not a glutton, are you? And I've trained you so well that you have no need of a gold ring to stop you eating fish. Go fetch me a carp."

Immediately, the heron drew nearer to the boat, stretched out her long neck, opened her huge wings, flew off and settled on the water, where thousands of fish were swarming, thanks to the progress obtained by the art of pisciculture. She dived, and came up with an enormous carp in her beak.

"Well done, my beauty! Well done!" Azrael said to her, throwing the carp back into the water. "I'd like a pike now."

Rosamonde raised her intelligent head toward Azrael with an expression of doubt and hesitation.

"Are you afraid?" Azrael asked her. "Haven't I taught you the fashion in which it's necessary to take hold of the pike in order to have no fear of its teeth? Go on—I want a pike. Obey!"

The heron flew off again, glided, and plunged into the water, but it was evident that she had found a redoubtable enemy with which she was fighting. After a couple of minutes Rosamonde reappeared, her feet bloody and her feathers bristling; in her beak she was holding, not a pike but a small alligator, which she threw, dying, on to the deck. Then, suddenly taking off again, she did not take long to disappear into the Seine and bring back a pike.

"You're a good, brave bird! Here, I'll give you this whole pike for your dinner." He turned to me. "But let's think about ours, my friend," the continued. "Let's go back to the Café Carême-Dugléré."

We climbed back into the locomobile, which only took 1.4 seconds to transport us this time.

"You've got your revenge, my dear mechanic. Well done! Here, this is to help you to forget my grumbling just now." And Azrael slid a hundred-franc bill into the mechanic's hand

"Well?" he asked me, afterwards. "What do you think of my flock of herons and pelicans? I'm sorry that you weren't able to see Flock fish. One of our most celebrated sportsmen offered me thirty thousand francs for him, but, in all conscience, he's worth more than that—and besides, I wouldn't want to get rid of him for anything in the world. Can you imagine that the bird is so intelligent that he can bring back a specimen of each of the fish you list for him before sending him forth? The other day I bet that he wouldn't make a mistake in a list of thirty different fish, and I won my bet. There wasn't a single one missing from his beak-pouch.

"What you'd have to admire even more are my falcons and my dogs, for, although hunting is a cruel pleasure, at least we don't procure it any longer by treacherously killing an unfortunate defenseless animal with the brutal weapons that our ancestors called rifles and shoguns. Pooh! The mere thought of the explosions they must have produced gives me a headache. Someday, I'll take you to hunt one of the kangaroos that swarm in the forests around Paris—the beautiful forests that date back a century and keep the capital's air healthy. You'll see then what my dogs are worth."

While he was speaking we arrived at a kiosk on the fronton of which the word *Journal* could be read in fiery letters, and into which a numerous crowd was incessantly pouring. We followed the crowd and found ourselves in front of a machine, an artful combination of electricity and mechanics, which produced thousands of printed sheets instantaneously and relentlessly, which were distributed to everyone in exchange for a five-franc gold coin.

"I'm distinctly behind the times with regard to the news," said Azrael. "I only read the first eight issues of the *Journal* this morning. I still need to peruse these six to get up to date. Can one believe that in the 19th century a single issue of a newspaper appearing in the evening sufficed the worthy individuals of that era? The poor souls! They were not like us, brought up to date on an hourly basis with the serious or frivolous events that succeeded one another by the minute throughout the world. However, the still-too-restricted mode of publication of our present-day newspapers will be subject to a further development that has become indispensable. The *Journal* has announced that it will appear every ten minutes henceforth. Within a week, the nine hundred other newspapers in Paris will be forced to do likewise if they don't want to lose a quarter of their five hundred thousand readers.

When we emerged from the offices of the *Journal* we went into the Café Carême-Dugléré and took our places in the room where we would be dining, and where a table was already set, served with a sumptuousness of gold plate and crystal that is indescribable. A bookcase of carefully-selected and elegantly-bound volumes containing the most celebrated works of all eras permitted the diners to keep the tedium of waiting at bay by means of riveting reading.

My God, I thought, *since I'm here, although I don't know how, in 2865, I'm curious to know which French authors have survived the test of time. Let's see: Molière and Walter Scott, complete works; Le Sage*, Le Diable boiteux;[97] *Bernardin de Saint-Pierre*, Paul et Virginie; *Augustin Thierry*, Conquêtes des Normands. *Good! Let's pass on now to those who were alive in 1865...*

At that moment, the door of my study opened noisily, and instead of my friend Azrael, I saw my friend and physician Dr. Amédée Forget,[98] who hastened to establish a current of air by opening both battens of the window, with no less noise than he had made opening the door.

"Are you mad?" he demanded. "Staying shut up like this in a study full of ether vapor! It's enough to anesthetize you to death! Thank God nothing unfortunate has happened, if not to you, at least to my friends Flock and Mademoiselle Mine. They're both asleep, in what seems to me to be a singular and perhaps troubling slumber."

Master Flock stretched and came to caress my friend, barking; Mademoiselle Mine leapt on to his shoulder in order to embrace him better, and I rubbed my eyes.

"Oh, my dear chap!" I exclaimed. "What a fine thing progress is! In 2865..."

---

[97] A wry acknowledgement to one of the story's models: in Le Sage's novel the hero is taken by the amiable demon Asmodeus on a tour of a great city in order to penetrate the secrets concealed by its roofs and walls. Azrael, of course, is not a demon but an angel: traditionally, the angel of death.

[98] Not the Canadian politician of that name but the Parisian physician who published a numerous scientific papers between the 1830s and 1860s, including *De l'emploi du chloroforme et de l'éther dans la pratique chirurgicale* (1853).

"Come on, you're still asleep! Wake up and come with me for a walk on the boulevard."

Alas, I said to myself, with a sigh, picking up my hat in order to go with my friend, *we won't see the marvels that my other friend Azrael has just shown me!*

SF & FANTASY

Alphonse Allais. *The Adventures of Captain Cap*
Henri Allorge. *The Great Cataclysm*
Guy d'Armen. *Doc Ardan: The City of Gold and Lepers*
G.-J. Arnaud. *The Ice Company*
Charles Asselineau. *The Double Life*
Cyprien Bérard. *The Vampire Lord Ruthwen*
S. Henry Berthoud. *Martyrs of Science*
Aloysius Bertrand. *Gaspard de la Nuit*
Richard Bessière. *The Gardens of the Apocalypse*
Albert Bleunard. *Ever Smaller*
Félix Bodin. *The Novel of the Future*
Louis Boussenard. *Monsieur Synthesis*
Alphonse Brown. *City of Glass; The Conquest of the Air*
Emile Calvet. *In a Thousand Years*
André Caroff. *The Terror of Madame Atomos; Miss Atomos; The Return of Madame Atomos; The Mistake of Madame Atomos; The Monsters of Madame Atomos; The Revenge of Madame Atomos; The Resurrection of Madame Atomos; The Mark of Madame Atomos*
Félicien Champsaur. *The Human Arrow; Ouha, King of the Apes; Pharaoh's Wife*
Didier de Chousy. *Ignis*
Jules Clarétie. *Obsession*
Michel Corday. *The Eternal Flame*
Captain Danrit. *Undersea Odyssey*
C. I. Defontenay. *Star (Psi Cassiopeia)*
Charles Derennes. *The People of the Pole*
Georges Dodds (anthologist). *The Missing Link*
Harry Dickson. *The Heir of Dracula*
Jules Dornay. *Lord Ruthven Begins*
Alfred Driou. *The Adventures of a Parisian Aeronaut*
Sâr Dubnotal *vs. Jack the Ripper*
Alexandre Dumas. *The Return of Lord Ruthven*
Renée Dunan. *Baal*
J.-C. Dunyach. *The Night Orchid; The Thieves of Silence*
Henri Duvernois. *The Man Who Found Himself*
Achille Eyraud. *Voyage to Venus*
Henri Falk. *The Age of Lead*

Paul Féval. *Anne of the Isles; Knightshade; Revenants; Vampire City; The Vampire Countess; The Wandering Jew's Daughter*
Paul Féval, *fils. Felifax, the Tiger-Man*
Charles de Fieux. *Lamékis*
Arnould Galopin. *Doctor Omega*; *Doctor Omega and the Shadowmen* (anthology)
Judith Gautier. *Isoline and the Serpent-Flower*
Léon Gozlan. *The Vampire of the Val-de-Grâce*
G.L. Gick. *Harry Dickson and the Werewolf of Rutherford Grange*
Edmond Haraucourt. *Illusions of Immortality*
Nathalie Henneberg. *The Green Gods*
V. Hugo, P. Foucher & P. Meurice. *The Hunchback of Notre-Dame*
Romain d'Huissier. *Hexagon: Dark Matter*
Michel Jeury. *Chronolysis*
Gustave Kahn. *The Tale of Gold and Silence*
Gérard Klein. *The Mote in Time's Eye*
Fernand Kolney. *Love in 5000 Years*
Paul Lacroix. *Danse Macabre*
Louis-Guillaume de La Follie. *The Unpretentious Philosopher*
Jean de La Hire. *Enter the Nyctalope; The Nyctalope on Mars; The Nyctalope vs. Lucifer; The Nyctalope Steps In; Night of the Nyctalope; Return of the Nyctalope; The Fiery Wheel*
Etienne-Léon de Lamothe-Langon. *The Virgin Vampire*
André Laurie. *Spiridon*
Gabriel de Lautrec. *The Vengeance of the Oval Portrait*
Alain le Drimeur. *The Future City*
Georges Le Faure & Henri de Graffigny. *The Extraordinary Adventures of a Russian Scientist Across the Solar System* (2 vols.)
Gustave Le Rouge. *The Vampires of Mars; The Dominion of the World* (w/Gustave Guitton) (4 vols.)
Jules Lermina. *Mysteryville; Panic in Paris; To-Ho and the Gold Destroyers; The Secret of Zippelius*
André Lichtenberger. *The Centaurs; The Children of the Crab*
Jean-Marc & Randy Lofficier. *Edgar Allan Poe on Mars; The Katrina Protocol; Pacifica; Robonocchio; Return of the Nyctalope;* (anthologists) *Tales of the Shadowmen 1-9*
Xavier Mauméjean. *The League of Heroes*
Joseph Méry. *The Tower of Destiny*
Hippolyte Mettais. *The Year 5865*
Louise Michel. *The Human Microbes; The New World*
Tony Moilin. *Paris in the Year 2000*

José Moselli. *Illa's End*
John-Antoine Nau. *Enemy Force*
Marie Nizet. *Captain Vampire*
C. Nodier, A. Beraud & Toussaint-Merle. *Frankenstein*
Henri de Parville. *An Inhabitant of the Planet Mars*
Gaston de Pawlowski. *Journey to the Land of the 4th Dimension*
Georges Pellerin. *The World in 2000 Years*
Ernest Pérochon. *The Frenetic People*
Pierre Pelot. *The Child Who Walked on the Sky*
J. Polidori, C. Nodier, E. Scribe. *Lord Ruthven the Vampire*
P.-A. Ponson du Terrail. *The Vampire and the Devil's Son; The Immortal Woman*
Edgar Quinet. *Ahasuerus*
Henri de Régnier. *A Surfeit of Mirrors*
Maurice Renard. *The Blue Peril; Doctor Lerne; The Doctored Man; A Man Among the Microbes; The Master of Light*
Jean Richepin. *The Wing; The Crazy Corner*
Albert Robida. *The Adventures of Saturnin Farandoul; The Clock of the Centuries; Chalet in the Sky; The Electric Life*
J.-H. Rosny Aîné. *Helgvor of the Blue River; The Givreuse Enigma; The Mysterious Force; The Navigators of Space; Vamireh; The World of the Variants; The Young Vampire*
Marcel Rouff. *Journey to the Inverted World*
Han Ryner. *The Superhumans*
Brian Stableford. *The New Faust at the Tragicomique;The Empire of the Necromancers (The Shadow of Frankenstein; Frankenstein and the Vampire Countess; Frankenstein in London); Sherlock Holmes & The Vampires of Eternity; The Stones of Camelot; The Wayward Muse.* (anthologist) *The Germans on Venus; News from the Moon; The Supreme Progress; The World Above the World; Nemoville; Investigations of the Future*
Jacques Spitz. *The Eye of Purgatory*
Kurt Steiner. *Ortog*
Eugène Thébault. *Radio-Terror*
C.-F. Tiphaigne de La Roche. *Amilec*
Louis Ulbach. *Prince Bonifacio*
Théo Varlet. *The Golden Rock. The Xenobiotic Invasion; The Castaways of Eros; Timeslip Troopers* (w/André Blandin); *The Martian Epic* (w/Octave Joncquel)
Paul Vibert. *The Mysterious Fluid*
Villiers de l'Isle-Adam. *The Scaffold; The Vampire Soul*

Philippe Ward. *Artahe*
Philippe Ward & Sylvie Miller. *The Song of Montségur*

MYSTERIES & THRILLERS

M. Allain & P. Souvestre. *The Daughter of Fantômas*
A. Anicet-Bourgeois, Lucien Dabril. *Rocambole*
A. Bernède. *Belphegor*; *Judex* (w/Louis Feuillade); *The Return of Judex* (w/Louis Feuillade); *The Shadow of Judex*
A. Bisson & G. Livet. *Nick Carter vs. Fantômas*
V. Darlay & H. de Gorsse. *Arsène Lupin vs. Sherlock Holmes: The Stage Play*
Séamas Duffy. *Sherlock Holmes in Paris*
Paul Féval. *Gentlemen of the Night; John Devil; The Black Coats ('Salem Street; The Invisible Weapon; The Parisian Jungle; The Companions of the Treasure; Heart of Steel; The Cadet Gang; The Sword-Swallower)*
Emile Gaboriau. *Monsieur Lecoq*
Goron & Emile Gautier. *Spawn of the Penitentiary*
Rick Lai. *Shadows of the Opera: Retribution in Blood; Sisters of the Shadows: The Curse of Cagliostro*
Steve Leadley. *Sherlock Holmes: The Circle of Blood*
Maurice Leblanc. *Arsène Lupin vs. Countess Cagliostro; Arsène Lupin vs. Sherlock Holmes (The Blonde Phantom; The Hollow Needle); The Many Faces of Arsène Lupin*
Gaston Leroux. *Chéri-Bibi; The Phantom of the Opera; Rouletabille & the Mystery of the Yellow Room; Rouletabille at Krupp's*
Richard Marsh. *The Complete Adventures of Judith Lee*
William Patrick Maynard. *The Terror of Fu Manchu; The Destiny of Fu Manchu*
Frank J. Morlock. *Sherlock Holmes: The Grand Horizontals; Sherlock Holmes vs Jack the Ripper*
Antonin Reschal. *The Adventures of Miss Boston*
P. de Wattyne & Y. Walter. *Sherlock Holmes vs. Fantômas*
David White. *Fantômas in America*
Pierre Yrondy. *The Adventures of Thérèse Arnaud*